THE MAGPIE

J.G. Harlond

Eloquent Books
New York, New York

Eloquent Books
New York, New York

Eloquent Books
An imprint of AEG Publishing Group
845 Third Avenue, 6th Floor - 6016
New York, NY 10022
www.EloquentBooks.com

ISBN: 978-1-60693-119-6
SKU: 1-60693-119-9

Printed in the United States of America

Book design by Wendy Arakawa

With sincere thanks to:
Antonio Arredondo del Rio, Guy Bowden,
Izabella and Peter Hearn, Ninu Sumray-Roots
and Carolyn Whittaker.

In memory of P.A.H., who taught me to observe.

PART I

Chapter 1

MALABAR COAST, INDIA, 1901

Millicent Cleaver, well accustomed to snail-slow Malabar trains, sighed as they came to yet another halt. She tapped the fingers of her right hand on the window ledge and watched a family of women in bright saris gathered around a plump young matron in western dress holding a baby. Each of the women kissed and fussed over the baby, then kissed and fussed over its mother. After some minutes a large, moustachioed patriarch paced down the narrow platform with a railway employee at his heels. The door to Miss Cleaver's compartment was opened and the railway employee entered with the young mother's travelling valise.

"Madam, madam, so sorry madam. There is a confusion. This lady, she has no seat, madam. Is it possible for you, please, to allow her to be here?"

Millicent Cleaver sighed again, "If there is nowhere else."

"Not first class, madam. Not a ladies' carriage, no madam."

"Then what choice is there?"

The ticket had been more than she could afford on her meagre salary but she had paid, believing the status of the compartment would ensure her some privacy; something unobtainable in her employment. Knowing she would have to scrimp later and now had to forego that which she had purchased, she was angry. "Well?" she said, fixing the carriage servant with an icy, school-ma'am stare.

The railway servant was lost. "Does that mean 'yes' or 'no', madam? Sorry."

"Oh, yes," she sighed with exasperation.

He placed the heavy leather valise in the rack above the free seat and stood by the door. A cloud of noisy flies began to swarm in, he batted at them idly. Millicent Cleaver, angry but polite said, "Please do not leave the door open," in cut-glass English.

The railway employee looked at her without comprehension.

The young mother eventually climbed aboard carrying her own bulky carpet bag and the patriarch handed up her child. The railway employee flushed with nerves and relief at a catastrophe averted, grinned broadly at the ladies, bowed twice, and closed the door to the stuffy compartment. Once safe on the platform, he wiped his brow and blew his nose on a square of red rag then wafted it energetically in the air, shouting, "All aboard the Bombay Express! All aboard!"

The old engine struggled back to life, ready for another climb up the Western Ghatts. The young mother smiled at her poker-faced travelling companion and settled herself into the seat opposite, adjusting the position of the large baby on her lap. The child gazed about him and waved his plump arms in the air. Millicent Cleaver swallowed hard and stared out of the window.

The family was now waving furiously, the women dabbing handkerchiefs to their eyes. Such a palaver over catching a train: all money and no manners, as her father would say. Millicent Cleaver pursed her lips and focused her attention on the flamboyant scenery, managing a watery smile in the direction of her Goanese intruder when their eyes met. She made no attempt to converse because she loathed long-journey companionship: talk, talk, talk about nothing; if one was never going to meet the person again why bother to be nice? Through half-closed eyes she studied the young matron. Seated sideways on the seat opposite, gazing at the retreating figures of her family she looked remarkably like a black-haired Queen Victoria: small head, small hands, ample curves. Millicent Cleaver closed her eyes and tried to doze but two flies had sneaked in to compound her annoyance.

After some minutes the baby became restless. The woman placed him on the seat beside her and ferreted in her carpet bag for a wedge of bread and an embroidered bib. The bib was tied around the child's neck while it opened and closed its mouth in anticipation of food. He was, thought Millicent Cleaver, exactly like a cuckoo: large compared with his dam and getting larger by the day. The mother caught her eye and looked embarrassed.

"His *ayah* left this morning. It is so inconvenient. I told her two days ago we were going to Bombay and this morning she was not in her room. I shall have to do everything for him now, until a suitable girl is found."

"Oh dear, what a chore," replied Miss Cleaver, who was a governess by profession.

"We are going to meet my husband, he's a diplomat, you see. In the new Russian consulate . . ."

Oh Lord, thought Millie Cleaver, here we go.

"I just came back to Goa to be with my mother, you see, for the lying-in. Then I stayed until Leonid found us a nice house on

Malabar Hill. You know Malabar Hill?"

"Yes, very nice."

"And he's got one. A little palace he says. With servants already installed - but no *ayah*. But at least I can go there and the furnishing is ready. Do you, by any chance, happen to know of an *ayah* in Bombay?"

Millicent Cleaver shook her head, but added "I'm sure you will find someone soon."

"I hope so. You see my husband is Russian, and a diplomat and I shall have to accompany him to social occasions; not stay at home like an ordinary wife. His father was an explorer, you know. They are very high class and well-educated family, not traditional at all."

The baby spluttered out a yellow masticated pulp, sending a daisy chain of soggy crumbs across his mother's white blouse. "Leo!" She pronounced the name the Latin way.

Portuguese descent, decided Millicent Cleaver; hence the fussing over the baby. She had once spent three months in a Goan household and resigned because the children were so spoilt they were unteachable.

"My name is Catalina Figueroa da Silva," said the woman extending a sticky palm, "Oh, sorry." She wiped her fingers on the boy's bib and settled him back on her lap. "We are pleased to meet you, aren't we Leo?"

The baby obviously felt the same way as the angular lady sitting in front of him. He closed his eyes and promptly fell asleep, but that did not deter his garrulous mother. "He's big for his age isn't he? Ten months now. Born in the hot weather. I cannot bear hot weather. Perhaps I shall like Russia, when we go. My husband says I shall visit his mother as soon as Leo is big enough to travel.

It is a very long way to go, of course. I don't know if I shall like the travelling, so inconvenient isn't it?"

"Yes."

"Do you have children?"

"I'm not married."

"Oh, so sorry. No offence."

"None taken."

For the next few hours Catalina Figueroa chattered on and Millicent Cleaver tried to stop gazing at the baby. She was not married, no. And never likely to be now; over thirty and obliged to work for a living. She continued to supply discouraging monosyllabic replies to satisfy her travelling companion and eventually the train pulled into a station. Tea, fruit and water sellers were lined up along the platform singing out their wares. The carriage servant came into the compartment and said they would be in the station for ten minutes but he would be stopping here. The two women handed him a few pice.

Catalina Figueroa moved the heavy child off her lap. Her blouse was soaked with sweat under the armpits and the boy's nappy was so sodden it had stained her skirt. The English lady then told her the train would probably be in the station for much longer than ten minutes, ample time to take advantage of the station's First Class Ladies Waiting Room facilities. A woman selling guavas, mangoes and fresh limes tapped on the window.

"Oooh, delicious fruit! Would you like some Miss . . .? Sorry, we travel together and I do not know your name."

"No thank you. But let me hold the boy; you go and freshen up and buy some fruit before we set off again."

"Yes, how kind."

The damp child was transferred into Millicent Cleaver's arms. He looked into her face with big green eyes and blew a bubble. His mother alighted the train.

"Now then, young man," said the governess, "let's see if Mummy has a clean nappy for you and let's see if I know how to change one."

Catalina Figueroa da Silva hastened into the First Class Ladies Waiting Room, holding her bag in front of her to hide the embarrassing stain. The cool air of the room was scented with lemon leaves, such a pleasant relief after the hot train. She put her reticule on the side of a basin and began to splash water over her face, but she was so nervous about hurrying she knocked the bag off. Bending to retrieve it she felt dizzy then, on standing upright again, she fell into a swoon, fainted to the floor and cracked the back of her head. A young woman who had no right to be in that particular waiting room bent to help her. Catalina Figueroa was unconscious.

The impostor looked around. They were alone. Coolly she exchanged her cheap fabric bag for the soft leather reticule on the floor, ripped the gold crucifix from Catalina's neck and slipped out of the door onto the platform as fast as she could. She climbed back on the train unnoticed and remained quite impassive when the train started to pull out of the station.

Millicent Cleaver felt her heart pounding as the train gathered speed, but the little boy on her lap seemed to find its rhythm soothing; he popped a thumb into his mouth and closed his big eyes.

A different railway servant came in with a pot of tea. "Tea or fresh lemon, madam?"

"Tea, please."

"What a nice boy, you have madam, very healthy,

very round."

"He is, isn't he," responded Millie Cleaver proudly. "He eats up everything."

Chapter 2

"It's more than a question of trust, you see," said the moon-faced Englishman. "We can accept the child to be educated, but you will have to pay a proportion of his tuition."

Millicent Cleaver stared at the man. She hadn't considered this.

"But this is an orphanage," she said.

"Exactly."

"The Bombay Anglican Boys' Orphanage, correct?"

"Correct. It is also a school, remember. Staff have to be paid. It is my belief," said the Reverend Johns, folding his soft hands over his stomach, "and I am sure you will agree, Miss Cleaver, that those of us who *have*, have an obligation to help those who *have not*. It is our Christian duty. That is why we are here in India, is it not? Not living comfortably in Hove."

Millie Cleaver was losing her patience. The reference to Hove made her nervous. Where was Hove? The man was clearly trying to trap her into a confession or a financial commitment beyond her means, or both.

"Reverend Johns," she said, "I will sign a document swearing under oath - on the Bible, whatever you like, to say that I am not the child's mother. I repeat: I am not the boy's mother. I found him: that is to say the child was abandoned in my arms. I have simply been trying to do what I can for him. It is my Christian duty, as you so rightly say."

The indignant spinster took a deep breath and looked out of the window at a wall: clerical grey stone covered in exotic, sinful colours. "I could just leave him with all the other little urchins in the street. Lord knows, there are enough of them, nobody would notice. Nobody cares about *them*. I could just walk down a busy street and . . . Obviously, I am not going to. The child is innocent. I must do what I can for him. But I cannot pay you." Her breath came in gasps. "I thought this school belonged to a Christian organization." She hoisted the heavy child into a more comfortable position on her lap. "And I will not be morally brow-beaten. He is not mine."

The principal of what was known locally as the BABO, nodded, "No, no, of course not. You said."

"Good heavens man, look at me! Do I look like the brat's mother?" The word brat had escaped her, she loved the child - had never, not once in four years, thought of him as a brat.

The Reverend Reginald Johns glanced involuntarily at the tight-lipped, thin face before him. Then he looked hard at the chubby features of the quiet child sitting on the woman's knee. It was, indeed, most unlikely that Millicent Cleaver had brought the boy into the world. So he said, "Well then there's the question of identity; name, date of birth, nationality."

The woman moved the boy off her lap. He stood beside her, gripping her grey skirt in a tight fist and stared straight at the round face in front of him. The man was like an owl. There was an owl in his grandfather's garden. It came every evening to sit on a tree stump. It could sit still for ages then suddenly there would be a flap of wings, a squeak or a screech and a limp body lifted into the sky. Owls had nice faces, but they weren't always nice.

The thin woman opened her cracked leather music case. She handed the man a sheet of yellowed paper. He read it through twice. "Leo Kazan Figueroa da Silva. Quite a name for a little chap. Goanese I see, but the Kazan? The father's nationality is not registered? Do we classify him as Eurasian or Indian? Or would you call him Anglo-Indian?"

Millie Cleaver's tight lips pursed out of sight, "Figueroa da Silva is clearly Portuguese. Kazan, I am not sure about, Armenian perhaps. It could just as easily be British. I am told England is teeming with foreigners these days."

Touché. "I'll put Indian, then. That covers another multitude." Reginald Johns dipped his pen into the inkpot and began to scratch at a sheet of paper on his blotter. The boy's large eyes watched each move but apart from the repeated clenching of the hand holding the long, plain grey skirt, he made no move.

"Now, I just need your full name and the name and address of your bank. Will you fill in this form for us, please?"

"So, in order for this child to be saved from the streets I must open a bank account. Mr. Johns I do not have a bank. My father dealt with all financial arrangements."

"Then your father's name and address."

"My father died three weeks ago today. That is why I am here; that is why I can no longer care for this child. I have to obtain employment to support myself. I am a governess; I can hardly take this boy . . ." She swallowed hard.

Mr. Johns had the courtesy to be abashed. She wasn't the mother. No need to punish her further. "I'll call Miss Tibbs: she's in charge of the under-fives. Perhaps you would like a cup of tea?"

The thin woman lifted the plump little boy back onto her lap. He snuggled into her arms and placed a pink thumb in his mouth. It was gently removed. Millie Cleaver breathed into the boy's soft black hair, trying to hold back her tears.

A strange case, the principal thought; this was no unnamed street child. There was something not right. She wasn't entirely innocent. But her crime? For all that he had to keep charity within manageable limits he was not a hard man, the unspoken affection before him pricked at his own eyes. He moved to the door, and without looking back said, "While you are having tea with Miss Tibbs you can tell her all you know about this young man. I'll go and get her myself." He nodded and left the room, closing the door gently behind him.

The little boy called Leo cocked his head on one side. "Not nice," he said.

Millie Cleaver smiled at him and kissed the top of his head. Now what was she going to tell this Miss Tibbs? The truth? She hadn't actually told a lie so far, but evasion had not been easy. Now he was gone she was tempted to confess to Mr. Johns. Explain to him how an adorable little boy had come into her arms for just a few minutes - and why she had kept him for nearly four years.

One hot, airless night in the summer of 1905, about a week after the admission of the Kazan child, Reginald Johns, principal of the Bombay Anglican Boys' Orphanage, woke up in a cold sweat. The name – Kazan – he had remembered. The next morning he contacted his bishop. The Bishop advised him to say nothing to anyone and contact Sir Lionel Pinecoffin, a senior IPS officer, immediately.

Looking at it from the point of view of the Indian Political Service, Reginald Johns could see that this was indeed a very delicate affair; the son of Russian diplomat abducted by a woman with a British name was now living in a British orphanage. It might start an embarrassment: a scandal. The Indian press would go to town. The Indian National Congress would have a heyday making mischief between the two nations. More than a scandal, the whole thing would be blown into a major international incident.

"Least said soonest mended," said Sir Lionel. "He is in good hands after all, won't starve. And if someone does discover his identity, well that will be wonderful. A happy ending for all involved."

Reginald Johns stared at the Political officer, who was perfectly relaxed, leaning back in his chair lighting a cigarette with cool hands. The austere office seemed to press in on him. The office belonged to the Raj and the Raj, in effect, had spoken. "Yes, yes. What can I say?" he said.

"Nothing, dear chap, obviously. You might just check the entry register when you get back, though. I think you'll find you misspelt the boy's name. *Leonard Curzon*, wasn't it?"

Sir Lionel appeared to find this amusing. The child was to be named for the British Viceroy of India.

The principal went straight back to his orphanage and took out the entry register. He dipped his pen in the ink pot then put it down again. No, the boy had a name, his own name and a genuine birth certificate. If he were to be found by his true family, that *would* be a blessing. A happy ending as Sir Lionel had said. In the meantime young Leo would be well cared for. As an ordained Anglican priest . . .

As an ordained Anglican priest of humble origin . . . In his mind's eye Reginald Johns saw his benefactress, his father's employer. She was sitting in the front pew for his first sermon. He saw her smile of encouragement - and remembered very clearly that she was Sir Lionel Pinecoffin's aunt. It was a small world: especially this part of India, where everybody seemed to know everyone's connections. But no, he could not, would not change the boy's name.

Chapter 3

Leo kept a pet python and fed it on frogs. It was not a wholly benevolent arrangement: the python was expected to guard Leo's treasure. The treasure was in a biscuit tin. On the lid of the tin were a lady in a poke bonnet and a young man in plus-fours riding a penny-farthing bicycle. The decoration meant nothing to Leo: he was only interested in the tin's contents. The tin and the python lived in the hollow bole of an upside-down banyan tree in the orphanage grounds.

One illicit evening, while eating sweet pastries in the bazaar, Leo heard an old man spinning yarns for his supper. He talked of the fabulous wealth of the independent princes. They had palaces three miles long and electricity and telephones (he called them speaking machines) and white concubines. They were so rich they kept their treasures under nests of cobras. They had so many rubies and diamonds, the old man said, they only knew they had been robbed when a thief dropped down dead before their very eyes. It was a splendid idea, and the python had been in the banyan maze for years.

The following Sunday afternoon, he and Skinny Eddie Sartay walked out of the orphanage servants' entrance, down to the dead-end of Lime Grove and then cut off down a rough track leading into the tall grass of India. They passed a group of houses, where chattering children played around women bent over cooking pots, and went on until they came to a track bordering a rice paddy. They were on a frog hunt. They were, of course, expressly forbidden to leave the orphanage unsupervised, and under no account was any boy ever allowed out on the Sabbath, but Leo had to go frog hunting. Sunday afternoon was best: watchful masters snoozed and so he only had to give his bored dormitory companions the slip, and that was usually quite easy. He played the role of the dorm fat boy to perfection. The butt of jokes and jibes, he was quite content to demonstrate how little intelligence he possessed. It was a relatively painless means of liberation. He kept Skinny Eddie as his best friend because boys who were loners aroused suspicion. Loners were scrutinised. Leo had also, reluctantly, come to accept that lone frog hunting was unwise. Not all snakes were as benign as his python. If he were to be bitten his companion would run for help. Or better still, his companion would be bitten instead.

"What d'you want frogs for Leo?" asked Skinny Eddie, skipping along beside his big friend.

"To put in Matron's bed."

"Oh."

They ambled on down the track to where a sort of dyke would keep them out of sight. It meant walking one leg up, one leg down, along the slippery bank, tricky but fun. Hiding in flat scenery had its challenges. For some time they crouched and grabbed, splashed and squelched until Leo's dirty linen bag was bulging with juicy frogs. Then they climbed up onto the top of the muddy bank and shared one of the Latin master's evil cheroots. Eddie was sick almost immediately so Leo finished it off, poking his bag now and again to make sure the fodder was still alive and kicking.

"Hey," said Skinny Eddie pointing, "look."

Two memsahibs were strolling down the track twirling frilly parasols. They were very pink in the face and giggling like schoolgirls. Leo pulled Skinny Eddie down into the warm mud and the women passed them by. Then Leo was up out of the mud and mincing at a safe distance behind the *mems* – a parasol in one hand, his precious bag of frogs tucked onto his hip like a baby. "Now then young Sartay, recite me your nine times table and you shall have jelly for tea."

"One nine is nine, two nines are nineteen, three nines are . . ."

Leo slapped his free hand over the boy's mouth, "Get down!"

One of the women had dropped her parasol and bent down to tie a bootlace. Across the tall grass on the other side of the paddy there was a ripple, a breeze of movement on a windless afternoon. The boys froze, watching the ripple shimmer closer and faster in the direction of the women. Suddenly the boot-tying lady sat down on the track, laughing. And then she wasn't laughing because she too had seen the grass move.

"Aaaaaagghhh," screamed Leo at the top his voice, charging towards the women.

"Aaaagghh! Yeaaaayy!" He was running full tilt waving his arms in the air. The leopard burst out of the grass and leapt straight over the track down onto the other side and into the paddy. Leo stopped. Nobody moved. The air stood still. Then the lady on the ground slowly raised a hand. Leo looked down at her, "I think it's gone," he said.

The other woman started to cry. "It's all right lady, don't be afraid."

The tableau stayed in place, staring in silence at a retreating ripple of bright spots.

"Hey!" came a voice from behind them. "You dropped your frogs."

The two boys were invited back to Lady Hermione's colonial bungalow in Acacia Avenue for tea. They had jelly and cakes, and tea with fresh milk in porcelain cups, on the veranda. They were introduced to Lady Hermione's children, two snivelling sneaks in white-drill safari suits. Then came Lady Hermione's Scotty dog called Hamish, who took too much interest in Leo's bag of frogs and had to be shooed into the garden by the house-boy. And then, just as they were about to leave, Sir Lionel Pinecoffin arrived.

"Lionel, come and meet a hero. This is . . . I'm sorry," the beautiful lady looked down at the boy, "you haven't told me your full name."

"Kazan, ma'am. Leo Kazan. But everyone just calls me Leo, even the masters at school, ma-am."

"Leo's different," piped the knowing voice of Skinny Eddie Sartay.

Lady Hermione looked across at her husband to share her amusement, but all his attention was focused on the boy.

"Well," she said, "a meeting of lions! Leo, this is my husband Sir Lionel Pinecoffin, he is the District Political Officer, if you know what that is?"

"Lavinia," the tall Englishman turned to his sister-in-law, "what is this all about? My wife is positively babbling." The question gave him a few extra moments to scrutinise the swarthy boy covered in mud, drinking from Crown Derby on his bungalow verandah.

"This young man," answered Lavinia, "is a hero. He saved Hermione from a leopard!"

"Good Lord. What happened?"

The story was retold and elaborated; the leopard brushing past them as Leo waved his arms in the air to deflect its murderous dive.

"Goodness gracious! I shall have to reward you. One cannot let one's wife's life be saved without compensation. What can I do for you, Leo Kazan?"

Leo cocked his head to one side, noting a silver cigarette box on a low table, "Actually, sir, nothing, thank you. That is, I would rather you didn't do - or say anything."

"Out of bounds were you?"

"Mmm." And there was a thin silver dagger-shaped thing on top of an envelope on a pretty silver tray. Leo looked up at the District Political Officer, a person of authority, and gave a sheepish grin. "I like your house, sir."

"And I like your cake," said Skinny Eddie, helping himself to another slice of Victoria sponge.

It was now time to leave. Despite Leo's protestations Lady Hermione insisted the garden-boy accompany them back to the orphanage. Once out of the bungalow's ample grounds and on the tree lined street however, Leo easily negotiated a deal that left them free to return unescorted. It cost him the last of the Latin master's cheroots.

Leo and Eddie sneaked back in through the servants' entrance. Eddie went straight up to the dorm and Leo went to feed the few remaining live frogs to his python. He pushed his way under the upside-down banyan roots and branches and untied the linen bag into the hollow. There was space in his round tin, he thought, for the silver box, but he wasn't sure the funny dagger knife would fit. He would have to find an oblong container. There was time: he would have to leave the new treasures in the bungalow for a few days to avoid linking his visit to their disappearance.

The following Wednesday was Sports Day, the last outdoor event before the monsoon. The tension that had built up during the humidity of May over-spilled into over-excitement. There was a general disruption in school routine; masters were relaxed; boys and servants were all over the place; Matron was in a constant panic trying to be everywhere at once. Leo was delighted to find exactly the tin he needed on a table in the dining hall. It was a long rectangle: the lid was covered in red tartan and had a man with bulging cheeks blowing into a contraption of sack and pipes. It was a sign. He helped himself to a finger of sugar-coated shortbread, stuffed his pockets with two more and tipped the rest into an empty dish. Then he put the lid on the tin and placed it on top of a pile of used plates. Dissembling the helpful schoolboy, he headed in the direction of the kitchen quarters. Nobody stopped him. Nobody asked him what he was doing.

On the evening of Sports Day, the orphanage entertained local benefactors, there was whisky and bonhomie. Pupils were sent up to their dorms a little later than normal. The runners, jumpers and throwers all fell asleep as soon as their heads touched their pillows. Leo, who had been in charge of tying finishing lines and measuring long jumps, was not in the least bit sleepy. He waited for the snivels, snores and mutters to form a steady rhythm; waited until a cloud obliterated the almost full moon then slipped out of bed and pulled on his darkest clothes. As he crept down the back stairs he double-checked his toffee supply. Still there and getting stickier. By the time he reached his destination it would be just the right consistency. Then he was out over the servants' gate with an agility that would have surprised many. It was quite a long walk to Acacia Avenue, and once there he had a little difficulty identifying where they had actually drunk tea from paper-thin cups. All the houses seemed the same in the dark.

And then he knew he was in the right place. The two women were sitting on the verandah steps sipping from tall glasses; Sir Lionel was leaning back in a low chair behind them, his hands cupped round a begging bowl of brandy. Keeping close to the bushes but not making a sound, Leo crept close enough to hear their conversation: something to do with a Cicely and a wedding. Where was the dog?

He was lucky: he almost always was. He was lucky now because he was able to get round into the garden undetected, and the back door was unlocked.

Which room first? Would the house-boy be waiting for the family to finish their drinks? Did the *ayah* sleep in the house? Would the two boys be awake?

First a bedroom: two boys sleeping under cathedrals of netting. Another door; a dressing table, a trinket box, a brooch, a long hatpin with a star at the end, a low growl. Hamish.

"Sshh . . ."

The dog growled, yellow teeth suspended in darkness. "Shut up you stupid dog," whispered the thief in street Marathi. He bent down and offered the squat demon his hand to smell. The growl ceased, the teeth disappeared and the tail stump wagged. "Good boy." Leo extracted a lump of toffee from his pocket and popped it into his mouth, all the time stroking the smelly creature's stiff fur. Then he removed the softened toffee and stuck it firmly onto a canine tooth. The dog licked. Mmm, it seemed to say, lick, lick. Leo considered using more toffee on the other tooth. He took another lump from his pocket, popped it in his mouth - and left it there. Why waste good toffee? He'd be out in two wags of the dratted dog's tail.

He checked the dressing table - nothing out of its place, made for the door, shutting it sharply on a black nose, then he was out through the back door, round once more to the front of the bungalow and under the shelf of the verandah. They were still dribbling on about Cicely and a baby. He squirmed into a comfortable position and finished his toffee. He didn't have long to wait. Cane chairs were shuffled, English voices said, "Goodnight." He pulled himself into a crouching position, ready, steady, "Sweet dreams," go. He was at the bottom of the steps. Between the English leaving and the house-boy arriving, Leo had grabbed the silver box, but the silver tray and the dagger thing were no longer visible. Never mind, another time. Then he was off up the path, over the gate and into the road. Hamish started yapping. A bigger dog barked. A voice shouted, "Who's there?" Then a long awkward run, hands closed like clamps over pockets, and then he was climbing the stairs to the dorm, out of breath.

He flopped down on his bed.

"That you Leo?" asked Skinny Eddie.

"Mmm."

"Whatsamatter?"

"Collywobbles."

"It's cuz you're greedy."

"I know."

There was silence. Leo pushed his loot firmly under his lumpy pillow, all except the sharp hatpin. He tried to sleep, but he was too excited. Outside, the moon pushed through a cloud and glinted just once on the star in his hand.

Would she like the pretty things in his tin? He felt her bend over his bed and tuck the sheet up under his chin; he felt her soft face against his and heard her say, 'Goodnight, my darling', the way she said it every night. Come and fetch me Mummy. You said you would. He gulped back his tears and the moon went out.

*

"Leo, I have here a request from Lady Hermione Pinecoffin. She wants you to go her home this afternoon." Mr. Johns looked at the twelve-year old standing to attention in front of his desk. "I have to admit, I was not aware that you were socializing in such circles. Do you know the way to Lady Hermione's home?"

"I think so, sir."

"I think so . . . So you have been before?"

"Yes, sir."

"When?"

"Only once, sir."

"When, once?"

"With Sartay, sir."

"When?"

"With Sartay on a Sunday, sir."

"Leo I am not conducting a quiz, nor is this meant to be an interrogation . . ." The boy's shoulders relaxed. "I am simply trying to ascertain how an orphanage boy has got into - how shall I put it? Oh damn it! What on earth have you been up to now, boy?"

"I expect it's because I might have saved the lady's life, sir. I didn't mean to. That is I didn't mean to be in a place where she was in danger of being attacked by a man-eating leopard and having to save her. It just happened, sir. Ask Sartay."

"Lady Hermione hasn't included Sartay in her invitation, so we can leave him out of this interview." Leo couldn't help grinning. If this wasn't about the shiny box and the star pin then there would be more cake, just for him.

"Well, I shall accompany you. I cannot allow my charges to go running off to the civil lines on Sunday afternoons without ensuring they are in appropriate company for the Sabbath."

Reginald Johns watched his pupil's face and there was just the faintest tweak of a smile, a dimple appeared and disappeared. He had to bite his lower lip and fuss about in a drawer until he was sure he could maintain his serious demeanour. "In the mean time, young man, I should like you to write a composition entitled *How I Saved a Lady from a Man-eating Leopard.* Dismissed."

Leo came back to attention. He didn't actually click his heels because the mission school was not a military academy, but he did march straight-backed to the huge black teak door. "Thank you, sir. Goodbye, sir."

"Half past four at the main entrance, clean uniform and the composition."

"Yes sir."

The door closed. The principal leaned back in his chair and chuckled. He wrote a note and sent for a runner. Then he sobered. An unfortunate set of coincidences, if indeed they were just coincidences. No, not even the scheming Sir Lionel Pinecoffin would, could, arrange a leopard attack.

After that first visit Leo went to the civil lines each Saturday afternoon for nearly two months. He was to 'accompany and entertain' the snivelling sons at weekends before they were shipped off to their English boarding school in July. Miles and Craig did their best to make his task as onerous as possible. Leo, who coveted his independence, was forced to invent games, accept perpetual defeat at interminable rounds of gin-rummy and tolerate a name-calling and physical abuse that would have shocked even the toughest BABO bully. That he did so was to his credit - and to his benefit. He swallowed his ouches because he knew Sir Lionel was watching him.

Leo also knew that his destiny as an orphanage boy was in the balance. If he passed muster he might be taken on in some very menial capacity by the Englishman. If not, he would be apprenticed as a life-long under-clerk in some British Bombay shipping firm, or worse still, in one of the stifling cotton mills. Charity boys were a source of easily trained clerical labour. Only those well above average in mathematics ever reached the more comfortable offices of cotton exporters or shipbrokers. Leo was not above average in mathematics: the very thought of dealing with three columns of figures made his head spin. Boys like him became filing clerks. And if he didn't mind his p's and q's this was going to be quite soon because he was already over twelve.

Occasionally one of the brighter boys who shone at Latin and Natural Science was given the chance to stay on at school until he was sixteen, then, if he was a very special scholar, he might achieve a bursary to study in Britain or at Bombay's own university. Not that this appealed to Leo either. Sitting still for hours on end, stuffing one's brain with facts and figures seemed a pointless waste of time. The facts and figures had already been gathered and documented, what was the point of memorising something you could find in a book if you needed it? Studying just filled up valuable space in your head that could be used for something more rewarding.

So, if putting up with Miles and Craig were to be his test,

even if it might only lead to fetching and carrying for Sir Lionel, he would do all that was required of him. Over and above that, he would, of course, prove himself to be resourceful and reliable. This very regrettably prevented the little lords from having any damaging 'accidents'.

"I see you get on famously with Ayah, Leo," said Sir Lionel, taking a seat beside the podgy youth on the verandah steps.

Craig and Miles had gone to change their wet clothes, they had been playing monsoon hide and seek in the garden; they did the hiding and sheltering, Leo did the seeking and soaking. He'd got them this time, though. They had been in the gardener's shed, he had passed the shed and simply said, "I say you chaps, I hope you aren't in there, garden matey told me he saw a cobra this morning." The boys were out of the door in a flash and off toward the house. But Leo had locked both the front and back doors of the bungalow. And now he was sitting next to Sir Lionel like an old-time friend. He cocked his head on one side, the way he did when he was contemplating the right response. Of course he got on well with Ayah: no boy should miss an opportunity to butter up a maternal woman.

"What language do you use?"

"Language? I'm not sure, sir."

"But you obviously understand Ayah very well, and you do not use English."

"No, I think it is the language they speak in the kitchens, sir."

"In the orphanage?"

"Yes sir."

"And are there other languages spoken in your school, apart from English?"

"Oh yes, sir, many."

"Leo, how do you know, that there are many?"

"Well . . ." Leo felt guilty. He wasn't sure why he felt guilty - or perhaps he was. He listened in on other people's conversations - and this man seemed to know it. How much should he acknowledge? "Well . . ."

How much is he going to tell me, wondered the Oxford graduate, who had passed his IPS entrance with flying colours because he too had what his chums called 'the gift of tongues'? "Mmm?" he nodded encouragingly.

"Well there are the languages some boys use with each other, in the dorm when . . ."

"When they don't want anyone to listen in."

"I suppose so," agreed the boy, knowing full well the man was right.

"And?"

"Well, sometimes it is more convenient for boys to just speak to each other - without everybody knowing what they are saying."

"Absolutely."

"And there's the language they speak in the kitchen. The sweeper, and the gate-keeper and the principal's syce, and the gardeners, they all speak a similar language."

"Similar?"

"I think some words, or phrases are different. They come from different villages, you see. Some are from the coast and some are from up country. Anyway they speak differently when they are together than the way they address Mr. Johns and the other staff."

Sir Lionel placed his old-fashioned pipe in his mouth and spent a while lighting a match, then puffed until the tobacco took hold. He watched Leo watching his every move, while apparently shifting an ant from one foot to another.

"I see. And you can speak to these people, the boys in the dorm and the servants, in their own languages?"

Leo grinned a half dimpled, conspiratorial grin. "I seem to sir, yes."

"Tell me, Leo," said Sir Lionel, "How do you get into the kitchen? And don't say through the door - I know about Indian kitchen ramparts - they can only be breached by a full-scale Agincourt strategy."

Leo felt uneasy about the Agincourt reference: he knew he should know it, but didn't. He transferred the ant to his other foot: it was a tenacious creature. "Cakes, sir," he said at last. "I'm very fond of cakes. We only get them on Sundays, for tea. But, you see, cook's assistant has got a brother who's got a pastry stall in the bazaar, and they are excellent, sir. I mean I know I shouldn't go sir, but you see sometimes I – well, I just escape. The bazaar is out of bounds, very strictly out of bounds, but *I* can get there. And I get those lovely sticky pastries with honey. And then once I got punished. But cook's assistant has got a sister who's a cleaner and she lets me into the kitchen - now that I can never go back to the bazaar." Leo was humbled; he hated having to admit that he had been caught.

"So the boy who knows cook's assistant has been banned from the bazaar. And does this boy take it as a life ban?"

"Oh no sir! It is a temporary ban, while . . ."

"While you grow out of your school? Or while you think of a strategy? Hamish come out of those rose bushes," called Sir Lionel. The man pushed a hand out toward the orphanage boy, "Go and get him, he'll bring mud into the house and there'll be hell to pay."

Leo ran his tilting, swaying run down toward the rose bed, "Dratted dog," he muttered under his breath.

Sir Lionel Pinecoffin watched Leo cross the sodden lawn.

The bustling backside was ample testimony to the story of the cakes. Now a lad who could learn a new lingo for a sweetmeat was a lad to nurture. But this particular lad came with an embarrassing family history. He would have to be very careful. He would have to play this one *very* carefully. The role he had in mind for Leo demanded absolute, unconditional loyalty.

There was no great hurry: for the next month Leo could continue to keep the peace between Miles and Craig. It would give him time to investigate Millicent Agnes Cleaver, and the man whose name was written on the birth certificate in his desk drawer.

Chapter 4

In 1900, when Britain granted Russia permission to establish a consulate in Bombay, Russia and India already had well established trade links: Russia imported tea and exported vast quantities of kerosene for Indian kitchens. Because of this successful, ongoing commercial link Russia had been harrying Britain for permission to set up a trade mission on Indian soil for over forty years but viceroys such as Lord Curzon, had held out, insisting that Britain needed to protect her source of raw materials, her jewel in the crown, from potential thieves.

Monitoring trade from a political perspective, as far as Sir Lionel was concerned, meant not one Ivan moved in or out of 'the gateway to India' without him knowing about it. This required constant vigilance, which in the British Raj was a standard arrangement. Everybody watched everybody in India; rajahs and parliamentarians, nabobs and businessmen, they all maintained a string of informants. Indians in the professions, particular the politically inclined and lawyers; begums and maharanis out of purdah; over-exuberant memsahibs and ordinary white box wallahs; itinerant ministers of religion; peripatetic princes - they were all subject to scrutiny.

In the so-called autonomous princely states, eccentric rajahs had kept British sub-secretaries scribbling away for generations. Dowdy clerks from Clerkenwell and Tunbridge Wells spent their dull lives minuting oriental peccadilloes. Some of the more startling extravagances, such as stealing Hill State virgins for dubious religious ceremonies, might on the surface, be nothing more than titillating nonsense, but if a Hill State tribal leader became an aggrieved father, or, heaven forbid, suffered a loss of dignity, retribution would be sought. That could lead to interstate trouble, which in turn would upset the delicate balance of the Raj. The Mutiny in 1857 had proved how vulnerable the British in India really were: it still informed the colonial popular consciousness. In this respect Britons attached to the Indian Civil Service and Indian Political Service all wanted to know what was going on everywhere, all the time. Watching who did business with the Russians was no different.

Sir Lionel's particular brief was to 'monitor commercial enterprise in the light of a changing diplomatic climate'. In other words, he was to watch and note and inform the India Office the moment a foreign diplomat stepped out of line. He was also told to keep a close eye on intellectuals. Cultural exchanges between St. Petersburg and Bombay, Delhi and Moscow might easily lead to insurrection. The Tsar was weak; there had been bad harvests; the peasants, organized by student agitators, were ready to revolt. Trouble was contagious and if the peasant class caught it there might well be an epidemic. It was in the best interests of all concerned, he was told, to prevent India's children from mixing with undesirables who spread germs. Hence the most diligent watching and reporting. Knowledge was power.

Sir Lionel had a modest office near the Stock Exchange; he also rented rooms near the Sassoon timber docks and maintained a network of remunerated beggars among the godowns: old men and young, who spent their days and nights hunkered down in ones and threes, chewing betel nuts and apparently gazing into space. His principal observation post operated from dockland premises. Here new arrivals and commercial travellers of all nationalities could insure their luggage for overland journeys and where, if in need, they could consult a firm of 'Legal and Contract Translators' that operated from rooms at the top of the building with panoramic views of the harbour. Sir Lionel rarely entered these rooms and only very few British officials knew of his interest in their whereabouts.

This is where Leo was sent when he was thirteen. He made the tea, did some filing and learned how to write some of the languages he could speak so readily. From six to seven each morning he was tutored in Russian and then the manager, a Eurasian by the name of Sydney Timpkins kept him busy for another twelve hours or more with clerical tasks. Once his working day ended he was sent off to a box room at the back of the building, where there was a mattress, a bucket and a brass washbowl that had once belonged to somebody's grandmother. Each night Leo had to practise his Russian grammar for the next day.

Sydney Timpkins was not an unkind man, nor was he generous, amusing, tall or good-looking. Despite his special status within the Raj he believed Life had dealt him a severe blow: being of mixed race set him apart. He saw himself as a second-class citizen. So, when cheerful young Leo was sent to him as an apprentice he took one look at the swarthy features, listened to the pukka English accent and decided that this boy should learn his place, be made to feel the humiliation incumbent on all Eurasians.

Before coming under Sydney Timpkins' tutelage, Leo had always avoided thinking about his origins. The orphanage had been home to boys of many types, they had ranked themselves according to personality, not according to colour or nationality. At first Leo was unaware that he was being treated badly, he just assumed this was what happened to juniors. He thought that as his clerical skills improved so would his life in general. Unfortunately, his rapid progress in Russian had a negative effect on every employee in the dockland premises.

Leo learnt too much, too quickly. Sydney Timpkins and the scribes employed as legitimate clerks ensured that Leo's working day in the office went long beyond the initial twelve hours, and there was never a day off. To Leo that meant never a free moment to look at his collection of treasures, and certainly no time to add to it. And that was another worry - sooner or later his precious tins were going to be discovered. The two clerks were always poking about, nothing was private. Leo had quickly developed strategies to defend himself during cross-questioning regarding his reasons for being in the BABO, and he ignored the insults related to his orphan status, but what concerned him above all else was that nothing material could be kept secret in the barren rooms which constituted Timpkins' private Raj. He shifted his tins as often as he could and lived in dread of discovery. Life became unbearable, his head swam with verbs and he was losing weight.

One evening, after Sir Lionel had terminated one of his sporadic meetings with the Legal and Contract lawyers and left the building, Leo ran after him.

"Sir Lionel!" he called, waving an arm. The man stopped in his tracks, furious.

"Are you completely stupid, boy?"

Leo was taken aback; he had never heard this tone before. What had he done?

"You will never call my name aloud like that again. Do you

understand?"

"Yes sir." Then, dismayed, Leo shook his head, "No, sir."

"Look," the man sighed, resigned to a conversation. "I'll explain one day. What do you want?"

"Nothing sir. Just to say that I um, er, I'm er learning the Russian verbs, sir."

"And doing very well, I hear. As it should be."

"So can I stop now? Please."

"No Leo, not yet."

The boy's face fell.

"Why do you want to stop when you are doing so well? Does Timpkins keep you on short rations?"

Leo lowered his head and nodded. Sir Lionel controlled a smile and his tone softened. "No you can't stop learning, especially not Russian. Not if you are going to be of any use to me. You might need it yourself one day, you know. You might even be grateful."

Leo had nothing to say. "Shall you tell Timpkins you have spoken to me?"

"I don't think so, sir."

"That might be wise. A lot wiser than keeping me here, talking." The tall Englishman looked around then ostentatiously reached into his pocket, took out a red leather change purse and gave Leo a four-anna piece: his standard tip for well-behaved servants and deserving vagrants. Leo stared at the coin in his hand, confused by the short interview and its termination.

"There, now run off and buy some of those disgusting fried cakes you used to like so much." The boy looked up. "Go on, or I'll ask for my money back."

So Leo did what he was told. Forgetting everything, he ran down the quayside clutching the coin tightly in his fist as he passed the beggars. Some of them made a mental note of his passing. One of them informed a man, who told another man, who knew the porter of the Russian consulate.

Chapter 5

"Leo, I'm moving you out of the translation business."

Leo, who had been watching rain lash Sir Lionel's office window, turned around, a smile scythed once across his face and disappeared.

"Timpkins feels you have become too much of a threat to him. And that is quite a compliment. What are you now, fourteen, fifteen?"

"Fourteen until August. My birthday falls under the sign Leo."

"Does it? Have you ever had your horoscope read?"

"No. I just needed a birthday and it seemed appropriate to have one in August."

Sir Lionel was tidying his desk, putting papers, pens and pencils under lock and key. The blotting paper on his desk pad was carefully torn to shreds over the waste-paper basket. Leo watched him.

"Blotting paper absorbs," he said. "It absorbs and can inform. Do you follow me?"

Leo nodded. Like you, thought the political officer, like you my lad: soft, innocent, apparently innocuous on the outside and jam-packed with personal data that could cause all sorts of trouble.

"I used to wonder about having *our* horoscopes done. Lady Hermione was very keen to see someone about the boys' birth dates. But, you know, people say they are frighteningly accurate, so I said, no, better not. Ignorance is sometimes wiser in personal matters."

Leo wasn't paying attention. "Where am I to go, sir?"

"Mmm, well. Sit down boy, we may as well discuss that here and now. Time to put things straight."

The tall Englishman sat down in his leather-backed chair and ran a hand through his thinning hair. The monsoon wore him out. He yearned for a very long, very cold gin and tonic with a twist of lime, then cool linen sheets and a good night's sleep.

"Where was I? Ah, yes, your future. Well, sit down, sit down. And just for *future* reference, if you are going to stare out of a window it is better to do it at an angle, and make sure there's no light behind you first."

Leo looked round sharply then moved to the bent-wood visitor's chair. On the other side of the desk Sir Lionel appeared distant and shivery. Either he had indulged in a very liquid lunch or it was malaria.

"Do you have your quinine tablets, sir?" asked Leo.

Sir Lionel laughed out loud, "I do, I do. You are very observant. And I think you are right. But first we'll get your future sorted out then you can make sure I get back to the bungalow before I become a dithering wreck."

He lit a cigarette, the match jittered; the smoke had made a spiral in the thick air before he spoke again. "Now then, you mastered the translation tasks in double-quick time, but you'll have to keep up with the Russian. I'm going to arrange private evening-classes. But for now I want to send you in a different direction. Have you ever heard of The House of Craven?"

"Is that a Sherlock Holmes?"

"Do you read Conan Doyle, Leo?"

"Whenever I can get a story, sir."

Lionel Pinecoffin was amused, he hadn't thought of his protégé as a reader. "Do you read a lot? I wouldn't have thought you had much opportunity."

"I did at school. It was a way of being on one's own." That is, people got used to me being in the little library or under the banyan tree and they left me alone. But he didn't say that. "A couple of the masters used to let me borrow their books, sir. I like Walter Scott and Robert Louis Stevenson especially."

I bet you do, thought the older man. Adventures! He chuckled to himself: here is a boy, whose own life is the stuff of novels, and he likes the vicarious word. Life was a conundrum. He brought himself back to the task in hand.

"Well Craven's shop is a real place. It would make a good setting for a murder mystery, though. The Cravens, father and son, are perfectly real." Except, he thought, Old Man Craven isn't altogether real. He is neither normal nor . . . He searched for words in his head. He would be sweating soon. The brain fog rolled in. "The House of Craven is a group of connected businesses dealing in precious stones, jewelry, antiques, that sort of thing."

Leo swallowed. Did he know? Had he found his collection and not told him? That is just exactly what Sir Lionel would do. Find the evidence and then set a trap for him. "What am I to do in the House of Craven, sir?"

"First you will be in the Oriental Curiosity Shop. Dust the ornaments, help at the counter; keep an eye on the customers - who comes in regularly, who leaves items to be repaired and sends someone else to pick them up. Keep a mental note of who comes in selling loose stones, uncut rubies, emeralds, that sort of thing."

Sir Lionel swiveled his chair round to look out of the window. Leo didn't know how to react. His first impulse was to shout 'yippee'! His second, to say 'spy'. Instinct told him to do and say nothing.

"So, that all right with you?" said the Political Officer. "Start tomorrow. I intended to take you there this evening, on the way home, introduce you." The chair returned to its normal position. "But I feel so terrible now, I'm not sure I can. Let me get down to the street and I'll see how I feel." He opened a drawer, withdrew a strong buff envelope, a leather wallet and a set of keys. "Shall we go?"

Leo went round the desk to help him to his feet. "Where shall I sleep, sir?"

"Tonight you can stay at the bungalow with me. I'm on my own. Lady Hermione won't be back until we've got the all clear on this warmongering. Not until the cool weather, anyway. I got a lad to pick up your stuff from the dock office. It's all quite safe in my boys' room."

So he did know. It must have given Timpkins great satisfaction to reveal that the boy, who was too clever by half, was also a thief.

"If you give me the keys sir, I'll lock up as we go out."

"Keys? Yes, here you are. Make sure you give them back before we leave the building."

They stepped out into a world of steaming dampness and pushed their way down to the Stock Exchange and into the commercial district, where the buildings so resembled parts of London only the bicycle rickshaws gave them the lie. There was a mist that was not a fog but a veritable cloud of humidity. Sir Lionel indicated a shop front, a wide step flanked by mullioned windows:

'Craven's Oriental Curiosity Shop'.

Straight out of Dickens, thought Leo. Would Quilp be inside, threatening to bite him if he didn't do as he was told? Sir Lionel had begun to shiver from head to toe, so they did not go in but hired a tonga, tucked themselves up under the leaking canopy, and the pony trotted and splashed them all the way back through the city out to Acacia Avenue.

As soon as they arrived at the bungalow Sir Lionel's bearer adopted his traditional role of field-nurse-cum-bodyguard and Leo was left to his own devices. He went straight to the boys' room to see what had been collected from Timpkins' rooms. His battered biscuit tins had been placed side by side on the white coverlet of a bed. He checked their contents. All his shiny objects were there, each item wrapped in paper and each layer separated by a filched lawn handkerchief. All there but no longer a secret. Would, could, a serious bout of malaria erase a recent memory? A few days of fever would give him just enough time to establish himself at the curious Curiosity Shop and find somewhere for his collection that was safe, safer, safest.

The next day he set off early for the House of Craven. He was there at nine on the dot. The shop was opened by a very tall, disjointed, ageless man who reminded Leo of the whippets he had once seen at the race track: pink eyed, anaemic but athletic. This was Young Mr. Craven, who ushered him in through the door as quickly as possible; telling him the staff entrance was "round the back" and never to use the customer entrance again.

The interior of the shop was ill lit, perhaps by design. The poor lighting came from wall-bracket kerosene lamps, whose fumes added to the strange mélange of odours that Leo noticed before his vision had adjusted itself. There was the lavender and beeswax of furniture polish, the old, rather damp smell of floor boards; there was incense and sandalwood, and a cloud of bhang that hung about a sweeper as he pushed his broom around the back room of the shop. Having identified some of the odours, Leo took stock of his surroundings. Above him were crystal chandeliers; to the right of the doorway, a small filigree cage containing a stuffed goldfinch hung from a brass stand. On the floor to his left, two green, square-faced Chinese dogs barked at his intrusion. Behind them stood a small jade lioness carved into a perpetual growl. There were a pair of less than oriental King Charles spaniels made out of porcelain, a stone toad, and two flat marble cats curled up on a counter; a mangy stuffed mongoose challenged a bronze cobra on another. Around the outer walls were large tureens and elaborate urns made just for umbrellas; there were waist-high, wax-faced dolls in oriental costumes, their tiny deformed feet nailed to wooden plinths. Behind a bamboo screen there was a commode decorated with scenes from the *Kama Sutra* and a pair of crimson Persian slippers. And there, behind the long, polished teak counter, under the only electric light in the shop were rows of sparkling stones nestling in beds of crimson velvet. There were ruby rings and sapphire brooches, pearl tipped hatpins and onyx tie-pins, emerald necklaces and diamond bracelets, gold collar-studs and silver cufflinks. Aladdin could not have been more pleased with his cave.

On his first day as a shop assistant Leo was introduced to the staff and given long-winded instructions on how to clean the ornaments, how to register watch repairs, how to fill in forms for this and that; which envelopes to use for jewelry to be valued and which for bracelets and brooches needing safety chains. Then, having spent the morning giving him instructions Young Mr. Craven said he could have a bowl of plain rice and fruit for lunch. Nothing spicy, nothing smelly, understood? At all times he must put customers first. After a half-hour break Leo was handed a small lined exercise book.

"Write down what I told you this morning, boy. Do it in categories: ornaments, stones, watches, brooches etcetera. Let's see what sort of memory you've got."

So Leo sat in the backroom and visualised the contents of the next room, and filled the pages under more categories than he was instructed. Young Mr. Craven showed neither surprise nor pleasure. "You'll do," he said.

Two weeks later there was a change to the quickly established routine. Leo was told he was being given the opportunity to increase his knowledge of the business.

He was led out of the back door and Young Mr. Craven's other shop boy whistled up an urchin, "Follow him," he was told.

First he was led down the narrow side-alley that led back to the main shopping street. They wandered among the colourful clients of The Fancy Mahal Bazaar for a few minutes and then they stepped out of the Victorian gothic of colonial Bombay into a very different land of commerce. Colonial emporia gave way to sari shops and trinket markets, out of this they crossed to a street of palladium and minaret facades, and then they were among street vendors and cooking pots; the smell of sizzling cardamom seeds and onions frying sweet golden brown in ghee. Then suddenly they were in a labyrinth of tall wooden tenements, stepping between bags of bones begging for life and painted boys lurking for business. Leo followed the urchin and knew that if he were abandoned or assaulted the outcome would be the same; he could run in any direction and never get back to British India a quarter of a mile away.

They turned into forbidding alleys that became canals in the rainy season. The tenements above seemed to lean in to suffocate the intruders. A rat ran down a gutter in front of them for a number of yards, a Pied Piper in reverse. They turned again, and again and again. The underfed urchin skipped and slipped down alleys that had never seen the light of day. They turned again, this time into a closed courtyard. A dead end. The urchin pushed open a door and the noise of Bombay, the clamour of humanity stopped. For one single moment there was silence. The urchin beckoned Leo to follow him into the empty black entrance. And then Leo jumped out of his skin.

A giant was hiding behind the door. The genie had escaped from its lamp. A huge, turbaned head lowered itself to examine him. Leo's eyes were on a level with a wobbling belly overlapping a sashed waistline, and a scimitar.

"Hah!" breathed the creature.

"Huh!" retorted the urchin.

"The water-rat returns, and with a fine fat frog for supper," whispered the giant, knocking Leo sideways with inhuman halitosis.

"The water-rat returns," said the urchin in his street Marathi, "on legitimate business."

"Legitimate!" exploded the giant, tossing the little guide some coins.

"Legitimate. What would you know, freak? Your mother was an elephant, your father was a toad, your arse is covered in warts and you fart like a . . ."

The giant lifted the urchin by what remained of his shirt. The shirt collar tore apart; the urchin fell, landed like a cat, looped beneath the archway of bandy legs and was through the door. "I have to take him back, you devil worshipping lump of pig lard! Call me." And he was away before Leo had a moment to realize he was on his own. But then he did, and he was terrified.

Leo had read about trolls but didn't know they existed in India. The creature lowered itself again to scrutinise him then reared up and a haunch of wobbling oiled flesh that was an arm stretched out to inch the door open a little further. Leo stood motionless, his white drill suit almost luminous in just one ray of light.

"Good Lord above and bless my heathen soul," said the monster in perfect schoolboy English. "A young *sahib*. Or yes, or no?"

He turned Leo with a plump, ringed finger. "The clothes say you are, young sir. But my nose tells me something else. Hmmm, fee-fi-fo-fum - not the blood of an English mum!" The creature sniffed Leo's hair, stared into his pale green eyes and tweaked his nose up and down, then he straightened up to his full height and adopted a quite different attitude.

"Now, please follow me," he said.

The turbaned doorman stepped into a foetid stair well and began to rise. "Follow me. Follow me. Come along, chop, chop, and take care to watch your step."

Leo watched his step and it was as well he did, for many of the steps were not there at all. Then a banister appeared as if summoned by the genie, and then they were on a landing and going up a more solid, safer set of steps. And then they were on another landing and the giant knocked delicately at a stout door. It was opened by a dwarf.

Leo was ushered into Victorian England. Velvet and chintz, tassels and hunting prints; three large-globed oil lamps, and in the centre of the room a carved mahogany table. Across the other side of the room an ancient seated mummy: a collection of leather-clad bones dressed in a burgundy smoking-jacket and wearing a fez, was propped behind a large, ornate desk beside a narrow window. It was Old Mr. Craven.

"You are Leo Kazan. Welcome, welcome. My son says you have the makings of an excellent apprentice. Come here, where I can see you better."

Leo stood rooted to the spot. Light entered from the barred window and as the old man stood Leo could see him in profile. His nose had been eaten away, his mouth had disappeared but his eyes bulged out on stalks. The urchin had indeed brought him to a house of freaks and - lepers! The man moved: it was a mask. He was in a madhouse: a masquerade. There were bars on the window; this was Bedlam in Bombay.

"Come closer," beckoned the decrepit creature that was to be his master. Then, with two yellow claws, Old Mr. Craven removed his bulging eyes.

Leo felt the floorboards disappear beneath him; he was falling, falling through the floor. He would land on the genie and . . .

The old man tutted, "Arnold," he said, addressing the small man that had opened the door, "call the Pathan back and get the boy some water then get back to Lionel and tell him my apprentice has arrived as arranged."

Eventually, Leo yawned a huge air-gulping yawn and found himself sitting in a high-backed armchair flanked by the vast doorkeeper, his arms folded across his chest, a scowl on his face, and an immaculate dwarf in white tie and frock-coat. The dwarf offered him a glass of water. The room swayed back into focus, but reality lay just out of reach.

A distant voice said, "Well now, young man, if those two

flights of stairs are too much for you I do not think we have a future together. Mmm?"

He was just a normal old man. Thin and wrinkled but neither wasted nor shrunken.

"I am most sorry, sir. I am - I am not a weakling."

"No indeed, you look very well-fed to me," said the elderly antiquarian, coming over to the chair and patting the boy on the shoulder. He nodded at the doorkeeper, who said something under his breath in English and left the room.

"Shall we start again?"

"Please."

"Well come over to my desk. Can you stand? Good. You are here to learn about precious gems, are you not?"

Leo drained the water and handed it back to the diminutive servant who stood waiting with a tiny silver tray. He dropped his shoulders, took a deep breath and levered himself out of the armchair. "Yes, I have been sent to learn. Well, that is, I want to learn." He walked over to the desk. Nothing seemed quite right; he was still a little woozy. "I am most dreadfully sorry about this disturbance, sir."

"Tut, tut, a momentary failure." Old Mr. Craven was back behind his desk replacing his magnifying goggles. "Nevertheless," he said, gazing at Leo with sightless eyes, "nevertheless, being quite serious, I shall say that this is something that you may not let happen. Not if you are to work for the House of Craven. If you are employed to take valuable items from here to there you need your wits about you. A slip, a trip, a stumble, whatever the environment, you will be stripped. Do you follow me?"

Leo nodded and went closer to the desk. On its green leather top there was a large sheet of pink blotting paper. On the pink blotting paper were two sheets of white paper. And on each sheet of white paper there was a small pyramid of irregular dull pebbles.

"Your task, young man, is to tell me on which sheet lie the more valuable stones. Shall we begin?"

Four hours later, Leo was back in the maze of alleys, trying to keep up with an underfed urchin who demanded four annas when they reached Victoria Terminus. Leo gave him two. It was still too much because they were probably of an age, but one of them had a future and the other faced mere survival. Two days later, Leo learned that the tenement occupied by his master had another doorway into another alley, and at the end of this alley lay Craven's Oriental Curiosity Shop and the land of the box wallahs. In less than a minute he could be back among the pompous emporia of the Raj. He revised his ideas; a street urchin who tried to protect a business investment deserved respect!

Exactly one week after that, Leo was standing behind a vast teak counter trying to thread soft, soggy string through the tiny holes of cardboard price tags, when his attention was drawn to a face pressed up against the shop window. It was a woman. More than that it was impossible to say so flat was her face against the glass. He had already learnt that women could spend ages gazing at the baubles Young Mr. Craven put on display in the window (anything of real value was kept behind the counter), so to start with he was not at all disturbed by her interest. But she didn't go away. The fiddly task was tedious and the woman's presence began to irritate him. He tried staring back at her, willing her to go away. It didn't work. He left his task and went to drink a glass of water. She was still there when he returned. He resumed his task; she stayed in place.

Unable to resist the temptation any longer, Leo lowered

himself from sight and re-emerged with crossed-eyes, and lolling tongue like a dribbling idiot. Suddenly the door bell tinkled and he nearly swallowed his tongue.

"Yes, madam, can I help you?" His voice squeaked up and down out of control.

She was tall, thin, wearing a spinster's uniform of high-necked blouse and long grey skirt. "May I look around? I want to buy a gift for . . ." She bent to examine two mother-of-pearl boxes on a three legged table, "How pretty."

Leo tried to get his features and voice back in order and came round from behind the counter to be of assistance. She looked up at him almost in fright.

"Oh, oh, dear. Yes, well thank you. Another day." She was gone.

Leo shrugged and went back to the price tags. He tipped the box containing the cut string pieces into the box containing the cardboard tags and pushed them to the very back of a drawer marked 'watch repairs'. The incident had unsettled him. He needed a more demanding task: he didn't want to think about her or anyone like her.

Chapter 6

Some time in the autumn of 1916, Sir Lionel Pinecoffin, who had just seen a colleague off on a voyage to England, was taking afternoon tea in the Taj Mahal Hotel. He enjoyed taking tea at the Taj. The absurdity of the place amused him. It was an ostentatious, French-designed building, erected on an unwanted swamp once gifted to England in a Portuguese princess's dowry. It was the only establishment in British Bombay to permit the Raj and wealthy citizens of all colours and creeds to meet in informal circumstances. The hotel also served the best tea-cakes outside the Home Counties. It was absurd, it was amusing. It pleased him to sit among the tall, cool columns and watch Indian rajahs and their retinues; ranis in gold edged saris, clinking priceless bangles as they lifted their cups; American businessmen in safari suits; Goanese spice-merchants, rich as Croesus and smelling of turmeric, selling cargoes. He liked to see how other nationalities conducted their lives, albeit the sheer expense of the hotel set them on different social strata to the rest of their fellow countrymen. Each and every visitor was in someway atypical. If the city of Bombay was a social melting pot, the Taj Hotel was where the wealthiest and best dressed of each race mingled.

On this particular afternoon, Sir Lionel had just ordered tea with lemon and Madeira cake, for a change, from one waiter when another came to his table bearing a business card on a silver salver.

"The gentleman to your left, sir, sends his regards and asks me to give you this."

"Thank you."

The man sitting to Sir Lionel's left was examining his finger nails. The name on the card was Leonid Kazan.

"Please convey my respects to the gentleman and ask him if he would care to join me."

The waiter crossed between the tables. Leonid Kazan looked in Sir Lionel's direction, inclined his head in acceptance and rose from his seat. He was a large, thickset man of indefinable middle-age. His hair was straight and black, his collar exceptionally white against a swarthy skin. Something about him reminded Sir Lionel of a seventeenth century courtier, the sort who ill advised his monarch for personal gain.

"Sir Lionel, how charming. Well met by lamplight, as your Bard nearly said." He lowered himself into a chair and smiled around him. "Midsummer Night, or was it Twelve Night? Yes, yes, charming. I have been meaning to make an appointment to see you for some time." His English spilled out in unpredictable bursts like rusty water from an aged watering-can. "So very congenial to see you in these delightful surroundings. I cannot understand at all why the architect suicided because the hotel was not quite altogether just what he wanted. Such a perfectionist must have had a sad life, don't you think?"

"Indeed," smiled Sir Lionel. "Perfectionists are their own worst enemies by definition."

"When one has to contend with so many petty enemies, why bring trouble to oneself through mere dissatisfaction? Not being satisfied is just a trivial excuse, don't you think, for being miserable?"

Sir Lionel inclined his head in agreement. "Are you resident in Bombay, Mr. Kazan, or just visiting?"

"Both. I have come from Calcutta on business, but also to see my house. I bought a charming property on Malabar Hill some years ago. The view, the jasmine - just a perfect place. Staff is a nuisance of course. They don't have anything to do when I am not there and expect to be paid. It defeats me. They live in this little palace, a perfumed palace, ah the jasmine . . ."

A waiter brought fresh tea and a cup and saucer for Sir Lionel's guest. The Russian lifted the lid of the tea-pot and peered into the hot liquid. "I only drink leaves," he said. "None of that dry powder your English think is tea." He stirred the pot with his teaspoon. "A proper home is so important, don't you agree?"

"Indeed, and your family are here or in Calcutta?"

"I am to re-marry very soon. We shall live where I am posted."

"Congratulations. Your new wife is from Bombay?"

"God forbid it, no. She's Russian - from a most excellent family. Pedigreed."

"Yes. Well that makes life easier; chatting to one's spouse in a foreign tongue must be a chore. Your first wife passed-away? I am sorry to hear that. Not the best of climates, Bombay."

"No, not the best of climates, nor perhaps, I may have to say it, always the best of people. Traders!"

He spoke the word 'traders' with such disdain Sir Lionel wondered if he had heard "traitors". Then, without more ado, the large man leaned back to watch someone entering the tea room. Addressing the room in general he said, "My first wife went mad."

He turned back to address his interlocutor in a more discreet tone, "She had delicate mental health; she was born in India of course. Her father was a trader. Perhaps the climate?" He shrugged and sipped his tea. "It is a sad case. And it has taken me *years* to acquire the divorce . . ."

Unsure whether he wanted to hear anymore about the first Mrs. Kazan, Sir Lionel moved the conversation in a new direction. "Forgive my curiosity, but you clearly recognized me here. I regret I cannot recollect us ever having been introduced."

"Yes, yes, many years ago. A vice-regal reception. There was some little joking about my name, some of your young fellows calling me Lord *Curzon*. A silly joke of course. It was you, Sir Lionel, who put a stop to the embarrassment."

"Ah, yes. I think I remember, your name wasn't . . ." Sir Lionel took a sip of scalding tea to silence a foolish statement. A political officer for so many years and he could still put his foot in his mouth! Hermione would laugh. He thought about her waving goodbye, waving a wide, white hat like a flag of surrender, and for the first time in many years wished that he too were on the ship going back home. Surrender to climate, the constant vigilance, give in to indigestion, mosquitoes, scorpions in slippers - give in to the whole caboodle and go back home, saying, 'pax: India you have won'. But of course he wouldn't. Nor, thinking about it, would the gentleman stirring a third sugar lump into his tea. So why the silly chit-chat?

Sir Lionel placed his cup on its gold-rimmed saucer. He was about to speak but Kazan said, "Interesting thing these names we have. Take mine for instance, fairly obvious its origin, Kazan, from the khanate: a province now, on the Volga. My ancestors were the Khans of Kazan, naturally."

"Naturally."

"Your name too is interesting. You attend many funerals?" The Russian chortled and some of his tea spilt into his saucer.

"No - that was an old school joke, of course. Also, that I am a good sort deep down." The word play was lost in subtlety or translation, or both.

The Russian said, "I still have land there, farms and villages. They bring me a comfortable income. Not princely, but something for a son to inherit. Which leads me indirectly, in this roundabout way, to why I wished to meet you. However, I pause. I see more people coming in to take their tea and perhaps this conversation should be less conspicuous. Is watched, you know? Shall we meet quite by chance in similar circumstances for an early cocktail in three days' time?"

"You were going to make an appointment to see me in my office. Why not come there?"

"Yes, yes, less clock and dagger. Our Empires are no longer enemies; they are brothers-in-arms in this tragic war. The habits of our old Great Game die hard. I was so used to you chappies keeping an eye on me I stopped noticing, until . . ."

The big Russian leant forward, straining the button-thread of his double-breasted suit, then apparently decided to withhold the next comment and sat back, cocking his head to one side and giving a dimpled grin. "Shall we say Wednesday?"

"Yes, I believe I am free."

"Good. Wednesday: the day of Woden, the warrior god, the transformer, the poet. Do you know Norse mythology, Sir Lionel?"

"No, I regret I don't."

"You should read the myths, my friend. They are the keys to our cultures. Every people have them. They serve to explain our origins. Names have meanings, they give us our belonging."

"Yes, quite."

The Englishman remained impassive, but he was formulating a response to what had become a diatribe of innuendo. He was saved however, by the Russian himself. Suddenly the man was on his feet and saying, "Well, thank you for a pleasant tea. Goodbye."

Sir Lionel rose from his seat but the swarthy Russian was already striding out, tugging his napkin from his jacket front as he went, tossing it onto an unoccupied table, nodding to a family coming in, not looking behind him as he left the room.

Lionel Pinecoffin sat down again, exhausted. It would all have been quite absurd, he thought if there hadn't been a quite definite element of menace. Origins: an estate in Mother Russia, a mad wife, a house on Malabar Hill - a perfumed palace no less. What did he want? What did he know?

Sir Lionel's sense of loss without his wife was compounded by his need to tell her what had happened at the Taj Hotel. He wanted to consider the implications of letting his Mowgli wander out of the jungle with someone who knew the boy well. Hermione was in every sense his helpmate; she would listen and perhaps offer suggestions. He *could* let Leo go. Kazan was right, the two empires had, albeit perhaps only temporarily, set aside their rivalry over the Indian sub-continent: the boy's return to his father could be stage managed as a glorious re-union. It could even be used in the press as confirmation of how the two nations had come together. The whole thing had all been a sorry mistake. Reverend Johns had rescued a lost child, who in fact had a family. The family had been located. End of story. And whatever the press did with it, no one could deny the orphanage had done its very best for the boy.

He would get Arnold Mackay, his personal secretary, to locate Millicent Cleaver - she was the only weak link. Johns would mind his p's and q's, whatever was said, he had too much to lose. But the governess woman would have to be dealt with, she was the weak link. He'd have to sound her out: perhaps a gentle threat of prosecution would be sufficient. The Cravens were not a problem: discretion was their family motto.

Unwilling to be alone with his conscience, for it did bother him, he finished his tea and took a cab to his club. He regretted the decision as soon as he entered the bar. Ha-hawing old-fogies were gathered in groups like grounded homing pigeons, too old to fly, too fat to get off the ground. He bought himself a whisky, exchanged pleasantries with a barman, then took another cab back to the docks and strolled down the only sweet smelling bunder in Bombay - the Sassoon timber terminal. He would call in on Timpkins for a chat. There were two important details to be ascertained before the Wednesday interview; the whereabouts of the mad wife, and how mad was mad.

On the following Wednesday morning Sir Lionel realized that when he had insisted on Kazan coming to his office he had not specified a time. Leo was with the Cravens, ancient and modern, it was unlikely he would come to the office, nevertheless the doorman was instructed to say the office was closed, should the boy appear.

He assumed the Russian bear would make his appearance during the lunch hour when the office building was empty. He was right. At ten-past one the lift clanked to a halt on the second-floor landing. Its metal cage scraped open and there was a tap, tap on the office door. Before going to open it Sir Lionel opened the door of an adjoining, interior room. A very small man was perched on a chair writing in a ledger.

"He's here?" enquired the scribe without lifting his head.

"Think so. I'll call if necessary." Sir Lionel straightened his jacket, smoothed a hand over a pocket and strode over to greet his visitor.

"Mr. Kazan, come in, come in."

The Russian was more subdued. He wore a dove-grey tie and had a matching silk handkerchief in his top pocket. He was carrying a crocodile briefcase. Just a little too elegant thought the Englishman, yet not vulgar.

"Good to see you, please take a seat." He ushered Kazan into an overstuffed chair in the corner of the room and took another that he had earlier placed at a suitable angle.

"Comfortable? I can send out for some tea, or would you care for something a little stronger? I have a bottle of vodka, a gift from a member of your consulate when it was first opened. It's rather 'aged in the bottle' by now, I fear."

Kazan looked at a silver timepiece on a chain. "It's after one, yes, why not? You show me the vodka bottle and I shall decide." The vodka was taken from a cabinet, its credentials examined, it was poured into appropriate glasses and the two men settled back as best they could in their uncomfortable chairs.

"Now Sir Lionel, I shall not be beaten about the bush, I am going to come straight to the point. This is in our both best interests and we are both to suffer if we cannot resolve the issue *tout de suite*. So here it is . . ." He paused, the door to the adjoining room was ajar, he inclined his head in its direction and raised a bushy eyebrow.

Sir Lionel followed his gaze. "My private secretary. Trustworthy. Has to be."

Kazan sniffed. "In both our interests, but not for secretaries,

Sir Lionel. I must insist."

The Englishman rose, closed the door. The small man in the interior office clambered down from his cushioned chair, took a stethoscope from one desk drawer, a small pistol from another and went to stand behind the closed door.

"Diamonds," said Kazan with the smugness of one playing an unexpected ace so early in the game.

"Diamonds?"

"A fortune's worth of diamonds."

"Diamonds here? Where? I understood Indian diamond sources were mined out last century. Very few or none left."

"Alluvial diamonds, picked like pebble stones on a beach. A river bed in Hyderabad."

"Good lord. The richest nizam in India and they find diamonds in one of his rivers. To he that hath shall be given. Are we talking about Golconda diamonds, by the way?"

"No, not Golconda, I don't think. I understand it is just a dry stream and someone found some interesting stones and he went to see somebody, who spoke to somebody else -you know the way these people are. Probably a brother-law of a cousin who is the washerwoman's grandfather. Who knows? *I* cannot say. My informer, you understand, is very shy with actual facts. However, the Nizam, this small man who is so rich man, doesn't know the local peasants are selling them to an agent. And he would have a blue fit if he knew this agent has links to a Bolshevik group in Moscow. Into the bargain, this agent is a Hindu and brother of a man in the National Congress."

"Sounds a bit of a rigmarole to me," said Sir Lionel. "You have, I am sure, checked the veracity of the claims."

"Naturally, Sir Lionel. We are not colonial amateurs, you

know. It is what I am told by a safe, honourable, very concerned source." The Russian picked up his drink, but before the already empty glass could touch his lips he exploded righteously, "Independence! Home Rule League agitators with more money than sense, now putting ideas to some damn stupid college boys in my country."

"Yes, well that link is nothing new, is it? Marx did after all stress the *International* aspect of class struggle - that's what this is, no more no less. Your students and the Indian hot-heads are basically acting out of what one might term petty jealousy. Know thy place, as my mother would say: lord in the manor, peasant at the gate." He sighed. He had been drawn into a popular opinion he didn't altogether share. "Are the gems going to Moscow or St. Petersburg, do you know?"

Kazan huffed. It was not the response he had desired. This English cold blood. Damn men had no passion. They deserved to lose their empire. If Tsar Nicholas only realized how easy it would be to wrest this treasure chest called India from their grip while their attention was turned fighting the Germans and Turks. Ah, how he disliked the British - whining hypocrites. He pushed his empty glass forward and watched his whey-faced opponent refill it. "Some get to the diamond exchange in Antwerp," he said "I do not know how in this war, but I am told they are traded for good prices. They are the best ones, the small ones go straight to Russia; apparently they are useful for our new industrial machines. A complete waste, if you ask me."

"You do seem very well informed."

"Of course! We have our patriots, Sir Lionel. There is mischief in my country . . ." The Russian diplomat searched for a word, "Disturbances! Strikes! Factory workers, farm boys, they are marching in the streets causing trouble. And who is organizing this? Students! There are groups of students and ex-soldiers with weapons, guns and God forbid it, bombs. And to get these guns, these damn nuisance students need finance. And some cheeky boys here in this country are providing it. This is *your* problem Sir Lionel. It is *your* job to find who is organizing this and why." The Russian tossed back his vodka with a flourish.

Sir Lionel adjusted his position. There was something not right in all this taradiddle. Kazan had rattled off the details as if he had been practising them for days. "Have you come all the way from Calcutta to tell me this, may I ask?"

Kazan nodded, which confused the Englishman. *Niet* was said with a nod.

Was the student threat in St. Petersburg that strong? Could these diamonds really be helping to finance rebellion against the Tsar of Russia? If the information was that they were being sold to finance the Home Rule for India campaign it would make sense. Could the two groups of revolutionaries be collaborating that closely?

Kazan broke the short silence, "You do not seem surprised, Sir Lionel. I thought you would take the matter more seriously."

"Well, yes and no. I mean I am surprised and not surprised. If anything, I am surprised at the apparent sophistication of a group of coolies discovering what must just look like ordinary stone chippings, examining them and then hiring an agent."

What actually troubled him was the Russian diplomat's involvement. He had known about the diamond find for months. Old Craven had told him about it. But Craven had said the stones were on Kapasala territory, which was a petty autonomous state belonging to a Sikh rajah who was running into serious money trouble. His idea had been to leave the rajah to his own devices then eventually bale him out, and buy his loyalty. Knowing the stones were on Hyderabad territory meant he would be obliged to take up the matter with the Nizam. Delicate. Or was the Russian throwing a red herring back into a dry river bed?

Lionel Pinecoffin stared into the colourless liquid in his tumbler. Kazan had unearthed this bit of illicit trading and brought it to him for something more than concern for a wartime ally.

It would be easy enough to stop at source. On the other hand it might be a real chance to trace Home Rule finance back to members of the National Congress and then remove them, once and for all, from circulation. Either way, he needed names and evidence. Ughh, vodka on an empty stomach was not a good idea. First he would have to warn Old Craven to get *his* finger out of the pie.

Looking Kazan in the eye, he said, "So the small diamonds go straight to Russia: overland, then boat across the Black Sea and through the Ukraine?"

The Russian shrugged his shoulders. "The usual trade routes. My country drinks a lot of tea. We think they go with the tea."

"And the end-users of the finance? Do you have names?"

"Our enemies, Sir Lionel. Mutual enemies. I told you. Revolutionaries who will kill our royalty, yours and mine. The same maternal line from your good Queen Victoria. These students will commit regicide as soon as they get into the palaces. They will, Sir Lionel, they will kill. The clever students organize and the stupid peasants follow their orders. Peasants, brutes with no learning, they do as they are told like dumb animals for the promise of a crust of black bread. Tchh."

Sir Lionel sighed, he would have to pour more vodka and let the bluster run its course. He reached for the bottle and refilled the glasses.

The Russian tossed back his vodka and barely pausing

for breath continued; "This war has shown them the power of the ordinary *ignorant* with a gun in his hand. Any uneducated son of a butcher can kill people like pigs these days. I told you, they are even marching! Thousands of killers are out on the streets every day, they pretend to be waiting in bread queues. They hang around outside factories, but they wouldn't accept a job if it were offered. No, no. They are just waiting for their weapons. These men and boys are not in uniforms on our battlefields, oh no. These *hoi polloi* are waiting their chance to stir up trouble. Sir Lionel, we need to identify our enemies within, and then we must exterminate them. All of them. No good just finding a few. Oh, no, we need the leaders. Look what happened to beautiful France. Destroyed forever by the unwashed *sans culottes*."

"Indeed." Sir Lionel wanted to laugh but the implications were too grave. He placed his empty glass on the low table before them and smoothed the creases in his trousers. "Tell me," he said, "does the Nizam of Hyderabad know about the alluvial diamonds?"

The man opposite him shook his head.

Damn it, was that yes or no? "He would intervene on your behalf, you know. You just have to tip him the wink. He would rush to your assistance. Independence is definitely not in his favour. Have you considered approaching him?"

"Sir Lionel, this is not my country. This is for you to do."

"Yes, absolutely. I just want to be sure of the facts before I go any further. This may just be a - well a coincidence. Some coolies find some stones and someone who has Home Rule sympathies and knows a couple of your students gets involved. I cannot see how a few industrial value stones can really be that significant."

Kazan was exasperated. His neck had gone red and he was clenching and unclenching the fingers of his left hand. "Yes, I see your point, Sir Lionel. Some precious stones are found fortuitously by accident in a dry river. Some local men contact an agent, who in this case happens to advise the Rajah of Kapasala. Next we know the third son of Kapasala is making arrangements and taking a percentage of the Antwerp price."

Sir Lionel frowned: a new twist. He was either being deliberately misled or Kazan was inventing details to elaborate a tiny bit of potential scandal. He decided to play a similar game for a round or two.

"Kapursala? He's the fat chap with the Spanish wife? They say she's very beautiful."

"She is. We dined in Paris. But that is the Rajah of Kapurthala. I am speaking of a another small state in the west; Kapasala. The princes have been educated in Britain, of course."

"Of course. You dined in Paris?"

"They travel widely these Indian princes."

And so do you, thought Sir Lionel. What were *you* doing in Paris? Chatting to the French about free-trade on the Indian sub-continent? The French were no longer Napoleonic empire-builders but they were very serious trade rivals. Or was it Indo-China? A way in through the back door. Was he just making his own post-war plans? Or had he made the trip with his own pockets full of shiny stones?

"They are princes," the Russian pronounced the words with a certain reverence. "They are wealthy from the tributes their peasants pay; they travel, they meet people, they spend their wealth. But," Kazan leaned forward, his double chin overflowing his dove-grey cravat, "now is a new fashion to have a European wife. To be more western. So they go looking to find a pretty woman, who can eat with a knife and fork and will not hide with the other bibi-wifies in the zenana. This is another of the symptoms, have you thought about that? You British educated them in your own schools then you cannot expect them to settle back into their traditional life. Here is the rubbing. The young ones get bored; they want to mix more in society; like all naughty boys they like to be with the less desirable types. They get ideas: political ideas, which they do not exactly understand. They should be kept at home. Quite honestly, Sir Lionel, it has to be said, your Government has an unnecessary sense of generosity regarding this country. It is education to blame. You let them go off and learn, any Tom, Dick and Hari! You even teach them here in Bombay in your missionary schools."

Sir Lionel fidgeted with a cuff. But Leonid Kazan made no significant pause at the reference. He was lost in the dangers of literacy and numeracy. His cheeks were growing redder, blowing out like nursery pictures of the wind.

"Look what happens, Sir Lionel," he continued, "a born prince who supplies revolutionaries, it is not natural. It simply should not be permitted. You cannot educate them to use their brains and then expect them to be docile like humble coolies. These chaps are looking for trouble."

"British ambivalence: we're good at that. Kapasala I take it is acting behind the Nizam's back? Is he just one of our naughty boys, or is he seriously acting out of patriotic principles, would you say? He could be just trying to pay off his gambling debts and have one up on us."

Kazan stared at the Englishman. "Such irony Sir Lionel may not be appropriate here. *We* are looking for immediate action. *We* have identified our enemies. Now, because they are on *your* territory we need your government and police to cut them down, root and branch."

"You may be right. But I am still confused regarding some details. Rajahs aren't interested in Home Rule, it would ruin them. They stand to lose income, land, status - their entire lives are rooted in the ancient laws of divine right. Why would young Kapasala be involved?"

Kazan looked at him as if he had just failed a spelling test. "Because he is not a first born. He will inherit nothing. Like all these Indian boys, he is considering his future!"

"Alright, let us recap. Let me see if I have enough facts to go on. Someone or some peasants locate a source of alluvial diamonds. They contact an agent, who somewhere along the line sells, or passes the stones on to obtain finance for revolutionaries. These revolutionaries are active in both this country and in Russia. Can we really assume one group will aid the other? Is their combined strength sufficient to overthrow your Tsar and our centuries' old status here?"

"Yes!"

"Well then can I ask why you have come to me with this and not taken it straight to Delhi?"

Kazan half closed his eyes, "Do you want an honest answer or a diplomat's answer?"

"I think I am simply asking what you stand to lose or gain, sir."

Kazan got to his feet and stood leaning over the back of his chair. "I have my enemies, Sir Lionel. People who have taken advantage of my past misfortune and my periodic melancholy to undermine respect for me. I believe this is a very dangerous matter. I have colleagues who . . . Let us say they do not take this seriously because they have less to lose. There is a very serious possibility of these revolutionaries being successful. Now . . ." Kazan removed a handkerchief from a pocket and wiped his forehead. "I am taking a big risk to tell you this. Being honest is not what a diplomat should do."

Sir Lionel was sobered by the man's tone. For as much as he wanted to set him down as a pernicious buffoon there was something very genuine about his concerns. He opened the palm of his right hand as if to encourage the Russian to proceed.

"If there is a revolution and these Bolsheviks win - if it becomes known that I was the one to cut a supply of finance for their revolution - once they are in office I shall have no job. I shall not only lose everything I possess in my country - that goes without saying, I shall lose my post. If this happens I have a double dilemma. I can never return to my family estate and I shall have no income here. I am, as you say, batting a sticky wicket."

Lionel Pinecoffin sighed, the human face of international politics. "So you want me, in my role as the British Political Officer for Commerce to be the one to put a spanner in the works?"

"Yes. Exactly."

"In that case, may I suggest a spot of lunch? There is an excellent restaurant just round from the Stock Exchange, we can have a private booth."

Chapter 7

Arnold Mackay heard them leave the room. He waited for the lift to clank shut and start its descent then he let himself out of the inconspicuous office, locking the door carefully behind him. A few minutes later he was entering a shop with mullioned windows. As a rare Bombay breeze squeezed in through the door behind him, there was a waft of lavender polish and bhang.

"Well?" said Clive Craven from behind the counter.

"It wasn't what we were expecting."

"What did he want?"

"Wants Lionel to nip the diamond deal in the bud. Kapasala's rumbled."

"How did he find out about that?"

"Oh, God, I don't know. You can't blow your nose in this country without someone minutes it. Everybody watches everybody: I should know."

"Only Kapasala?"

"No mention of us, whatsoever. And if that Russian knew about our little game, believe me he would take the greatest pleasure in informing our dear Lionel."

"What about father?"

"Nothing. He only mentioned Kapasala and the agent. Calm down, Clive."

The dwarf spent a few moments getting himself settled on a velvet-covered chair provided for the comfort of older customers and looked around him, "Nobody here, I suppose."

"No, business is not good. This damned war."

"There is a small complication." The small man fixed his gaze on the stuffed mongoose and brass cobra. "The Russian says that the stones are being sold to finance certain revolutionary . . . Um, that Bolshevik student types in Russia and Home Rule Leaguers here are using the money to get weapons."

"Oh my God! Oh dear Lord! Oh heavens above!" The jeweler began to hyperventilate. "I knew we shouldn't have got involved."

"It was your father's idea!"

"My father reads far too many penny-dreadfuls. Goodness knows what goes on in his mind." Young Mr. Craven, whose father was in his eighties, wrung his hands, "Oh dear, dear, dear me."

"Well it's not *such* a catastrophe. Could even be turned to our advantage. Put up the 'closed' sign Clive. We don't want to be interrupted. I have a plan."

Clive Craven winced. Nevertheless, the shop was duly closed and darkened, and the spindly jeweler returned to his habitual station behind the counter. The dwarf pulled a square silver case from an inside pocket and smoothed his plump fingers over his engraved initials; he opened it and removed a cigarette. Slowly, deliberately, he tapped down the Turkish-blend tobacco on the counter and struck a match.

The jeweler watched every move as if mesmerized. His mind had gone quite numb. All the adventure in his soul was expended on the purchase and resale of antiques and items of jewelry. He kept meticulous accounts: what was bought at one price and sold at another: each transaction entered in its appropriate column. Colonial politics worried him at the best of times; diamond dealing that financed revolutionaries scared him. Being *involved* in colonial politics and financing revolutionaries *and* benefiting from unregistered diamond dealing scared him to death. He gripped the counter with both hands.

He had been doubtful about his father's diamond scheme from the start, but even his cautious nature hadn't foreseen such a disaster. "I think we had better go into the workroom," he said "I don't think we can be observed, but one cannot be sure. I need to sit down."

"Clive, you are over-reacting. I come here most days of the week. Nobody will remark on this visit." Nonetheless, the mismatched friends made their way through the glories of the overstocked shop and into the dingy workshop.

"Lord, I forgot," said the dwarf, "where's the boy?"

"With father. He's learning about emeralds this week: cutting, clarity, settings. He'll know more than me soon."

"You want to watch that!" Arnold Mackay, who had also spent some years in the Bombay Anglican Boys' Orphanage, loathed Leo. This chance to get him out of his boss's orbit was too good to miss. He had a plan. He sat on the watch mender's stool and fiddled with the tiny, delicate brass tools.

The jeweler closed the communicating door and leaned against it, forgetting he had wanted to sit down. He said, "If they know what young Kapasala is up to why don't they get him arrested?"

"He's done nothing wrong. A fellow told him about alluvial diamonds, he got some and consulted your father; no crime committed, unless his Highness, the Nizam of Hyderabad decides to take him to court for stealing something on his land, there's nothing anyone can do. Finders keepers: oldest rule in the book."

"But they aren't keeping them. They're selling them. And look where the profit's going. Heavens above, we're in very serious trouble."

"Rubbish. You - well, your father has given advice, facilitated the polishing nothing more. Still," said Arnold, blowing a set of perfect smoke rings into the still atmosphere, "we do need to be a bit more careful. I don't want to be linked with undesirables."

"Undesirables! Arnold, we are talking about treason. If what that Russian says is true, we are linked with Russian revolutionaries there and bloody Home Rule revolutionaries here. We could be shot!"

"Now who's acting out a penny dreadful? Calm down for God's sake. I'd rather run the risk of upsetting the British government than get on the wrong side of those bloodthirsty dacoits Kapasala's using as runners!"

There was silence. Cigarette ash was tapped into a common brass ashtray. The dwarf said slowly, plainly, "We have to advance in the knowledge that pulling out of the agreement could be infinitely, infinitely more dangerous than continuing. If you get my meaning?"

The tall man peered at his small friend and fellow conspirator. "No, no I don't get . . . Oh God, yes! We know too much."

"Exactly."

"Tell me everything. Start to finish. What the Russian said and what Lionel said."

"Well, the Russians have found out about how young Kapasala's getting money for his unruly friends. They know about the riverbed, possibly where it is located, but I'm not sure about that.

They know that the stones are sold and that some of the proceeds also end up in St. Petersburg. They think there are two groups working to their mutual advantage. I don't think *we* constitute a group, do you?"

Clive Craven shook his head uncertainly.

The dwarf continued, "The stones are polished, then taken out of the country; at least I think that is what he told Lionel. No mention was made of our cut. Or that you or your father value some of the bigger stones before they leave Bombay."

In a low voice, Clive Craven said "Arnold, did *you* know about the finance aspect?"

Sir Lionel's private secretary examined his burnt down tube of tobacco then looked up with a rueful smile. "More or less."

"Oh, dear," sighed the jeweler, visibly shrinking with dismay. "And now Lionel knows."

"Oh come on, Clive! Your father and Lionel have been working hand-in-glove for the best part of twenty years. Do you honestly believe Lionel didn't know about this?"

"No, I suppose not."

"It wouldn't surprise me if it wasn't our dear Lionel who got *us* involved in the first place!"

"You mean he could be using us? Why?"

"I don't know. He's too devious even for me sometimes. Look, you and your father know nothing about the final destination of the gems. None of your business. Simple as that."

Clive Craven shuddered and started to bite his nails. His friend tried to appease him. "All right, we will extract ourselves. But not," he tried to snap his podgy fingers, "not just like that. It would arouse far too much suspicion. You do a couple more trips, then you say you can't continue because your father has had a heart attack and you are too busy looking after him to do any more."

The jeweler stared in horror. "I can't!"

"Clive, be reasonable. They know where to find us. Well, where to find you and your father. We keep the arrangement going as agreed for one more month, okay? Then you back out for a reasonable reason."

"I cannot make another trip. I get sea sick as it is."

Arnold Mackay sighed dramatically then, as if it were their last resort, he said, "I suppose we could use the boy: Lionel's personal flunkey. We'd be quite safe then. If Lionel *is* watching, he will make damn sure nothing happens to his beloved Leo."

"Leo saved Lady Hermione's life," said the jeweler.

"That's the story."

"It's true. You don't like him I know, but it's quite true. Lady Hermione told me about it herself."

Arnold Mackay shrugged, "Must be true, then."

Clive Craven paced around the small workshop with his arms folded, considering the new proposition for a moment or two, then he came back to where his friend was seated and said, "I don't like it. The boy doesn't need to be involved in this, too. It would just be one more in . . ."

"Trouble?"

"Yes, trouble."

"A clever man once said 'the end justifies the means'."

"Machiavelli."

The end, for Clive Craven and Arnold Mackay, had been some financial security in turbulent times. The Home Rule movement was gathering momentum and most Indians seemed to be expecting self-governance in return for their country's participation in what they saw as a European war. If they could not achieve independence through diplomatic means, they would simply resort to violence. The new hero called Gandhi, recently returned from a non-violent racial campaign in South Africa, might preach peaceful tactics but everyone knew his words wouldn't stop an angry mob on a hot night. Sooner or later incendiary devices would be thrown into British-owned shops and topee-wearers would be attacked on the streets.

The Cravens had been in India for generations but that hadn't changed the pink of their skin or the tone of their voices. Their business would be targeted, of that there was no doubt. The real situation facing father and son was the fact that if they were called to quit India the contents of their shop would be worthless. They would not be able to sell their business and they would have nothing to take with them when they left. But, above all else, they had nowhere to go.

Arnold Mackay had been born in Rawalpindi and orphaned by cholera in Bombay. His father had been an army corporal. He had joined up because there was no future for him as a farm labourer in Suffolk. His mother had joined him in India because her only alternative was working sixteen hours a day as a house-maid in a lonely rural area. They had only been in Bombay that summer because they had a passage back to England: they were taking their only son to a doctor specializing in growth disorders in London.

The problem facing Arnold was ultimately the same as his friends: he had nowhere to go, India was his only home. The income from the Kapasala diamonds was to provide a fund for his future refugee status.

Chapter 8

During the early months of 1917, Leo made three sea trips in a fishing boat to a small harbour some miles down the Malabar Coast. On each occasion, a gaunt individual wearing the yellow scarf of Kali gave him a stitched-up rag wrapped package. The rag package was ridiculously easy to unstitch. From the first two rag packages he extracted one small dull stone. Just one. Not the smallest, not the biggest. Just an average dusty, uncut diamond.

It occurred to him that this might be one of Sir Lionel's tests. If so, was he succeeding or failing? Were the errands a matter of trust or to see how sharp he was? He had assumed from the beginning that Sir Lionel was involved because he couldn't believe even Old Man Craven was capable of hatching such a dangerous scheme. However, no matter who was running the deal he was determined to have his cut. On this third trip the bag he was given was significantly bigger than the previous two. So he took significantly more stones.

Sitting in the prow of the evil smelling bark on that last return voyage, he watched white birds swooping between the blue sky and the green sea. Noisy gulls harassed the fishing boat for part of its catch. They bullied the more delicate terns, stealing shiny little fish from their very beaks. A couple of years before, a gull had dived out of the sky and stolen a cake from Leo's hand as he walked along the beach: he had been more scared than he cared to admit. They were brazen, abusive thieves; vicious, noisy, no style, no saving graces.

He liked being at sea, though. The boat trips had been a revelation. He had lived near the sea all his life and never really noticed it. Out here on the water there was a sense of cleanness. It was everything that the city was not. Despite the clamour of the gulls there was a particular tranquility. The patched sail flapped and the woodwork creaked, and Leo thought they were the finest sounds he had ever heard.

The gentle lurching of the boat lulled him into a reflective mood. He normally avoided introspection; tried not to look back at the past, what he saw there was too upsetting. But now it wasn't a question of thinking about the past, now he was examining the present. Uppermost in his mind was the image of a yellow Kali scarf looped around a dirty brown neck. Did these men in offices, who wore starched collars no matter what the heat, these men who drank tea at five and only ever mixed with their own kind, did they have any idea who they were dealing with? Or more to the point, who he was dealing with? Had they ever heard the word *thag?* Did they know anything about the cult of the goddess Kali? Thinking about it, Leo became angrier and angrier. These ignorant colonials had sent him to men who were obliged, compelled to kill - to make regular sacrifices - human sacrifices. It was not as if he even had a chance of escape if he were chosen. Kali's men worked in threes: one to confound the victim, one to hold the victim, one to slaughter the victim. Leo shuddered. He had been sent to collect a small bag of uncut stones from known killers, because for sure the man with the yellow scarf had not been on his own. Old Mr. Craven had some dubious contacts but these were just plain dangerous.

He was irate, fuming. Who the hell were these people to play with his life? Just because he had no home: no parents to complain if he went missing. Even the Cravens' urchin runner was better off than him. He had a family and a home. It was a tin shack, but it was where the family lived - together.

Leo leaned over the side of the boat watching the white spray grow taller. He was always being sent here and there; do this and that 'and not a word to anyone'. Not that you could talk to anybody and expect them to take your words at face value. Nothing could ever be taken at face value. There was no one to trust and nobody was what they seemed. Even the hillsmen that sent the rubies down from the frontier 'only for Mr. Craven, Sahib' had private or political interests beyond purses of rupees. That's why the Pathan was employed. He could translate their cryptic messages into English, Arnold Mackay would then set them out in official form for Sir Lionel, and the IPS officer would include them in his regular dispatches to the India Office in London. And all those messages ever contained were a few lines on who had been seen off the beaten track in hill areas. The Great Game with the Russians, the geo-political struggle for the right to pass unchallenged through mountain areas, for the freedom to cross from Afghanistan and travel down into India for trade, was not over yet. International politics all tied up in scruffy bags of rubies.

But oh, those rubies! The gem of gems: the lord of stones, worth three times more than these trifling diamonds. Rubies to protect a man in war and peace, to keep body and soul safe from injury and evil.

And the emeralds, so cold and clean to the touch. Emeralds the colour of a temperate spring, symbol of beauty and eternal love. It was written in the Veda, the Hindu book of Life, that emeralds had the power to heal and brought the wearer good luck.

Diamonds had their value, he supposed, because they were all things to all people, they possessed not one colour but all colours in the universe.

Learning and working with Old Mr. Craven in his stuffy old room was fine. Handling the uncut stones, weighing them, pricing them, that was fine. Cleaning up old jewelry, watching lights glint off facets, examining unusual settings, this was more than fine. Learning juggling and disappearing tricks with the Pathan giant, was fun, too. But was this what they had been training him for? Had he learnt all this just to be sent on crazy errands? Was he of so little value that it mattered not if he were killed in the process? He was useful, but not valuable.

The closer the boat got to the Bombay docks the more resentful he became. The thought crossed his mind that he ought to pocket the rag package for himself. When he reached the docks he could buy a passage to – anywhere, or stowaway on a liner. Stay at sea for a few weeks. This was the life for him! He'd get a job on a boat, sail away and live his own life. Everybody wanted something from him and nobody gave him anything in return. It wasn't fair. Even his grandfather . . . But he wouldn't think about that. He stepped across to the other side of the boat and watched silver-scaled fish swimming too close to the net for their own safety. His mind started to replay a scene and he couldn't stop it.

Don't wriggle dear. You'll fall off the wall like Humpty Dumpty.

Fidgety bottom, never still. Tell him he'll fall off. Crack his head one side the wall, drown on the other. That'll stop him.

Her arm tightened round his waist. He could smell her warm hair and skin, like vanilla and the roses in Grandpa's garden.

Millie, for God's sake put him on the ground, and leave him there, nobody will notice. You can't keep him for ever. Fidgeting like a cuckoo, shifting his fat bottom until he's pushed us out of the nest, eating us out of house and home.

Down, down now.

I've just put you up, dear. Look at the pretty boats Leo. Off they go for the fishies, bobbing up and down. No don't bob dear, you really will fall and drown like Grandpa says. Look at all the boats. That's right, big boats going to other countries. Ships, they are called ships. We'll go on a ship one day.

Will you? And where'll you go, I'd like to know? Millie you put more nonsense into that child's head than is good for you – or him.

Down, down now.

All right, let's go to the beach.

I'm not going to Chowpatty, I told you I wouldn't and that's final, bloody kids and squawking women all over the show.

They walked along beside the sea wall instead. Mummy bought him a stick with a wooden monkey at the top. Grandpa carried him on his shoulders. They stopped to watch a fleet of little fishing boats coming in. The sea had been calm that day.

Now the sea had begun to churn, his head ached and for reasons he could not understand he wanted to scream, shout. Out at sea, the water had begun to boil up, black waves tumbled into a tumult then threw themselves in an ecstasy of spite at the vulnerable little vessel. The spray soaked Leo's shirt and dampened his lank black hair. He brushed it back off his forehead. He would wear his hair brushed back like this now, he thought. It would make him look older. He felt older. He stared into the ocean, willing it to drench him; daring it to knock him over. As if in response a huge wave hurtled straight at him, leapt into the boat to clasp him with monstrous claws, sink its frothing fangs into his throat. Involuntarily he stepped back. 'Coward,' he said to himself. The wave, accepting defeat, licked his feet in submission. He stamped on it, splat! Killed it dead. He turned back to his seat on a greasy coil of rope; he was too old for kids' games.

The boat got back into port at sunset. Leo stuffed the small rag bag deep into his left trouser pocket and stepped onto the foul smelling quay. The reek of the half-dead catch combined with the overpowering stench of drying Bombay Duck nearly knocked him flat. Clamping his left hand over his trouser pocket he swayed down the quay and into the city. Keeping to lighted paths whenever possible, he hurried straight back to The Oriental Curiosity Shop and entered through the back door. Young Mr. Craven was doubled over a ledger doing accounts. Leo placed the rag package right on top of the ledger, slightly smudging a group of numbers. Young Mr. Craven tutted, just like his father, but said nothing. Not a word. So Leo had no opportunity to comment on his errand. A long-fingered hand waved dismissal and Leo was sent on his way.

Outside the darkened shop the night was cooling; nocturnal street-life was crawling out from warm, rotting woodwork; every delight for was up for sale and so much to choose from. Leo returned to his tiny apartment in the building guarded by the Pathan, changed his sea drenched clothes and was back down the rickety staircase in a trice. The gatekeeper wasn't there but he left his cheroot offering on top of the door frame anyway.

The night was now wide awake and eating a hearty breakfast. Everywhere there was the smell of food; frying onions, cumin and coriander, ghee and cauliflower: a thousand curries crowded the narrow lanes. A painted boy called to Leo from a balcony; an elderly whore laughed at him and said she could improve on the offer, if Leo had the energy. Energy had nothing to do with it he called back, he was a eunuch! They all laughed - knowing damn well he wasn't. Walking backwards down the lane, calling up at the balconies he offered a cookhouse supper to the first one to tickle his fancy. The painted boy disappeared indoors- Leo squealed in mock horror and skipped off down the alley, through the tenement labyrinth and out into the shopping streets.

Some, but not all of the money in his pocket, was quickly spent. Then he slipped into a curtained doorway and joined a group of much older men in an elaborate den. Their headwear spoke of their religious differences but not their conversation. He shared their hookah and listened to their gossip. Hari had been in a fight. Ali Sayid had been called up to fight for the English. His younger brother had returned to their village to scratch a living out of dust. Gupta had met the boys from Hyderabad and had found a place for them to meet the Bombay nationalists. It had been agreed he could buy small stones for polishing but he wasn't to sell them in the city. They could send them to England with someone safe. Who might that be? asked Leo. Aziz said he wasn't going anywhere for anyone. He had found a girl with three breasts. He had fondled two, sucked the third and fucked her stupid. They laughed, guffawed, "Where, how much?" "Under the Towers of Silence." There was a silence. Was it a joke? One did not joke about sacred places. One did not offend.

Leo left and wandered through the bazaar, bought a cone of puffed rice and found himself on the sea front. Fishermen, holding long bamboo poles were angling for a catch before the storms. An urchin appeared from a shadow and grabbed his hand, "Hey, Leo, Sahib, an anna and a toddy and I shall be your friend tonight." Leo handed him the half-empty cone of rice, then squatted beside a beggar sitting cross-legged on a bench. The urchin hunkered down on the ground beside them. "Here child, go and rot your guts and don't blame me." Leo handed him two coins. The urchin jumped up with glee and ran off.

"So?" said the beggar.

"May the gods be good to us and bring us rain," said Leo.

"The gods will be good to you, never fear. Sit beside me and share an old man's thoughts."

Leo sat and listened and paid the old man for his intelligence. Then, as if pulled by the retreating tide he returned to the sea wall. The tide was pulling him, pulling him out beyond the rows of fishing vessels, out beyond the pretty boats Leo; out beyond the sea lane to the Gateway of India - out, out into the deep, deep sea. Now he was on one of the big ships. He was leaving the stuffy intrigues of Bombay, living his own life: voyaging to the lands of camels and dry sands; traveling over the sand now to the land of donkeys and olive trees, where Christ was crucified; now up to the snowy lands where Christmas trees grew and a man called Santa made toys for good boys that sat still and ate their bread and butter nicely. *Such nonsense you put in his head, Millie.*

A sharp pain split his forehead in two and settled in the left temple. He leaned over the sea wall to be sick. His head ached, his body ached. It was time to go.

"Not yet, Leo, not yet."

Lionel Pinecoffin looked at the young man seated in front of his desk. He was tall, well-set and good-looking in a swarthy way.

He held himself straight, did not slouch in the chair. He was as close to being a gentleman as became his circumstances. He was like his father only in build and certain mannerisms. There was a lot less bluster about young Leo now. He had learnt to measure his words. But then he had always known when to keep quiet, nobody had ever had to teach him when *not* to speak.

Getting up, Sir Lionel busied himself in a filing cabinet, extracting a sheet of paper to cover his discomfort. Seen from this corner of the room he could visualize the young man dressed in furs, riding across the Steppes, a crossbow-shooting Khan. He could also pass as a Balkan count, a Portuguese merchant, even, in a silk turban, a green-eyed upstate prince. In his scruffy pyjamas he was a Bombay coolie of indefinable heritage. What he was not, and never would be, was an Englishman, which was inconvenient given that he spoke English as his mother tongue. And that was something which would have to be dealt with sooner or later.

He had found Millicent Cleaver. He had her address in his top drawer. Leonid Kazan had given his without having to be asked. The wretched Catalina had finally been traced to her parents' home in Goa. She was, as her ex-husband had so unkindly stated, quite mad.

But, mad or not, Leo had a real mother, he also had grandparents and a real father. And what about the broken Anglo-Indian woman, who went to sleep every night clutching a small blue shawl she had once knitted for a baby boy now living not five miles away from her? He could send the boy to any of them.

But it was too late now. There never had been a right time. First, because of the scandal and its political repercussions, then because the boy was doing so well on the road he had mapped out for him he believed he could not do without him. Leo was an invaluable watcher: he mixed and went unnoticed. So many reports had been sent to the India Office in London based on Leo's observations. The information he was currently picking up about members of the Indian National Congress, the INC, was pure gold. No doubt about it, the boy had become an essential part of his machinery and he did not want to part with him.

But it wasn't all one-sided. He had done his best for the lad. Life wasn't a bed of roses. Leo was complaining, like any other adolescent about life not being fair. Since when was life ever fair? No one had offered *him* a choice regarding his future? No. It had been Winchester, Oxford, Indian Political Service. And think yourself lucky Lionel: you are the second son of not so wealthy West Country gentry.

In fact, right at this very moment he would like to be walking the home farm with a couple of gun dogs. Then back to a roaring fire and supper with Hermione. The colonial administrator sighed and pulled himself back to the present. He turned to his protégé.

"The fact is I have been waiting for you, Leo. Waiting for you to grow up, so to speak. I have some rather special plans for you. I wasn't going to tell you for a while yet, but as you seem so low perhaps I can cheer you up with what is to come. But, before you get too excited," he braced a fair hand in the air, "I'm not sending you to Britain until this damn war is over, too many ships being attacked to risk losing you."

He was fond of the boy, no two ways about it. His sons had been sent away but Leo had stayed. He'd maintained a healthy distance of course but he had watched over him just the same. "There *will be* a good deal of travel. I didn't send you to Timpkins for nothing. Your Russian will come in handy. More so now than when I first decided you should learn. Perhaps we should find a way to top you up, so to speak, you are probably a little rusty."

Leo said nothing. He watched Sir Lionel twiddle his left cuff-link, a sure sign the man was nervous and playing for time. He sat still and watched.

The Englishman continued, "And we haven't had you wasting your time with jewelry and curios either. You needed a trade. You needed to learn how to make an honest living." He looked the boy straight in the eye. Leo did not bat an eyelid. "I have tried to help you learn the ways of the world and I can see that you now want to be out in that world. Normal reaction at your age, so yes Leo, you can go, but I don't want to lose my investment: your skills and abilities. There is an important, perhaps even exciting role ahead for you. But we are talking about the future. I do not want you to leave Bombay, yet. You will go, but not yet."

Chapter 9

The beast that is Malabar Hill lies crouched, lapping the ocean, its head to the south licking the salty surf, its tail alert, wagging up country. Colonisers and better-off natives built houses along the beast's spine to escape the swampland and enjoy the spectacular ocean views. They built in every style and ostentation; pagodas and Palladian mansions, medieval castles, gothic horrors with more turrets than structure. The Hendersons' property was someone's idea of Ancient Greece, or perhaps Ancient Rome - in its decline. Whichever, the house itself was not out of keeping with the bacchanal planned for that night as a fundraiser to help send Indian boys to the European Western Front.

The cab driver kept his bony pony at a trot behind the other conveyances also taking party-goers up the hill. Leo sat back in his tonga thoroughly pleased with himself, especially his appearance. His silk tunic lay smooth and comfortable across his barrel chest, its long, pearl-buttoned front line made him appear even taller than his current six foot one. He was especially delighted with the pigeon-egg ruby pinned in his sky-blue satin turban; borrowed for the one evening only and to be returned to Old Mr. Craven before noon next day. For this evening (there might be more) he was Karan Singh - it was a common enough name. He had recently arrived in Bombay was looking for new chums.

The youngest prince of Kapasala had been placed high on the Hendersons' mixed guest invitation list and had accepted in writing. Leo was to attach himself to the Kapasala crowd.

It was the sort of function Kapasala enjoyed; joking with the British, playing at playing the old Great Game. It was far more fun than being trapped on his father's virtually bankrupt estate. His father, who had frittered away *his* inheritance, now lived well above his means and in dire fear of Independence; the tributes he extracted from his peasants would immediately come to an end, then there would be no one to pay for education and entertainment, for French brandy and Havana cigars, tiger hunts and week-long weddings. His troublesome third son laughed in his face: his father threatened to cut his allowance. What allowance laughed the son? That pittance doesn't keep me in cigarettes.

This third son, despite his youth, was a better businessman than his father ever could be. He now had his own spacious apartment overlooking the ocean; he paid his tailor and drove an Italian-built four-cylinder automobile with a mechanical starter. Leo was finding it difficult not to admire Sir Lionel's latest target.

Sir Lionel insisted young Kapasala was a dangerous, spoilt brat, and Leo had better watch himself because if he got wind they were playing him at his own game Leo would certainly lose, and in a very disagreeable manner. Kapasala had some nasty acquaintants - as Leo was well aware, from recent experience.

Leo's tonga drew to a halt on the gravel driveway of the Hendersons' pillared mansion. Sir Lionel was being admitted. The young Sikh in the sky-blue turban counted to sixty, paid the driver but made no arrangement for a return journey. Then he strolled up to the open doorway and mingled with a mixed group of youngsters who were gathering forces for their third sortie of the evening. "Fundraising for the Front is such fun!" squealed a girl to no-one in particular.

The vast, round hallway was lit with Venetian chandeliers; liveried servants were stationed at inner doorways like museum attendants. Envelopes, empty for the filling, lay on a huge marble-topped table, carefully scattered around a grotesque centre-piece cornucopia of soggy fruit and wilting flowers.

Mrs. Henderson, a robust matron dressed in swathes of rusty taffeta, a perfect match for her hennaed head, was crossing the hall with what appeared to be a dishcloth in her hand. She stopped in her tracks and cried, "Sir Lionel! Oh it is nice to see you! You're quite the stranger these days!"

Sir Lionel made a very short half-bow in response.

"How is Lady Hermione? We do miss her on the committee, you know, she's the only one who ever managed to keep us in order." There was a burst of girlish laughter.

Out of the corner of his eye Sir Lionel watched Leo enter with the gay young things. A waiter, hired for the evening, proffered a tray and without paying due attention he took a flute of tepid champagne.

The Henderson woman twittered on, "Let me just do this," she indicated the dishcloth, "and I'll go and find Albert, he'll want to show you what he's laid on himself. I'm not supposed to know what he's got out on the terraces. I do, of course, but it wouldn't be right for me to admit it." She giggled away, cupping her free hand round the side of her mouth conspiratorially. "He says Edna, you keep quiet or you'll get expelled from your own knitting circle - hee, hee, hee - all in a good cause he says, and if tonight we don't raise enough to win the war, we'll just have to come up with something that will. Mind you, after this I can't think what. You just wait and see what he's got outside!"

Sir Lionel was patient; what had Henderson laid on? The chap had the resources of course. Box wallah traders could get hold of anything, even genuine French champagne. Leo had disappeared from view. He watched the woman rush off to someone's rescue with her dishcloth, put down the warm wine, picked up a pink gin and sauntered out to the top terrace.

The night spangled around him. Men and women of all ages and creeds mingled in that particular cocktail hush that heralds a long evening of sweetened alcohol and tasteless canapés. He was collared by an earnest couple and grilled about his family, his plans for the near future, the distant future, his pension schemes and what would happen if they all had to quit India. He was polite, charming, bored. He extracted himself and made his way to the steps that would take him down to the next terrace.

Albert Henderson intercepted him from a distance, "Goodoh, off to find the fun. Edna said you'd arrived. Goodoh. Enjoy. There won't be another night like this for a long time."

Let us hope, thought the Englishman, who year by year seemed to have less in common with his fellow nationals. He descended and found a well-built young Sikh regaling a group of youngsters with the bawdiest version of the 'Charge of the Light Brigade' he had ever heard. In perfect classroom la, la, la, the voice came to the closing climax, "And climbing on top, again! she cried. Up, up, up with the Night Brigade . . ." Kapasala in western evening dress was holding his sides, doubled in mirth. Well done Leo.

Other voices drifted in and out of his consciousness; a group of older men beckoned him over, "We're just saying, Pinecoffin, bad business these disturbances in Petersburg and Moscow."

"Yes. Not unexpected, though."

"Not unexpected? Tsar Nicholas has abdicated! Daily Chronicle says the Empress is under arrest!"

"Where'll it all lead? That's what worries me," said a stooped greybeard.

"Should have thought that was obvious," replied another.

"We'll all be up the Khyber without a paddle," said a retired colonel draining his glass and reaching for a replacement.

"Trouble is our children here think Mother Russia might be their great deliverer from the north. If these hot head students, whoever they are, do succeed, we are done for."

"Not much a question of 'if', anymore. It's when and where. What d'you say Pinecoffin?"

Sir Lionel saw no easy means of escape, "I say we have to see this war out, get back on an even keel, and start worrying when we see what's left of Europe. Home Rule? Has to be discussed, no way out, no decent way out of it."

"Good Lord," said the greybeard, genuinely shocked.

"We didn't survive the Mutiny and this blasted climate just to hand over power," the other greybeard shook an arthritic index finger, "to a bunch of native amateurs."

"George, keep your voice down, we are in mixed company. We can't afford to upset anyone until we've seen off the Hun," said the Benjamin of the group. Then he bravely added, "Lionel's got a point, you know. The future should be discussed in open debate."

There was a collective intake of breath. Lionel watched the Benjamin's reaction, the poor chap was torn, but his cronies and his career won. A little too hastily he said, "Not that we shall ever let them dictate to us. We are the ones who have given them railways and sanitation. We call the shots, of course. But we can't upset them too much yet, we need Indian battalions in France and that's that."

"Indeed we do," agreed Sir Lionel. "And we have to accept that India will expect some form of recompense for their sacrifices in what they see as a European war. There are more than a few well-educated natives that want to see greater autonomy along democratic, British lines, and they deserve to be heard."

"And what about all these layabouts setting fire to godowns and threatening to booby-trap public services? You're surely not going to accept them in your 'dialogues'?" asked the first greybeard.

"No, no, naturally," replied Sir Lionel in measured words. "Aggression should always be dealt with . . ." Leonid Kazan in an immaculate evening dress had just crossed his line of sight. "If you'll excuse me gentlemen, someone I need to have a word with."

He left them gaping at his temerity.

"Great scot!" said one.

"He'll sell us down the river," said the colonel without a paddle.

Sir Lionel picked up another pink gin and surveyed the terrace. Perhaps in acknowledgement of Woodrow Wilson bringing the States into the fray, there were gaming tables laid out like an American saloon; roulette and twenty-one, black jack and poker. Leonid Kazan had joined a poker game. His son was standing not two yards away. But the boy's attention was directed elsewhere. He was completely focused on a woman in a gold frock playing at the roulette table. From her neck hung the famous 'Empress Emerald'.

So called, not because it had once belonged to an empress but for its shape: it was the exact profile of the late Queen Victoria. The head was formed by a lustrous pearl, the body a plump, pear-shaped emerald; the neckband was of thick, yellow gold, studded with smaller emeralds and pearls. The necklace was worth a fortune.

The woman wearing it was no beauty, though: her skin aged by the sun, her voice roughened by whisky and cigarettes. In Leo's opinion she did no justice to the fabulous ornament. The woman was oblivious to his gaze. She was playing with the intensity of an addict, watching the croupier's hands like a hawk scanning for rodents.

"Thank God the old Viceroy isn't here to see what we're up to," laughed a player.

"Curzon? He'll find out - wherever he is. He always did. I said to him once, you know, Lord Curzon, I said, I'm afraid you cannot expect us mere mortals to live in a country where we are permanently gated by the climate, not to look for something more daring than tea parties. If we have to keep ourselves indoors most of the year, you have to expect a bit of harmless gambling."

"What did he say?"

"Blessed if I remember. Something pithy."

"I wouldn't call Henderson's stakes all that harmless," said a hospital doctor. "I've just lost the equivalent of a month's private patients."

"Well, playing a few tables has kept me outdoors quite a lot recently," said the emerald woman's husband. "Last summer in Simla I picked up a whole new string of polo ponies."

"Yes," said a pretty woman in red, pretending to fasten a necklace, "We can see you're on one hell of a winning streak." She indicated the 'Empress Emerald', "Where *did* you get *that*?"

"Oh, here in Bombay. Old Craven chap, get you anything if you're prepared to pay."

The woman wearing the 'Empress Emerald' stroked the stone with a nicotine-stained finger. Leo flinched and stepped back into the shadow. He brushed shoulders with Sir Lionel. They did not speak.

"Hey, where's Johnny Sing-along?" cried a public school voice. "Come and see what's going on down here my new young friend." And Leo was dragged off down to the next terrace. Leonid Kazan watched the noisy young bunch pushing and pulling Leo down the steps. Sir Lionel went in search of a waiter, he needed another drink.

Some minutes later, he too made his way down to the third terrace. The steps were framed with an arch of well-established weeping willows, and at the bottom, on the green-lawned terrace itself was - dear Lord - an illuminated, Chinese willow-pattern plate bridge, complete with live fisherman and rod. Beyond the angler, however, was entertainment of a more sophisticated nature. Japanese girls - could they really be geishas? - were serving rice wine and . . . It took Sir Lionel's eyes a while to adjust to the shadowy dark areas. There was neither sight nor sound of Kapasala's wild bunch. Had they descended to yet another terrace? What could be down there? Had Albert Henderson read Dante? Very unlikely.

Sir Lionel returned to the house for some food. The evening was proving even more of a strain than he had anticipated. He hadn't noticed the Russian's name on the guest list. But his presence was logical, as the man himself had said; the British and Russians were brothers-in-arms in a World War. In Russia Bolsheviks had stormed the Winter Palace, Cabinet members had been captured, but that was still a matter of domestic politics, the Russians themselves had to sort that out. Nonetheless, Kazan hadn't exaggerated all that much it would seem. If the Tsar had gone, then the aristocracy would lose everything. And where did that leave the descendent of Khans? He would have to seek refuge somewhere.

Sir Lionel re-entered the house. He went into the dining room and surveyed a dead turkey, a sirloin of stringy beef, a mound of colour-coded fruit. Was there anything edible?

And he'd upset the greybeards, it didn't do to upset old timers: they still wielded too much influence. He would have to repair the damage, poor old buffers, still living in the 19th century. Life in India was changing. The nature of Great Game had changed and there were new players.

He helped himself to a sticky slice of smoked salmon.

"Lionel," said a colleague, "I was wondering where you were. Come and talk to these chaps. They have had the most extraordinary meeting with this chap Gandhi. He was half naked they say, and sat on the floor."

By midnight the Kapasala crew had exploited the Hendersons' entertainment to the full and were ready to move on. To everyone's surprise they stopped at the cornucopia table on their way out and left their anonymous contributions to the Great War. Sir Lionel followed in their wake, placed himself by the open door and watched Leo seat himself on the folded canvas hood of Kapasala's roadster. The car roared off, scattering sheets of gravel over dozing ponies and chauffeurs. As the noisy machine disappeared into the darkness the lonely Englishman was overcome with fatigue. If Hermione were here they would return home and finish the evening with a brandy and snigger over who'd worn what, and who'd said what to whom. Then they would go to bed. He sighed. He waited a for a further fifteen minutes to see if Leonid Kazan was going to make a move, then he made his contribution and bade farewell.

Reaching home, he sat on the bungalow verandah drinking warm milk to settle his stomach. Stretching out his long legs and loosening his collar, Lionel Pinecoffin of the Indian Political Service mused over Leo's performance. The boy had shown he was up to the mark; as good as a pro; if necessary they could go ahead with the plan to send him to London then, if necessary, on to follow up the contacts in Moscow and Petersburg. Young Kapasala was an apolitical sybarite with no thoughts beyond lucre, just as he had assumed all along. Still, Leonid Kazan had raised a serious issue: someone was using the Kapasala scam to finance trouble. Leo would have to play along until he got some names, or until they rumbled him.

Hamish, the Scottie dog sniffed his trouser leg, he reached down to scratch behind the scruffy ears and said, "Bedtime, Hamish," and pushed himself out of the low wicker chair, "our short day takes flight."

*

The car in which Leo was traveling soon screeched to a halt, its driver needed a pee. Leo took advantage of the stop to find out where they were going.

"Kapi's den. Then maybe over to see some of his tame girls and boys, depends."

"Which do you prefer?" asked a long-limbed Asian girl, touching his knee.

"Oh, I like girls," laughed Leo. And he cocked his head in his own special way and gave a lopsided grin. The girl licked her upper lip with a pointed pink tongue. Then the driver jumped back behind the wheel and fiddled in the dark to locate the newfangled ignition. Leo wriggled backwards. He intended to stage a fall off the back of the car as it lurched back to life. If they stopped to pick him up - well, so be it - if they didn't, he would be free for the rest of the night.

The fall was harder than he had anticipated but the turban, or perhaps the lucky ruby, saved him from concussion. The white tunic made disappearing into nearby bushes a challenge, but he managed it in a manner which did credit to the mad genie's training.

"Stop!" cried the Asian girl.

"Singsong's fallen overboard!" shouted one of the goodfellows.

"Let him find his own way home," said Kapasala.

"He didn't want to lose his virginity, Lucy Lee," quipped one of the backseat boys.

"Never mind, you can have me tonight darling, no charge," said another, putting a very hairy hand up Lucy Lee's skirt.

Leo waited until the car was out of sight and made his way back up the hill to the Henderson residence. He bribed a chauffeur waiting in the drive to let him have a nap in the back of a strategically placed horseless carriage. Then he nearly fell asleep waiting for the woman wearing the 'Empress Emerald' to leave. Two things kept him awake; what to do about his clothes and the gut-churning fear that the woman might have gambled the necklace away.

Chapter 10

The papers were full of it. 'Priceless Emerald Stolen!' – 'Malabar Jewel Theft' – 'Daring Robbery'. Editors had gladly latched on to a bit of light entertainment, the war offering only glum headlines. Sir Lionel scanned the newspapers headlines on his desk. Arnold Mackay tapped the 'Bombay and District Morning Herald'. "That's the best version," he said.

'The famous necklace known as the Empress Emerald for its kindly likeness to our late lamented Queen has been stolen from the Bombay residence of Mr. and Mrs. Ernest Wilson.

A distraught Mrs. Wilson told police that in the few weeks that she had been the proud owner of this very singular necklace (a wedding anniversary gift from her husband) she had of course kept it in a safe. The adornment had been left in her room only a matter of moments between removal and placing in the domestic stronghold when it was taken. Its disappearance is proving a troublesome mystery for the police.

Mr. and Mrs. Wilson have a number of dogs on their property including a bull mastiff but none of the dogs raised an alarum as to an unwanted intruder. Only one member of the domestic staff was present in the residence at the time of this heinous crime. The other two native servants have been arrested by police but our Morning Herald reporters report that the two servants, who have long been in the employ of the Wilson family, are most anxious to establish their innocence.'

"Who writes this stuff? Oh, never mind." Lionel slapped the paper down, picked up a more serious periodical and made a show of reading the war news. 'Russians Decline to Fight,' he read aloud. "What's this?" He ran an eye over the front page column and turned to the editorial.

'Ongoing negotiations with Bolshevik leaders were brought to a close yesterday when the otherwise oratorical Mr. Trotsky made the following brief statement, 'I just announce the war is over.'

Despite allied efforts at numerous peace conferences the new, and dare we say, cowardly leaders of Russia refuse to continue fighting the Germans.

Military strategists say this will enable enemy troops to withdraw from what has hitherto

been the Russian Front. These troops will
undoubtedly be used to strengthen enemy lines
in France . . .'

Sir Lionel looked at his private secretary. Arnold Mackay was reading a report on the Malabar Hill robbery with just a little too much personal interest.

"Blasted reporters," he said tapping the editorial, "they know more than we do."

"They make up most of it."

"Do you think this is fiction, then?"

"The robbery or the Bolsheviks?"

"Russians - 'declining to fight'."

"Sir Lionel, my job is filing, not speculating on international political issues."

"Arnold, you underestimate yourself."

No I don't, thought Arnold Mackay. His boss was watching him with a particular look, so he made a show of straightening the papers.

Sir Lionel took up his post at an angle to the window overlooking the street and fiddled with a cufflink. It was time.

"Arnold," he said, "Go down to the travel bureau and see what's sailing next week. Single passage, second class - no, first class - for one passenger. I'm only interested in Southampton - not Le Havre or Marseille."

"For you, sir?"

"Not for me, no."

Arnold was out of the door and down the stairs as fast as his stumpy legs could carry him. When he reached the street he slowed to a dignified waddle. A number of passenger vessels had been targeted by the Germans in the past year; how terrible if the boy's ship were to go down.

Sir Lionel accompanied Leo to the ship. There was a fresh October breeze blowing off the sea. Standing apart from anxious passengers and hopeful coolies, Sir Lionel ran through his litany of instructions. Leo was to pick up the keys to a small flat near Westminster from a Mrs. Smithers, who lived near Waterloo Station. He was to buy cold weather gear on arrival. He was to take a series of dispatches in person to India House. Then they ran through which packet was to be delivered to whom.

Sir Lionel said he was, on no account, to be separated from the documents, nor was he to mention that he was even delivering them to anyone, now or in the future. If the ship were hit, Leo was to destroy them as fast as possible. If there were a severe storm, Leo was to strap the documents to his body in the oilskin pouch provided. Sir Lionel tried to be cool and factual but the very real danger of the ship being targeted by the German navy had hooked into his consciousness. Was he sending the boy to his death merely on the suspicion of theft? But what a theft! Sooner or later the boy would be caught and it was better it did not happen in Bombay. He had to go, and they could not wait for the war to be over.

Leo, on the other hand seemed completely unperturbed about the risk. He was trying to be calm and serious, but Lionel could see the fellow was as excited as a schoolboy. The moment had come for him to hand over two more envelopes.

"Now listen, these are for you. Just you. I don't want you to open them until this evening. It might be wiser to wait until you have dined."

Leo reached out a hand for the two unaddressed, white

envelopes. One was fat, the other thin. As he started to put them in his inside jacket pocket Sir Lionel caught a glint of red and gold. Leo was wearing a damned great ruby ring.

"How did you get that?" he blurted. "No, don't tell me. I don't want to know." The boy was a magpie. An incorrigible magpie.

"It's to protect me, sir."

"Yes, well it's big enough to protect the whole ship."

"I hope so, sir."

Sir Lionel laughed and pulled the boy into an unconventional, uncharacteristic embrace. Leo, who lacked most forms of self-consciousness hugged back. Nevertheless, he was surprised by the gesture. English gentlemen never touched. A handshake was as close as they could get to emotion. Some couldn't even do that. Young Mr. Craven had barely even touched his fingers as he said farewell. But the genie had clasped him to his oily chest with genuine emotion, his street cronies had slapped his back, his favourite girls had given him the closest of good-byes, and now here was Sir Lionel, of all people, hugging him in public.

"Well, that's enough," said his patron. "Off you go. I'll be in touch as arranged." Sir Lionel turned on his heel and strode away through the crowd, a drowning man in a sea of unspoken words.

Leo picked up his cabin luggage, kicked at a coolie that tried to pull it from his hand and walked up the gang-plank alone. He turned once to look back at his city.

A woman in the crowd, a tall, thin woman in unfashionable clothes, raised her hand.

"Godspeed, my darling," she whispered. "God keep you safe." Tears rolled unchecked down her cheeks. "Mummy loves you."

A man, who had been standing in the shadow of the harbour

buildings, also raised a hand, an involuntary action. He watched the retreating figure, its height now exceeding his own, until it had disappeared among the other passengers on board, then he also pushed his way through the crowds, summoned a tonga and returned to his perfumed palace on Malabar Hill.

Sir Lionel headed straight for the Taj Mahal Hotel. He sat in a private booth in the elaborate bar and ordered a large whisky. He pulled out his handkerchief and blew his nose. His vision was blurred. Oh God, he was crying and someone was bound to notice. He blew his nose again and looked up to see who was in the bar. His nose prickled and he couldn't seem to swallow. He hadn't blubbed since the week after Hermione left. But that had been in the privacy of their bedroom. The thought of Hermione took him over the top. He got up and went to the gentlemen's washroom to splash cold water on his hot face.

As he lent over the white wash-basin he saw his lovely wife waving her favourite wide-brimmed hat, saying, 'Goodbye, darling. I will see you soon, won't I? You will come home if there is a war? Promise!' He hadn't promised; he had stayed away from her for four awful years. There wasn't a night that he didn't smooth her pillow and wish they were together. And his boys: he had lost their childhood. Who had taught them how to tie a tie like a gentleman, shown them which collar-studs were best? Now Leo had gone, too.

The bathroom attendant, who had missed nothing, handed him a lemon-scented towel and lowered his eyes. Sir Lionel handed him two coins and returned to his whisky. He downed it in two goes and stared at the rows of bottles behind the bar, wondering what to do for the rest of the day: he couldn't face going back to his office. The poison dwarf would have a field day. Perhaps he should have sent *him* with the confidential reports on the Home Rule connections. But then Leo, in his unprincipled way, was far more trustworthy than the devious little chap he called his private secretary. No, Arnold was safer kept on a tight leash at his side.

Leo did not obey his instructions. As soon as he was shown to his narrow cabin he locked the door, removed his jacket and pulled out the two envelopes. Which first: the fat one or the thin one? The fat one, it might be money.

It was money. He counted a thousand pounds in large bank notes. There was also a card with the name and address of a City bank. Leo sat back against the wall of the cabin and whistled. So much! Why?

Then he slipped his thumb under the seal of the thin envelope, opening it with a jagged tear. It was empty. No it wasn't, there was a very thin piece of official-stamped paper. He pulled it out and unfolded it. It was his birth certificate.

 **PART II**

Chapter 11

CORNWALL, ENGLAND, 1913

A roll of thick, white mist curled around the many-cornered house, sidled up the chimneys and settled down to await the sun. Below, between high willow herb and tall rushes, the old river barely moved. A late-night water rat cut his way home through the shallows. An early- rising trout snapped a fly. Along the waterside the never quiet ducks pattered and chattered. Coots gathered food among the reeds. A heron speared an unwary amphibian for breakfast. Morning had come to the final turn in a Tamar River valley.

  Davina awoke to the silent call of Hans Andersen swans. She buried into the feather down of her white pillow and pulled a blanket up around her ears. She was poor Elise alone in her prison garret. High above circled her white-clad brothers.

  She sighed and stretched her arms into the air. Today she would illustrate Andersen's tale in river-coloured watercolours. But first she had to finish all the different fruits in Christina Rossetti's 'Goblin Market'; 'Currants and gooseberries, Bright-fire-like barberries . . .' She rolled onto her stomach and poked around under her bed at a pile of books. The large, pink volume of Andersen's

Fairy Tales was just out of reach. Her hand groped into the dust balls and rejected a variety of small poetry books. She shifted and pulled and out came two leather bound tomes. The first was her beloved 'Morte D'Arthur', which had been given to her brother and, as far as she knew, he had never read. The other was a thick, mud-coloured volume embossed with the image of a medieval damsel in steeple hat and floating veil. From her precarious position, balanced over the side of her bed, she contemplated the image: all those pretty ladies that never got old unless they were changed into hags or locked up in turrets. How long *would* it have taken Rapunzel to grow so much hair? Why did so few have happy endings? Tristan and Iseult: such love, such sorrow.

She stopped trying to reach the book without leaving the warmth of the bed and retrieved her copy of Rossetti's 'Goblin Market' from under her pillow. At least that had a satisfactory ending, but then it was a made-up poem. She read, for at least the twentieth time, the goblins' cries as they trotted down the glen to tempt Laura to sin. Something told her the poem was full of morality but she wasn't altogether sure what morals. Her mother called it Victorian twaddle. She had even sent her the latest edition of 'The Girl's Own Omnibus of School Stories' to read instead. Davina thought they were silly stories: all about mean girls that gossiped, or feeble girls that sprained their ankles and had to be rescued from perfectly safe places. And in nine days' time she would be one of them, wearing a boater and cheering the Head Girl, and buying sweets and stamps from a little old lady in a little old shop on Saturday afternoons. She sighed. The very idea of it depressed her. Especially, and she wasn't sure why, the idea that the highlight of the week was fudge and stamps from a poky little shop. Not that *she* would be sending many letters home. Her mother was always up in London being fashionable; her brother, here, there and everywhere being dashing; her father always away in Bristol or London being busy with his wine business. They weren't interested in her, and she certainly wasn't going to write to miserable old Morrigan.

At that moment the door opened and Morrigan entered. She limped across to the window and yanked the curtains back. "You awake, then?"

Davina dived back under her blanket. "Mmm."

"Well, come on, get dressed, I'm not coming up those stairs again this morning, you'll have to sort yourself if you're not out of that bed this minute."

"I'll sort myself, Morry. I can, you know. I'm old enough to go to school."

"And not before time," said the old lady in the yellow starched collar and cuffs. "Keeping me coming up and down them stairs all these years…" She hooked the book of damsels up with her foot then bent down to pick it up. "All this nonsense! Time you was doing some proper learning. This won't get you very far in today's world, Missy."

Davina burrowed further down the bed.

"Proper learning, and manners, that's what you need. Left to run wild here, and me doing everything in this gert house. D'you hear me in there?"

"No, Morry. Yes, Morry." Davina poked her head up above the blankets. "Can I have porridge with honey and cream for breakfast?"

"No, you cannot! Toast's already made and getting cold and that's your look out. Now then, look sharp or I'll feed it to your precious birds." Her Cornish accent caught on the r in birds, making them sound unpleasant. She lumbered around the room, pushing in drawers, poking at the curtains, making a great display of her aching knees. "And I'll thank you to be a bit more considerate when you come home at Christmas. If you do. No more sleeping up here on the top floor. Not when I'm down there by the kitchen being cook, skivvy and lady's maid, and me with my roomatics."

"Yes, all right. I'll get up now, promise." Davina swung her tanned legs out of bed.

"Where's Matthew?"

"Lor' I don't know. Why have you put socks in your petticoat drawer? Bombay, wherever that is. Selling wine to blackies, I don't know, don't seem right."

"Bombay is on the West Coast of India, where the Imperial Sun never sets! See, I don't need to go away to a stupid school. Mr. Jones teaches me everything I need to know?" Davina was now out of bed and swishing cold water over her face with a threadbare flannel at her washstand.

"Back of your neck."

"Behind your ears," muttered the child. "He'll miss me, he says. Mr. Parry Jones says it has been a real education coming here to teach me the three Rs." She mimicked his Welsh accent, "A *real ed-u-cation*. For himself, I'd say; it's our library he likes . . ." Davina bit her tongue, she had no wish to betray her friend and teacher. "He'll miss the extra money, Morry."

"Ah, don't you worry about Mr. Parry Jones; he'll get his little extra just the same. Mind you, I dare say they need it. That ol' school up there don't keep them in food and fettles, I shouldn't think. His Mary will be coming here to skivvy, though. Your mother'll keep her bargain . . ." Martha Morrigan glanced quickly at the child: she had said more than she ought. "If there's a war like they say. Your Ma won't be safe in London then. Have to come here. That's, lest we all goes to that fancy house in Brizsol. Safer here, is what I think. Then we will need an extra pair of hands. I can't be up and down no more, not with my ol' roomatics. Here put this on."

Mrs. Morrigan, who had been handed down in Celia Dymond's family from generation to generation, held out a much-laundered dress to her last charge. Davina put her arms up and the elderly lady pulled the garment over her head.

"You're too big for this, now. I don't know, growing that fast, you are. Well, wear it this week and then it can go to someone who'll benefit. I'll make a package for Mr. Jones when he comes."

"No point giving it to him, Mary Peach is bigger than me. Davina pulled her thick blonde hair up off the back of her neck. "Why is she called Mary Peach?"

"Blessed if I know. I can't do these buttons, not with my fat fingers. They say it's because she was as pretty and soft as a fresh peach when she was a baby."

"Was I like that?"

"No, course you weren't. You were bald as a coot and the rest of you was like a pudding. Where's your shoes?" The crotchety old lady caught the dejected look on Davina's face. She sat down on the faded, over-stuffed window-seat and pulled the girl to her. "You was like a fairy; pale and silky and smelling of sweet violets and warm custard."

"Custard!" The girl slithered to the floor to hunt for her shoes. Morrigan had got whiskers like an old man. At least going to school meant she could get away from the old misery. "*Please* can I have warm porridge with honey and cream for breakfast?" she said.

"No you can't. Nobody eats porridge in August."

Mrs. Morrigan made for the stairs.

"You'd give it Matthew if he asked."

"Probly I would. But then he's not here to ask, is he? Away in vurin parts eating Lor' knows what concoctions . . ." Her voice drifted out of hearing as she turned onto the first floor landing. "Durn gert house; her up here, me down there. Doan' make no sense. And me and my roomatics . . ." The mumbling continued until a comfortable chair in the barn-like kitchen was safely reached.

Davina retrieved a shoe from under her washstand and bent down to put it on. A shaft of sunlight shimmered on the golden hair of her arms; "Swans-down!" she gasped, and jumped up and ran to the open window to call to her brothers.

Chapter 12

The room had begun to tilt. Not dramatically, the bottles and decanters were still on the tables, but the room was definitely listing. The maid that had smiled at her when she first came in, passed her with a tray of empty glasses and full ash trays. Her pinafore was stained with wine as if she had been shot in the stomach. "Happens every evening, but I can't change tonight, I've got nothing left," she confided.

"Have they spilt wine on you before?"

"Every night since the Armistice. Honestly miss, I'm dead on me feet."

"You mean they have been celebrating like this for a whole week?" asked Davina. But the girl had gone, chivvied by an ex-officer's pinch.

So that was why the house seemed so, so . . . She searched for a word: debauched. Her parents would be furious. They had hardly used the house during the war but her mother was due to arrive within a week; there would have to be a major clean-up. Davina examined her surroundings; she hadn't been here since she was a child – four years ago. Now she was old enough for the marriage market, why else would she have been allowed to come up to London to be with her brother?

The room tilted again and she grabbed the door jamb. It was a lesson; from now on she would fill a glass with water and pretend it was gin. She turned to go to the kitchen just as Jessie was admitting two strangers, complete strangers; one of them was definitely not English. He had the swarthy look of the Tamstock Gutteridges, dark Cornish stock. But this was no Cornishman, the clothes were too elegant. He was removing an opera cape; rather over-dressed for a week-old drinking session she thought.

Another older man separated himself from a group standing outside the library and went to greet them then the two Englishmen left the foreigner standing on his own in the hall. Nobody seemed to notice and Davina had no wish to embarrass herself by talking to a total stranger. She sneaked down into the kitchen then went into the scullery and kicked off her shoes. The floor was cold and reviving. The rancid odour of aging dishcloths hung in the air, but even that was preferable to the stale tobacco smoke and sweat upstairs.

She wriggled her narrow skirt up and sat down on the floor, hugging her knees. If this was her brother's London she would be happier back in Tamstock. What a disappointment; what a dilemma, this or a winter of boring hunt balls and all the same old faces in Cornwall. They would be old faces too: very few of the local boys had got through the war. There had been a bizarre, tasteless row about the height of the new war memorial; every week or so they had to add names. In the end the project had been delayed – to see who did and did not come home. The whole thing had been very embarrassing for everyone except her father. He couldn't see what all the fuss was about, but then his son had come home, wounded but in one piece – well two, counting his game leg. Davina rested her head on her knees and sighed a deep world-weary sigh.

Leo Kazan took stock of his surroundings, smiled a crooked smile at nobody in particular and sauntered in the direction of the piano. Someone with a good voice was singing something he didn't recognize; it didn't bother him - he was used to being *disconnected*. He paused at a make-shift bar and poured himself a large scotch and soda. The singing had reached the melancholy stage. Nevertheless, it was a pleasant tune, whatever it was.

The voyage from India had taught him how to steer through what he had come to think of as these *disconnections*. There was a lot he didn't know about the British; he didn't know popular songs or war ditties; he didn't know some people called luncheon dinner and had tea for supper. He wasn't familiar with the names of music-hall 'turns' and had never read any boys' comics. He was nothing like the rough public school toffs in the First Class smoking room or the less-educated commercial travelers, who sniggered at smutty jokes and gambled away their sales commissions at his card tables. He had, and he was quick to recognize it, much more in common with a few Anglo-Indian or Eurasian boys he'd met on the second class deck, sons of craftsmen and modest tradesmen who had chosen to make their homes in India and married native girls. They had been good company. Finding a suitable candidate to befriend and perhaps emulate however, had been a problem. 'Not too solitary to attract attention', Sir Lionel had warned, unnecessarily, 'nor too chummy to invite interest'. In effect he'd followed his old orphanage code: sociable and jovial when necessary and keep to yourself when not. He had been extremely sociable and jovial: he had entertained at table and smoked mediocre cigars with chinless wonders on deck. But it had been tiresome, and it had been so easy to beat them at cards, whatever the game. Fortunately, once his gaming success became common knowledge they left him alone.

Sir Lionel would be satisfied with his progress so far; he had made contact with the people from the India Office, he had settled into the mews flat arranged for him and he would be starting a training course of some sort within the month. He had followed all his instructions to the letter. Just that this particular party had not been on Sir Lionel's itinerary; this was part of his own, private arrangements. He needed to make contact with a young Hatton Garden jewel dealer, who, despite the war, was still trading uncut precious gems. Sir Lionel knew nothing about any of this, or so Leo hoped.

Leo surveyed his surroundings more carefully; expensive furniture, tasteful decoration, not a style he was familiar with, but he liked the pastel shades on the walls and the absence of flowery soft furnishings so popular with expatriates. "A very pleasant house," he said nodding to a fellow guest, "I wonder who lives here?"

The fellow guest shrugged his shoulders and lurched off with the scotch bottle.

"Oh, Miss Davina, there you are. Whatever you doing down here?" Mrs. Morrigan, looking fragile and furious like an angry wasp, entered the cold scullery, "You'll catch your death! Get up this minute."

Davina struggled to her feet and followed the elderly woman into the kitchen.

"I didn't know you were in town, Morry."

"Your mother's idea, as if I want to celebrate at my age. Anyways, never mind that, Jessie said you were here, and I am that glad you can't believe. Now you got to make them stop. It's not good for any of them. We're all worn out down 'ere. A week they've been at it. I told your brother, I said you'll get a sclerosis of the liver with all that wine, but he doesn't listen to me. Don't nanny me Nanny, he says!" Mrs. Morrigan had obviously had no chance to vent her feelings on anyone for quite a while.

"Morry, if Matthew won't listen to you, he most certainly won't pay any attention to me. I only arrived this afternoon; I haven't even seen him to talk to properly." Davina chuckled, "I thought the house was in a bit of a pickle."

"Bit of a pickle! It's a wonder *they* aren't all pickled - and bottled. It has *got to* stop before some real damage is done. What's your mother going to say when she gets here? I'll get the sack, I will. Then what's to become of me? I don't want to stay here in this Godforsaken city your mother loves so much and there's no room at my sister's place and . . ."

"No, of course not, calm down Morry. Let me find Jessie and we'll start to remove the bottles and decanters. Tell her to say we have run out of drink and not to serve any more of anything."

"I'm not going back up them steps Miss Davina. Not until all they – all those hoity-toity, spoilt . . . Not until they have gone. I will not be laughed at, not at my age."

"Have they made fun of you, Morry?"

The Cornishwoman sniffed and disappeared through the service door that led to the back staircase. Davina sighed. Her brother was ten years older than her, but she always felt the elder. She didn't really like her brother, not like some girls who worshipped their big brothers. He teased her for being 'mousy'. She wasn't mousy, just quieter than him. Now, with a new, unfair responsibility on her shoulders she decided that she didn't like being back in London at all; she didn't want to be with her brother and glory, glory, how was she going to sort this out before her mother arrived?

It had gone rather quiet above. Perhaps the party was dying

a natural death. But that was not the case. In the library they had set up a séance and were sitting in silence, sweaty fingers on upturned sticky tumblers, all eyes closed. A disparate group of party-goers were conjuring spirits less tangible than those which had led to their communal trance. In the drawing room a half-naked woman in slinky silk was lisping a love song; men still in uniform lounged around, trying to keep her in focus. In the sitting room couples smooched while four earnest young men re-established European borders.

Davina turned to look for Jessie and came face to face with the foreigner. He was leaning against the wall watching her. Close up he seemed much younger than the man with the cape. He suddenly cocked his head to one side and Davina was instantly reminded of a blackbird listening for worms on the lawn at home. Or perhaps a beady-eyed magpie, looking for rich pickings. A couple pushed past him, he was much taller than them. He was in fact tall and large and - sleek, that was the word: sleek. Not handsome but sleek. Nationality: Greek?

"You appear to know as few people here as I," he said. Was there an accent?

"Well, yes. My brother is here of course, otherwise I wouldn't be here." The stranger made her nervous. She looked around for a means of escape. "And you?"

"Oh I was invited by a third party, I fear. Without wishing to seem rude, who is our host?"

"Well, my brother, I suppose."

"Oh dear, how embarrassing." His eyes twinkled. He isn't embarrassed at all, thought Davina.

"So you are my hostess?"

"No, not at all," she laughed, relaxing her shoulders and smiling. "I don't know anyone!"

"Good, then stay and talk to me." Her hair glinted in the light of the chandelier like spun gold.

And Jessie and old Morrigan could have flown to the moon and back. Davina located a bottle of French wine and two glasses and they found a vacant sofa. They sat and chatted for what seemed ages, but Davina didn't find out who he was, or why he was in London, or how old he was or what nationality, or any of the things she really wanted to know. Then, when they left the house to go to a restaurant because they were both starving hungry, she had a sudden stomach cramping fear; suppose he was a Bosnian, someone from the Balkans, or a Turk come to spy, or for sabotage.

"Tell me about London."

"Can't, only been here a few times. I know the shops my mother likes, that's all."

"You do not live here then?"

"Heavens, no. There is - was - a war on, you know?" Davina looked up from her plate of veal in cream sauce. "I wonder where they get this divine food? We have been living on cheese and potatoes." The point was lost on Leo. To him the food was tasteless.

"Where do you live, then?" he asked.

"Well, mostly in Cornwall. But Mother doesn't like it there though she says it's boring. My father's business is in Bristol, he's got some agents in an office here in London as well, but he prefers Bristol. Anyway he's almost never at Crimphele - that's our house in Cornwall. It's been in my mother's family for generations. I like Cornwall best. It rains a lot, but in summer it's lovely. What's your family home like?"

Leo poured her another glass of wine and Davina, getting no response to her question, filled the silence with a description of summer mornings in Cornwall: how the morning mist floated up from the slow River Tamar and enveloped the ivy-covered walls of Crimphele making it look like a fairy tale castle. Leo couldn't visualize a fairy tale castle, but he knew about mists and damp places.

"So why are you here, in London, now?"

"Yes, well . . ."Davina tried not to slurp her wine; she was more than slightly dizzy and felt rather out-of-control. She knew she should be more circumspect, she was telling this foreigner far too much. He was definitely foreign, despite his perfect English, or perhaps because of it. Nobody she knew spoke like him, not even her mother's falsest posh friends. But it was impossible. He wanted to know everything. "My mother has this awful idea that she can get me presented at court. I tell her I'm too old now, but that won't stop her. She's a terrible snob. You do know about debs?"

"No, tell me."

"Oh, no, I am much too full and much too tired."

There was a pause while the waiter removed plates and served the dessert. The girl scooped up a spoonful of real ice-cream. "Wonderful," she sighed. The foreigner laughed and tipped the last of the wine into her glass.

"No, no, no! I shan't be able to walk home."

"Then I shall call a taxi."

"You'll be lucky. The London taxi is an endangered species."

"Then I shall carry you."

"Ha, after what I've eaten!"

The bill was paid. The restaurant owner ushered them into the street, glad to see them go. He tutted as he locked the door behind them: they were too young to be wining and dining on their own.

A Siberian wind was blowing down the narrow street. Leo pulled Davina into the warmth of his cape. It was, she decided, the single most romantic thing that had ever happened to her in her whole life. There was no taxi and Leo only managed to carry her for a few yards because she squirmed and squealed so much. He said it looked as if he were abducting her. Davina grinned and said, "I am really stupid sometimes. Pick me up again. I want to be abducted."

The front door was wide open, although the party appeared to be over. Davina suggested Leo have a cup of cocoa before he set off in the cold again. He shuddered at the thought but declined graciously, then asked her if she would be free the next day for afternoon tea. He kissed her goodbye and was gone.

Davina closed the door, leant against it and slid down onto the tile floor. Now she was home she could feel her feet; they were in agony; satin dance shoes were not made for London streets. Carrying her shoes as if they were Cinderella's glass slippers, she climbed the stairs to her bedroom. Exhausted from the long walk, dizzy on wine and emotion, she swore to herself she wouldn't sleep a wink. She washed her face, cleaned her teeth, taking care not to touch her precious, kissed lips. Then she fell onto her bed, wrapped herself in the eiderdown and slept like another princess until Jessie pulled back her curtains, said it was nearly lunchtime and did she want vegetable consommé or oxtail?

Chapter 13

Davina was dressed for afternoon tea and waiting for Leo by two-thirty. She sat in the front bay window, handbag, coat and dinky hat at the ready until he arrived at five. They went to the nearby Chocolate Sundae tea room and ordered cakes and a pot of tea for two.

Leo said he had spent the day with diamond dealers. Davina's eyes widened saucer-wide. Diamond dealers! If her mother only knew she was taking tea with a diamond dealer. But Mother probably wouldn't like the 'dealer' bit. Horse dealers, card dealers: the connotations weren't quite right. Still, diamonds . . . "Gosh," she said, "diamonds."

After much probing, Davina finally got Leo to tell her how and why he had come to London. As he related his story she converted it into the conversation she would have with her mother. This man had risked his life on a sea voyage all the way from India (*before* the war had even been declared *over*) to sell *some* of his mother's family diamonds. His father, Sir Lionel, had *begged* him to get a good price; it had been *so* difficult maintaining their social status on a reduced income during the war. And, this year, oh dear, his mother had lost a *little* too much at the gaming tables in the hill station during the hot weather months.

Then Davina stopped her interpretation of Leo's story and started to really listen. She wanted to know about India. He told her about the snow-topped mountains that cooled the blood just by looking at them. And yes, there were man-eating tigers and leopards. He himself had saved the Viceroy's wife from a man-eating leopard when he was only twelve. He described the incident in detail. Then he explained how leopards sneaked into villages and the outskirts of big cities like Bombay to steal babies during the night, and they wouldn't hesitate to attack an armed adult if they were hungry. They were far more dangerous than tigers. No, cobras were no problem, you just had to stamp the ground and they'd wriggle away. And pythons? He'd kept a ten-foot python as a pet when he was a child.

Leo spun his own special web of fact and fiction, of exciting events and exotic places. Then he reached for his hat and said he regretted he would have to escort her home early because he was to dine with the family lawyer on the other side of the city. Would she be free for tea again tomorrow?

Tomorrow and the rest of her life - Davina hugged herself with joy and anticipation. She had so much to tell. But who would listen? Certainly not brother Matthew. The only person available was Mrs. Morrigan.

The elderly Cornishwoman listened to the very end of Davina's breathless account of her new life and said, "You be careful, my girl, fancy words and fancy ways. It'll be a broken heart or something more serious or I don't know about vuriners!"

"He's not foreign, not like that, Morry"

"Vurin or no, he's a man and you're a maid and I know more about the girls in this family than your ma would want me to tell. Just be warned. Fancy words and fancy ways never done no girl no favours."

The following afternoon Davina and Leo crossed the Thames and wandered down the left bank. Then they re-crossed the river and stopped at another tea room near the Houses of Parliament. They ordered a pot of tea, a cream horn and a jam doughnut. Davina poured the tea and they tucked in. As there was no way to eat her cream horn elegantly Davina didn't try. She licked at the cone like an ice-cream and made fun of her own lack of dignity. Leo bit into his doughnut and jam squirted onto his white collar. They giggled like school children. Then, just as Davina bit into her puff pastry cone Leo tipped her hand so her nose was smothered in cream. The girl hooted with laughter and people turned to watch. Leo, ignoring everyone, leant across to lick the cream off her nose. Over his shoulder Davina caught the eye of an outraged matron in tweeds at the next table, the girl spluttered and slapped her white napkin up to her face.

She was still hiding behind the napkin trying to pull herself together when there was an almighty crack, a scream and then a moment of absolute silence. A teaspoon rattled into a saucer. The world stopped turning. Two waitresses bearing heavy metal trays stood frozen in their steps.

A man in an army greatcoat had got up from his chair. He was holding a gun.

"Shut up. All of you. Shut up!" He fired a shot at the ceiling and plaster fell on the tweedy matron. A small girl started to cry; the mother put her hand over her child's mouth and pulled her onto her lap. The tweed lady whimpered.

"You pathetic, fat cows!" the gunman shouted at the women. "Shut up!" he screamed, pointing the gun at the child. The tea room stopped breathing.

"Shut up! Do y'hear? Shut up!" He took a step toward the mother and child. There was a noise behind him, he spun round, the barrel of the gun panned the room. It came to a halt at the tweed lady.

"What have you got to cry about, grandma? Stuffing your face. Look at you! Great fat COW!" He went up to her and stuffed a piece of bread into her mouth. "Suck on that and shut yer face!"

Inside the coat he was skin thin, his wispy hair glistened with sweat in the steamy hot tea room. He kept the gun in front of him, his finger on the trigger. Nobody moved. Then one of the waitresses dropped her heavy tray; boiling water must have scalded her legs for she screamed out.

"That's it," shouted the man. "Scream, scream. That's what you should be doing. All of you." He panned the room again. "You sit here guzzling while we're out there, dying. Dying to save your fat arses. You bastards! You lazy, food stuffing fuckers, you don't give a shit about us."

The street door swung open, the bell mechanism above it sending out a grotesque 'ding-dong'; a woman with two small children in school uniform entered. The man's attention was diverted and a number of people took advantage of the moment to get down under their tables. The woman and children stood transfixed in the doorway. The gunman turned back to face the tea room and fired two shots at a row of copper kettles on a shelf.

Davina and Leo were seated at a table near the back of the tea room. Leo was slowly, very slowly edging his chair back. Davina turned to him, asking with her eyes what he was doing. A bullet ripped past her head and lodged in the wall behind them.

"Look at me, when I'm talking to you," cried the gunman

pointing the gun straight at her. "Yes, you, Miss. Look at me. I've been saving your fucking life for four years. Look at me, God damn you!" Davina was too scared to react. "All of you. Look at me when I'm talking to you."

The gunman turned back to face the door. Leo grabbed Davina, pulled her off her chair and under the table. She cracked her head on the floor and stuffed her hand in her mouth to stop herself crying out.

"So," said the man with the gun, advancing on a table of elderly ladies, "you don't like nasty bangs, do you? Well don't worry my hearties, you can die in quiet, too. Shall I go into the kitchen and turn on the gas? Let you try it for yourselves?"

He sat down at an empty table and reloaded his pistol. The people remaining seated watched in horrified fascination. People under tables peeked out to investigate the silence.

"Okay, my fat friends, ready when you are." The man in the army greatcoat stood up again and waved the gun around like a boy with water pistol. He was talking to himself now. Mumble, mumble punctuated with expletives and another shot at the ceiling. It went on for what seemed an age. Then he shouted in a high-pitched voice, "Get up you fucking cowards. Get up and face the fucking guns. You can't hide down there. Get up like we have to - have to - have to - to save you here, stuffing your faces. Fat cow cowards. There's men dying in mud, dying of cold and hunger and bullets and gas and you sit here, you fat bastards, drinking fucking tea."

He fired again: the bullet struck a thick metal teapot and bounced off. As if it were a cue, the swing doors to the kitchen opened and two policemen emerged holding brass trays in front of them like shields. They looked ridiculous.

"Ha, the porkies!" laughed the gunman, "Come to take me

back? Not bloody likely!" He pulled another pistol from his left pocket and fired straight at them with both guns. The bullets bounced off the trays. The policemen froze, then as one they dropped their shields and scooted back through the swing doors.

The gunman started after them but tripped over a foot sticking out from under a small table. He yelled filthy abuse and scrambled to his feet. Then he grabbed an old man still sitting at a table and pulled him in front of him: a human shield. The man's wife jumped up. "No! Please, no! His heart!"

The old man's face had turned purple, he was clutching at his chest. The gunman didn't hear her, he was focused on the departing policemen. He started to run, dragging his hostage toward the swing doors.

Leo peered out and saw the gunman's back. He mouthed the words, "Follow me," to Davina. Keeping to the floor, as low as possible, he started to swarm through the jungle of table legs, chairs and trembling tea drinkers.

The pensioner in the gunman's grip twisted and turned and crashed into a table trying to get away. The gunman pulled a trigger. Thick bright blood spurted across a white damask table top. It splashed the shirts of the people still sitting at the table, staining their clothes like doughnut jam. A young soldier still in uniform wiped his face and began to cry. Someone screamed. Someone called, "Get an ambulance."

Leo, checking to see Davina was still with him, began to crawl along the back wall in the direction of the main entrance. The gunman turned back to the tea room, fired another shot at random then made a dash for the swing doors. Shots were fired in the kitchen and there was a terrible clashing of metal against stone floor paving. Leo pulled Davina to her feet and pushed her in front of him until they got to the door. It was blocked by the terrified mother and children, he reached round them and yanked the door open, then pushed them all outside. The cheery ding-dong betrayed their escape but they fell through the doorway into a semi-circle of police.

The street had been cordoned off and already a crowd of gawpers were at the barriers like spectators at a dogfight. Before Leo and Davina could reach the barriers, though, there was a warning shout. From behind the tea room's cosy façade more shots were fired.

The two policemen, who had entered through the kitchen, now came charging down a narrow tradesman's alley and into the open. They were pursued by the gunman. The crowd stepped back, leaving an arena for the performance. As the thin soldier in the greatcoat turned into the open space a police sergeant took aim and fired. The soldier's body leapt into the air then fell back into the pretty mullioned window, squares of leaded glass tumbled out. The body jerked once more and finally slumped over the windowsill. Ignoring the glass, the two police who had been chased threw themselves on the body, pulled it onto the pavement, rolled it onto its front and clamped the mad, dead soldier's hands in handcuffs.

A police sergeant looked into the tea room from the outside and said, "All over, folk. It's all right, all over now." A few people left coins on their tables. Some ran out without collecting their coats.

In the street Davina began to tremble with shock and the cold. Leo took her hand and, side-stepping police and spectators, pulled her back into the tea room.

"Which is yours?" he asked pulling garments off a coat stand.

"The blue one."

"Put it on." He held the coat for her to put on. "Now drink

some sweet tea."

"Are you crazy?"

"Do as you are told, you need sugar."

Davina collapsed in a chair and started to sob. "There's blood."

"Ssshh. Just drink a drop and we'll go."

"I hate London. I want to go home." The girl was shuddering between sobs.

"Sshhh, I'll get you home now, don't cry."

But it wasn't that easy. Crowds of people had appeared from nowhere. Policemen were everywhere; some taking statements, some marshalling the onlookers.

"Excuse me sir, madam, excuse me dear people: would you be so kind."

It was a newspaper reporter, he panted up to Leo like an eager little mongrel anxious to ingratiate itself in the hope of food. "You were inside. What a terrible experience. How did it start exactly?"

Leo replied in an incomprehensible foreign language. The reporter's face fell. "Ah, you're not from here, sir. P'raps not, then." He turned in search of other witnesses.

Leo steered Davina forward. When they finally reached the street corner, traffic had come to a standstill. There was a line of three buses but none were going near St Anne's Terrace. All the taxis were occupied. Not being Londoners, neither Leo nor Davina thought of using the Underground.

"We'll have to walk again," said Leo. But he had lost his sense of direction. The need to take charge was over and he was starting to feel wobbly himself. "I think my flat is closer, we'll go there."

The girl said nothing and let herself be led away.

The flat was dark and cold, the coldness that goes with places left unoccupied too long. Leo filled a battered kettle in the tiny kitchen and struck a match to light the gas. Mrs. Smithers, who came in to 'do' for him, had stocked his cupboard with English food and drink. He opened the tea caddy and spooned what the English called tea into a Brown Betty teapot.

Davina collapsed on an uncomfortable two-seater sofa in the square sitting room. Neither of them spoke. Leo poured the tea English style and handed a cup to Davina. Bits of cream floated on the surface of the thick brown liquid. She looked at it and put it on the floor. Leo looked at his cup: blue and white willow pattern, it stirred a memory: he cocked his head and smiled a crooked smile.

Davina didn't notice. She was gazing up at a small, rather dusty imitation chandelier. "I'm a Dymond, you know. A white Dymond. My brother is black. Old Spanish blood they say."

"What?"

"Nothing. Just that I'm a Dymond."

"Is that your family name?"

"I told you at my brother's party."

"Oh, yes. Sorry."

"Davina Dymond. It's a ridiculous name, isn't it? I'm a white Dymond, from my mother's side. They aren't Dymonds, of course, they're Fulfords. They're all very fair."

"Diamonds aren't white."

"Aren't they? What colour are they then?"

Leo looked at her: she was bunched up on the sofa, her knees tucked underneath her like a beaten animal. She was harmless, and very pretty. He liked the way her wavy gold hair seemed to move as she spoke. "What did you say?"

"Diamonds. What colour are they?"

He got to his feet. "Stay there a minute and I'll show you."

Leo disappeared into the kitchen. Davina took a sip of the disgusting tea and put it down again. She leant her head against the prickly material of the sofa. It was very uncomfortable but she hadn't the energy to move.

Among the food Mrs. Smithers had assumed Leo would need, among the packets of biscuits and pots of potted meat, behind a tin of Oxo cubes and a packet of custard powder were two shabby old biscuit tins and three new Indian brass containers. One container contained rice; one contained marine salt crystals; the third contained brightly coloured boiled sweets. Leo had brought the containers all the way from Bombay in his trunk. He pushed the tins to the very back of the cupboard and took out the brass containers. He unscrewed each one and looked inside. The one containing sweets he returned to the musty cupboard. He took the other two into the sitting room and put them on the small dining table.

Davina looked up, sleepily. "Are you going to do a conjuring trick to make me happy again?"

"Yes. Come and sit here." He indicated a chair.

"Can't move. Too sleepy."

"Oh, no," he pulled her up off the sofa, "you mustn't go to sleep. Do you feel sick?"

"No, just sleepy. Why?"

"Basic first aid."

Davina let herself be moved to the table. "You know the strangest things Leo."

"Yes, I do. Watch." He took a small key from a jacket pocket and opened a nondescript bureau standing against a wall. From its inside shelves he pulled some sheets of heavy vellum writing paper and a small set of scales. He put them on the table in front of the girl. Then he put on the table a bedside lamp with no shade, three glass plates and a pair of tweezers. After that, he closed the sitting room curtains, put on the electric light and plugged in the shadeless lamp.

Davina removed her coat and sat down. "Alright, I'm ready for the show," she said.

Opening the two brass containers, Leo said, "What do you see?"

"Don't know."

"Lick a finger and taste." He demonstrated, licking a finger and putting it into the pot of rough, unrefined rice. A few grains stuck to his finger.

"Is it rice?" she said.

"Well done. Do you have rice in England?"

"Of course we do. Rice pudding. Children have to eat gallons of it. Didn't your nanny or your mother ever make you eat rice pudding?"

"Yes. Now, what's in this pot?"

"Salt?"

"Correct and incorrect." Leo shook out a small measure of salt on a plate. With a pair of tweezers he selected a large crystal. "Not salt, Davina, not salt."

"Is that a diamond?"

"This is a polished diamond. Big enough for a solitaire ring or it could be cut into smaller stones."

"Gosh. So what's in the rice?"

"Diamonds, as well, look." He sprinkled some of the rice he had brought from Bombay onto the second plate and selected a number of tiny pebbles. "This is a stone from the ground. Rice has to be washed well, there's always grit and stones in it. But this," he held a fragment of what looked like dusty quartz up to the light, "this is a very precious bit of grit."

Davina squinted at the object in the lamplight.

"You see," Leo said, "true diamonds do not start life as white. Let me show you. First you have to find them, and they are dirty and dusty. Then before you clean them or cut them you have to see if they are flawed and how much they weigh."

He selected one tiny stone with his tweezers and weighed it. "Diamonds are measured in carats, which I am sure you know. A carat is one-fifth of a gram." He held the stone up to the light again. "This is one is octahedral." He placed it on the third glass plate and held the plate over the lamp. "This helps to judge the clarity, even the tiny ones have to be examined for impurities. As with all things of value: purity is the essence."

Leo selected another stone and held it over a sheet of white paper. "This is what is called *glace*. You see the colour almost matches the paper. But it's only white because it's on white, if I move it next to your eyes it will become blue." He held the gem up to her eyes then put it back on the paper and picked out a much bigger stone. It was an irregular lump of dirty grey. He weighed it.

"Thirty grams: quite a whopper - but inferior. In Africa this is called *mackbar*. I like the name, it sounds like it is - inferior. Now, come round here and look at these three stones. They are quite different in size and value and yet all three are magic. They can only be damaged by each other; it takes a diamond to scratch a diamond. Did you know that?

"These are the truest elements of our world, they were formed below the deepest layers of Earth's crust maybe a hundred million years ago. It has taken volcanic eruptions to bring them to the surface and perhaps millions of years of rain to wash them out into the common dirt. And now here they are in London, ready and waiting to be shaped and polished; to make women prettier and men richer - or poorer, of course."

Leo smiled at the fair lady at his side and slowly put an arm round her waist. But Davina could see he only had eyes for the little lumps of carbon on the table.

"Can you see their beauty? I think they are lovely even in their natural state."

He watched the girl closely. The stones had no effect on her.

"Davina, Davina," he whispered into her hair, "Look at them closely. This is as close as you may ever come to the stars."

Davina felt guilty, was she so easy to read? If these were his stars would she ever figure in his universe? Did she want to? Oh, yes, yes. He was not so good-looking: he was dark and large and foreign. But he was brave and clever, and strong and kind. She smiled. He didn't notice: he was pouring the contents back into the pots and gathering up his paraphernalia.

"I should take you home," he said.

She was being dismissed. "No, not yet!" She pulled away from him and crossed the room to a low sideboard. "Do you have anything stronger than that awful tea?" She looked inside. "Yes, look; gin, whisky, rum, green cordial and . . . Oh yuk, what's this?" She held up a jar of mouldy cherries. "This has been in here for years."

She put the grey-coated cherries back inside the sideboard and looked up at Leo. "Bring some glasses, I am going to make a large gin and something, and prepare myself to face the world again. What do you want?"

In the tiny kitchen Leo laughed. "I'll have some of that

scotch. It's okay, I already tasted it."

Davina pulled out the bottles, talking nineteen to the dozen. "He was quite mad, of course. But it did scare me. You are such a hero, Leo. I think you must be more than a diamond merchant. That's what I am going to tell Mother; you're a merchant, not a dealer, sounds much better . . ."

The flood gate of relief had opened. There was no lemonade or tonic, so she swigged back a glass of neat gin and coughed. "Oh dear, better put some water with it. You haven't got any lemons I suppose? Do you know I haven't seen a lemon since . . . Oh, I can't remember when."

Leo sat on the sofa watching her. She handed him a huge measure of whisky and snuggled down beside him. They drank their over-strong drinks without talking for a few minutes then Davina broke the silence.

"I'm going to recite a poem," she said. "Then I want you to tell me what it means, and then, if you still want to, you can call a cab and send me home."

She went to stand by the fireplace, gulped some more gin and curtseyed.

"A little recitation by Davina Dymond." She lowered her head, suddenly embarrassed by her girlish behaviour. "Two verses from *Sing Song* by Christina Rossetti.

> *An emerald is as green as grass;*
> *A ruby red as blood;*
> *A sapphire shines as blue as heaven;*
> *A flint lies in the mud.*

> *A diamond is a brilliant stone,*

To catch the world's desire;
An opal holds a fiery spark;
But a flint holds fire.

"So what does it mean?"

"It means you are the loveliest girl I have ever met. Please come here."

She did as she was asked and was kissed like a woman for the first time in her life. The kissing didn't stop. His lips and tongue were moist and whisky warm; his skin smelt like ginger spice. His hands moved across her back, shifting her into a better position on the small sofa. Davina struggled for breath.

Leo pushed down the high cotton frill of her blouse and kissed her neck. "You smell wonderful."

"It's only rosewater."

Relax," he said, and unbuttoned the top two buttons. The girl did not protest, so he continued with the little pearl buttons until he could nestle into her freckled chest, lick the tiny gap between her breasts. A hand ran down over her ribs, over her hip, went down to her knee and then back to her chin. He ran a finger over her wet lips and kissed her again with his tongue. Davina made no attempt to resist. He opened the remaining buttons kissed her breasts above the silky liberty bodice. She put her arms up around his neck and sighed, "I nearly wore wool because it's November."

The words brought him to a halt. He moved apart from her. "Oh, heavens, I am sorry," he said. He got up. "Please, you must go home."

Davina went cold then hot tears came into her eyes. "You don't want me?"

"Of course I do! That's the problem."

Leo scanned the room for an escape. "Where's your coat? No, oh no, don't cry, please don't cry. It's just the shock of what happened this afternoon. You aren't thinking straight, and I am taking advantage. I can't take advantage of a girl who's . . . Look, you'll be better tomorrow." He snatched up her coat and held it out to her.

She made him wait with his arms stretched out whilst she buttoned her blouse, keeping her head down away from his concerned gaze. Then for the second time that day, Davina turned her back to him to put her arms into her coat sleeves. As she did so she leant back against him and he closed his arms around her.

"Please don't send me away," she said.

He kissed the back of her head, took her hand and led her into his bedroom.

As he closed the bedroom curtains Leo mentally disappeared into a stuffy, incense-scented room across the ocean. Except that now it was different. Now he was the instigator and teacher; his hands led, his lips warmed and wetted. This girl was so round and soft: so unlike any of the bony women and girls in Bombay. He loved the way her hair fell loose over her shoulders. He nuzzled into her neck again: rosewater.

He was a small boy running his fingers through velvet rose petals in a basket. *Shall we make rosewater, Leo? Don't the petals feel nice? Softer than velvet.*

They put some of the petals in bowls. With the rest they made rosewater.

Davina was cocooned by his gentleness, the tone of his voice. As his body moved into her she felt a sharp pain, but it dissolved, and as they moved together she drifted across water in a place far beyond

London, until he brought her to a shouting, gasping, back-arching halt. Then, as he began to move again, this time more urgently, she found herself among the tall rushes of her old river. She came back to consciousness as his act of love terminated in a pumping spasm and collapse.

He licked the sweat from between her breasts, touched her nipples with sticky fingers and rolled away to the other side of the bed.

While he slept, Davina traced the fine black hair that covered his chest and came to a point beneath his ribs.

For the next five afternoons Davina was initiated in the gentle, slow, sensuous art of Indian love-making. For her, each afternoon was a new heaven on earth.

For Leo, each afternoon was time given for no reward save the pleasure of lying with Davina. He realized he had never done anything voluntarily that was not in some way an investment calculated on long-term gain. But here was this lovely girl, who could offer him no advantage or benefit for his future except her presence, and he just wanted to be with her.

Chapter 14

On the morning of the 25th of November, a dark day of driving rain and grimy sleet, Leo was summoned to an anonymous office off Sloane Square. A grey man in city pinstripe kept him standing beside his desk and cross-examined him like a schoolmaster. Now and again the grey man consulted a sheaf of papers. It was evident to Leo he knew the answers to his questions; he just wanted some form of confirmation. Behaving like a schoolboy, he became taciturn and said no more than was required. Eventually, the civil servant placed the papers on his blotter and covered them with a book, but not before Leo had glimpsed Sir Lionel's handwriting.

Leo was to go to Russia. It would be similar to what he had been doing in Bombay, except this time he would be entirely on his own and his reports would be coded, they had yet to agree on transmission. Leo was astonished, then angry; and then his time with Sir Lionel slotted into place. Of course, this is what it had all been leading up to. Memories, snatches of conversation charged around Leo's head; the grey man took his silence for acquiescence. He gathered the papers from his desk and left the room. Leo sat down uninvited. Some minutes later, another man entered the office. He was altogether larger, more portly, but otherwise another grey man in black jacket and City pinstripe.

"Mr. Kazan, our very own Kim! Have you read it? Tremendous story! My name's John Shepherd."

Leo jumped up, annoyed at being caught off guard. The Civil Servant offered a smooth hand. Older, more genial and more senior, calculated Leo, but he still fell into the category of 'grey men': civil servants who moved pieces of paper from desk to filing-cabinet and had the beige-grey pallor of office-dwellers. The nearest they had ever got to India was opening an atlas.

Mr. Shepherd seated himself behind the plain desk and smiling good-humouredly, gestured to Leo to resume his seat.

"Well, I am pleased to tell you that you have passed muster with my colleague so we can go ahead with your training and placement. Not very orthodox but then these are hardly orthodox times." He took some paper and a fountain pen from a drawer and wrote down an address in Canterbury. "Present yourself at this address this evening; they are expecting you. During the next few weeks we want you to learn to drive and pick up a few of our special skills. You will also have a Russian tutor."

Leo's heart fell: Sydney Timpkins and verbs all over again.

"Once you are ready," continued the Civil Servant, "you'll be sent to enrol in St. Petersburg or Moscow, depends what's happening and who's where."

"Enrol, sir?"

"Yes. You are going to be among students. You will need to study something."

"Study!" Leo was horrified. "What must I study?"

"Whatever you like to start then switch to whichever faculty has the greatest number of Indians. Russians have been sponsoring Indian students for a good while now. Some chaps are genuine of course, good students - eager to learn and all that, but they're told that all forms of monarchy are evil and independence is a virtue, and then they become proper little Reds. Mother Russia has always been interested in our family jewels, she'll use any means to get them and anybody to do her dirty work in the process. You need to see what's going on."

John Shepherd stood up and went to his window. The view, what little there was between brick buildings, depressed him. He suddenly wished *he* were off to join a bunch of over-excited students in a foreign land. "I'd start with philosophy. That leads to anything and everything. You could try Russian literature, good stuff if you've got a morbid turn of mind. Take advantage, not many young men your age able to study these days. You can always go back to Bombay and teach; this business won't last very long. None of these Bolshevik types have got any idea about leadership. Personally, I give them another year. One more bad harvest and they'll get booted out. Mark my words, people vote with their stomachs."

He returned to sit at his desk, reached into a drawer and withdrew a buff envelope. "You'll need these papers. Name: Leonard Kapadia. Nationality: Indian. All the rest corresponds to you. You'll have to fill in 'religion' yourself. You know more about that than we do, I expect. Now, we'd like you to sign this document to say you accept our terms. This is a formal arrangement, albeit of limited duration."

Leo looked at the fake papers: a new identity but more or less the real him. As to religion, except for the Malabar Hill lark, he always played for the Christians - some things couldn't be faked. He examined the document for small print. It was straightforward. It meant nothing. Learning to drive would be useful. He signed.

"Good, well done," said Mr. Shepherd retrieving and

countersigning the document. "You must be one of our youngest recruits. Speaking of which, I have to make a particular request." He looked at the dark young man sitting very upright opposite him. "We would like you to make a commitment not to make contact with your 'family'."

"Family?" Leo cocked his head to his right shoulder.

"Yes, I understand that lately you . . ." The young man was staring at him, unblinking, daring him to make eye contact. He looked away. "That you have rather adopted Sir Lionel Pinecoffin. Ha, ha, ha. Jolly decent sort, Lionel. Same school, lot younger, of course. Won all the cross-countries . . . It wouldn't do, though."

Leo dropped his gaze, touched a rather too fancy cufflink.

The grey man said, "Fine, fine. No need for you to return to that flat, we've got everything you need here, unless you've got anything personal to wind up. Obviously you can't take personal belongings. Leave them where they are: quite safe in the flat. No mementos, souvenirs, personal effects we'd want anybody to see, nature of the game. We'll kit you out with suitable clothes – socks, shoes, the lot. Ha, ha. You *won't* take anything compromising, will you?"

"No, nothing I would want anybody to see. What about money, sir?"

"Don't worry about that. You'll be well remunerated. My colleagues in Canterbury will go through all these details with you. Anything else?"

Yes, Leo had a very important question. "Why, sir?"

"Why Petersburg? Or why you? I can give you answers to both. Petersburg is where Indian agitators are drumming up support for some sort of Russian alliance for their silly Home Rule ideas. The sharp ones know damned well they can't manage on their own;

they'll need trade, industry, financial and governmental support of one sort or another. Not just us concerned, either, it's got all the little princes in their Princely States wetting their knickers - afraid they might have to give up all their lands and luxury if the Communist ideas take hold. Not without reason. That chappy Kapasala, the one they set you to flush out in Bombay, may be playing a key role somewhere along the way, or he's being used by someone more important. Keep your eyes peeled for anything to do with that little set up.

"India House has also put in a request. They want anything on Hindu-Moslem relations. This Moslem League is growing by the minute. They may be looking for sponsors on their own. Not too far-fetched to suspect they may be planning a government take-over in Delhi, they've got a lot of advantages already with the extended franchise. We want to know who's mixing with whom. Any chance to upset friendships, we want to know. Divide and rule, as the great man said."

John Shepherd drummed his fingers on the desk then leant forward, as if about to impart a very great secret. "There's also another dimension you need to be aware of. Now you have signed the document, I can tell you there is a very strong chance we'll be sending British troops into Russia: an Intervention Force. We don't want too many Lefties calling the shots. Nip this Soviet nonsense in the bud. They'll explain all this in Canterbury. But mostly, as far as you are concerned Mr. Kazan, we want to know anything and everything to do with the Russo-Hind student connection. We do not, repeat, do not want these student types stirring up coolies, getting it into their heads that they can do to us what the Bolsheviks have done to the Tsar."

As if realising he was getting too agitated he eased his

cellulose collar and sat back in his chair. He drummed on the desk again with his right hand and said, "And why you, young man? Because a very highly thought of India hand tells us *you* are the one for the job. That answered your question?"

"Yes, sir, thank you."

"Right then," the grey man rose from his seat, "Let's get you started. We'll be keeping an eye on you, to start with then you are on your own."

"The same men sir?"

John Shepherd frowned, "Same men?"

"You've been keeping an eye on me since I arrived, sir. Two men wearing the same overcoats, taking it in turns. You might suggest they change their outfits now and again."

The civil servant got to his feet, laughing a little too heartily, "Ha, ha. Well done, well spotted. Pretty girl, they tell us. Country stock, fairly safe for you I should think."

He led the Indian student to the door, they shook hands. John Shepherd held Leo's hand for just a second more than necessary. "Your situation with Lionel Pinecoffin was nothing like this, you know that, don't you? Anything goes wrong in Russia you are, as I said earlier, on your own. We are just as likely not even going to hear about it. Understand?"

Leo nodded, but said nothing more than, "Thank you, sir. Goodbye."

John Shepherd, who had had three sons and lost two in the war, waited until the door was closed, then let out a sigh of relief. Lionel hadn't exaggerated; he was indeed a quite formidable young man.

At twelve noon of that same day, a motorcycle messenger

delivered a letter addressed to Miss Davina Dymond. It said:

I regret I cannot see you this afternoon I have to go out of town.
I may be away for some time.
I shall think of you often.

     Yours,
     Leo Kazan

Chapter 15

Matthew Dymond settled back into his chair, lit a cigar and looked at the Spaniard seated next to him in the lounge bar. "My father has asked me to sort out the new arrangement for your sherry: price per barrel and per bottle, we'll look at all the options. Then we need to discuss shipment. Now this bloody war is over we assume your shipping rates will become more lenient - stands to reason. My father sends his regards by the way."

He drank from his tankard, put it back on the low table in front of them and tried to ease his game leg into a more comfortable position. The Spaniard watched him; he watched everything. His father had warned him; 'Don't underestimate the playboy, latino style; this one doesn't miss a beat'.

"Your father is ill? I hope not. Such a strong gentleman."

"Strong physically, strong mentally when it comes to business, not so strong when it comes to his little girl," replied Matthew with rancour.

"Your sister is ill?"

"My sister is flaming pregnant! Family scandal, eighteen and unmarried and all my fault for not looking after her. She should be able to look after herself, I told them. Molly-coddled country bumpkin. You'd have thought she'd have known . . ."

He stopped, but it was too late, and that was the war's fault as well. He would never have spoken to a business associate about such personal matters before. He had lost his temper for ever the day a bomb blew him out of a trench and into a hell of hospitals and nosy specialists. He had also lost most of his right leg which, as far he was concerned, was far worse than keeping or losing his temper. And everybody said he was lucky! Lucky to be an invalid; lucky to be at his father's beck and call; lucky to be stuck in a hotel in Bristol negotiating a wine shipment when he could have been living his own life, making his own decisions, driving a car, riding a horse, playing golf.

"Tell me about your sister."

"I hardly think you would be interested Mr. García. This is a family matter."

"On the contrary, I am always interested in family matters. I have three sisters: you could say I am an expert. One is married but without boys, she is a widow, two live with my mother. They are not married. They are," he searched for a word, "plain."

"Well my sister is not plain - obviously."

"She is good-looking, like you?"

Matthew shot the Spaniard a sharp glance; he had wondered; the enthusiastic hand-shake accompanied by pats on the back; a squeeze of the arm, an unnecessary closeness as they stood at the bar. "No!" he tried to laugh it off. "I am a black Dymond, from my father's side. Davina is mousy."

"Mousy? Like a mouse?"

"Like a country mouse, absolutely: fair, quiet, gentle. Does water colours, visits the poor and needy."

"But not so quiet, it appears."

"Hmm, and that's the grand mystery. They've got her shut up in her room until she tells them who."

"Who is the father?"

"Blessed if I know. Came to one of my parties, apparently. Must have done because she didn't go anywhere without me for over a blasted fortnight. I took her out to dine, we went to the theatre, met my friends for supper, et-bloody-cetera. She hung around me like a flaming puppy. Ruined my fun while she was having a bit of her own, that's what gets me."

"So?"

"So? Excuse me for asking, but why the interest? Morbid curiosity?"

Then it was the foreigner's turn to lean back in his chair and take his ease. He said, as Matthew was to tell his London pals - with all the bloody calm and matter-of-factness you can get in a Latin, "Mr. Dymond, please convey to your father, that apart from the wine shipments, I am in the market for a wife."

Matthew spluttered into his beer, "What?"

"Just that: a wife would be convenient."

God all bloody mighty, thought Matthew, I need a brandy.

"What d'you mean 'convenient'? Convenient to get into our business? Convenient to get higher prices? Convenient to do a bit of blackmail?" roared Fred Dymond, his Cornish accent asserting itself in his tension. "Mind you, he's got a tasty bit of business himself. Family must be worth a fortune; they've got everything; vineyards, bodegas, bottling plants. Old family, too. We could do worse. Gawd'nbennet, we could be stuck with her brat. Tell him I'll talk to him tomorrow evening. Tell him to come here to the house. We don't need anyone listening in on this deal."

"You mean you are ready to marry her off? Just like that?" Celia Dymond snapped her well manicured fingers before the varnish was quite dry. "Damn you."

For spoiling her nails or exiling their daughter? After nearly thirty years he still couldn't tell what his wife was thinking or feeling. Then she added in her own special accusing tone, "You might have told me before. I need time to prepare myself to meet this – what's his name? Really Frederick, it is rather precipitate."

"Course it's bloody pre-ci-pi-tate; she's three months gone! You got any better suggestions?"

Celia repaired a nail, keeping her head low. Fred Dymond went back into his dressing room and put on a stiff white shirt.

"Have you told her?" called his wife from their bedroom.

"That's your job."

"Mine! I hardly think so."

"Well you should think so. If you'd been around to tell her how to look after herself we wouldn't be in this situation. Got to be said Celia, you've left her to grow up on her own. In that barn of a house every school holiday and you off with your fancy friends somewhere else. You should have looked after her better."

"That's not fair. I always made arrangements for her."

The stocky Cornishman came back into the bedroom fiddling with a collar-stud.

"Do this will you?" he asked his wife.

"Can't, they're not dry," Celia held up a freshly manicured hand. "Anyway, Morrigan was always with her."

"Your Morrigan is old enough to be Methuselah's mother. What she remember about courting? If she ever did." His face was growing redder, his jowls trapped beneath his chin as his stumpy fingers tried to twist a collar-stud into place. "Oh, fuck it!"

"Frederick, language!"

"Frederick, language! Gawd, fuck a duck and tup the cow, it weren't like this in my mother's house."

"Don't you start on about your sainted mother, she drank tea out of a saucer; she could barely read or write . . ."

But the usual barbs missed their mark. Fred had crossed the landing in search of help. He tapped on Davina's door and went into her bedroom. Davina was sitting at her dressing table fully dressed, hair brushed, nails buffed but not polished; one of her beloved poetry books lay open at a Bronte poem but she didn't appear to be reading it.

"Davy, do this for me my 'eart." They exchanged places and Davina screwed down the three studs over his black tie. "You all ready then? Best bib and tucker." He was trying to see what she had been reading, maudlin stuff by the look of it. Her face was white as a sheet. Involuntarily he sought a bulge in her straight dress. "I got a bit of news for you."

The Cornish was very pronounced; Davina knew that meant he was under stress. All her fault, of course. She wanted to hug him, tell him she was sorry; she wanted to be hugged and told not to worry: it would all be all right. But it wasn't going to be all right.

She had tried to cry on Morrigan's shoulder but received no compassion there. Had she been raped at gunpoint she would probably have received the same comment; *I warned you, fancy ways. You can't trust vuriners.*

Her mother had just been furious; first because she had ruined their Christmas with her miserable face then, when she continued to refuse breakfast Celia Dymond had guessed and challenged her. After that, her elegant mother had withdrawn into a tight-lipped silence.

Barely a word had been exchanged since. They were together for more than a week, mother and daughter for the first time in years, and the act of transgression separated them more physically than all the miles between London, Bristol and Cornwall had ever done.

"Daddy, please don't make me come to this dinner. Please."

Poor maid, thought Fred, she ought to be told before they came face to face. He would leave aside the business-angle; just tell her he wanted her to meet a valued associate. He'd tell the Spaniard to do his own proposing. He moved over to the window seat and said, "Come and sit here my dove. Sit with your old dad a moment."

They dined on venison at the Limes Park Hotel. Being a Saturday evening there was a Palm Court Orchestra and people danced before and after dining. The location met with Celia Dymond's approval, as did the young man. He was fine-boned, close-shaven, quite fair, certainly not as dark as her English husband. Indeed, save for the cut of his evening clothes he barely looked foreign. He would do nicely, and Davina should be more than grateful.

Matthew Dymond watched the Spaniard watching his sister during the meal. She appeared to pass inspection. What a set up, he thought, better than a bloody novel.

Fred Dymond had watched the girl, too. She'd pushed the ripe meat to the side of her plate and hardly touched anything else. He wondered what his mother would have said and done. *She* had been a tartar, no mistake, but she'd loved them all. A tin miner's widow coping on less than five bob a week, she'd raised five out of seven, and all the boys had done well for themselves. He still missed her, missed her common sense, her bad language and sense of humour. Celia had been a prize, of course, what with that old house and all, but she was no mother: no maternal instinct and no humour. The last time she'd laughed in his presence was when he tripped over her ruddy lap dog, damned thing, always sniffing and farting and no use to anyone.

The men went to take coffee in the lounge; Davina and her mother went up the ornate staircase to powder their noses in the ladies' room. Celia had latched on to what Alfonso - shame about the name, a touch too Gilbert and Sullivan - had been saying about his family home. Four floors built around an open patio. Carriage and horses still kept on the premises.

"Obviously, you'll accept darling. Quite a catch under the circumstances."

Davina adjusted her hairpins and sat on a pink chair to await her mother. She said nothing. Then the word clicked into place.

"Accept?"

"I thought your father had told you. He told me he'd explained why we're here."

Davina replayed her father's little speech; so this was what it was all about. If she wasn't able to marry the father of the child she had 'better settle for someone else, quick like'. Very quick like! A matter of three hours between suggestion and conclusion. Well, no, darling parents, she would most definitely refuse.

"Naturally it's your choice. But I think you should remember you are not twenty-one yet. And I, for one, am not going to sit out six months in some dreary little *pension* in Belgium, or wherever it is that girls of your sort go." Celia tapped her daughter on the chin. "You *have* examined the usual options, haven't you? Under other circumstances France might be an option, but I don't think poor old France will be much fun for a year or two. Pity, it would have been a good excuse to go down to Nice and enjoy some decent weather."

The girl wouldn't even look at her, sulky madam.

"Shall we join our menfolk? As your dear ol' Granny would say. Now that would have been the perfect solution: you could have gone to her." She sighed. "People are never around when you need them."

Celia Dymond snapped shut her little beaded bag and patted her hair one final time: she looked quite ash-blonde in subdued lighting. The Spaniard was really quite dishy, in an angular sort of way. She opened the ladies' room door. "Come on, it's hardly lamb to the slaughter. You could do a lot, lot worse!"

They went down to join the gentlemen. Davina counted the stairs, trying to get her nerves and anger under control. There were nineteen, not enough.

The men were waiting in the doorway of the 'Palm Court'. Matthew greeted his mother then headed off for the bar. Fred took his wife's arm and led her onto the dance floor.

Alfonso Ignacio Jose Maria García del Moral Lopez-Rey took Davina's right hand and bowed over it just close enough to touch it with his lips without actually doing so. "Shall we dance?"

He led her between ailing aspidistras onto the chess board dance floor, a hand barely touched a vertebra and they began to waltz in a circle. There was one palm in the centre of the floor, its poor leaves bitten back like chewed fingernails. Staid couples waltzed around it, bored beyond words.

"You like dancing? You dance well."

"I used to enjoy dancing."

"I may call you Davina?"

"Of course."

"I like your name. Is it from the name David?"

"I suppose so."

He was tall and thin, a head taller than her. Not ugly but his features were not pleasing in the kind, warm way she had thought a prospective husband should look.

Her parents were dancing in silence: her father's hand held an inch from her mother's back. The Spaniard's right hand however guided her firmly: his left hand was smooth and cool. But he kept his body separate from her, independent of her as if trying to keep her face in focus. She in turn tried to focus on the dowdy lady playing the violin. What a story she could tell, if she only knew.

He was pleased she danced well. She had grace; she held herself well; she had self-discipline, that much was clear from her conduct at the dinner table, his sisters would have made such a fuss over the dreadful food – she had just pushed it to one side. It bode well. And she was good-looking in an unsophisticated way. Her youth was an advantage, he could mould her appropriately. She would be no threat to his mother.

"Davina, we will go to a quiet place now."

"Oh, really, I am so enjoying this dance."

"I wish to talk with you."

"Oh, yes, I know. Might we talk while we dance?"

"If you wish."

They danced on in silence. The orchestra came to the end of a nameless melody, people stood and clapped. Her parents left the dance floor, ignoring them. The orchestra took a lifetime to rearrange music stands and scores, sip water and wipe their fingers. There was no alternative they would have to sit down. Davina led the way to a low table in the furthest corner. Her heart was beating so fast she feared he would hear it. Alfonso held a chair out for her then seated himself beside her.

"Davina I will tell you immediately. I would like to be married with you."

"You know of my - situation?"

"Yes."

She wanted to ask him why? Why did he want to marry a pregnant girl he didn't know? But she didn't because she was too embarrassed. And afraid of the answer. Afraid of what her father had arranged. Fred Dymond had a formidable reputation as a businessman. The possibility that the engagement was Alfonso's idea never occurred to her.

"I am honest," he said, "when I tell you that you will like my home. Your father is pleased with the arrangement."

"Arrangement? It is all arranged, then?"

"Well, not without you, clearly." Alfonso reached for her hand and gave it a squeeze,

"I am not a monster, Davina. You can be happy with me and my family."

"Well, if it is all arranged, what can I say?"

The orchestra had struck up something a little more lively. They returned to the dance floor. "You may return to England as often as you wish," he said as he whirled her round. "My ships will come nearly every month now. So you can return to be with your Mamá."

"Oh, yes. That will be nice."

"So we are agreed?"

"Arranged, agreed, engaged. You can say, *veni, vidi, vici.*"

"Good, you know your Latin. That will help." The Spaniard laughed, pulled her closer to him and traced a vertebra with his thumb. Her pelvis responded: she was appalled. He had no right to do that. And her body had no right to respond. He was a complete stranger. All that about his house and bodega could be a pack of lies. She had not said 'yes'. She had been waltzed into an arranged marriage.

Chapter 16

"Well, you can't say as I didn't warn you." Nanny Morrigan sat back in her old tapestry chair and folded her arms. Davina stared into her meagre fire. It was the first time she had ever been in Morrigan's London room. It was an attic room at the very top of the house. She remembered how the old lady used to complain about her sleeping in a turret in Crimphele. The sudden memory of Tamstock, of calm, misty Cornwall gave her a start. If she went to Spain she might never see the swans or hear the gentle river again.

"What's to do, then?" asked the elderly woman.

Davina hunched her shoulders. "I shall have to go."

"You considered the alternatives?"

"That's what Mother said. Are there any?"

"Dear Lord, course there are. But I don't expect your mother helped you any along that line."

Davina looked up. "Tell me. What are the alternatives?"

"Well it's too late for a back street job. Anyway you're too precious for that. But you could stay here. Have the cheel here, with me to look after you. Then we could look for a home for it - wouldn't have to look far. Take it down to Tamstock and pop it in with the Parry Joneses."

Davina shot her a glance, "The Parry Joneses? What do you mean?"

Martha Morrigan looked at the girl from the corner of a rheumy eye. "Aye, Missy, you're not the first and I dare say you won't be the last. Not in this family. The sins of the flesh, they was called. Fine ladies, fine food, fine clothes, fine airs and graces and not one of them any better than she should be. You're not the first and won't be the last if I know what day o' the week it is." She paused for a moment. When she got no response, she said, "You haven't been told about what your grandma arranged for your auntie, I suppose?"

Davina didn't move a muscle. "Granny Dymond?"

"No, not her! Nobody ever had a word to say against the Dymonds! Nothing to tell about them, or nobody ever dared. Everybody was scared to death of her. She'd skin you alive with the words of her tongue, she would. And her boys, all as big as trees and winning the wrestling. No, God-fearin' and clean and tighter than the Wesleyans they Dymonds. Oh, no, not Granny Dymond. It was the other side. A pretty girl, your auntie, but too much imagination and an eye for the boys, specially one, who wasn't so much a boy anymore. A poor school teacher, and married to a silly girl who couldn't add up her grocery bill. Obvozly there wasn't going to be no marrying off there. But your Grandma Fulford was sharp and knew a man's measure. I think she was sorry for him. Daft about young Caroline he was, daft enough to risk his home and his job. And their house went with the job, as well." She shook her head and sighed. "You ever looked twice at Mary Peach?"

"Mary Peach? Parry Jones' daughter?"

"His daughter, yes. Mary's his cheel. Least ways he was happy enough to claim her – and the pension that went with her.

No doubt about that. And his silly wife, saying 'yes', all sweet and Christian-like then weeping and wailing and running back to her ma and pa in Wales, and leaving him to manage with the baby and all the other little ones. Nice bit of revenge that was - leaving him holding the baby. I had a laugh I can tell you."

The woman twisted a thin circle of gold around a gnarled finger. Davina had never noticed that she wore a wedding-ring before. Martha Morrigan continued, following her own train of thought; "I can't think of any man deserving a good woman. Can't be trusted, any of them. Billy Morrigan left me with a sick baby and no pay-packet to go off for the rich mining in Africa. If it hadn't been for your Grandma Fulford and my milk for that Caroline I wouldn't be here now."

"Morry, what happened to your baby? I didn't know you had a baby."

"Course you didn't. Women like me don't have families. We don't have lives. We give 'em up the day we're taken on to care for them with bathrooms and three meals a day on the table. My baby died the week it was left with the other poor little bastards in a cold, stinking cottage with no running water."

Davina shuddered. Baby farms, she had read about them.

There was a silence, each woman thinking about life in a quiet riverside village in Cornwall.

Davina conjured a baby called Mary, who was as soft and pretty as a peach, who was illegitimate but loved and cared for by her father. Parry Jones, the school teacher, was a good man.

As if reading Davina's thoughts, Martha Morrigan said, "He's a good man, can't deny it. 'Twas all that silly tart Caroline's doing. She *would* have him. And she had him and then she had the baby. Then it was given over to its pa and his wife to care for. They even had her christened. Mind you, look what's happened to her. She's in the family way to that gert brute Jim Hawkins. His family's a bad lot, always getting drunk. 'Cept the mother, and there's another case. Look at the way she's been trodden down by her menfolk."

She blew her nose with an embroidered handkerchief. "So there you are. Your aunt Caroline had her cheel and they packed it off where it belonged, and then packed her off to America. She's still there, isn't she?"

Davina nodded.

"So now you know. That Mary Peach, as they call her, is your cousin. What d'you think about that, then?"

Davina swallowed hard. Mary Peach was her cousin. Yes, of course, they were very alike. Mary was broader, softer, a few years older, but yes, there was a strong likeness.

Failing to get the response she was seeking, the old woman said, "Well, this don't help you, do it?"

Davina shook her head. "Not really, Morry."

"No, knowing 'bout skelington's locked in closets don't help."

Then the woman slapped her hands down on the hard wooden arms of her chair and looked up accusingly at Davina. Her tone changed abruptly, she was angry, spitting out words. "That's the way, with your lot. I'm telling you, my fair lady," she wagged a misshapen index finger in the air, "you don't come as no surprise to me. Oh, no. You're none of you any better than you should be. But you sleep sound in your beds, all of you. You have fancy crystal jam pots and a wench in the scullery to wash your dirty linen. Hah! Your mother, when she found out about her precious sister Caroline! Had to send for the doctor for *her* we did, hysterical, or pretending to be. She always was a hoity-toity madam, your mother. And now she says *I* can't be staying here in London, and they're closing down the old house in Tamstock. So if I want to go back home to Cornwall I got to look out for meself. I'm long past seventy, you know that? Where am I to go? A lifetime I've given to your mother's family; and for what? Well missy, I'll tell you. Have the brat and farm it out. You can pay. And the likes of us need the money. We spend a lifetime up and down stairs and eating humble pie in the scullery then when you're done with us, when we're too old to be useful anymore, kick us out on the street. They pension off the poor ol' mine ponies in a pasture, but the likes of us is out in the street with no food and water."

Martha Morrigan leaned out of her rocker and aggressively pushed at a slow coal with a sharp poker. A blue flame licked the air and died in the act. Davina sat exactly where she was. She watched the woman who had always been in her family home and realized that all her life she had taken the woman's complaints in jest. She had ignored the woman's aches and pains and moaning as 'just Morry's way'. And it had all been genuine. The woman had once had a baby and it had died. And she had had to live with the people, who were ultimately responsible for that death, for the rest of her life. And now . . . could her mother really have dismissed Morry? She felt her childhood lurch into the fireplace. A flicker of dusty coal smoke and it was all over.

Davina got to her feet, saying nothing she crossed to the woman that had been her Nanny Morrigan and kissed her on the forehead. She wanted to say something but could find no words. She got to the door, opened it then turned back as Martha Morrigan spoke.

"There's one thing I always say, my mother said it and it's as true as true: what you worrit about you draw on yourself. Think on it. You got to survive, so take the best path for your journey. You can't come back and start again: you can't never come back and start over. So you just got to move forward best way possible."

"Thank you Morry," Davina whispered.

She shut the attic door behind her and counted the narrow service stairs down to the kitchen. Leaning her belly against the cold stone sink, she picked up a tumbler from the draining-board and filled it with water. She began to drink then stopped. She tipped the remaining water into the sink and went into the drawing room. Kneeling on the floor, she pulled all the decanters out of the drinks cabinet. They were all completely empty. She sat back on the floor. So that was that. No alternatives, mother dear.

Davina placed her hands on her growing belly, smiled ruefully to herself and said aloud, "Well, little one, you are safe. And you always will be. We shall make a life together and *I* shall never ever leave you."

Chapter 17

He was named after his father, maternal grandfather and Saint Ignatius Loyola, the Jesuit. He was tall and always immaculately turned out; the sort of gentleman who never wore brown. He had a long, thin neck and a long, thin face and a sharp, beaked nose. As he leaned across her to put the wedding-ring on her third finger Davina caught the gesture; a vulture reaching out for a tasty morsel of carrion. She shuddered. He smiled into her eyes and confused her.

Outside the registry office, icy confetti fell from the sky, the early March wind ruffled Mrs. Dymond's furs. Davina, in a dove-grey cashmere coat with a high collar, smiled obligingly for the photograph. They lunched in an anonymous restaurant. There were no speeches. Nobody tried to be jolly. Matthew drank too much. Her parents said goodbye. Nothing was said about when they would meet again. Fred Dymond gave his lovely daughter a brief, tight hug; there were tears in his eyes. Then he grabbed his elegant wife by the elbow and steered her into the everyday London streets.

Alfonso paid the bill and escorted his wife to their hotel; he had not requested a suite. Then he left her alone. That afternoon was the first time Alfonso absented himself without explanation. But that evening he returned to dine with her and take her to bed.

It was the first occasion they had been together for any length of time unaccompanied. It was easier than Davina had anticipated. He made conversation during the meal, informing her in greater detail about his family home, his family business. She was not required to participate or make conversation above a nod or a smile. After the coffee he went to the lounge to smoke a cigar and she went up to their room.

When he arrived she was propped up in the large bed, her hair loose across the pillows behind her, she had a poetry anthology open on the gold satin eiderdown.

He sat on the side of the bed. "You have beautiful hair. My sisters will be very jealous. You will not cut it to be fashionable." It was an order not a request. He curled his fingers into the tresses and bent to kiss her. He smelt of tobacco and brandy, his mouth was dry. "Mmm," he murmured, "now we shall see."

He disappeared into the bathroom and Davina was almost asleep when he emerged in burgundy silk pyjamas. Slowly he selected and lit a cigarette then went across to sit in the bay window. "Please, get out of bed," he said. "I want to examine my acquisition."

Davina did as she was told. The floor was cold despite the thick carpet. Should she put on her slippers?

He lounged back in his chair, "Please, remove your . . ." He didn't know the word but she understood. "Now come here, please."

She moved toward him.

"Stop. I can see you well there. You are trembling. Are you cold, or excited?"

"Cold."

"Of course. Not excited. Not yet. Please, turn around."

My God she was white. Her waist had thickened. Her buttocks were dimpled. He was reminded of white lard. This would not do. "Wait, please." He stubbed out his cigarette and opened the fly of his pyjamas. His hand would be Maribel; Maribel's deft fingers, Maribel's warm lips. He conjured her dark skin, her black hair spread across his belly, her lips and tongue licking and gripping his penis. He went up to his new English wife and rubbed his penis across her bottom: he was tempted to take her from behind but her buttocks were not appealing.

"Get into the bed, I am ready," he said.

Davina pulled back the eiderdown and her poetry book tumbled to the floor, she looked at it then lay back on the spotless sheet. Alfonso kicked the book under the bed and sat beside her as he had done earlier, but now he put his hand between her legs.

"You are dry." He pushed her legs apart and licked her fanny then he hoisted her legs up and pushed his tongue into her vagina. Then, keeping her legs up, he pushed himself into her. She gasped, it hurt.

"My God," he laughed, "I have married a pregnant virgin!"

It did not take long, few thrusts and it was all over. Davina lay absolutely still, she wanted to cry but bit her lips; would she lose the baby?

Alfonso rolled on his back and said, "I thought a woman with a full belly would know more how to please a man." He got up, adjusted his pyjamas and went over to the table for his cigarettes. "Montaigne said a woman should drop her shame with her underclothes. Here." He threw Davina's nightgown onto the bed and settled himself against his pillows. "drop her shame with her petticoat – that is the word – petticoat. That is what Montaigne said,

I believe."

"Montaigne? Is he French?" said Davina, putting on her nightgown clumsily.

"He was French. A wise man for a French."

"My mother does not allow me to read French writers."

"She sounds like a good Catholic mother."

"She is. She's Roman Catholic."

"*Vaya*! That will help you with my dear mother. Be sure to go to mass as soon as we arrive."

"No, I can't do that. I was confirmed by the Church of England when I was at school. Mother was furious, but she never mentioned anything about her being a Catholic, and she never went to church, at least not when I was around. So when all the girls in my year were preparing for confirmation I just went with them. I didn't think I was doing anything wrong. We were confirmed by the bishop at the same time you see."

"Bah, one church another church – they're all the same. Candles and bishops, saints and relics." He stubbed his cigarette into the ashtray on the bedside table and rolled over as if to sleep muttering, "A pregnant virgin. Mother will be ecstatic . . ."

Davina surreptitiously pulled the sheet up to her neck. She would wait until Alfonso was asleep then she would go to the bathroom and wash herself.

"Huh, a pregnant virgin . . ."

Suddenly her husband was wide awake and staring down at her in the lamplight.

"But my mother will never know. She will never know. Do you understand?"

He pulled back the covers and pushed up the silk nightgown and spread his long-fingered hand over her naked belly, "No one will ever know. And if you ever tell the child I shall kill you – both of you."

He watched his nails dig into her flesh then twisted his head around to look her straight in the eye. "This is not a threat English lady, this is a promise."

*

The crossing to Cadiz was stormy. Davina felt the end of the world was upon her. Once the sickness had abated, however, Alfonso became solicitous and charming. He arranged for her to have chamomile tea and chatted to her in their cabin. He was clearly pleased to be returning to Spain, and once they docked in Cadiz to make the transfer to El Puerto de Santa Maria he was in high spirits, joking with the lighter-men; exchanging news with other well-dressed young men on the quayside. If this were his natural temperament on home territory, Davina thought, perhaps she might come to like him.

Standing on the deck of the sailing vessel she noticed the way his fair hair blew in the wind. He caught her looking at him and put an arm around her shoulders.

"I should have been a sailor," he said.

"Why didn't you?"

"Ah, duty and obligation, you know. I am now the only man in the family; I have to run the business, keep my mother happy and all the rest."

"Do you not like your business?"

"Yes, I like it. My grandfather made a successful business with the sherry, I am proud to follow him and my father. And I want my son to feel the same."

Davina wanted to say; *but what about the boy who is not your son?* She didn't.

Alfonso looked at his English wife. The breeze had brought the colour back to her cheeks. She was presentable, not as good-looking as her mother but in time she would lose her plumpness and become more stylish. He would mould her. So far, he thought, no regrets.

Davina watched seagulls circling and swooping around a fishing boat. "If I were a boy I'd probably go to sea, too. I love the fresh air. I love the way water ripples in the wind. I can stand and watch water for hours."

Alfonso laughed and hugged her to him. She was still a child.

Davina was numb with apprehension. He could be charming one minute, cold and tyrannical the next. Perhaps, if she just did as he requested he would be nice to her.

A car collected them from the quay in El Puerto de Santa Maria and they were driven in stately silence up from the coast and over the long, white hills to Jerez. Up here it was colder and a knife-edged wind cut right into the interior of the vehicle. Davina, wrapped in her voluminous grey cashmere wedding coat, shivered and hugged her arms across her stomach staring out at her new country. The landscape was wide, wider than she had ever seen in her life. Open rolling hills with nothing but occasional rows of stubby bushes and random fields of round olive trees: no streams, nothing green and not even a hint of springtime.

As they neared the town they passed between rough, tumbledown dwellings, chickens scratched in the dirt road. There were no pavements, no street lights. A skinny mule tied to a post, skittered around at the approach of the car and a mangy dog ran across the road in front of them to snap at its heels. Suddenly they were behind a herd of goats, the nannies' udders nearly scraping the dust. A rickety old man, stubbled like the hide of one of his dirty herd, ambled up after them occasionally poking a long stick at a straggler, but making no attempt to move them off the road for the car to pass. Taking advantage of the slow progress, barefoot urchins appeared from nowhere and started to run around the car calling out for coins, then calling out abuse as they received none. A black-haired, square-set woman with a fair-haired toddler clamped to her hip emerged from the doorway of a neater, whitewashed single storey dwelling and yelled something sharp at the children. The calling immediately ceased. Davina turned to watch her through the back window as they crawled up the hill. The woman stared after the car. Alfonso lit a cigarette and said nothing.

Eventually they reached the town and bumped down a cobbled boulevard lined with Alice in Wonderland orange trees. On their left was an imposing church.

"The Parish Church of Santo Domingo," said Alfonso, wafting a gloved hand at his window. "My mother's week day church. On Sundays she goes to the cathedral. Mass every evening and twice on Sundays." He opened the window and tossed his cigarette through the church railings. "Personally, I can't stand piety."

The car turned a corner into a street of tall, grey buildings, which appeared to grow out of one another. In this street there was no green save for the painted railings of high, narrow balconies. To Davina the street appeared austere, grim, closed in.

The driver stopped the car outside two vast doors, blackened with age and reinforced with iron. Davina was instantly reminded of an illustration in one of her big picture books: Bluebeard's castle. As if by some sinister magic the door swung open. Alfonso ushered her into a fern-infested patio. It smelt dank and very uninviting. Davina looked up and around her. The patio was open to the sky, but on all four sides above and around her there were windows. She sensed watching eyes and lowered her gaze.

The driver unloaded the last of their luggage and tipped his hat. Alfonso nodded in response. A maid appeared from a side door and grabbed two of their cases. Then, allowing them to pass before her, she followed them up the steep staircase to another vast, bolted structure of varnished wood and oiled hinges.

Alfonso rapped twice. The door jerked open and Davina was immediately pulled inside a narrow corridor with windows opening onto the patio below. Two large, brown, squawking hens set upon her, pecking at her clothes, tugging at her gloves, removing her hat. Davina clasped her hands to her head to protect herself as beaks and claws scrabbled at her hair, squawking over its wheat and barley waves. Alfonso pushed past and disappeared behind thick, brown velvet curtains. Then, before she could either focus or speak, Davina was pushed further along the corridor, around a corner, down another corridor and into a heavily curtained room. She could see nothing in the gloom and stood trembling with shock and confusion. Tears welled in her eyes. It was precisely in this moment of weakness that she first met her mother-in-law.

As her eyes became accustomed to the dark, she saw a fine-boned, grey-haired woman seated in a high wing-backed chair. Two grubby Pekinese snuffled at her feet.

Doña Mercedes said, "Where's Alfonso?"

"I'll get him!" cried a sister.

"No, sister, I'll go!"

The plump sisters heaved themselves simultaneously into a

narrow door-frame becoming jammed in the process. As they huffed and puffed, Alfonso appeared in another doorway to their right. Their darling brother had arrived; the sisters subsided in a mutual sigh of relief and returned to normal human dimensions. Davina, no longer afraid of what she could not see, was suddenly amused by the ridiculous women. But her smile met with disapproval. Alfonso was in no mood for hilarity. He swung into the room and kissed his mother on the cheek.

"Here we are Mother," he said. "Here is my wife Davina Dymond, who has a variety of other names and none to be ashamed of, but I haven't troubled to learn them." He signaled to her with a wave of his arm. Davina stepped forward to be introduced and politely offered her hand. The woman looked at the hand, pursed her lips and nodded.

"And here are Esperanza and Gloria," said Alfonso, introducing his sisters in English for Davina's benefit. "Hope and Glory: my dear, older, unmarried sisters. My eldest sister Mari Fey - that is Mary Faith, who has actually been married but unfortunately, as I informed you, lost her husband and son, will no doubt be here as soon as word reaches her."

Alfonso arranged himself in a chair. "Well, this is cosy," he said, reverting to Spanish. "Your dogs haven't moved Mother, have you had them stuffed?"

Davina could not understand what was being said in Spanish but it was quite clear to her that Doña Mercedes was not prepared to stand to greet her newly arrived daughter-in-law. And Alfonso was afraid of his mother.

Esperanza and Gloria clucked on either side of her. They pecked at her sleeves for attention then started to argue across her as to whether she was to be called 'sister' or 'sister-in-law'. Alfonso quickly lost his patience.

"For God's sake just call her by her name - Davina."

"Dabina, Dabina," echoed the two fat spinsters, trying out the name and giggling over its foreignness.

"Enough," stated Doña Mercedes. "Take her to their room. Then leave her alone."

The matriarch nodded: Davina was dismissed. Alfonso got to his feet but was signaled to remain. He hovered for a moment, then reached inside his jacket for his silver cigarette case and tapped a tube of tobacco onto his initials. He lit the cigarette, watching the backsides of Esperanza and Gloria waddle down the windowed corridor. The women were taking it in turns to give Davina a little push until they reached the assigned door.

Which room was she – they - to have? He had checked first thing to see if any of his belongings had been shifted from his old room: they had not. It had been a tremendous relief. His bureau looked untouched. Not that it really mattered: he never risked leaving anything personal of importance in the house.

Doña Mercedes waited until her daughters were out of earshot then looked up at her son. "Sit."

Her son sat.

"Now, tell me."

Alfonso related a version of his extended visit to England, glossing over the date and details of the marriage. "And she is - no doubt you noticed - already expecting a child."

His mother gazed at him, clenching and unclenching an arthritic hand. He was her one last joy. Her only other son had died of typhus before he was two. Then there had been three big, healthy girls and a long, long wait. Alfonso had been a gift from God, but not endowed with Christian grace. He was not to be trusted. They had all spoilt him, that was true, but he lacked any form of charity. Her only consolation was that his mercenary nature meant he was astute in money matters and the family business was safe in his hands. To the rest she had long turned a blind eye, a deaf ear. Nevertheless, she had very mixed feelings about this marriage. It was convenient that he was finally, legally married. A legitimate child was a blessing, but marriage to a foreigner of unknown provenance . . .

On the other hand the girl was young and spoke no Spanish. That would make her more manageable. She would make it quite plain she was not going to accept dowager status in her own home. If Alfonso chose to purchase a house of his own, which was unlikely given that he was so close with money, but if he did choose to set up his own home, so be it. No, all things considered it was not so bad. Better perhaps than having an uppity Spanish bride strutting around the house wanting to decorate rooms and buy new furniture. That would never do: the house must stay as it was before Alfonso's father died. It would not be right to change things for change's sake. She would have to make it very plain, from the start, that the girl need not concern herself with household matters. She was to content herself with raising Alfonso's sons.

Nonetheless, a curious choice, she thought. The girl lacked style, still very immature, perhaps too nice for her own good, which, no doubt suited Alfonso's plan, for he would have a plan. That was his way. The girl wouldn't put up any opposition to his old lifestyle, to begin with at least. Doña Mercedes put out a claw-like hand and tried to stroke her son's sleeve, like mother like son.

"Bring her to my room before dinner. I shall give her something from my jewel box; it is her due. Now you had better go to her or your stupid sisters will exhaust her with their nonsense."

Alfonso stood, stooped to kiss his mother on the cheek and

left. He took the corridor that bordered the right-hand quadrant of
the patio below, dipped into his old bachelor room, collected his hat
and gloves and went straight down to the street, saying not a word
to his wife or anybody else.

Some hours later, Davina stood in the doorway to her mother-
in-law's room. There was a bed with a carved walnut headboard, a
vast wardrobe, a round table covered in lace and a pink armchair
with a matching foot stool. What seemed like hundreds of miniature
paintings in silver frames were arranged in groups on three walls, on
the fourth wall and arranged around the dressing table mirror were a
dozen or so plaster cherubs. The cherubs rather spoilt the effect but
otherwise it was very much how she had imagined Miss Havisham's
room in *Great Expectations* – without the cobwebs and the wedding
cake, of course.

Doña Mercedes sat at the crowded dressing table. Before her
was a large, fancy casket. Alfonso pushed Davina gently into the
room and remained slouching against the door jamb.

"Tell her to come here," said his mother.

Alfonso reached out a long arm and touched Davina's
shoulder. "Mother has something to give you. It is a normal
tradition."

Davina went to stand beside the woman. She could smell
her hair, it was not pleasant. At this distance she could see where
powder was clogged in the wrinkles around the mouth. Doña
Mercedes ceremoniously opened the casket. The lid was lined
with faded purple velvet, parts of which had moulted leaving bald
patches. The woman then ran a finger across a shelf littered with
mismatched earrings and dull rings. She lifted out this shelf and
placed it carefully on the stained white lace runner. The next layer

in the casket held a jumble of necklaces. Some bright with precious stones, some muted and sedate with coral or pearls. This layer was removed and set beside the top shelf. In the base of the casket there was more jewelry.

"I shall give her the earrings *my* mother-in-law gave me." She selected a pair of earrings from a section of the first layer. "What else do you want her to have? Nothing from here mind!" Doña Mercedes waved a long twisted forefinger over the bottom of the casket and hastily reinserted the second layer. She looked up at her son, "Mmm?"

"Whatever you like, Mother. She doesn't wear much, anyway."

"Will she appreciate something of value?"

"Well her mother will."

"Ah, yes," Doña Mercedes turned to her son with a quizzical look, "her mother. It did occur to me. Is she beautiful?"

"Yes."

"And is this mother also glamorous and a socialite?"

"Yes."

"But you chose the . . ." She looked at Davina's soft hands, her smooth features, her rounded figure, "the innocent daughter."

Alfonso's lips widened into what was neither smile nor grimace and shrugged his shoulders. "I told you. It is a good family, they have a successful business. The father is a good type. There is only one son and he is a fool."

Doña Mercedes chuckled, "You should have informed me before today, I would have bought the child something modern that she - and her mother might appreciate." She poked at some glass beads and a tarnished silver locket. "So she brings you a good business. Then we had better make it our business to keep her happy and raise her son appropriately. In the meantime, she'll have to make do with what I've got here."

She looked now at Davina, "Choose my dear. What has your new little mother got that you would like?"

Davina turned to her husband for translation.

"She says take your pick from either of those two trays. She keeps the valuable stuff in the bottom of the box, don't expect anything of that."

Davina was too embarrassed to speak and bit her lips in confusion. She had the distinct feeling she was being insulted. "Just what is the tradition. Thank you."

"Give her the earrings and something that will go with them. Sooner or later she will have to attend social events with me. We don't want her letting us down, do we? Not those beads or the locket. Can I go now?"

Alfonso was not going to wait for permission to leave but his mother was quick off the mark.

"No, wait until I have finished." She picked up a strand of pearls. "Here, I wore this with the earrings. The clasp is broken, Alfonso will get it fixed."

She held the pearls in the palm of her hand and proffered them to Davina with a sigh. The woman was upset with her son; the sigh was one of disappointment. But it seemed to Davina that her mother-in-law begrudged the gift; she felt she was taking something she should not have and the woman was angry. She had no idea what to do.

"Here," the woman insisted, "they are for you."

The pearl necklace slipped from the palm of Doña Mercedes' hand and fell to the floor. Davina instinctively bent to pick it up. By the time she had reached under the dressing table, the woman was on her feet with the closed casket in her hands. Davina went down on her hands and knees to reach a pearl that had separated itself from the strand and rolled into a crack in the marble tiles. The floor was very dusty.

Neither mother nor son stooped to help. She felt them watching her. It was all too humiliating, tears rolled onto her cheeks. She stayed with her head lowered so they should not see her cry. Doña Mercedes eventually stepped round her to give her more space. As Davina pulled herself up with the help of the dressing table stool her head swam. She stayed in that position waiting for her head to clear and watched her mother-in-law place her precious casket into an open niche in the wall beside the bed. She pushed it as far back as it would go then closed a plain wooden door over the hole and locked it with a key from the many on the chain at her belt.

Davina got to her feet and dusted her knees. Addressing her son, Doña Mercedes said, "I thought you were in a hurry to go. Go!"

Davina was desperately trying to control her tears. Alfonso looked at her and raised an eyebrow. "An emotional ritual I see. One has to be a woman to appreciate these things I suppose." He put an arm around her shoulders. "My wife is lost for words, Mother. I shall say thank you on her behalf." He blew his mother a kiss and steered Davina out of the room.

They stopped at the door to the room they were expected to share. Davina said, "Alfonso, your mother is angry with me. Please, take these back to her."

"She's not angry with *you*. She's angry that you are young and she isn't. And I told her your mother was beautiful."

"Is she?"

"Is she what? Which she are we talking about now?"

"My mother."

"*Por Dios,* women!" He strode past her and disappeared into his own bachelor room. A few minutes later Davina heard a door slam and feet running down the stairs. She went to the corridor windows and looked down; Alfonso was crossing the patio. He did not return for dinner. That was her first night in her husband's family home.

She thought she heard him come in well after everybody was in bed. He did not come to their room. For which she was grateful.

Chapter 18

Somewhere across a harvested corn field, a lark rose and fell, leaving its short song hanging in the early morning air. A mile away, the memory of bird song interrupted a valerian-induced sleep and Davina opened her eyes. The room that had become hers alone had no window save that of the glass door opening onto the corridor. She looked around at the austere white walls. It was like a convent cell. There had been adornments in the room but one by one she had removed them. A plaster-cast bleeding heart had been popped into a bottom drawer; a chipped Jesus, arms extended to a dusty multitude, had been placed at the back of her musty wardrobe. The rosary placed for easy access on her bedside table was now hanging with her long necklaces over the side of her make-shift dressing table: just another set of beads among glass baubles. Apart from the large wooden crucifix that hung precariously over the bed and which Davina did not dare touch, the only remaining adornment was a small picture of a gaudy Mary in bright virgin blue. The Madonna, wide-eyed in her innocence and motherly love, gazed down at the plump, rosy-cheeked babe cradled in her left arm. Davina was happy to sit gazing at it this picture, tracing the heels of the baby that had begun to move inside her. She had never held a baby in her arms.

The room that morning was more stifling than usual. Davina tried to roll into a more comfortable position. So early and already so hot. She had learnt why windows had to be kept closed during the day, but hated the way the shutters were bolted against the sun, and then the curtains drawn across to hide all trace of the outside world. The house became blind, inside and out. Except that is, for the early evening hours when Hope and Glory were obliged to sit on their respective narrow balconies and make an attempt at embroidery. Stabbing at their linen squares, they would stare down at the street below and fill their silly heads with ideas for gossip. They rarely saw any 'suitable' young men, which was the object of the exercise. Doña Mercedes still maintained a room on the ground floor, where a daughter might sit safely behind black iron bars and converse with a prospective *novio*, who naturally could not be admitted to the house until an official engagement was announced. But the sisters, Davina believed, were content in their spinsterhood, for all their silliness they knew they had never been beauties and were never likely to marry.

The eldest daughter, Mari Fey, had been married though, to bring a lesser sherry firm into her father's business. Within a year her father had died and then her husband; her sickly child was born posthumously under her mother's roof then it too expired. Mari Fey had had enough strength of character to insist on returning to her marital home. She visited her mother every day, as was expected, but was free to return to the peace and quiet of her own house each evening. Davina envied her, but recognised that in having her own home she would have to share it with Alfonso – unaccompanied. She didn't know which was the better alternative, her mother-in-law and the silly sisters or her husband on his own.

Davina sometimes felt she was living through a chapter in an extraordinary book: everything was different, everything was alien. She had quickly learnt the petty rituals of her new abode. Having a good ear, she picked up enough vocabulary to make herself understood when she was obliged, or permitted to speak. Her sisters-in-law never stopped asking questions, but these questions were either attention-seeking devices or pathetic attempts to ingratiate themselves and did not require complicated answers, more often than not a smile would suffice. Esperanza and Gloria repeated themselves constantly and argued incessantly. It was tiresome but Davina used it to her advantage. It enabled her to live within herself, which was the only way she could survive. And she had to survive and be strong for her baby.

Days merged into weeks and the weeks into a suffocating summer. In the morning the house was cleaned; rugs and washing were taken to the roof; dust was disturbed from one place and shifted to another. A cook with a face like a melon clattered about the primitive kitchen abusing the scullery wench and concocting evil stews out of dried beans or chickpeas. Occasionally, she served up a piece of unidentifiable leather and called it pork. Her salads were to be approached with caution. During one interminable supper, Davina had watched a weevil-like creature weave its way round the crystal bowl, in and out of the limp lettuce, under and over the soggy tomatoes. Its progress fascinated and revolted her. No one else noticed it, the salad was eaten and the bowl left clean.

When it became too hot for the sisters to continue their balcony watches, they all sat in Doña Mercedes' darkened sitting room. The matriarch did nothing save watch her daughters ruin their eyesight crocheting ochre-coloured circles or stitching shapeless baby garments. The three sisters shared tidbits of gossip. A random comment could be spun into a fine thread of dubious facts and used to stitch a patchwork of conjecture. As the weeks dragged on and her Spanish, perforce, improved, Davina came to realize their gossip was not as harmless as she had at first supposed. When the mood was upon them they could cut a saint to the quick. Nobody was safe - except Alfonso, who was never mentioned.

Alfonso kept a strict daily routine. Monday to Friday at nine a.m. he would eat a bread roll for breakfast then take his coffee and newspaper to his room. He left the house at ten to go to his office. He would return at two-thirty to change his shirt and have lunch with the family at three. At five he would go down to the town *casino*, which was essentially a gentleman's club, then go back to his office for an hour or two. He did not return home for the evening meal and despite the fact that they did not share a room Davina knew he almost never got in until well past midnight. She slept badly and Alfonso made no attempt to come in quietly. Here was a very juicy morsel for the sisters' afternoon dissection sessions, but nobody ever mentioned it.

The labour pains started one afternoon in early August. Doña Mercedes and the two sisters had retired for their siesta, Alfonso had left the house. Davina was trying to read by the dim light in her room. She stayed seated in her chair and waited for the pain to lessen. The spasm passed and left her breathless. Then her bones began to disconnect. Her head was heavy, hanging like that of a wooden puppet over a body that was no longer hers. Sweat trickled down her neck and between her swollen breasts. She got up clumsily, crossed out of her room and opened a patio window. It was a cardinal sin but she had to breathe. She hung over the window sill and stared down at the patio ferns and began to see her river moving between rushes. Ducks chattered, a swan paddled by. The next pain came and she staggered back into her room to the bed. From a sitting position she swung her legs up and crouched sideways over the stiff pillows. Her head swooned. Was it possible to faint lying down? Now she and the bed were soaking wet with sweat and broken waters. But still she did not call out.

She must have slept a while before the next contraction gripped her. Holding her abdomen she tried to lift herself, the walls were closing in on her, trying to suffocate her. A caul of humidity was strangling her – she had to escape and she could not move. Now she wanted to call out but no words came, just a desperate scream.

The next time she looked up there were faces at the bottom of her bed. Angels. Angels with black hair, facial hair.

"Mother sent us," said one.

"Are you all right, sister?" asked another.

"No, I'm bloody not!" she screamed. "Get out!"

They were back again, the faces around the bed. Someone was mopping her brow with tepid water, someone else stood with a bundle in her arms. So she wasn't dead. Oh, God, why not? She most desperately wanted to never wake up again. Then she focused.

"Your daughter," said a stranger.

Davina put out her arms to take the child. The nurse turned to the woman standing in the doorway. Doña Mercedes nodded her assent.

"She may feed it for a week or two, it won't do any harm. Don't tell anyone."

"Of course not Señora, I am always discreet."

"Well, it doesn't matter anyway, she doesn't have any friends and no one invites her anywhere. It's the hair – too blonde. Decent women don't approve, they assume she's a . . . you catch my meaning?"

The midwife glanced at the wet, mousy strands across the young mother's forehead and felt sorry for her; she wouldn't want to live in this house for all their class and money.

"She doesn't have much of a figure to lose," continued the matriarch, "let her feed the child for a week or two. Now, you stay with her, everybody else leave. I shall send someone to clean up the mess."

Davina gazed down at her baby. Tears welled in her eyes. The floodgates of relief, of physical and emotional exhaustion broke, she sobbed, heart-rending, shattering sobs. She cried and cried for all the things she had tried to forget; for her home by a slow, old river, for her father calling her 'Davy', for her books and her poems, for mist and rain and fresh air. For a world which had ended one cold London morning a lifetime ago.

"The child will be named Maria de la Inmaculada, Mercedes, Josefina and something else. I could ask the priest to include Davina in the list but I doubt he'd allow it. Women in Spain are not normally named for David. Names have to come straight out of the Bible anyway. She will be baptised on Friday. If you are well enough, you may accompany us."

Alfonso began pacing around the stuffy room. "It has a certain irony about it, don't you think? Inmaculada! Do you think the old witch knows?"

"Inmaculada? I don't understand."

"Maria of the Immaculate Conception."

"Oh. But I want to call her Marina. It's a Spanish name and it's English, too."

"You can't. Mother has decided."

"But . . ."

"I thought you understood, Davina. You live in Spain. This family is Spanish. We do what is done in Spain. I admit that normally a girl is named for her mother. However, in this case my mother is naming the girl for the Virgin and for herself. You should be honoured. What is your problem?"

Davina wanted to say that her problem was that she did not like the names; didn't have one iota of belief in the Virgin; and hated his blasted mother. She said nothing because she had in that instant decided that *she* would always call her daughter Marina and only ever speak to her in English. Maria Inmaculada could easily be shortened to Marina. She also didn't want to aggravate him further: she had never seen him quite so discomposed. She sighed and said, "Alright. I am sure I can get up now. I feel fine."

"Fine." Alfonso nodded in approval and turned to leave. With his back to her, he said softly, kindly, "She is your child; you can call her the name you like. I do not oppose it. At the baptism my mother will name her, and my sisters will be Godmothers. Mercedes is a good name for a girl born in Jerez; she is our patron saint. It will make your daughter more Spanish. Do you follow me?" He turned around and smiled at her. "You feel better, that is good. I should like you to be well, as soon as possible."

For a moment she thought he was genuinely concerned about her. Then she realized. He still needed a son.

Chapter 19

Propelled by Hope, Marina had reached heaven. Her sturdy, white-stockinged legs thrust out before her, her wavy, jet black hair streaming out behind like a banner, she took the swing as high as it would go then tucked her legs under her and bent forward to sustain the return trajectory. "Look Mamá, look!"

Davina, sitting on the park bench below, smiled an uncomfortable smile. "You be careful. You'd better come down now."

"Oh no, sister!" cried Gloria, bustling into the path of the swing. "It's my turn to push."

Davina jumped to her feet and grabbed Gloria out of danger. "For heaven's sake, there'll be an accident! Marina, come down immediately. That is enough."

"You can push her tomorrow," said Hope, pulling her round, brown sister away from the swing.

"That's not fair, we agreed . . ."

The two sisters fell to squabbling. Marina slowed her movements and gradually returned to earth. Her aunts were fighting over nothing as usual. At school the nuns told children not to fight. But *Tia* Esperanza said that she and her sisters never went to a real school. So, obviously, that was why they did it. She reluctantly brought the swing into its final, gentle arc but stayed on the seat, hoping her mother would relent.

Gloria made a grab for her niece and the swing jerked round dangerously. Marina called out, "Mamá!"

"Stop it! Stop it both of you! She'll fall off," screamed Davina in fluent Spanish.

The middle-aged spinster looked shamefaced. "I only wanted to have my turn. It *was* my turn."

"For heaven's sake," said Davina. "The girl is not an object for ownership, she's a child."

"Yes, you are right," sighed Esperanza, folding her arms over her ample bosom and shaking her head in exaggerated commiseration. "Just one little girl."

"Yes, sister-in-law," added Gloria, picking up her sister's thread. "One little girl, that we all must share."

"Such a pity for our brother, he would so like to have a boy. A man needs a son. He cannot take a girl to the bullfights, or buy her a fine white horse, or show her the fine gold pens on the desk in his office and tell her the desk will one day be hers."

In her annoyance Davina caught hold of a swing rope herself. "Mamá!" screamed Marina as once more she nearly fell to the hard earth beneath her.

"Sister!" cried Gloria, "Take care, our niece is not a boy but she is very precious to us."

Davina grabbed her daughter's hand and marched out of the children's playground. Her head raced with resentment and angry retorts - all the things she wanted to say, but never dared. Was there nowhere she could go to get away from these women? They were insufferable. Would no one rescue her from their incessant taunts?

Ten years of their vicious stupidity. Ten years of doing what she was expected to do. Ten years of marriage to a husband who didn't care for her or about her. A decade of suffocating summers and cold, damp winters in a cheerless mausoleum. And the utter, utter loneliness of it all. If it weren't for Marina she would most definitely have left by now. But where could she go? She had a little money of her own but she also had a child to take care of. She couldn't just pack up and return to England, though God knows that was what she desired above all things. But she couldn't because her mother wouldn't have her.

They turned the corner of the street and Marina's hand slipped from her. "You're hurting me, Mamá," Davina stopped and looked at her daughter.

"I'm sorry, sweetheart. It's just that they make me so cross."

"They can't help it," said Marina sagely. "Can we get an ice-cream?"

Davina purchased two tubs of vanilla ice from a street vendor and they sat on a bench like a couple of tourists. Marina became intrigued by two scruffy lads playing marbles in the dust. She collected marbles herself but never played with anyone for fear of losing them. The girl looked up and caught her mother's eye, she smiled her wide, guileless smile and Davina bent to kiss her forehead.

And that was another thing she couldn't fathom. Her own feelings for her daughter were so strong it seemed incomprehensible that her mother could be so cold. She had never written to her, not even a Christmas card. Her father came once a year, but he spent more time in the bodega and Alfonso's office than he did with his daughter and granddaughter. He always said his wife would join him for the next visit – but she never did. And he had never once hinted that Davina should return with him for a holiday, which for sure was her mother's dictum. She had been an exile for ten years now – had she not paid for her crime?

Davina sighed, "Finished? We'd better get back before your aunts start telling tales."

"They're worse than children," replied Marina.

Mother and daughter set off back to Doña Mercedes' mansion. How nice it would be, thought Davina, if we were really on our way home – to our own apartment, or one of those lovely new houses they are building on the Seville road. She took Marina's hand gently in hers. "I'm sorry about your play time - I lost my temper, didn't I? What would your nuns at school say about that?"

"Oh, they'd say it was very wrong, but they do it all the time. Most of them are very bad-tempered. Like Grandma. Anyway, I think I'm getting a bit old for the swing. I've been to the top. Can I learn to tap-dance?"

"Tap-dance! Wherever did you get that idea from?"

Marina chatted on about her school friends, their hobbies and pastimes. Davina half-listened and then got lost in her own train of thought. She knew it had become a bad habit, but she spent her days living through scenes and conversations in her head – to the point that her mind would go off on its own track even when she had someone to talk to.

. . . How lovely if they could be a normal family; father, mother, daughter – and perhaps one day a son. Just them: no mother-in-law, no sisters-in-law - Hope and Glory were so irritating. But you couldn't hate them, not with real hate - they just made a difficult situation ten times worse.

And so it went on, until one afternoon in the autumn of 1932, quite by chance, two men entered Hope and Glory's lives.

The first was a little man wearing a jacket two sizes too small and shoes five sizes too big. The second was a dashing Robin Hood hero in leather jerkin and close-fitting hose. The sisters discovered Hollywood.

Either because she had finally accepted that her daughters would never marry, or because she had simply given up caring, Doña Mercedes ignored their increasing visits to the town centre. Esperanza and Gloria had been watching a building being converted into a cinema, and on the day it was inaugurated they dared each other to enter.

The new cinema satisfied their wildest imaginings; Sheiks of Araby delivered them from marauding hordes; a poker-faced bachelor defied runaway trains to save them; the sad-happy tramp called Charlot lived out tragedies more profound than they could ever fabricate. Mary Pickford and Clara Bow: here were women with stories more scandalous than any snip of gossip they might acquire.

They lost interest in their English sister-in-law almost immediately. There were new magazines devoted to the lives of stars: they had far more interesting foreign women to scrutinise, envy and criticise.

Curiously, the more the sisters left Davina in peace the more time Alfonso spent at home. He no longer stayed out until the early hours on weekdays, only troubling to sleep with her if they had been to an unavoidable dinner party or a concert on a Saturday night. Now he returned for the evening meal during the week and often took Davina with him for 'a stroll' before supper. They would encounter other local businessmen and their wives and exchange comments on the weather and recent or forthcoming events. There were more invitations to dine, more concerts: Davina was now expected to accompany him to all sorts of social events and chit-chat about nothing to other local burgers' wives. And then Alfonso started going to church on Sundays.

Davina could not say precisely when she first realized her husband had lost his swagger; it had been a gradual process. His hair had gone quite grey and with it he had acquired a more staid personality. It became increasingly evident that Alfonso was a worried man. His newspapers featured reports on labour unions wresting power from their employers in Barcelona and Madrid. The dangers of syndicalism were anxiously discussed in the *casino*. There were serious labour disputes going on with the men who transported sherry down to the coast. A group of wagon-drivers had started a trade union and now the men working in the sherry bottling plants were demanding improved conditions, too.

There was a lot of scandal mongering, mostly focused on how communists were planning to annihilate the middle-class. People said the Republicans were going to secularise education and sack priests. There were increasingly violent incidents involving agricultural labourers in the south and factory workers in the north. Davina assumed Alfonso simply felt safer at home during long, dark winter evenings.

That winter was dull and cheerless for all. So as the days lengthened and lightened and the new year shifted forward into the short Andalusian spring, everyone began preparing for the big fiestas in April and May.

One bright afternoon in late March, Davina took her daughter to collect a frock from a new dressmaker living on the Cadiz side of town. Coming out of the dressmaker's house into the daylight carrying her cumbersome, cardboard dress box, Marina caught sight of Alfonso walking along the opposite side of the street.

"Papá, Papá!" called Marina. Alfonso didn't hear her. "Papá, Papá," she insisted, running awkwardly with the box in her arms across the dusty road. "Papá!" she screeched.

He turned. He was embarrassed, annoyed that the girl was making a spectacle of herself, but above all he had no wish to be seen in such a location. He stopped and turned to speak, and as he did so he saw how pretty Marina had become. No longer dark and stocky, she had raven's wing black hair tied back in a large bow and her eyes, as green as rare emeralds, gazed up at him with undisguised affection.

"*Cariño*," he said, "what are you doing here?"

"We've got my dress for the *feria*, come and look. It's soooo beautiful."

"Not now darling. I'm busy."

"Later on then. I'll put it on for you before dinner."

"Well . . ."

"After dinner then - before I go to bed. Please!"

"Not tonight, darling."

"But Papá I look beautiful, like a film star. You have to see me. Please!"

"I'll try. I have to sort out some business. I'll try to get home before you go to bed - if I can. Now run back to Mamá."

Davina had stayed where she was, watching the scene. She saw her daughter's excitement evaporate as she turned away from the man she thought of as 'Papá'.

Alfonso looked across the street to where Davina was standing. He seemed to see her, too, as if for the first time after a long absence. She had lost her youthful roundness and acquired a certain style and sophistication. Her gold-blonde hair, so despised by his mother, moved in the breeze. She smiled; she had a lovely smile. Suddenly he wanted her. He *would* go home with them. See Marina parade in her dress, then perhaps he would take his wife out for dinner. Just the two of them.

He had not taken two paces across the street, when a swarthy workman ambling home came along-side him. He acknowledged Alfonso with a gesture of the hand; "*Buenas tardes, Señor*," he said. Then he looked across the street at *la Señora* and the pretty young lady with the fancy box. What they said was true then; the girl didn't look a scrap like her mother and she didn't look a scrap like the pasty García del Morals, either. And what were mother and daughter doing down this way, out of their territory? Had the English woman finally caught on to his little game? He raised a bushy black eyebrow; "*Hasta mañana*," he said and sauntered off down the hill toward the area where the poorer labourers and gipsies lived.

Davina saw immediately that this workman had stopped Alfonso in his tracks. He was clearly at a loss, wondering what to do. She waited for him to say something.

When he spoke he was brusque, not angry but clearly giving an order. "Get her home. You shouldn't be out and about on your own around here. It's not safe in this area."

"Oh," said Davina, looking around her. "I didn't think about that. Can you take us back home?"

"No, not now. I'm sorry, I - I have things to do." He stepped forward as if to kiss Marina on the cheek, but didn't, instead he pushed her in the small of the back, "Off you go home now. Quick as you can. And not a word to Grandmother. She worries."

They went their separate ways. 'She worries?' thought Davina. About what? Doña Mercedes knew where they were. All this so-called trouble with the new unions. Alfonso was exaggerating. Who on earth would be interested in them?"

"Where's Papá going?" asked Marina.

"To see a man about a dog."

It was what her father had always said when she asked him where he was going. She caught a glimpse of her father winking at her and disappearing out of the back door. Davina sighed: she never stopped missing him. She turned to look at her daughter; she was as stubborn as her grandfather, and as dark as a black Dymond. "Come along," she said, "Papá is right, we shouldn't be dawdling in an area we don't know."

"Why?"

"Because there are people in the street who do not like . . ."

She was going to say 'us' and what she meant was 'them' - the García del Moral clan. Alfonso's increasing involvement in right-wing politics was viewed very negatively by his workforce and his new *paterfamilias* persona convinced very few, even the family cook had developed a scornful attitude. Davina quickened her pace but Marina dragged behind.

"Come on now. Do as you're asked, please."

Marina hung back then ran to catch up with her mother. Struggling with her dress box she said, "He doesn't like dogs."

"What?"

"You said he's gone to see a man about a dog. But he hasn't."

"How do you know that?"

"Because he doesn't like dogs."

"He might do. He didn't like those stupid Pekinese your grandmother used to have. But they were disgusting creatures."

"Well I've told him I don't want one of those. Every birthday and Christmas, I tell him I want a puppy, and he always says they smell and make a mess. He doesn't like dogs."

Davina didn't reply. Marina was just an adolescent looking for an argument. But as they walked briskly back towards the town centre she thought; who knows what he likes? He never really talks to us. He makes comments about this and that, shouts at his sisters, fawns over his mother and reads the newspaper. That's all we know about him. We've spent more time together during the last winter than ever before and all he ever talks about is his blessed fascist Falange party. He's certainly never said a word about Marina nagging him for a puppy.

As they neared the centre of town Marina said, "Let's look in the shoe shops for a pair to match the dress, while we've got it with us."

As Davina was taken from shop to shop the incident in the Cadiz road area slipped from her mind. It wasn't until they had reached the black portals of her mother-in-law's mansion and she was crossing the patio that a thought struck her; if it wasn't safe for them to be in that area of town, what was Alfonso doing there?

The following afternoon Davina said to the women gathered in Doña Mercedes' sitting room, "I'm just going back to pay the dress-maker. I shan't be long." And she was off down the stairs and through the patio before Marina had a chance to say she was coming, too.

She saw Alfonso before reaching the area where the dress-maker lived. He was some distance in front of her, which was better, as long as he didn't take one of the narrow side-streets. She just managed to keep him in view. Where the taller Jerez town-houses stopped he crossed an unmade road and headed off down the hill in the direction of the coast. Some way down the hill he stopped under a wide chestnut tree, and Davina watched in amazement as he loosened his tie then took off his jacket. It was a warm afternoon but that was no excuse for a gentleman to remove his jacket outdoors. Alfonso swung the jacket over his shoulder and carried on at a jaunty pace like a man without a care in the world.

I've been here before, thought Davina. We come up here in the car from El Puerto. This is the way the mule trains come. She followed as best she could, her heart pounding in her chest. If he saw her she would say she was looking for the dress-maker's house and she'd somehow got lost. The excuse was ready but in her heart of hearts she knew he wasn't going to notice her. His mind was fixed on wherever he was going. The man in front of her was a very different man to the one she knew.

She paused at the chestnut tree to get her breath back. She wouldn't go any further: she suddenly didn't want to know any more. Alfonso was entitled to his own life. She swept her hair off her face and swallowed hard. Just a second to calm herself and she'd go home.

At a bend in the rough road ahead there was a single-storey white-washed dwelling, surrounded by a rickety, painted fence. Chickens scratched in its yard. From where she stood she could see a kid goat playing with a brindled puppy outside the gate. Alfonso stooped to scratch the puppy's neck and shooed the kid back into the yard, then he went up the short path to the low doorway and opened the front door without knocking. The brindled puppy scampered up behind him and began to whine when the door was closed on him. The door was pushed open and the puppy disappeared inside.

Davina stood frozen to the spot beneath the tree, her heart

racing. She couldn't move. There was the sound of bells in the distance: a mule team was labouring up the hill. She mustn't be seen skulking under a tree in this neighbourhood. She tried to gather her wits but then the door of the little house opened again. She grabbed the bark of the tree for support. He would see her for sure.

But it wasn't Alfonso. A short, square-set woman with a tiny baby in her arms came out and paced around the small yard. The baby was screaming, the way only very young babies scream, and the woman was rocking it. She hoisted the tiny creature onto her shoulder, patted its back and started to sing. Then a small, pretty woman with tumbled black hair came to the doorway. Laughing, she called, "Mamá, come in. Let him hold her, see if Fonsie can stop her squealing!"

Fonsie! The crying baby was Alfonso's daughter! Alfonso's daughter . . . Davina felt herself go hot and cold. She was jealous! The thought crowded her mind: jealous. He had another woman: had always had another woman. And he was happy with her. And he held their baby. He had never once picked up Marina, held her in his arms.

But then Marina was not his daughter.

PART III

Chapter 20

AMSTERDAM, THE NETHERLANDS, 1934

The metallic heels of the red shoes tapped sharply over the uneven cobbles. The woman walked purposefully, avoiding the deeper puddles but never deviating from her way. The man walking behind was delighted by the red shoes; they were so smart and bright in the drab afternoon. The shoes clicked down the street and he followed: they were going his way. Tall buildings held the two forms in a labyrinth of early afternoon lights and admitted a third. Another man. A man in a grey gabardine, collar turned up, hands deep in pockets. Leo registered his presence as they passed a modern shop window; he turned round, as if naturally curious to see who else was out on such a filthy afternoon. The man's hands were thrust too deep in the gabardine's pockets - it wasn't that cold. Wet and nasty, but not winter cold.

Leo stiffened, the hair on the back of his neck prickled. He moved his left arm across his body checking the small bag tucked safely into his inner jacket pocket. He had nothing else of value on him. This chap wasn't a petty thief anyway. Perhaps he was over-reacting. His visit to Levi had rattled him. He had gone expecting to conclude a deal for the cutting and polishing of stones, which would then be traded by the Jew in Antwerp. The elderly Jew had turned him down. Precious stones were losing their value by the hour, he said. Sensible people were hiding their money in safe Swiss bank vaults not parading it these days.

"If you are so interested in the diamond trade, join the legitimate dealers in the *Diamantclub*," the old man said. Huh, he'd been trying to join the international *diamantaires* on the Pelikanstraat in Antwerp for years and had never been accepted - he lacked the 'necessary credentials'.

Leo was annoyed, more so because he knew the old man was right; it was time to shift his focus. But to what? The industrial diamond business with Moscow and Leningrad was lucrative but it lacked élan. He needed to maintain strong links with the Soviets and the industrial deals provided a safe cover, he could travel around more or less where he chose and not arouse suspicion - but it was boring. He had come to Amsterdam looking for a private arrangement that might lead him into something more exciting, not that he intended doing much business in The Netherlands: the guilder was in free-fall, same as the deutsche mark.

Leo suddenly realized he was distracted, not concentrating on what was happening around him. A sure sign of tiredness. He quickened his pace: he would get back to his rented room, get packed and get out; back to Dover, pass through debriefing then a passage home to Bombay. It was time for a complete break, his nerves were on edge. He turned round making no attempt to disguise the action: the man in the grey gabardine was still behind him, why?

The woman in the red shoes turned left to cross a narrow pedestrian bridge. The same bridge he would have to take if he were going back to his rented rooms. The gabardine man stopped to read a menu on a restaurant wall. Leo decided to follow the red shoes. A school-girl in convent brown was crossing the bridge in the opposite direction. She had a satchel on her back. It would be easy to stop her, ask her for directions, grab the satchel straps and use her as a shield – if necessary. He stepped to one side to let her pass, unhindered.

The red shoes tapped over the wooden planks then turned left again. Leo followed, as did the man behind him. They were now walking down an otherwise empty street. Half way down they all turned up a side street, walked another block and came out alongside another canal. They crossed another, wider bridge, each now looking over the low wall at the green-black length of silent inland water then back in the direction they were going. They turned left again and started down the other side of the canal. The buildings were taller, more elaborate and elegant here. Wide stone steps led up to the heavy doors of respectable burgers' houses. Some houses were divided into apartments. Apartments with long rooms and high windows, where lonely people or nosy people with binoculars sat peering out, hoping for a glimpse of someone else's life. A delivery boy on a heavy bicycle overtook them, whistling cheerily in defiance of the weather.

Just before the steps to number 105, the woman in the red shoes stepped into the shelter of a book-seller's doorway and rested her body on the narrow window sill, extending her legs before her. She opened the cheap bag she carried over her left shoulder and extracted a pack of cigarettes. Leo watched her until he had to pass and then ostentatiously averted his eyes. She was just a tart, after all.

As he ascended the five steps to the front door of 105, he saw the man draw level with the woman, watched him light her cigarette. Then, as he opened the door, Leo saw the man step into the middle of the empty street and bend down to tie a shoe lace. The hem of his long mackintosh fell into a dirty puddle. Because of the weight in a pocket, thought Leo. He suddenly moved fast to close the door behind him, but it was too late: a smart red shoe prevented it.

"Can I help you?" he said in English. "Oh, so sorry, do you live in this building, too? How charming."

The woman smiled what should have been a winning smile. She had pink skin, under the thick mascara her eyelashes were white; her white-blonde hair was natural. She reminded Leo of undercooked French lamb.

The woman said, "Charming? Well, yes, if you say." And she brushed herself up against the door jamb.

A Soviet sex-kitten! Leo wanted to laugh.

"Do you think I could come up for a moment?" she continued. "Just to get warm. It is a horrible afternoon. And you're all on your own, aren't you?" She ran her tongue over her upper lip.

Leo watched her with stony eyes. "I'm sorry, that won't be convenient," he said. Because, even if he were tempted, which he most definitely wasn't, not with this scraggy cat, he never, under any circumstances, played at home.

"Ya, well, never mind," She pushed her way into the gloomy hallway.

Leo made a business out of ignoring her and selecting the key for his rented apartment, as he did so two very strong, gabardined arms locked around him and the keys dropped to the floor with a clang. The woman searched his pockets and removed his small pistol.

"Shall we go up?" she said, signalling the stairs with the gun, "Or do you want to try calling for help?" She stuck the gun dramatically into his neck, "You can try if you want. But we have three guns, you have no gun."

She led the two men up the flight of steps, opened the

apartment with a key from her own shoulder bag and stood back for them to enter. The man in the gabardine raincoat pushed Leo through the doorway.

Fool, fool, fool; Leo was furious with himself – so absolutely, bloody obvious.

The woman with the red shoes and the foreign accent switched on the electric light and pushed the door closed with the heel of a red shoe. She stood square in front of Leo and said; "Now listen, we do not want to hurt you. That is not our intention. We just need your co-operation. You must give us any documents, papers, letters, that sort of thing. And then you must come with us. We do not want to hurt you, but we can and we will if necessary. Do you understand?"

He had two other guns in the apartment. How could he get them? Then his eyes focused on the state of his lodgings. The sofa had been gutted. Through the open bedroom door he saw clothes strewn everywhere, the mattress skewed across the bed.

The man in the raincoat said, "Bit of a mess, isn't it?" and looked questioningly at the blonde. She shrugged her shoulders. Then the man looked at his watch and said, "Hey, we've got time for a cuppa." He was English. His accent was London English. He pushed Leo into the kitchenette.

The apartment had been ransacked. They haven't found what they were looking for and expect me to help them, thought Leo. What were they after? What documents? Did they think he was a complete idiot that left interesting items lying around for any little streetwalker to lay her hands on?

They may, of course, have followed him all the way from Leningrad. Or maybe they had picked up his trail while he was with the Labans and Rosenthals in Hamburg. If they had anything to do with the German fiscal police they might, justifiably, be suspicious.

What did they think he'd got? Photographs of people talking to people they shouldn't even know - of precision machine tools the West hadn't yet invented? Code books? Pilfered documents? Family jewels to be sold to raise cash for beleaguered German Jews? What were they after? And for whom?

Leo said, "There's no money here."

"Wrong," said the woman. "There is a Thomas Cook traveller's cheque worth twenty pounds sterling. Here, take it."

Leo took it then looked at it as if he had never seen a traveller's cheque in his life. He nearly laughed, what the hell was going on?

"Right then," said the Londoner, shrugging off his wet raincoat. "Let's make ourselves at home for ten minutes. I'm John, she's Mary and there's the kettle. No funny business lighting the gas sir, if you please. You've got no reason to hurt us."

Leo filled the kettle, lit the gas and spooned loose tea from an upturned caddy into the teapot. They had emptied the tea caddy but not the sugar bowl. The salt jar was intact, too. So they weren't after the Rosenthal stones. Or they were and they wanted to make him jumpy. Or they wanted to see what else he might have smuggled out of Germany. Or they were amateurs acting on their own.

The woman called Mary, but more probably Marie or Marietta had now disappeared into the bedroom; it sounded as if she were banging empty drawers. In the kitchen, the man stood legs apart, arms folded across his barrel chest, with his back to the door. The 'sir' clicked into place. Well, well, well, a London bobby. Leo went through the motions of making the tea, his mind racing backward and forward over the past few days, then weeks and months. What had he acquired that these two might want?

The woman came into the kitchen and placed a bundle of dog-eared, well-travelled letters on the green gingham table cloth. Letters.

Never put anything in writing; never keep anything personal with you – 'no mementos, souvenirs, personal effects . . .' Rules were made for reasons. Fool, fool, fool.

"Well?" she said.

Leo cocked his head on one side and gave her a half grin. How best to deal with this - friend or foe? London Johnny could have sold his limited skills to any number of firms, and she was his boss. But whose outfit?

"Well this isn't very clever, Mr. Kazan. I'm sure you were advised against it. Keeping letters. Tut, tut, tut . . ." said John, turning the bundle of envelopes over with a podgy hand.

"They're love letters," said Mary. She didn't sneer, she didn't need to. Her statement was sufficient. She was almost certainly Russian. A modern Russian. Product of a Leninist high school and a Stalinist finishing school on some snowy Ural alp.

"Oh dear," said John. "I hope this doesn't complicate things." His patronising nasal voice made Leo want to smack him very hard across the mouth.

"They are from his wife."

"Blimey."

Leo did not speak again. He stood watching the kettle, waiting for it to boil, every sense trained on the woman's movements. She had gone back to the bedroom.

John opened and closed the drawers of the kitchen dresser. He ran a hand behind the water heater. Plaster flaked off the wall and clung to his cuffs. He tried to brush it off but it clung to his fingers. It was a good moment. Leo calculated the moves to get out of the kitchenette then out of the building. He didn't move. Even if he set fire to the tea towel hanging by the sink, he was still in a very weak position regarding the speed of bullets. As if picking up his thoughts,

John picked up the tea towel and made a fuss of wiping his sleeve with it. Mary came back into the kitchen area and tapped her watch.

John said, "Kettle's just boiled."

"No time."

"Ah well, time and tide wait for no man, or so they say." John buttoned up his gabardine and slapped his hands over the bulging pockets. "Time to go. The lady's right, we'll miss the tide."

"Tide?" asked Leo.

"The tide, Mr. Kazan. We are off to the seaside. And just in case you don't fancy our little excursion remember, that apart from this little chap," he waggled a pistol in his right hand, "I've also got these." He flipped a pair of handcuffs from his left-hand pocket, grinning. "Shall we tell him where he's going?"

"No!" Mary replied sharply. "You talk too much. Shut your mouth." She stuffed the letters in her shoulder bag.

"I need to use the lavatory," said Leo.

"Yeah, yeah," said John.

"Go," said Mary.

Leo went to the bathroom and stood looking into the toilet. Amateurs, he thought. But no less dangerous for that. He closed the wooden seat, stood on it then pushed up a cuff and inserted a hand into the cistern above. They had got guns, he hadn't. He located a flat, square-shaped package covered in oil cloth. They said they wanted him 'to help them' then didn't ask one damn question. He wiped the waterproof cloth with his fingers and checked its sealing. Not that the packet needed to be dry; pearls were created in water, and diamonds didn't melt – anything except a silly girl's heart. His wife had no time for them. She liked red, red rubies, clever girl. He stepped down, wiped the seat with a sleeve and pulled the flush. Then he popped the damp package down the front of his underpants and jiggled until it was in a tolerable position.

Now what? If these two goons hadn't raided his rooms, they knew who had. So, run? Play along? Was there an option? Yes; find out what the options were first.

He returned to the demolished kitchen and sat down at the table. "Look," he said, making eye contact first with Marie-Marietta, then London Johnny. "This is all rather confusing, not to say unpleasant. You have turned my temporary home upside-down. The place is a complete shambles. Tell me what you are looking for and I can tell you where it is. Then you can leave, and I can try and tidy up before my landlady arrives and faints on the doorstep. My wife is always accusing me of untidiness, but this really isn't fair."

There was an exchange of glances. John said, "Tell him."

The woman looked straight at Leo then focused on a point behind him. "At two o'clock yesterday afternoon there was an explosion outside your father-in-law's shop. It happened during a street demonstration. Your wife and her parents were killed."

Leo looked at the two people and then said slowly and clearly, "That is not true."

"I regret it is."

"And my daughter?"

"I didn't know you had a daughter," said Mary, too fast.

"No, you know absolutely nothing about me. You have just got your orders and you are making a total fuck up of carrying them out. My wife and family live in the centre of Bombay. How do you know what happened there *at two o'clock yesterday afternoon?*"

"The building was destroyed. Completely. There was rioting in the street. Many people have been killed and injured."

There was silence. Eventually Leo said, "What do you want?"

"You - and any documents of any description in your possession." Mary tapped her shoulder bag. "If you have anything else, please tell us. It will be worse for you if you do not."

"This is nonsense!" cried Leo. "Absurd. How the hell do you get information from Bombay that fast? Who the hell are you?"

"If you have a warmer coat than that mac, sir, you'd best put it on," John said quietly, "it'll be arctic out on the water."

Leo could not move. John took an arm pulled him gently to his feet and directed him into the bedroom. Leo silently moved over to the wardrobe, the key was in the door but the door was hanging like a broken limb from one hinge. His heavy winter coat was on the floor. They hadn't even slit open the lining. He picked it up and put it on. The last time he had seen Elena she had been sitting in her high-chair waving a spoon in the air. He had kissed her fluffy head and she had smeared egg yolk over his shirt and the lapel of his jacket. He'd rushed into their bedroom to change. His wife had laughed at him. He'd been cross and rushed out of the door in a hurry, forgetting this thick, winter coat. Then he'd turned round at the bottom of the stairs, dashed back up, grabbed the coat from his wardrobe and left again - without saying a proper goodbye.

But it wasn't true. Couldn't be true. When he got back to Bombay . . .

"Can I take that suitcase?" He pointed to the top of the wardrobe. "I don't know why you've wrecked this room and left a suitcase like that untouched," he said with scorn.

Mary looked at her partner. John shrugged and said, "Just some old pictures on blocks of wood. Let him have them, they're no use to us." He pulled a chair round to the wardrobe to stand on.

"I can reach," said Leo, who towered over inner-city Johnny.

"Open it," demanded Mary.

Leo placed the leather case on the bed and opened it. There was a cotton draw-string bag inside containing exactly what John had described: pictures of the Madonna and child painted onto thin blocks of wood. Some were chipped and very old. Leo had 'rescued' them from various churches around Leningrad. The churches had been converted into warehouses or children's nurseries. In one he had found some women burning ikons and bibles for warmth. Leo ran a hand over the bag.

"Here," said Mary. She scooped underwear and shirts from the disrupted drawers. Leo packed them around the bag. John threw a jersey and some socks onto the top of the bed.

"That's enough," Mary said.

Leo snapped the locks of the suitcase and was escorted by his unpredictable kidnappers down the stairs, Mary in the lead and John, with a gun in his right hand, keeping as close as possible behind him. Once out on the street again they walked back past the bookshop and turned onto the Princengracht. They had a car parked alongside the canal. John motioned to Leo to get into the front passenger seat. Mary sat in the back, immediately behind him. She tapped his shoulder with his own pistol but said nothing.

As John reversed from the parking space, another car pulled out further down the row. It followed them onto the new road between Amsterdam and Den Haag. John appeared not to notice it - either because he knew who was in it, or because he really was a complete amateur.

The car followed them through the evening rain all the way to the North Sea harbour of Scheveningen. The quayside was strangely deserted unless they had missed the tide - or they were too early. There was a man sitting on a bollard, he signalled to them as they drove up. John parked where the man pointed and they all got out. Leo was marched at gun-point to an evil-smelling fishing trawler. He looked around for their followers but apart from a handful of genuine looking fishermen and a couple of scrawny dogs scavenging among abandoned fish crates there was no one.

So they were shipping him off somewhere: north or south? Or were they going to ferry him west, across the North Sea? If they intended to kill him, they were going a long way about it, unless they planned to dump him at sea, which on a foul night was a fairly safe way of disposing of a trouble-maker.

A fisherman climbed aboard the trawler and alerted the skipper. A huge Dutchman in sea boots and jersey appeared on deck and said, "Come, come, I am expecting you." He stepped forward and held out a hand to Mary, she ignored it and hoisted her skirt up to climb over the gunwale. John poked Leo in the back and said, "Now you sir." Then he followed them aboard. The skipper directed them to a poky cabin and went about his business.

John pushed Leo down a ladder: the awkward suitcase banged against each step and bruised his legs. The woman squeezed into the cabin after them. There was an element of humour about the whole manoeuvre: Leo wanted to laugh at the silliness – because he was frightened.

John put his hand on Leo's shoulder and said, "Skipper will drop you off, when he sees fit."

"Where?"

John gave his habitual shrug and went up on deck to light a cigarette. Under other circumstances Leo could easily have grabbed the woman and used her to get away. But he didn't because his brain was not functioning at its usual speed. He just looked at her and said, "Is it true?"

She lowered her eyes, "Yes. I am sorry for your loss."

It was a direct translation. Leo said, "Whose side are you on?"

"I think you must ask yourself the same thing." She closed the low door and Leo heard a key turn in the lock.

Keeping his head down to avoid cracking it on the low ceiling, Leo looked around him. An oil lamp on a tiny desk, a thermos flask and a snug looking bunk. He took off his overcoat and sat down on the bunk. Above him feet ran to and fro. A good few years had passed since he had last made a trip on a smelly fishing boat. Then he grinned and ran a hand over the lining of his coat; he never travelled without sharp scissors and a needle and thread.

He must have slept for some time because when the door opened it took him a good second or two to register where he was. They were still rolling with the sea. Had they reached their location? They weren't about to put him ashore. The skipper stood over him, his right hand raised directly over Leo's chest. He had something in his huge right fist.

Leo rolled over and fell to the floor, but there was no space - he was lying on the Dutchman's boots. They were of a similar build, but the Dutchman had all the advantages: he was on his feet, he was obviously stronger and he had a weapon in his right hand. Trying to escape was pointless – his only chance lay in dialogue.

"Aagh," moaned Leo in mock agony. "I forgot how narrow bunks are." The Dutchman was off guard – he had a knife and wasn't using it . . .

The Dutchman bent and helped Leo to his feet with his left hand, saying nothing. Leo sat back on the bunk rubbing his side. The big man looked down at him, grunted something in Dutch and dropped a package on the bed.

The door was shut and locked once more. Leo put his hand on the package - Kitty's letters. He put his hand on them and knew it was true.

These letters were the sum of his marriage. He had married a pretty Eurasian girl but hadn't stayed at home to love her. For the three years of their marriage they had been together for perhaps a matter of months. His daughter had been born while he was away. And now she had died - while he was away - doing dirty work for the British government. Where were the British during this street demonstration? He'd been running around for twenty years helping them to keep their precious Raj in one piece – where were they when his family were threatened? His father-in-law was an ex-soldier, who had fought for his country in a shire regiment uniform during the Great War. Why had they done nothing to save him? Or his mother-in-law: a tiny Maratha woman who had no argument with anyone, why should Bombay 'demonstrators' involve her? And Kitty and little Elena . . . why them?

Anger kept him awake for the next hour or so until exhausted, he rolled onto his side and hugged the letters to his chest; Kitty; gentle, good-humoured, innocent Kitty. He should have been there - not chasing after fat-bellied Marxists - or lining his own pockets for the fun of it. The woman was right; whose side was he on?

For the rest of the dark night he wallowed in self-pity, sleeping in snatches and waking to the injustice of his existence. Just when he wanted to go home and, for the first time in his life, had a proper, loving home to go to – it was taken from him. Let them dump him at sea. The game was up.

Chapter 21

They landed him at Lowestoft and left on the same tide. He booked himself into a boarding house and stayed in his room until the landlady asked him if he needed a doctor. On the third day he asked her to buy him a razor and a new shirt. Then he tidied himself up, converted the traveller's cheque into cash at the nearest bank, paid the landlady and purchased a train ticket to London.

He went straight to India House. He was tempted to go in through the main entrance and up the fancy staircase, throw open the door to his section and demand an explanation. But histrionics would get him nowhere with civil servants.

Going up the back stairs to the third floor, he realized he had only ever used the tradesman's entrance, which put his so-called job in perspective. He provided a service; he was a handy extra, not even a pawn in the Game of State.

The third floor corridor was alive with people. Men and women trotting to and fro with sheaves of paper, a harassed tea-lady carrying a huge tray, a post-boy pushing a trolley: two southern Indians in snow-white cotton and thick black, rubber-soled shoes were conferring in whispers outside a closed door.

Leo knocked and entered his usual office. There had

been changes; a non-descript female secretary with a smart new typewriter now occupied the ante-room where he normally wrote up his reports in long hand. She said, "Yes, how may I help you?" in a tone suggesting she would do nothing of the sort. Leo looked around him, took in the pile of correspondence beside her typewriter and gave her a beaming smile.

"Hello, you are new here. Leo Kazan, to see Sir Gerald."

She was impervious to charm. "Wait here. Sir Gerald is in Downing Street."

Leo beamed, "Good for him! He deserves it." She didn't catch on.

"I'll tell Mr. Howard. He's here." She opened the door of the main office and said, "Mr. Howard, Mr. Kazan is here. Do you want to see him now, or shall I tell him to come back later?"

Leo, riled by her tone, entered the office before Mr. Howard, whoever he was, had a chance to speak. There were now two desks instead of one. A ferrety little man was sitting at the smaller of the two. He was wearing a brown suit. Times have changed, thought Leo.

"Mr. Kazan, a pleasure to meet you. My name's Howard, Jim Howard."

The ferrety man had got to his feet behind his desk but made no move to come round and greet Leo man to man.

They shook hands over the desk and Leo, out of custom, removed his hat and coat and hung them on the stand behind the door. Howard resumed his seat and observed his visitor with a mixture of intense curiosity and trepidation.

"Take a pew," he said, indicating an upright chair in front of his untidy desk. Leo settled himself on the wooden chair, adjusted the crease in his trousers, touched each of his garnet cufflinks and cocked his head to one side. Would this Mr Howard be doing the debriefing?

"Cup of tea, Mr. Kazan?" Howard had heard about the suave Leo Kazan, who ran a tight little business in precious stones whilst he kept his eyes and ears open for the India Office. He had been expecting someone rather more film starish, better looking, nevertheless, the elegant cut of the charcoal suit, the fancy cufflinks and matching tie pin set him apart from the usual jobbers.

Leo declined the tea. He was curious to see how this little man, corporal made up to captain perhaps during the war, was going to cope with international intelligence gathering. Howard spent a few moments making a space on his cluttered desk for a new block of lined writing paper. Once he had that in place, he began to fiddle about with a fountain pen and blotter. Leo was irritated by the effective clerk charade and simply handed over the list of names he had compiled during his stay in Lowestoft; members of the Indian National Congress who were active Marxists.

The ferrety man was clearly uncertain what to do. He looked at the list, looked at Leo and said, "Yes, yes. Perhaps you had better explain it to me. That way I can make sure Sir Gerald gets all pertinent details."

Playing for time, thought Leo, he's a bumped-up clerk, nothing more. He made a mental note of the contents of Howard's desk while the man's whining voice recited the names. Sticking out from under the blotter was another list of names. Leo leaned over the desk and picked it up, giving Howard a quizzical look. Jim Howard stopped reciting and said, "Ah, yes, that came in yesterday, from Delhi I believe."

"Why don't we check to see if they match?" Leo was becoming angry.

"Well, we've got Pran Seth and Narandra Dev Prakasa on both lists. I know Prakasa from somewhere else, too. I think he's been in the limelight for some time. Sir Giles says these are mostly Hindus, a few Sikhs. Yes, yes, this list came in from Delhi."

"Did it? Should you be telling me that?" Leo watched the clerk squirm. "Never mind – you don't have Daniel Gopi and Mahesh Lakh. They're on my list and not the Delhi one."

"Gopi and Lakh?"

"They are teaching in Leningrad. Lakh is a mathematician - it's a good name for a mathematician. Gopi is an expert on Katha Kali."

"Sorry," said Jim Howard. "I don't claim to know any Indian languages; I'm just here as a sort of general assistant to Sir Gerald, during the crisis, they're very busy with this new Government of India Bill. I used to be in Transport, actually. Not a lot I don't know about trams."

Leo smiled, he'd scented blood. "What would you like me to tell you about Gopi and Lakh? They are influential in academic circles; we'll need to watch their political contacts. I know that Gopi has arranged a limited amount of finance for a campaign in Delhi. He's very popular with students, quite a character, gets invited to all sorts of events." Leo extracted another neatly folded sheet of paper from his jacket pocket and handed it to Howard. "This is a brief outline of the financial links in the chain."

"Oh, good, good; that's very useful."

"I should hope so, took months to achieve. Do you want me to explain it to you – or to Sir Gerald?"

"Oh, well yes, erm . . ." Howard pressed the nib of his pen onto his pink blotting paper and stared at the shape of the blot."

Oh, Lord, thought Leo, he's way out of his depth. Whatever

were they thinking of putting a tram man in the India Office? Suddenly he felt sorry for the small man who had to work for the larger than life Sir Gerald and didn't know a turban from a tea-cosy. No games with this one, he'll burst into tears.

As if rejecting Leo's sympathy, Jim Howard waved the Delhi list and said, "We do know about a lot of these people already, you see. Not that you've been wasting your time, don't get me wrong. It's that they have come into the open, they've actually set up a separate party and . . . come into the open. While you've been in Russia – it is Russia you do, isn't it?"

Leo nodded and said nothing: even the timidest animals snap when cornered.

"Yes, well we now have the Congress Socialist Party no less. On their way to taking over Gandhi's 'self-governing, independent India', they say. I wonder what the little chap thinks about that when he's at his spinning wheel?"

It was an attempt at humour. Leo was not amused.

"I'll just chase up that tea, shall I?" Howard was out from behind his desk and through the door to the ante-room in a trice – he needed a breather. As he closed the door with his right hand he lowered his head and dragged oxygen into his damaged lungs. Lifting his head he caught the secretary's eye: she looked straight through him. Eventually his shoulders relaxed and trying to keep his voice under control he said, "Joyce, get us a cuppa, will you?"

Joyce scowled, "I am Sir Gerald's secretary, Mr. Howard."

Jim Howard opened the door and wandered down the corridor. Sir Gerald called his network of informers 'intelligencers' and kept their files under lock and key. That had made him curious for a start - not being allowed access to folders on the men whose reports he had to decipher and write up on official paper. So, naturally, the day

Sir Gerald left the filing cabinet open and then went off for a long lunch he'd had a look.

The dossiers, which contained personal data and operational background details, all made interesting reading, but in personal terms Kazan's dossier was a corker. The chap had spent fifteen years in and out of Russia, first as a student then as a merchant peddling industrial diamonds. Reading the file it seemed that Kazan spent his life picking up tidbits here and there, keeping a check on who moved where and when and taking advantage of open windows to obtain little gems of information. It wasn't all that dangerous, as far as he could see. Of course if anyone found out who he was really working for there would be trouble. But that wasn't what interested him. It was the stuff about his young life that made interesting reading, made him feel a bit sorry for him, too. Chap had never had a proper home as a kid, even when he got married he'd never settled down to a proper life. Not what he'd call a proper life; taking the kiddies to the seaside, listening to the radio with the missus of an evening, watching a game of footy on a Saturday. Fancy hotels and posh suits didn't make up for a nice suburban semi. Not after what he'd been through in France. Wife and two kids - mow the lawn on Sundays and a safe job with a regular income. No, this chap Kazan had got his priorities all wrong. So he had no right to play the superior, make fun of a decent chap who was just doing his job. Jim Howard inhaled deeply for a count of six and exhaled for a count of eight, the way they'd shown him in the hospital.

When he returned to the office, Kazan was sitting where he'd left him staring out of the window. There had been a young sparrow on the windowsill that morning. Poor creature seemed afraid of heights, hadn't got enough strength to get back to its nest. He had put some water in a saucer for it to drink. Perhaps the bird had come back.

"There was bird on the window sill this morning. Learning to fly, I think. Poor little devil needed a parachute."

"Really?" Leo shook himself mentally He wanted to finish his report and get away as fast as possible.

"No sign of the tea-makers, sorry."

"Better, I never drink English tea. We were comparing lists, can we get on with it, do you think?"

"Yes, yes, the lists." Jim Howard controlled his respiration. "I was telling you about the Congress socialists. Listen to this," he extracted a typed document from his overflowing in-tray, "'independence must mean the establishment of an Independent State'- nothing new there. They've been banging on about that since before you started, haven't they? But now we have a new twist for the old tale; 'wherein all power is transferred to the producing masses'. Producing masses! They couldn't make a decent cup of tea between them when I was out there before the war. And then, get this! 'and such objective involves refusal to compromise at any stage with British Imperialism'. What do you think of that, Mr. Kazan? Refusal to co-operate and we're all breaking our backs trying to make life better for them with this new Act." He looked at his visitor for a reaction, and got none. "Yes well, ours not to reason why, eh?"

Leo didn't move a muscle, but the final phrase, spoken with ignorant sarcasm, flooded his mind; *refusal to compromise at any stage with British Imperialism*. It made sense. It made perfect sense. It had taken his homeland three centuries, and him personally three decades to realize it, but it was neither too late, nor too early to stop compromising. It was time to start making one's own decisions: time to sort out the muddles and accept the consequences.

Leo looked at his interlocutor, produced a rue smile and

nodded. The pen pusher in the brown suit grinned back in gratitude, and then remembered Sir Gerald's plans and stopped. He sat down behind his untidy desk and said, in a quite different tone, "Sterling work, Kazan. Links confirmed. You've been on their trail a long time. Patience rewarded, eh? Now we can keep an eye on the blighters *in situ*."

"Not me, Mr. Howard."

"No, no, not you. You have done your bit. And you're blown - as they say. Sorry about the travel arrangements, Sir Gerald wanted you to be seen to be removed from the scene. If you see what I mean? Exciting stuff, I must say. Mind if I smoke?"

The man kept a packet of Players in his drawer – not in a silver case in his jacket. Leo watched the clerk's hands shake as he lit a match.

Leo cocked his head on one side. "Am I being dismissed?"

"Dismissed? Good heavens, no!" Sir Gerald strode into the room all brandy fumes and bonhomie. Leo jumped to his feet and they shook hands like old colleagues. Jim Howard hastily stubbed out his cigarette on the window sill and flicked it into the courtyard below. Sir Gerald dropped his briefcase on his side of the room and came over to perch on the edge of Jim Howard's desk. Leo was not asked to resume his seat.

"Call it *resting*, like the actors. There'll be other work for India hands and Russian speakers like you, for sure. That girl Marietta, the one in Amsterdam – Bulgarian, she tells us – as do many others - that Joe Stalin has his sights on the Balkans. Makes sense - access to warm sea ports, that's what they've always been after isn't it. And if they do get any power in India, God help us!" He shook his head of thick brown hair like an indignant lion. "Then I'm sure you'll be back in demand. Trouble with India is that many fools still see Mother Russia as their great deliverer from the North. But you've done enough in this context Leo. We think it's time you lay low for a while."

Jim Howard picked up Leo's list and the financial links report and held them out to his boss. Sir Gerald glanced at the sheets of paper and said, "Excellent. Well done. All double-checked, no dropping any innocent fellow travellers in the mire I hope."

"Time will tell," replied Leo.

The senior civil servant caught the edge in Kazan's voice but maintained his casual approach. A lot could be achieved through purposeful banter: it usually helped to avoid unnecessary scenes. "We may need to call on you sooner rather than later, as it happens. I've just been called in to update members of the Cabinet regarding the Princely States. Most of the petty rajahs want nothing to do with the Muslim League or Congress, for obvious reasons of personal finance. Socialism, in any form, is anathema to them, as you well know. So make sure we know where to find you."

He looked at Leo Kazan. Give him a close shave and dress him tails he was a gentleman, put him a dhoti and he was a coolie. A well-fed coolie, but his hair was just the right shade of oily black. Put him in a silk turban and he was another princeling. A chameleon, but chameleons were only required to be there and watch, not interact and use their situations to feather their nests. Except chameleons didn't make nests – or did they? He would consult his wife's Pear's Encyclopaedia the minute he got home.

"I've booked a passage on the 'Viceroy'," said Leo "This Friday. I wasn't intending to stay."

"Fine, fine. Well if you and my splendid *aide-de-camp* here have finished, our little lady next door has a nice fat envelope ready for you." He moved to his feet, placed a hand under Leo's elbow and directed him into the secretary's office. Keeping a hand on the door handle behind him, he said, "We'll be in touch."

Leo suddenly came to his senses. "About my wife, sir . . ."

"Yes, that was a bit naughty, getting married and not telling us first. Families have to be vetted you know. We've always been tolerant with you, you know, but there are limits."

"Marietta, the Bulgarian woman, she said my wife and her family – had been killed – in rioting."

"Oh God, yes, that's right. Slipped my mind. These disturbances are getting very nasty in some areas. Her father was ex-Hampshire Regiment I believe. Should have put his wife's name on the shop, English names are being used for target practice these days. Fact is we're not too popular. Anyway, all things Indian from now on: dominion status. They say the Act will be through by November. Things should quieten down soon."

Leo was on the verge of physical violence, he wanted to shout, 'Tell me you stupid bastard, tell me what you know, or shut your fucking mouth'. He swallowed hard and stared at a crack in the wall plaster, trying to erase any emotion from his features. He was just about to speak when the secretary came up and quietly offered him a buff envelope.

"Can you sign for it, please," she said, "in my accounts book."

He went up to her desk and signed his name against a set of digits and the date.

"Pinecoffin, too, you know," said Sir Gerald opening the outer door onto the corridor.

Leo turned, "In the rioting?"

"No, natural causes. He was getting on, and that climate was no good to him. Pity you weren't at the funeral. Your father was there to represent you, of course."

"I think you are mistaken, Sir Gerald."

"Hardly, the chap got a three column obit in the 'Telegraph' and two in the 'Times'."

"No, sir, about my father. I went to a British orphanage school."

"Well, where else would they have sent you? British education, logical choice. My parents sent me back to Blighty when I was seven and I bet you can decline Latin as well as any of us. Julius Caesar's Julius Caesar, Gallic wars are the Gallic wars in any school. Well, can't stand here chatting - seeing the P.M. first thing tomorrow and got a bit of homework to do." He clapped Leo on the back and strode back into his office. The secretary sat down and began to rattle away at her typewriter.

Sir Gerald closed the door to his shared office and looked at Jim Howard. Howard was in a dither again. The little man made some unnecessary mime of wiping sweat from his brow and said, "Phew, he's a cool customer."

"Not any more he isn't: red hot as we speak. He has just lost all members of his so-called family. He's reached saturation point with his Russia job and now we have effectively said don't call us, we'll call you. Not cool at all Mr. Howard. Hopping mad at me, too. Silly blighter's too emotionally involved to see what's what, of course. We play the same game, use similar tactics you see. "

John Howard didn't see.

Sir Gerald went to his desk and stroked an alabaster paperweight. "What will he do now do you think, Mr. Howard?"

"Oh, I really couldn't say, sir. If it was me, well I'd - erm. Well it's all is a bit - erm - drastic. All his family you say, in street riots . . . They're blood baths from what I've been told. Dear me, I don't know. He won't go and do anything stupid, will he?"

"Top himself? No, not Leo. He'll probably flash on the charm, fleece a wealthy widow, pick up one of the fishing fleet and . . . and he may very well decide that he is after all not a true Brit and go very *pro patria*. I'd lay bets on all three."

"Fishing fleet, sir?"

"The wenches who still go off to India for the cool season hoping to hook a husband, if not on the voyage then once they get there. Heaven help them with Leo."

"His father is still alive, though. He wasn't erm - in the rioting?"

"Well done, Howard, you are learning to winnow."

"Winnow, sir?"

"Glean, sift and sort the chaff from the grain. Now, fast as you can, run up to Mike Lee and tell him to get himself down here double quick. We can't allow our Indian magpie to be out of sight for a while yet, not in the state he's in. He's angry with us and he knows much too much."

Leo got on the first bus that passed but it got so crowded he jumped off on the station side of Waterloo Bridge. Taxis were pulling into the station, delivering passengers on the first stage of their journeys west. Sir Lionel had used this station. He used to say . . . what? Something about a cup of tea and a Bath bun at Waterloo, he'd forgotten. Dodging people who had somewhere to go, he crossed the road and went down the steps to the embankment. The cold and damp were palpable, he knew he should keep moving but suddenly he was drained of energy – could go no further. He sat on an elaborate wrought iron bench and pulled the collar of his overcoat up around his ears. For a matter of moments his mind was empty: he could have been anywhere – his mind had simply closed down.

Slowly, very slowly, he came back to consciousness and began to register his surroundings. Dolphins curled up lamp posts on dry land. Cats were eating bread tossed for pigeons. A seagull landed on the paving stones and strode towards them with felonious intent. Nothing was where it should be, as it should be. Leo looked around, trying to locate something that made sense and realized how close he was to Dickens' villainous waters. But even the river looked wrong for its element, it was solid, unmoving.

He turned his attention to the grey sky lurking above the city on the other side of the river. Gradually, his surroundings took shape and he remembered he had been here before. Perhaps not the same bench, but very close. The girl at the Armistice party - fifteen, sixteen years ago. And that dreadful incident in the tea shop. He hadn't thought about it for years. And now, when he should be mourning his mentor, his wife, his daughter – an entire existence for God's sake, he was thinking about a soft, fair-haired girl, whose only meaning to his life was that she had made him realize sex could be more than a series of gymnastic exercises.

Had he been born without a soul? Kitty had asked him that once - perhaps twice. But he loved - had loved Kitty, for her gentle ways, her kindness and honesty. She had never, ever tried to be anything other than what she was. Was that because her parents thought she was so wonderful; that she had never had to *try* to please? They were good, honest people. Perhaps that is why he had wanted to marry Kitty: to share in the security of their home.

In which case, Lord tell me why I spent more time away than with them?

He stood up, ready to move on, ready to erase sentiment

through action. And as he did so, the certainty that he had been on this very spot before overwhelmed him. The girl at the Armistice party - the one he had dropped because he had been sent to do a man's job in a dangerous situation, when he was still a boy. The dalliance he had discarded because he had suddenly become important. Except, and it was now abundantly clear, he wasn't and never had been important – useful but of no intrinsic value. Like an industrial diamond.

That English girl had been a sort of Kitty, fair instead of dark, but very similar - the same innocence. Perhaps she had been his first love and he'd never realized it.

Love. Why couldn't he cry for Kitty and Elena?

He leant over the railings staring down at the sludgy Thames. A steady drizzle rolled in from the west and disturbed the water. He shuddered; no wonder Lionel Pinecoffin had stayed on in Bombay. He walked back and set off across the bridge in the direction of the City. Had Lionel's sons arranged a memorial service at Westminster, or somewhere in the West Country? Sir Lionel Pinecoffin had been more than a father to him and he had missed his funeral.

'*Your father was there to represent you, of course*'.

"What bloody father?" he shouted to the wind. "Why are you telling me this, now?"

A woman carrying a shopping basket scuttled past him, nearly losing her groceries in the passing traffic. There were strange people on the streets these days and that was a fact. This one looked too young to have been in the war, but he was talking away to himself like a madman. She inadvertently caught the eye of a bag-lady crouched in the lee of the wall. The toothless crone screeched with laughter, pointing at the posh fella looking over the side of the bridge and yelling at the water.

Had Lionel known? He had a real father – and nobody had ever told him. Lionel would have told him – surely. Well, it didn't matter now: father or no father, he was never going back to Bombay. End of a story never begun. He reached into his jacket and extracted the envelope containing his passage to India. He pulled the ticket out and held it up to the wind and rain.

The old crone was up on her doddery feet: he was throwing his money away, Lord luv'im, throwing his dosh away! The paper ticket fluttered up for a moment then hovered over the Thames. She'd lose it, damn him. No, it was blowing her way. She watched it drift across to her and drop down into a puddle right at her feet and screeched in delight. Then she cursed him and all his kind; it weren't no tenner, nor a fiver nor even an IOU - and she'd found a few of them in her day. Nah, this wasn't worth having. She left it in the puddle and hobbled back to her niche out of the rain and traffic fumes on Waterloo Bridge.

Leo watched her and turned away. He had taken perhaps ten paces when a thought struck him. "Bugger, shit," he shouted. "Damn, fuck . . ." He rushed back, shouting a stream of filthy abuse in English, and street Marathi.

"'Ere, you!" shouted the crone. "Mind yer language."

Leo stopped in his tracks, "Sorry," he said. "No offence meant."

"And none taken, but you'd better watch yerself, sonny. You'll get picked up by the peelers, you will."

Leo bent double and retrieved the limp, muddied ticket from the puddle.

"I have to get back you, see. It's my biscuit tins; I'd forgotten all about them."

Barmy! Potty as a public lav. The crone huddled into herself and watched him march off across the bridge. Too many strange buggers on the street these days, yer weren't safe in broad daylight no more.

His precious biscuit tins, wrapped in green and gold sari material that he'd pinched from a washing line expressly for the purpose, were buried under the floorboards of his late mother-in-law's outside kitchen. Had that survived the rioting? He had to get back as soon as possible. Amongst other, lesser treasures, the round tin contained the 'Empress Emerald'.

Chapter 22

The P&O steam ship passed Trafalgar as the sun appeared over the horizon and was piloted into Gibraltar's North Harbour as late-rising passengers finished breakfast. Leo Kazan was up on deck early, arms akimbo over the rails, watching for the twin Pillars of Hercules. A pretty blonde joined him and snuggled up against his left arm.

"This sort of morning in November only happens after Finisterre and before Port Said," Leo commented. The girl murmured assent. She was pleasantly drowsy, a catlike grin lingered around her rouged lips; she had secured a beau before the second port of call and her friends were green with envy. He was so dashing, sophisticated and funny - he'd had them all in fits. And he was the sort that *always* traveled first class. Her brother had been right: the extra expense was worth it. She rubbed her cheek up against the grey tweed arm on the polished rail. Lovely.

As if speaking to himself, her new beau sighed and said, "I'm like that rock."

She giggled, "What, big and surrounded by water?"

"No, silly - Gibraltar is not a true island, it's linked to Spain - to Europe - by a narrow isthmus."

"Fancy," said the blonde.

Leo looked down at her peroxide parting. She wouldn't do.

"It was like he suddenly went cold on me," she told Edna over a nice cup of milky coffee later that morning, "and that sort of made me look at him properly, if you know what I mean?" She glanced around to see who might be listening. "In the daylight he's, well, you know, very dark . . ." She whispered the word 'dark' like an evil secret then raised her tone; "So I said to him; are you Anglo-Indian? Because I'd just had this awful thought, perhaps he's not, you know, *pukka*. And he said, do you mean am I an Anglo Indian? That is, a Briton living in India. Or am I Eurasian? That is, of mixed parentage. Well, it was embarrassing, him putting it like that. But I said yes, and he said, which? So I said the last. And he said - all la-di-dah; if you mean the latter, the honest answer is: apparently.

"Well! I mean, that was that, as far as I'm concerned. Just think . . ."

"But Mavis," said Edna in a horrified whisper, "he was in your cabin last night. You slept with him!"

"Not much! Sleep I mean." And Mavis giggled in spite of herself. "But don't, for God's sake, don't breathe a word. If my brother gets to hear about it, I'm up the Khyber."

Once the ship was safely anchored in the deep sweep of the bay, Leo took the lighter that ferried passengers to the quayside. He had done business over the years with various jewelers in Main Street. Stopping off on London-bound trips he had sold them all sorts of interesting items; rare black pearls, lapis lazuli, rings with unusual settings. On an outward-bound trip a few years ago, one establishment had commissioned uncut rubies. Old Mr. Craven's hill tribesmen had served him well then. Cheating nobody, he had made a small fortune. Americans on world trips still had plenty of money in their pockets by Gibraltar. The Wall Street crash of '29 had destroyed many companies and private investors in the USA, but there were still enough wealthy travelers to keep the luxury goods business afloat.

He had also, over the years, developed a special relationship with the Indian merchants on the Rock. Many just sold fabrics and curios that could be found in any Bengali street bazaar; some used this as a cover for more lucrative business in hashish and opium, but regardless of trade, they all retained a strong interest in their homeland and in particular the progress of the Home Rule movement. Most ships to and from the Indian sub-continent put in at Gib. and their network of contacts covered the length and breadth of the Raj. Back in 1921, a Hindu on Main Street had tipped him off about the boycott arranged for the Prince of Wales' November visit to Bombay. He had taken it seriously and tried to get a message to Sir Lionel but it had either not arrived, or made no impression. To the Raj's appalled embarrassment, the Prince of Wales was driven through deserted streets and there was not a native flag-waver to be seen: all the shops were shut and everyone stayed at home for the day.

Patwardan of the 'Empire Store' had a brother who was arrested during the 1930 Salt Law disturbances at Dandi. It had been Patwardan who had told Leo about the proposed march on the Dharasana Salt Works. Leo had passed that on, and much, much more - whilst keeping his nose to the to the INC-Marxist trail. One way and another he had spent the past fifteen years working like a trained spaniel.

He watched a seabird swoop for a fish. Its wings barely

touched the water and it was away with its morning catch. No, thought Leo to himself, his retriever days were over. Better to be like that bird, dive and catch, for sport or sustenance, the prize was your own. Except that today's transaction wasn't for him, it was for the Rosenthal widow. Let it be his final European obligation: once her valuables had been safely delivered to the Laban brothers he could sail out of the Mediterranean a free man.

Sitting in the bows of the 'Viceroy' lighter he turned the well-traveled, waterproof package over in his jacket pocket. If he sold this on for his own benefit and added to the sum using funds tucked away in various bank accounts, he could probably buy a decent-sized mansion on Malabar Hill and retire to dabble in whatever took his fancy.

He looked around at the women in the boat: well-heeled, well-fed: safe in the belief that money could protect them from all evil. Perhaps the widow Rosenthal had been one such as these, but now her home had been stripped, her bank accounts frozen and her dignity destroyed. He wouldn't harm her further. There was something about her, the way she carried herself, the way she poured tea from her one remaining silver teapot that reminded him of . . . He couldn't name it but her manner of dress: the high-necked blouse, the long grey skirt - something touched a chord. He would do as he had agreed take her most treasured possessions to a shop in Gibraltar to be sold by her cousins. The money would be placed in a safe account until the time she or any of her remaining family could get out of Hitler's Germany.

Once they reached the quay, Leo waited for everyone to step onto dry land then went to queue for transport up to the commercial area. A row of dusty black taxis and smart horse drawn gharries were lined up, ready to take passengers on sightseeing tours of the

Rock, but the drivers were more interested in two men brawling in the street than customers.

"What is going on?" asked an elegant American woman.

"I have no idea, Madeleine, you're taller than me, can't you see?"

"Oh, yes. Oh, honestly, would you believe it? Some men are fighting."

"Latin types, hot-blooded," said Beryl, the elegant woman's dumpy companion, nodding at this regrettable fact of life.

"No, they're not Latinos, at least not many, I don't think. Gibraltar is part of England, remember."

"Oh save me! More blimey-limeys. Well they can keep their squabbles for another day I am *not* walking up those streets." With that Beryl opened the catch of her capacious alligator handbag and extracted a metal whistle, she pushed up her fluffy mauve coat sleeves and blew a long, sharp blast.

Madeleine nearly jumped out of her skin, "Beryl!" she cried, "whatever are you doing?"

"My mother always kept a whistle in her bag, it often came in handy. Lot of foreign types in the Bronx."

Madeleine looked around her, it was as if her director had said 'freeze', except now all faces were turned toward a steep narrow street, from whence came a regular clip, clip, clip of hobnailed boots. As the noise increased a British bobby, his face beetroot red under his domed helmet, rushed onto the scene and slithered to a halt.

"What's going on here then?" demanded the policeman.

No one spoke. The taxi drivers shrugged and opened their car doors, the gharry drivers were suddenly very busy bustling fares up into seats, tucking rugs over the elderly, jerking reins.

"Pure Buster Keaton," said Madeleine.

Beryl looked up at her employer, "Well, we going round this dingbat island or we stopping here all day? Hey, we was here first," she snarled, elbowing her way in front of a dowdy memsahib and daughter. "Blow your own whistle, lady, this horse cab's for us!"

Leo watched the scene, laughing to himself then realized the dowdy memsahib had taken the last gharry and only an aged donkey, head drooping to the dust, was left for hire. A shifty looking lad with a check cap over his eyes pointed at the poor little beast with the stub of his cigarette.

"No, thank you," said Leo. "Shanks's pony for me."

The youth shrugged.

Leo set off on foot up the steep hill. He had barely gone fifty yards when he came alongside the American women's gharry. Beryl and the driver were in hot dispute about the price of their tour.

"Can I help at all?" he asked, doffing his hat.

Beryl gave him the once over, decided he was a gent and said, "Yeah, d'you know the going rate for doin' this lump of rock?"

"Actually, no I don't. But if you would allow me to accompany you as far as Main Street I will more than gladly pay your total fare."

Beryl's jaw dropped. She was just about to say get your own cab ya sleazy limey when she realized her employer was leaning across her saying; "That won't be necessary, Mr. . . . We can easily afford the fare, Beryl just likes to haggle. It's her peasant blood."

Beryl huffed, made a show of securing the vast handbag on her lap and settled down to sulk. Leo spoke to the driver and climbed into the seat facing the elegant American woman. Looking into her eyes he said, "Leo Kazan. I am very pleased to meet you."

"Madeleine Marshall," replied the woman offering a gloved

hand. The gloves were the exact grey of her eyes. Such attention to detail, observed Leo to himself, such a pleasant change from cultureless Soviet girls and off-the-peg Mavis.

As they shook hands Beryl sniffed loudly. Leo turned to her, included her in his charm; "I am most grateful, it is a mission of mercy you see."

"Not at all," drawled Madeleine, "Beryl and I need a third party. I'm afraid we are going to be rather tired of each other by the end of today."

"Take no notice of her," said Beryl. "I been with her for more years than she'd want me to tell. She's always complaining but she always takes me along - *ever-y-where*."

Leo looked at the elegant Madeleine Marshall. She wore her clothes like a Parisienne, even her perfume matched the morning. He looked at the hunched woman at her side, mauve coat, blue rinse escaping from under a blue hat, pink cheeks and beady eyes. She reminded him exactly of the plump little budgerigars the English kept as pets. He raised an eyebrow.

"Take no notice," said Madeleine Marshall, "her familiarity is sheer contempt."

He swallowed a smile and indicated the ships anchored out in the blue water bay as they appeared in a gap between tall, whitewashed walls.

"You are on the 'Viceroy'?"

"Yes."

"We are going all the way around the world," informed the irrepressible Beryl. "New York to Liverpool – Liverpool, what a dump. London, nice shops, I like the palace with the funny soldiers. Does the King actually live there?"

Leo nodded, but had no time to get a word in. "Now it's

India; the ship's okay. The soup's always cold but I told the waiter - he said he'd fix it. Then Calcutta to China. China! We bin there already, China Town, Los Angeles. There's enough Chinks there – who wants to see any more? Then Australia - kangaroo, didgeridoo, what's to do in a country of criminals and poisonous spiders? And *finally* home sweet home, Belvedere Park, Santa Monica, California, hallelujah."

"What a splendid trip," said Leo. "And today we are all in Gibraltar. Perhaps you would both care to have lunch with me at the new Rock Hotel or dinner on board - at least once before you get back to Belvedere Park, Santa Monica, California."

Madeleine looked at his twinkly green eyes. He looked solvent, was wearing a large but not tasteless ring (was it set with a real ruby?); he didn't appear to be the lounge lizard type and his accent was absolutely divine. "Not lunch," she answered, "dinner. One has more time - one can be more leisurely over dinner."

Beryl rolled her eyes. "Hey driver," she said, "when we get to this Main Street drop me off at a wool shop. Looks like I'm going to be all on me lonesome, might as well take up knitting - again."

Sitting with his back to the driver Leo noticed the little grey donkey that had been parked on the quay, labouring up the steep bends behind them. Its owner was poking it with a short stick as he ambled along behind it. A man in an unnecessary mackintosh was perched uncomfortably astride the narrow beast, his feet nearly touching the ground. When Leo alighted the gharry at the top of Main Street the donkey was just breasting the hill behind them.

He signaled farewell to the lovely Madeleine Marshall and winked at Beryl, slipped a pound note into the gharry driver's hand and crossed the street to a shop that bore the sign: 'Laban Bros. Gold and Silver bought and sold'. Then he had second thoughts. He waited for a moment until the gharry had trotted off and walked to the end of the street to admire the portals of the Governor's residence. Within a minute or so the little grey donkey tottered past, empty.

Leo walked back down to the shop and spent a few moments perusing velvet lined shelves of rings, bracelets, elaborate silver pocket-watches and ladies' gold wrist-watches, but he saw no one reflected in the spotless panes of glass save himself. He tapped his pocket and sniffed *a la* Beryl; someone with training? Or was he being over cautious? One of Sir Gerald's lackeys? Or someone with a National Socialist fiscal interest? Or no one at all? If the first – so what? If the second, a little deviation was called for. If the third? He consulted his own watch - there was time to spare and better safe than sorry, as Matron used say.

Making a fuss about tying a shoe lace he gave the donkey-rider time to get his bearings then he led him off down the busy shopping street.

Johnstone's Temperance Hotel: three floors, plus attic windows. Perfect. He banged his trouser pockets as if searching for a key. Then with a hop and a skip he was up the steps, past reception, and up the first flight of stairs then he turned down a green carpeted corridor and popped into an open doorway. A bed had been stripped, the windows were wide open and the occupant was out for the morning; a long-term resident judging from the open wardrobe door and the contents of a dish on the dressing table. Jet brooch and earrings, an enamel hatpin and – oh pretty, a flower brooch set with amethyst petals and aquamarine leaves. Something to appease Beryl, perhaps? He popped it into his top pocket. And what might be in the bottom of the wardrobe? An outside shutter rattled, a breeze moved one of the windows, the door swayed on its hinges.

"Damn." Leo shot back behind the door just as the

chambermaid pushed her bed-linen trolley into the room. She was singing a Spanish *copla* and took her time about unfolding a sheet. As she shook the starched linen over the bed Leo nipped out of the bedroom. There was no one to be seen, he strolled down the ill-lit corridor peering at door numbers then turned up another flight of stairs, along another dim corridor then down the back service stairs to the ground floor, passed the kitchen and into a mulligatawny dining room. A spotty young waiter asked him if he would like to reserve a table, which he did to oblige him: table for two, by the bay window and would he be a good chap and rustle up a cup of coffee. A shilling piece sealed the deal. Then he was seated near the window of the coffee lounge opening a day old copy of the 'Sketch' and watching the mackintosh man trying to persuade an officious Spanish receptionist he had not entered the hotel simply to make use of its 'sanitation facilities'.

The mackintosh man was obliged to leave the premises. Clearly rattled, he took up a very conspicuous position across the street and opened a packet of Navy Cut. Leo drank his disgusting chicory coffee and examined him from behind the net curtains; English, small fry, pink around the gills and the cigarettes were a clincher. Nothing to fear on Widow Rosenthal's behalf, but if Sir Gerald was so interested in his movements he was happy to provide some action. He folded the paper, replaced it on its rack and walked out onto the hotel entrance steps then, as if remembering something, he slapped his forehead dramatically with the heel of his hand. Giving the mackintosh man time to stub out his cigarette he headed back toward the dining room, where he had indeed remembered there was a door with the word 'Gentlemen' in well-polished brass lettering.

Once the mackintosh man had followed him into the gents

and the officious receptionist had dashed in behind to prevent *un abuso* of the hotel's sanitation facilities by a non-resident, Leo simply squeezed past them, exited the dining area, nodded to the girl on the reception desk and sauntered back onto Main Street.

At the Laban brothers' shop he made arrangements for the sale of the diamonds and pearls in Mrs. Rosenthal's package then spent some time discussing Hitler and the situation in Germany with the owners.

"Our father's family left Russia because of the pogroms, Mr. Kazan. One brother went to Hamburg, two went to Berlin. We came to Gibraltar five years ago – my father has a nose for trouble – but he stayed in Hamburg." Jacob Laban sighed. "Where should we go next? Gibraltar isn't so safe anymore. If there's another war it will be one of the first places to be occupied. We just want a home, a peaceful home – to be together. We don't make trouble for no one just run a business, a legitimate business."

Aaron Laban held the door for Leo, he said, "Home is where the heart is, but our hearts yearn for a home Mr. Kazan, they yearn."

Leo nodded. "Yes, I understand that very well. But I have no answers. Sometimes it seems that whatever you do it's wrong."

They shook hands and Leo walked out into the street. Jacob closed the door and turned the 'open' sign to 'closed'.

"He's another one, brother. You can see it - he has no home, either."

"But he's not one of us," replied his brother.

"His family might have been once."

"No, I think not. His eyes are wrong. I've seen those eyes before. A long time ago, but I've seen them. They aren't so very slanty but they are the green eyes of the Steppes. Green seas of grass, brother. Those are the eyes of a Tartar khan."

That evening, back on board the 'Viceroy', Leo sat down to write a brief note on plain paper to Mrs. Rosenthal. It would be posted in Marseilles.

My dear Aunt,

I was received warmly by your cousins, who send their best wishes. They are delighted you are safe and well, and strongly recommend you join them. They say the Mediterranean has a pleasant climate, I too, find it warm and peaceful. Personally, I support their idea. From what I have seen of Europe these last few months an extended Med. cruise seems just the thing.

The atmosphere in London was also very chilly; I do not recommend it, even for a short break. Going north, of course, is now out of the question.

Mother's belongings are all being taken care of, nothing to worry about there. The cousins say you can write to them at the address you gave me, but they will be neither surprised, nor in the least inconvenienced should you drop in on them without warning.

I wish you all the very best, and once again encourage you to come south before the unpleasant weather you are currently experiencing worsens.

Best wishes,

L

Leo folded the letter and tucked it into a plain envelope. As he slipped it into the dispatch section of his letter case his eye caught the edge of a postcard. He pulled it out. A picture of a white Scotty dog in a blue ribbon, sitting by a white birthday cake tied with a matching ribbon. It bore a Royal Mail stamp and was addressed to Miss Elena Kazan in Bombay.

Dear Little Miss Muffett,

By the time you get this picture you will be two year's old and Daddy will nearly be home. Be good and blow out all your candles.

Give my love to Mummy and Grandma and Grandpa.

Big kiss,
Daddy.

He had bought and written it in defiance in London. But he hadn't posted it. Slowly and very carefully, he tore the cute little dog into tiny shreds and brushed the remains into his waste-paper basket. He got up and stared at the grey circle of his porthole. Then he stretched his arms above his head, flexed his shoulder muscles and loosened the tightness that had crept up around his neck, he turned briskly to the narrow desk and put the letter case into a drawer. Then he put on his evening jacket, straightened his cuffs and stepped out of his cabin to dine with the lovely, if perhaps not so youthful, Madeleine Marshall. A wealthy widow or a widow and no longer so wealthy? Or gay divorcee? Whichever, there was little doubt that the lady would have made suitable arrangements for her companion's evening meal. 'Keep yourself busy, lad, that's the ticket,' said Sir Lionel.

Chapter 23

Leo booked himself into a modest hotel on Marine Drive under the guise of a commercial traveler. His cabin trunk was carried up to his room by a couple of voluble porters, who were very taken aback when he addressed them in their own tongue.

"And," he said, "I want this room watched. Watched, not investigated, do you understand? Because if I return one afternoon to find one item out of place, one wrinkle in a sock . . . Then you can be sure, best beloved, that this yellow scarf, which is always in my pocket waiting - this pretty yellow scarf will be round both your necks and your eyeballs will be bouncing across the floor before you can say Kali!"

Their dark faces blanched to the colour of their cotton pyjamas. They looked at his shoes and did *namaste* ten times, they vowed on the souls of their departed mothers they would be on guard day and night, that no one would enter, not even over their dead bodies, and they backed out of his room with their foreheads touching praying fingers but their eyes firmly fixed on a sliver of yellow silk poking out of the sahib's jacket pocket.

For two days Leo wandered around the colonial city of Bombay. He took a tonga up Malabar Hill, ambled around the

Hanging Gardens; he strolled along the sea front in the evenings and ate in anonymous restaurants. On the third day he left his hotel after breakfast bearing a cheap but larger than average leather briefcase: the sort used by commercial travelers, the sort large enough to hold two biscuit tins, and disappeared up a side alley into India. He spent an hour with a pretty girl named Mumtaz - *very clean, very respectable, a delight in every way* and reappeared in a scruffy grey kurta and what was now called a congress cap. He tossed a generous handful of coins at some street urchins and headed for the commercial district around Central Station, the urchins in his wake.

The street where his father-in-law had established his haberdashery was intact and utterly alive. Tongas squeezed between barrow boys, ancients on bicycles wobbled between basket-bearing coolies, beggars crouched in doorways and dogs wound their thin frames round bony legs. A few people in western dress marched purposefully from one purchase to another, taking care to make eye contact with no one. It was as if nothing had happened. So it wasn't true. Leo's heart lifted, he skipped a step round a bevy of nuns, forgot himself and doffed his congress cap like an English gent. The street was alive, Kitty and Elena were alive - nothing had happened.

And then he was staring at the space where the shop had once stood. He looked up at what had been the first floor, where he and Kitty had come to live while they looked for their own house in a decent suburb. But Kitty soon said she felt happier with her parents while he was away so he had settled into their lifestyle. And it had been so good to come home to a warm welcome and people round a table for meals: to be part of a real family.

It was as if a tooth had been pulled. All that remained was an ugly hole. Leo stepped down into the debris. The premises had been thoroughly looted except for a box leaking black ribbon and the empty cash register. He felt his stomach dive into his abdomen but he took a deep breath and walked across the small premises, through the remains of the partition wall into what had been his mother-in-law's domain. Then his stomach involuntarily lurched again – but with relief. The wooden boarded floor, swept twice each day and scattered with pellets each evening to keep the cockroaches and vermin at bay was still intact. Some of the boards had been chewed by fire but not consumed.

He pushed at a board with a sandaled foot. It wouldn't budge. That was good. Very good. He beckoned to the group of urchins that had trailed him from the girl's tenement block. "Take what you can find for your mothers and sisters," he said, throwing a handful of coins across the cinders and soot of the shop floor.

The boys instantly started pulling at rubble, exclaiming over charred ribbons and squabbling over metal buttons found under the cash register. Once they were sufficiently distracted Leo crouched down and prized at the floorboard with his manicured finger nails. Nothing, it wouldn't move. The wood must have swollen with the heat of the fire. A knife, he was in the kitchen area, where was a knife damn it? The kids would be round him any moment ruining his plan, hurry. He pulled open the black teak food dispenser. Nothing. Looters had taken the lot. Frustration made him clumsy and he fell back on his haunches: he caught sight of a fork under the primus stove. Yes!

A fight broke out among the boys - excellent. He shoved the prongs down between the boards, they bent backwards and the wood did not shift. Sweat dropped into the dust, shit, damn, bugger, fuck, then the Marathi abuse and finally the fat end of the fork moved the swollen plank up and he was able to get the fingers of his left hand under it, then using the toes of his left foot to hold it up, his right hand squeezed into the space below and he touched the cloth-covered treasure trove.

He looked up and leaned back. Oh, no! A local policeman, hands on hips was shouting at the boys. With a lunge that tore skin from the back of his hand he tugged at the dusty green material and pulled the receptacles to safety. In a flash the briefcase was opened, closed and the floorboard stamped into place.

Leo stood in what had been the partition doorway; "Little vultures! Be off with you," he shouted in English, kicking emaciated backsides. "Thank you officer, thank you, thank you," he said, wobbling his head like a simpleton with each phrase. "It is a crime that such creatures take advantage, why are they not in school for the benefit of Mother India? Now please to be telling me, sir, how it is that this shop that purchases my wares and sells so nice handkerchiefs and the suchlike is no longer? And please, what has happened to the also so nice family who live above if indeed, not upon the very premises. Such a pretty baby they have, just like my own sister's girl child Uma."

The policeman confirmed what Sir Gerald had so gladly thrown in his face. The shop had been targeted because it was owned by an Englishman. Rioters had thrown in an incendiary bottle bomb during a rally organized by textile workers. The firemen had recovered three adult bodies. The street had been chock-a-block with angry, shouting demonstrators, the army had to be called in so the firemen could reach the shop; shots were fired to calm the hysteria; some hotheads had been injured. The family could not escape because of the crush in the street, and look - there is no back exit. So they had been asphyxiated and then burnt to death. Very sad. No one had mentioned a child.

*

The sign on the door of the Oriental Curiosity Shop said 'closed', which surprised Leo. He peered through one of the mullioned windows, the shop was in darkness but there appeared to be a light on in the back room. He gripped the greasy, badly cured leather handle of his commercial traveler's briefcase and walked round to the side alley that led to the labyrinth wherein had dwelled Old Mr. Craven and a mad Pathan genie. No urchin now led him higgledy-piggledy round the houses, he knew the route by heart. He turned left at a street pump, left again under a decrepit gallery and was at once in the alley leading the to the 'Oriental Curiosity' back entrance. A rim of light around the door suggested someone was on the premises. He tapped three times with his knuckles.

"Yes?" said a weary voice in English.

"It's Leo."

Bolts were dragged open, the door opened a few inches and a weasely face peered through the crack. It was Arnold Mackay. "What you want?" he demanded.

"Arnold, it's Leo."

"I can see that. What you want?"

"I was just passing. Thought I'd pop in. I've got something that might interest Clive."

"Not anymore it won't."

The small man gazed up at Leo in the shadows of the alleyway, the light was poor but it was evident the golden boy had lost his glow. He noted the grey rings under Leo's eyes; he was wearing a shirt and trousers, but no tie. He looked very different to the sleek young man that had fascinated his boss for so many years. He actually felt sorry for him. "Here, come in," he sighed and opened the door.

Leo looked down at Mackay's small figure: he looked even smaller now because he was hunched under a thick woollen shawl.

"Are you ill, Arnold?" he asked. The weather was cool but by no means cold. Arnold ignored his concern.

"Clive's not here."

"No, well in that case . . ."

"Come through."

Arnold Mackay picked up some matches, lit a brass oil lamp and carried it through to the main shop. He put it on the counter. A wall-mounted figure of Ganesh, the elephant god, scowled down at them, the brass cobra reared out of the gloom, a glass eye of the perpetually arched mongoose winked in the meagre light. Arnold shuddered and sat down on the balding velvet of the chair provided for older and long-stay customers.

Leo stepped behind the counter out of habit and put the briefcase carefully on its shiny surface. The contents rattled against each other, he smoothed his hand over the thick leather as if to calm them.

"What's in there?" The small man threw his woollen mantle back and extracted a cigarette from an engraved silver case.

"Clive might be interested. Why is the shop so dark? Don't they leave lights on in the evening anymore?"

"*They* don't, anymore. And *I* don't either. No need to court danger."

"Arnold, you are speaking in riddles."

A series of perfect smoke rings hovered in the dusty air.

"Clive's gone, too."

"Gone?" There was a brief silence. "You mean . . .? When? How?"

Arnold shrugged. "After his father passed on - nearly a hundred, the old devil - Clive just seemed to run out of steam. No one to tell him what to do. The old man was a bully, remember?"

"Oh I remember!"

"Well, Clive sort of, I don't know - lost direction. Happened this time last week. Just keeled over where you're standing now."

Leo shifted in spite of himself; he pushed the cut-glass ashtray that was always kept on the counter closer to Arnold to cover his discomfort. "What happened, though? Was he ill?"

"Must have been, it was a heart attack. I don't think he was eating properly, and he was scared to death they'd torch this place as well. Sorry," Arnold flicked ash into the ashtray and looked at Leo. "Didn't mean to . . ."

"No, no, of course not. Difficult times."

"Difficult! Difficult!" Arnold Mackay had lost his short temper. "I'll say difficult. He left all this," he waved his cigarette at the contents of the shop, "the shop and every blasted thing in it to me."

Disappointment punched Leo between the ribs and winded him. He swallowed hard and brought an imaginary curtain down over his features. He had always thought, assumed, the Cravens would pass the shop over to him. What did this bloody-minded little man feel for its glorious contents? How would he ever find the curios and artefacts, the gems and golden goblets to stock it? How would he convince dithering clients to choose the more expensive item? The stuffed animals would rot before he found them a caring home.

Then he realized Arnold was angry because he didn't want the shop.

"What will you do? Sell it?"

Arnold Mackay had served Sir Lionel well because he lacked imagination; he had been trusted with information because he was naturally secretive and knew not how to exaggerate. Having never pictured himself outside the routine of his job with a civil servant, albeit a political civil servant whose post demanded a degree of cloak and dagger work, his new circumstances distressed him. Sir Lionel had kept him on as P.A. after his retirement because they were both at the age when men value stability above all things. But now, within the space of a month, he had lost all that had once given purpose to his life. His job had disappeared because his employer had died; his best and only friend had also died, but instead of leaving him with fond memories he had left him a business he had no interest in, whose accounts book read like a work of fiction and whose bank balance leaned heavily into the negative. He stubbed his half-smoked cigarette severely into the ashtray.

"Who the hell would buy this, now? I can't sell it and I can't keep it. We are a doomed race. Everyone that can is getting out before Congress comes into power and nationalizes everything we've created."

"That's scare-mongering talk," retorted Leo. He was getting fed up with this self-imposed Anglophobia; the steamer had been rife with it. "That's box wallahs giving each other the willies. There is no evidence that is going to happen. Hell, I've just been in London – 'Dominion Status' doesn't mean they can nationalize anything, just more provincial autonomy: it doesn't give us anything like the right or power to make our own decisions."

"Us! Our!" Arnold's head shot up. "Us? Whose side you on now? Those murdering coolies have just killed your wife and her family and you say 'us'! Jesus Christ Leo, you're a cold-blooded bastard if ever there was one."

Leo opened and closed the drawers under the counter. "Forget it. It wasn't what I meant. I'm not thinking straight these days. Look, there's no reason to think British owned properties will ever be confiscated, now or in the future."

"Well, that may be so. But financially this emporium is . . ." Arnold, still shaken by Leo's lapsus, searched for a word on the walls around him, "moribund! The cash register is not going to ring out when jolly mems buy their Christmas gifts any more; no more jolly Raj boys with hot polo winnings to spend. And if the communists in Congress get their way, there'll be no more jolly rajahs, either."

Leo laughed out loud.

"You can laugh," sniffed Arnold, "but it's no joke. What's a man like me going to do? No job now Lionel's gone and now this. I don't even need the money." He bit his lip and grinned in spite of himself, he'd said too much, and to the Kazan brat into the bargain.

"Well," said Leo, feeling considerably more relaxed. I suggest we shut up shop here for the night and get ourselves an evening meal. We might see things in a more positive light in brighter surroundings. You're not the only one reassessing the future, you know."

"No, sorry - got a bit carried away. Shame about your wife and that. Nasty business. I'd like to get my hands on the organizers of these so-called 'rallies', inciting good people to cause havoc."

"That's one of life's little ironies," said Leo, picking up his bag so as not to jostle its contents. "I have more than likely been drinking with the very chaps who were there winding things up. Very likely I've sat in their dens, smoking their pipes, sharing the bhang, and you know I never for once took it seriously. I just listened to the gossip the way I was told to, got the information back to those that wanted it - the way Lionel and that mad Pathan trained me, and that was that. Now it seems quite different."

He looked around at the contents of the shop he had loved so much: something else that had acquired true value by being taken from him. He said, "Just when I want to come back and make a proper life here, I can't. I can't even nail the bastards that caused Kitty and Elena to die. I've been given my cards. I am no longer needed by our great and good Imperial government. What d'you say to that Arnold?"

Arnold looked Leo in the eye, something he had always avoided before: he was surprised, but then he no longer had access to the IPS network. "What you got there?" he said nodding at the counter.

Happy to change the subject, Leo opened the catch of the smelly leather briefcase. "I'll show you. It's another little irony." He moved the lamp closer to the bag and carefully removed, one by one, three cloth-wrapped wooden blocks and laid each one flat on the counter. Then he began slowly and gently to unwind the white sheet material torn from a rented bed from around the ancient paintings. Arnold did not speak until the last one was revealed.

"They're Russian ikons, aren't they?" he said.

"Mmm." Leo traced his fingers around the gold leaf halo of a Virgin.

"Are they valuable?"

"That's what I wanted Clive to tell me. I don't think they'd get much at the moment. Probably only of interest to émigrés, and they don't have much money these days, from what I've seen."

"Have you only got these Madonnas?"

"No, I've got more. I found the first one in Kazan."

There was a silence. Then Arnold said, "Kazan?"

"Russian town north-east of Moscow on the Volga, where I

probably come from."

"Do you know that, for sure?"

"No I don't. But I think you do, Arnold. It's my father's name according to my birth certificate. I think you, and Sir Lionel and Lady Hermione, and the Cravens - father and son and half of Bombay city know – knew an awful lot more about my life than I do."

"No Leo, it isn't like that. Lionel knew perhaps, but he never confided in me. And, if there had been a conspiracy, believe me, I would have known about it. I always keep an ear close to the ground – no choice when you're my height." He smiled and folded the woollen blanket into a neat square. "I feel better now. Funny old world. I never thought you'd be the one to help me through a bad patch. I've never trusted you further than I can spit, and I don't spit."

Leo felt his shoulders relax and gave a dimpled half-grin. He started to wind material once more around an oriental-looking Madonna. Her angular child looked hungry. "I found this one in a church where they were burning bibles to keep warm," he said. "It had been converted into a nursery for factory workers' kids. They'd pulled down all the screens, the altars and everything. Place was like a barn. The little ones were freezing to death. I nearly stepped on her," he said, indicating the ikon. "She was next for the bonfire."

"Have you got any saints? Or is it just the mother and child figures that caught your fancy?"

"I didn't notice any saints. I don't know anything about saints." Leo looked at Arnold, "What happened to your parents?"

"Cholera. I was five or six - don't remember much. That's why I was sent to the BABO"

"Were you at the orphanage? I didn't know that." Leo

wrapped the second Virgin and placed her carefully in the bag. "*I* remember it very, very clearly. I remember the day my mother left me there, and I was much younger than you were."

"She wasn't your mother."

Leo kept on winding, "I thought you said you didn't know anything."

"I don't know about your real parents," Arnold lied. "I do know about Millicent Cleaver."

Leo stopped. Millicent. *Millicent*! shouted an impatient voice in his head. *Millie, put the kettle on.*

"Is she still . . ?"

"Oh very much so. Very sprightly. I'll tell you over supper. Not something to be rushed. Finish what you are doing and let's get out of here. These things," Arnold indicated the mongoose and cobra, "give me the creeps."

As they were leaving through the back door Leo said, "What about setting up shop elsewhere?"

"Like where?" said Arnold turning the key.

"It crossed my mind a couple of weeks ago Gibraltar might be a good place for a business. Pleasant climate: British but not England. You've got the steamers dropping off rich American tourists on round-the-world trips, all anxious to buy 'cute' little curios to show the folks back home."

"I thought there weren't any wealthy Americans anymore."

"Ah, there's a new brand. They start on the stage in New York and then the movie industry picks them up and makes them rich just as fast as you can say 'Zeigfeld Follies'."

Unable to sleep for the fourth night running, tossing, turning, wide awake and being led down thought paths he didn't want to tread, Leo came to the conclusion he would not stay. He would not make any attempt to visit them.

Millicent Cleaver, who had looked after him when he was a baby but was not his mother, was a bus ride away. Go? Not go? And his father? Seek and find? No. No. He did not want to see these people. Not now, it was too late.

Sleep crept in. He was conscious of his limbs sinking into the mattress – sleep, finally, sleep. And then a little round face framed in a mop of black hair was looking up at him, her plump caterpillar arms reaching up; *Daddy, Daddy . . .*

Leo was on his feet, the curtain tugged back, the window wide open – he was gulping for air. He pulled on his worn cotton kurta and his down at heel sandals, pushed the coins on the bedside table into a pocket and stumbled out into the night. He walked, going nowhere, down to the sea front, onto the sand and along the beach. The tide sucked at his feet. The chilly sand squeezed between his toes and told him he was awake, alive. But if he turned toward the ocean – and he did – and he walked into the water – and he did - then if he went in a little deeper, a little further, soon, soon he would be floating and safe and not awake or alive anymore. Pushing against the heavy waves, he waded in right up to his chest then suddenly he stepped onto nothing, his head was under, he was swallowing gallons of salt - he was . . . struggling to the surface, beating at the waves, gasping and retching, stumbling back onto dry land.

He sat on the sand, his back up against the sea wall and put his head between his knees. And he cried. He cried from the shock of going under; from fright; for his cowardice; for his mother, who wasn't his mother; for a pretty woman who had been his wife; for a black-haired baby with big green eyes. He cried until his body heaved and rolled sideways, until he was sprawled on the beach like flotsam thrown up by a storm.

He must have cried himself to sleep for he awoke shivering with cold. A pi dog was sniffing around him. "Scavenger," he said, "nobody wants you either."

The skeletal mongrel came up to his hand, licked it then hopped away on three legs, the fourth dragged a pattern in the moonlit sand.

"Oh, God!" shouted Leo, "Stop! Enough! That is enough! I give in. You don't have to make me feel bad for anyone or anything anymore! I'm sorry, for all the things I should and should not have done, I am sorry! Please, no more, please!"

Leo waited for an answer. He waited until his instinct for survival asserted itself once more and he knew he would have to get warm and dry or risk pneumonia. He got to his feet, pushed his hair back off his face and turned toward the steps that led up to the city. He had lost his sandals: he would have to go back to civilisation barefoot.

A *sadhu* holy man and an elderly beggar were perched together on the back of a park bench like two old vultures. Leo passed them and wished them a pleasant evening.

"Stop, and speak with us," said the *sadhu*.

"Speak with us," echoed the beggar.

"What must I say?"

"What is in your heart, sahib," said the beggar.

"What is in your soul," said the *sadhu*.

"My heart and soul are empty of words, masters."

"Then go, and God be with you."

"God be with you."

"And with you."

He started across the promenade on his way back to the hotel, stopped and looked back. "Which god, masters?"

"Shiva, Vishnu, Allah . . ." said the *sadhu*.

"Jesus Christ and the Buddha . . ." said the beggar.

"They are all of the One Being," affirmed the *sadhu*.

"God is merciful, sahib." said the beggar, scraping his black talons across an empty clay dish.

"God is not!" retorted Leo. "Tell me, wise men, who have nothing left to lose - how can God be merciful if he takes the lives of the innocent?"

"No one is innocent in the universe," answered the *sadhu*.

"Except the little children," interrupted the beggar.

"Each man comes with a part to play that involves deception, then, when he has played his part and deceived his fellows – then he goes."

"Some by cholera, some by typhus, some by birth itself," rambled the beggar, "God gives, God takes them regardless of age or status."

"God gives God takes, according to His divine plan. Sadly for us, some that are chosen can only be taken by force," said the sadhu.

"Why?" shouted Leo. "Why does that happen?"

"It is the Wheel."

"The good Lord gives, the good Lord takes away," nodded the beggar.

"Oh, shut up you old fool. What do you know? What on earth am I doing here talking this nonsense?" Leo was furious with himself and ready to go but the beggar reached out and clawed at his sleeve. "You must listen, sahib."

"Zeus, Jupiter, Jehovah, Tew, Jesus, Yahweh," said the *Sadhu* to the sky. "They are all One; they are all cruel. Gods have power: power is cruel. When Man acquires power he too is cruel, but the same power destroys Man."

The *sadhu*, who had once been a college principal, rocked on the back of the park bench, his feet barely touched the seat. The beggar, satisfied that he had prevented Leo from leaving loosened his grip and he too, rocked back on his perch.

"I was told at school," said Leo, "that God is love and God is good and that we are created in his image."

"The white Christian says this. But it is not my belief." replied the *sadhu*. "The white Christian *says* Christ is benevolent because *he* wishes to be seen as benevolent. Have they, best beloved, created *you* in this image of deceitful benevolence?" The *sadhu* stuck out his head and long nose and fixed Leo with a stern look. Leo said nothing, for now he was engaged in thought. It was his upbringing that was to blame for this torment. He was not British and he had been reared by people who had imposed their ideas upon him.

"The conquering Christian says, 'suffer little children to come unto me', and expects us to go to him like children."

"And be treated like children and punished for our misdemeanours?" said Leo.

"That is true," said the beggar, coming into the conversation. "The British Christian makes promises to us all the time, like we are children - and then lives his own life with his own people and forgets his promises. Never make a promise to a child or a beggar. All good people know that."

"And when shall we be rid of this hypocrisy?" asked Leo.

"When the sun has come and gone. When the battle's lost and won." The bald-headed *sadhu* burst into a gale of laughter. He flapped his bony arms up and down, "Aiii, the white bard," he cackled, "the Swan of Avon always has the last word. We shall lose, my son, they have got Jesus Christ *and* Shakespeare on their side."

"It is," said the beggar, who inhabited another world, "that we are each nothing more than a grain of rice. Gandhiji says one grain is nothing but a whole bowl of rice, when it is full and ready, it swells. Only as many grains together shall we be both many and one, and strong, and part of the great Unity."

Leo dropped all of the damp coins that remained in his pocket into the beggar's clay dish.

"God be with you, sahib."

"And with you, master," replied Leo.

"Fair is foul and foul is fair, hover through the fog and filthy Bombay air," the *sadhu* was lost in the scenery of his previous existence.

Leo ambled back along the silent water front. Now and again he stopped to look at the lights of the ships from the western world or the dip and spread of phosphorescent wings. This is what he had come for, the solace of the sea and the flicker of candle-white waves. As he reached the front door of the hotel some boys scuttled past him with brooms, mops and buckets, a policeman on a bicycle pedaled by half asleep, an empty bus coughed to life. Morning had come to Bombay. Its citizens were climbing down from their feather beds or up from the earthen floors of make-do shacks, ready to start once again the daily scramble for justice or survival.

"Poor city - poor country - what a mess we are in," Leo said to himself. "What an absurd life this is. Maybe the Mahatma is right, we should try passive resistance. Well, goodnight Mother India and good morning, and may all the gods be with you."

Unconscious of his bedraggled appearance he strolled

through the open doors of his hotel and into the reception area. A coolie employed as a night watchman came to attention on his mat on the floor. He took one look at Leo, his torn clothes, his bare feet, his haggard face and dashed to hide behind a potted palm. The Kali-worshipper had been out in the night – to give sacrifice. Look at him - exhausted by his acts! "Aiiii," he moaned involuntarily, "aiiii."

Later that morning, Leo stepped from around the night watchman's palm tree the very image of a very Anglo Indian. His face closely shaved and swathed in aromatic balsam, his clothes impeccable save perhaps for the rather artistic sprig of yellow peeping from his lapel pocket. The night watchman, who was now confined below stairs, was at that very moment regaling his compatriots with gory horror stories of the man covered in blood who staggered into the hotel in the middle of the night. Leo, unaware of the commotion below, strode up to the reception desk. He wanted to settle his bill before breakfast, enjoy his repast in comfort and move on.

He was stopped in his tracks by an envelope propped against a brass bell with his name printed clearly upon it in neat, school-room blue-black lettering. Trying to ignore it, he paid his bill and walked towards the breakfast room but just as he reached his table the receptionist came running up behind him waving the envelope. He had no choice but to accept it.

Chapter 24

Alfonso García del Moral Lopez-Rey straightened his collar, smoothed down his jacket and turned to examine his profile in the mirror. The khaki uniform was not elegant. The material was somewhat coarse, and inappropriate for the hot weather. The boots however, made-up for everything. Tall riding boots in conker-red leather. They were beautifully made and fitted perfectly. He gave himself another half turn in front of his dressing room mirror and jumped as his mother's figure appeared like a ghost behind him.

"May I come in?"

"Of course."

Doña Mercedes hobbled to the dressing table with the aid of her ebony stick and lowered herself into the chair with an involuntary groan. "You are going, then?" she said.

"I told you."

"You are too old for any man's army." She picked up one of his silver backed hairbrushes. "Did you buy yourself in? To get away?"

"No."

"You are a liar, Alfonso. You have always been a liar."

"I am doing what I believe to be right. For our country."

"Grown men playing soldiers. You'll be shot."

"I am joining the cavalry." Alfonso indicated his uniform in exasperation.

"They'll shoot your horse."

"Oh, for the love of God, mother! What is it you want?"

The old lady shook her head and picked up four hairpins one by one, the English woman's. They were sleeping together. She bit back her tears. "I came to say goodbye, that's all. A mother may bid her son farewell, when he goes away."

Alfonso went to kneel by her chair in remorse, but his new boots wouldn't bend sufficiently at the ankle and he was obliged to bend over her. He kissed her cold, scaly forehead.

"I shall be fine. As you said, I am too old to be in the front line. Please, do not worry."

"Why?"

"Why what?"

"Are you going, leaving me here alone with your stupid sisters and *la inglesa*?"

"Don't call her that. She's your daughter-in-law."

"Huh, by English law. I've never seen your marriage papers. That black-haired young madam may be a bastard for all I know."

"Mother! Marina loves you."

"Marina!" Doña Mercedes scoffed, "That's what her mother calls her."

Alfonso ignored the jibe, turned his back and opened the top drawer of his tallboy.

"What about the business?" his mother continued. "You haven't told me anything."

"Alvarez and the Alonso boys know what to do. Alvarez knows more about the business than me, and the Alonso boys are very sharp: their family has been working for us since last century, Mother. We can obviously trust *them*; we've been feeding, clothing and housing them for three generations."

"And you think that will keep the accounts straight and in our favour?"

"Yes. They wouldn't dare try to cheat us."

"Hmm. People are sometimes cleverer than you think. For all you know they are republicans just itching to get you out of the way and turn our business into one of their co-operatives. There's enough of that clan to keep the business running on their own!"

The thought had occurred to Alfonso, but he wasn't going to admit it. The Alonso brothers had been very congratulatory when he said he was joining Franco's rebels 'to keep the business safe': they were younger than him but had made no mention of wanting to join the fray. Nor had the chief foreman, Alvarez, whose son was a student in Seville. He was certain the boy had republican if not communist sympathies. But he said, "Everything is arranged and in safe hands, Mother."

"That's what you think. You shouldn't be going, leaving me, leaving the business. This war is going to cost us enough without you handing your inheritance on a plate to outsiders. What's she say?"

"If you are referring to my wife, Davina, she understands."

"Ah, we are so lovey-dovey these days. What about the other one?"

Alfonso opened another drawer in his tall boy and selected four handkerchiefs.

"That finished years ago."

"I know that. I'm not blind or deaf, yet. *La inglesa* found you out and threatened you with something serious - your pretty reputation with the big boys in town, no doubt."

"How do you know . . .?"

But she hadn't known for sure. He saw the little victory creep into her cheeks, her lips cracked into a smile. She gripped the arms of the chair to lever herself out: he bent to help her but she pushed him away so he handed her the ebony stick. She looked up at him and traced a scar along his neck with its silver and ivory handle.

"You've been in the wars already, my son. Was that the gypsy bitch? I don't blame her. Have you taken care of the brats? I don't want *her* coming round here expecting charity as well."

Alfonso refused to answer. He had settled an allowance on Maribel 'during his lifetime'; it was an arrangement designed to keep him safe from her brothers, cousins and uncles. He had nightmares about that particular threat.

As Doña Mercedes was about to leave the room, he said, "Please try to be nice to Davina. She has never done anything to harm you and she has put up with Esperanza and Gloria all these years."

"Yes, I know. But she hasn't given me a grandson."

"No, well . . ." Alfonso busied himself with his packing. "I have to go out now for an hour or so, I shall be back for an early supper. I have to be at the new headquarters by midnight." But he spoke to no one. His mother was tapping her way down the marble floored gallery, wiping the gnarled forefinger of her left hand along the window sills to check for dust.

Alfonso tugged at the hem of his jacket and gave an inadvertent shudder. The thought of money made him check his wallet. Enough to get by: not too much to invite leeches. Joining the cavalry might ensure a better sort of companion but they wouldn't all be out of the top drawer. His mother was right: the war was going to cost them serious money. Well, they could afford his absence for a few months. It wouldn't take Franco's professional troops long to subdue a bunch of airy-fairy reds. A republican government couldn't rule by definition; it had only been voted in by illiterate peasants, who should never have been enfranchised in the first place. It wouldn't take long to send that rabble running back to their hovels. Davina might get righteous over the poor needing education and hygiene, which according to her the city council could easily provide, but she didn't see the danger of letting the so-called poor take over. Let them get any power and everybody would be poor. Look at what was happening in Russia.

Alfonso patted his pistol in its holster, put on his cap and went into the corridor. He was intercepted by Esperanza, who was watering plants with a small brass watering can. As she turned, water squirted out and stained his new boots.

"Careful!"

"Ooh sister," she called, "come and see our brother! Ooh, you do look handsome, brother. Those boots! Go and show Mother."

"She's seen me. Let me get past without ruining my uniform, I have to go out."

"Are you leaving already?"

"No, not yet, I told you this morning."

"Yes, brother, but I've forgotten."

"Tonight, I'm leaving tonight. Have you seen Davina?"

"She's still in her room. Shall I fetch her?"

"No, I shan't be long. Remind cook about the early supper and tell Davina – after she has rested - that I didn't want to wake her and I'll be back about seven, if not before."

Alfonso left the house and stepped out into the leaden afternoon heat. September and still oppressively hot, the shops wouldn't open for another hour, the street was deserted. He set off in the direction of the Nationalist recruitment office. On his right was the main doorway of the parish church of Santo Domingo. A couple of decrepit widows draped in black were asleep in the porch, wearied from a morning of fruitless begging. One opened an eye in her dried fig features and pointed a stick finger at him.

"*Usted!*" she called out accusingly. "I've seen you!"

Her companion woke with a start and recited her plea for alms; "Señor, have pity on a poor widow."

Alfonso shuddered. He turned right again and headed down the wide street that led past the side of the church. One of the side doors was open, on impulse he entered.

It was slightly darker but not significantly cooler inside the high white stone building. His boots struck the paving stones and echoed around the nave. He genuflected in front of the altar and wandered around looking for something with meaning. In one of the ornate chapel screens he spied a small figure of Saint Michael, he paused: an angel with a sword. He manoeuvred his angular frame into a narrow pew, bent his head and tried to pray.

"Mary, mother of Jesus help me - help us in this time of . . ." What was he praying for? His own safety; was that a real issue? For the longevity of his mother; she was aging but hale. For his wife, who had become his real wife the day she discovered his mistress. For the woman his wife had become. Yes. If anything happened to him – which was highly unlikely – she might be in a difficult situation. When he came back on leave he would put the house in her name. She and the girl deserved some security. His sisters had their income from the business.

And then he began to pray in earnest for a son. It wasn't too late; he had fathered children, Davina had borne a child, why did God not grant them a child together? When he came back - when he came back . . . He had to leave first. Maudlin nonsense.

He strode back into the glaring sun. Coming out into the bright light he did not see a group of barefoot boys playing among the orange trees that lined the street. His leather-soled boots slipped on the cobbles and the inelegant move attracted their attention. The boys nudged each other, sniggered and fell into a parody of a formation behind him as he marched down the empty boulevard.

One of them said, "Look at his boots."

"Made for riding a mule!"

"Look at his hat."

"Made to keep his fat head from frying."

"Look at his posh breeches."

"Big enough for two bums."

"Made for Franco's farts!"

"Look at the pistol in his holster."

"Because he hasn't got one in his pants!"

The comments became more obscene, the laughter more aggressive. Alfonso heard the taunts and walked faster.

"Hey General, you don't need to run! We won't hurt you!"

"Much!"

With one accord the boys began to pelt him with fallen oranges. Alfonso was furious. He turned and started towards them, keeping an arm up to protect his face. The boys screamed in mock horror.

"Look out, the cavalry's charging!"

"Arm yourselves, lads. Defend yourselves to your dying breath!

Doubled with derisive laughter the boys stooped to collect more missiles. In the dry circles of earth around the orange trees there were small, sharp stones. They threw these at random as Alfonso, tall and imposing in his smart new uniform, bore down on them. The smaller boys ran off, hiding in ones and twos behind tree trunks. A bigger boy, one of Maribel's Heredia clan, fitted a bigger stone into his catapult and took aim.

"Enough," shouted Alfonso. "Stop!" He put his arms out in front of him in a halting gesture and the sharp flint caught him right between the eyes. He dropped like a rock, face forward onto the hot cobblestones and died in the instant.

*

A bolt had been drawn, a lock turned. Alfonso coming in or going out? No, not Alfonso. Davina was wide awake. Not Alfonso and never again Alfonso.

Davina listened. Heavy rain drummed against the shutters. Rain to wash a thin trickle of blood off a hot, dry street. Rain to fill the water butts and flush out the drains, rain to revive the rivers and feed the fields. Welcome rain in windblown blasts.

Their door was open, had she left it open? Had someone come in and left without waking her? She switched on her bedside light to see the time: four-thirty, her usual time to wake in the night. She stretched a hand across her husband's side of the bed. She should have gone back to her old room. Why had she chosen to sleep in his room? She lay back and begged for sleep.

He had been waxed like a tailor's dummy and laid out for exhibition in the Chapel of Rest. The whole town had come to gawp. A group of mawkish relatives had swamped the bereaved mother. All dignity destroyed, the stern matriarch had crumpled and sobbed through the brief funeral ceremony. Later, back in her house, she had sat silent beside the vast empty fireplace in the best salon, while visitors drank the family sherry and chatted about the weather and the price of fuel and said not a word about politics or war.

After everyone had gone they called the doctor. He gave Doña Mercedes sedatives. Mari Fey helped her mother take the medicine then went home. The two spinster sisters gently, quietly, lovingly settled their bereaved mother in bed but they soon forgot about speaking in whispers and spent ten minutes arguing about who was to sit with her first. Eventually, bored with their squabbling, they ate supper together in silence and they too went to bed.

Marina sat for a while with her grandmother until it was evident the woman was too heavily drugged to wake then she went to sit with her mother in the small parlour. As the clock struck the midnight hour Marina gave her mother a long, tearful hug and went to her room.

Davina had almost told her. Almost said, 'Do not mourn too deeply child, he did no more for you than was expected of him'. But she didn't. She was a real mother. Whatever else people might accuse her of, she always put her child first; she would never abandon her, never do what her own mother had done, what her aunt had done with her daughter, what Morrigan had done with her child. She would never leave her and never do anything to unsettle her world.

Marina had held her hand all the time they were at the chapel of rest, only letting go when the bodega foreman, Alvarez, and his son Pedro arrived to pay their respects. The girl and boy had stood side by side while the foreman spoke to Doña Mercedes, two healthy souls in a room of ritualized sentiment. Some time later they had briefly left the lobby of the chapel together, close but not touching. She saw them leave and then re-enter moments later just as serious as they had left. Alfonso had clearly succeeded in putting a stop to their romance. A shame, they looked good together. She would speak to Marina: love should laugh at class. The foreman was a good man - his son would care for her daughter.

But if Marina got married and had her own home what would she do? It would be unfair to impose on them. No Alfonso and no Marina, and more than likely no income. Had Alfonso provided for her in any way? She must go through his papers, find his will. And if he had made a will would there be anything for her save perhaps a small allowance? Would there be any provision for Marina?

Supposing his mother had the papers. It made sense. He might have left her instructions about what to do if anything happened to him. But she knew in her heart he had done no such thing. He had been as excited as a schoolboy that he'd been admitted to the cavalry at his age. It was absurd: someone had fixed it for him, one of his finger-in-every-pie friends.

It was still raining; a steady hum interrupted by an irregular patter as water fell from the broken guttering and dropped onto the narrow balcony above the main street. She lay still, eyes closed, and saw steady rain breaking the surface of a still river on a Michaelmas morning.

Sleep would not return without a glass of hot milk. Reluctantly she swung her legs into the cool room, pushed her feet into her slippers and pulled on a robe. She went to the window. The heavy wooden shutter opened onto blackness. She left it open to air the room, lit a short, thick candle and, sheltering it with her left hand, she walked down the draughty corridor. Beyond their glass-paned door the Ugly Sisters were snoring just as they spoke, constantly interrupting each other, neither separate nor in unison. Passing the heavy velvet curtain that cordoned off Doña Mercedes' quarters, Davina paused, there was no sound, perhaps she was dead, too.

The kitchen was still warm after the long summer heat, too warm for hot milk. She turned on the tap and held a glass under it while it gulped out metallic water. She ate a left-over honey pastry from a fancy dish and headed back to her room down the right hand corridor. As she past Marina's room she peeked in; the girl was fast asleep hunched under the counterpane. She went in, as she always had done, to check on her baby, to smooth her hair and tuck the sheet up under her chin. The candle flickered as she moved and flared up in a sudden draught, the bed was empty. A bolster had been stuffed under the covers. Davina sat on the bed, there was a white sheet of paper on the bedside table.

Mamá,

I am sorry that I have to leave like this but I know Grandmother will never permit me to marry Pedro. I do not want to leave you but Pedro is being sent to Córdoba, and then possibly to Madrid. I cannot live without him, I have to go with him. Father said he was not good enough for me – he was wrong, Pedro is good and kind and he will look after me, so please don't worry.

I am going away with the boy I love. You must understand! You left your family to come to Spain. You must know what real love is like. Please forgive me for hurting you.
Grandmother will probably be nasty to you because of me, I am sorry.

Please understand there was no other way to do this.
I shall always be your loving daughter,

Marina XXX

How right and how wrong the child was; 'you left your family to come to Spain' but only because the boy I loved didn't want me. Why did the only people she cared for leave her these notes?

Madrid? Pedro had joined the Republicans. He was going to fight; Marina would be a widow before she was a wife – if she weren't killed, too. They were dropping bombs on Madrid.

For some time she sat on the side of the bed. And then, with a set purpose, she got up and went to her mothering-law's quarters. She pushed back the heavy curtains and listened. The door to the bedroom was open. The woman had rolled on her back and was now snoring louder than both daughters put together. Davina went straight to her dressing table and put down the candle. The key she needed was on the bunch in front of her, but which one? It had to be small: she flicked through them, keeping a watchful eye on the sleeping dragon. There were three possibilities. Holding the bunch in her fist so it made no noise, she tried each in the lock of the wall niche safe.

The third key turned. The lock seemed to click very loudly but the dragon slept on. Davina removed the jewel casket and then realized she had nothing to put the contents in. The whole casket would be too awkward to carry. She grabbed a shawl from the back of a chair and quietly tipped the contents of each shelf into the middle. She ran her hand round the base of the casket and extracted a final ring then she returned the box to the niche, relocked the wooden door and replaced the keys on the dressing table. With the stolen treasure in one hand and the candle in the other, she moved out of the bedroom into the small sitting room.

Doña Mercedes' bureau was unlocked. Someone else had taken advantage of the sedatives; papers had been pulled out and put back untidily into their divisions; Mari Fey, anxious to know her situation, no doubt. The money drawer was still full of neatly stacked notes, though. She took all but the first two and stuffed writing paper behind them to act as padding. Hurrying back to her old room, she pulled out a traveling bag and rammed the shawl bundle down into the bottom, then she pushed in random items of clothing, took two dresses and a skirt from her wardrobe, emptied the contents of her dressing table drawers into the inside pockets, stuffed her robe on top of everything and closed the leather straps. She pulled on her favourite old blue dress and a pair of sturdy shoes then covered herself with the heavy waterproof cape her mother had bought for the crossing to Spain.

Picking up the bag she moved quietly back into Alfonso's room. The light from the candle was barely enough but she didn't want to put on the electric light. She put the candle on the bedside table then opened the shutters wider, but there was no moonlight in the downpour. The top drawer of his private bureau, where Alfonso put loose change, was empty. In a side drawer was their English marriage licence and her passport, used only three times since her arrival in Spain; once for the drunken farce that had been her brother's wedding, and twice for funerals, first her mother's then her father's. It had rained torrents the day her father was buried, too. She shivered at the memory then slipped the documents into the side pocket of her tapestry covered Gladstone bag. The rest of the drawers contained cardboard folders, titled and dated but in the gloom she could not see whether they were relevant to her or not. I should have gone through all this years ago, she thought. Too late now.

Turning around, she noticed that there was nothing on top of Alfonso's tallboy: the box containing his shirt studs, cufflinks and tie pins was missing. Strange. Quickly, starting at the top like an amateur, she riffled through the drawers. No cheque book, no bank book, no cash. There was nowhere else to look, except the wardrobe. She felt her way through Alfonso's jacket pockets. They were all empty. So she would have to manage. At least she had her passport and the housekeeping money from Doña Mercedes' bureau. Davina snapped the catch of her bag, closed the leather straps and left the room.

Just as she was about to open the door leading down to the patio she remembered Marina's note. Leaving the bag on the top step she dashed back to the girl's room, careless now of making a noise she grabbed the letter and ran back to the bag then she was off down the steps to the patio below.

It took what seemed a lifetime to slide open all the bolts to the huge double doors without waking the maid that lived on the ground floor, but finally she was standing outside the building on the rain-soaked street. Hood pulled up over her fair hair, bag hidden beneath her cape, she walked out into a damp, alien dawn.

She crossed the street and involuntarily looked up at their bedroom window. There was a faint glimmer of light: she had left the candle burning. And there, at street level, standing well back under the balcony of Alfonso's room was a man. Davina turned and ran. The traveling bag banging against her legs slowed her down but she kept up a steady pace until she was well past the church. The stranger did not follow, or that is what she thought.

The man under the balcony watched the caped figure disappear around the corner of the church. She had left the main door to the house wide open. Now was his chance to get back in and finish what he had started while everyone had been so busy comforting the Black Widow. He looked into the patio, stepped inside and froze; the ground floor door to the servants' quarters opened and little Maria Castro came out pulling a cardigan over her uniform. Rain was still falling; she covered her starched cap with her hands and ran across the open patio to the stairs. The door to the street was wide open but she hadn't noticed. It was five a.m. - time to clear up the mess from the day before and prepare breakfast and she was still half-asleep.

The maid hadn't seen him but he'd missed his chance - this time. The man slipped back onto the street and hurried after the caped figure. He saw her going down the long shopping street and ran until he was parallel. "Marina!" he called.

Davina froze. It was Alfonso - the height, the voice.

They stared at each other for a moment. It was not Alfonso - it had to be his son.

The boy who was not quite yet a man, said, "I thought you were . . . Where are you going?"

"I don't know." There were tears in her eyes.

"The bastard has left you nothing and the bitch has thrown you out!"

"No, no not that. Not yet."

"And Marina?"

"She has gone."

"Gone?"

"With Pedro Alvarez."

"They say he is a good man."

Davina nodded.

"Come," he said.

The tall young man, so physically like his father, took the Englishwoman's bag and escorted her across town to the Cadiz road, then down the hill to his mother's small white, single storey house.

As they walked into the one main room, Alfonso's ex-mistress, Maribel, came out of her bedroom, her hair was wild and her eyes red from crying. Her mother, as if triggered by an alarm, appeared from another room in a rush and stopped in her tracks. The square-set woman, aged beyond her years, looked at Davina and said, "So you're back. Nothing for you here, unless you've brought her," she nodded at her daughter, "your inheritance and pension." She moved out of the doorway and stood, hands on wide hips in the centre of the room. She was wearing a vast white nightdress and looked like an avenging angel. "Well?" she demanded.

"Leave it, Gran," said the boy. "Leave her alone, she's never done anything to you."

The gypsy sniffed and moved toward the hearth. She struck a match, revived a dead fire and prepared a pot of coffee. Davina watched her as if mesmerized.

Maribel said quietly, shyly, "Sit, please, Señora." She pointed to a small upright chair by a pine table. Davina sat down. Another silence followed.

"I found her," said Alfonso's son, who was called Sito - from Alfonsito.

"Why do you leave so soon, Señora?" asked Maribel indicating the traveling bag on the tiled floor. Davina couldn't begin to answer the question. She looked around her at the primitive conditions. Alfonso had never done anything for them except perhaps provide his mistress with this ill-built house and a maybe a miserable income.

"I'm sorry," she said. "I didn't think. You have less than I. He hasn't left you anything, has he? What a mess we are in."

"We?" demanded the gypsy woman, sitting on a stool by the fire.

The old woman's tone, Marina's letter, the stress of the past few days, not to say the past eighteen years, all hit Davina at once. She put up a hand to hide her tears and sagged forward in her chair.

"*Dios mio*, not you as well," said the old lady. "He was a selfish bastard! What you crying for?"

"Not him," said Davina, "for us."

"Well that won't put food in the pot. Here, take off that cape and make yourself comfortable, we'll sort ourselves out - us women together. Sito, get back up that hill and bring us some fresh bread. And not a word to anyone - absolutely no one, family included, understand?"

The young man nodded and opened the door to the street. A brindled lurcher bitch, which had obviously been waiting outside the door, jumped up at him. He bent down to scratch her behind the ears. Alfonso's son, without doubt.

He was in his early twenties, as tall as his father, better looking without the sallow skin or hooked nose.

"How old is your son?" Davina said, looking at Maribel.

"Nearly twenty."

"And the girl is just eighteen," added the grandmother. "A year older than yours."

"And your other child?"

"Died of the typhus two months ago," said the grandmother in a matter-of-fact tone.

"I'm sorry," said Davina. What had Alfonso been doing two months ago? Is that why he decided to join Franco's troops at his age? Had he broken his promise – or never kept it?

And then the image of the tiny baby crying in its grandmother's arms came to her mind, poor little soul. She hunted for a handkerchief then used her sleeve to wipe away the tears.

As if to terminate any further expression of sentiment the old lady said, "It was always sickly. One less mouth to feed."

Davina looked across at Maribel; the once pretty woman tried to smile.

Without another word the grandmother got up, went into her room and closed the door behind her. She reappeared some minutes later dressed in the peasant woman's uniform of black. From a rough pine dresser she produced a jug of olive oil, a bowl of salt and a heavy bread-knife; she put them all on a wooden board on the square table. Maribel didn't move.

Sito returned with two long loaves of delicious smelling bread tucked into his coat. The lurcher bitch tried to squeeze into the house behind him, he laughed and gently pushed her out, "No fresh bread for dogs, out you go."

The dog whined behind the door. "Haven't we got anything for her? She's hungry."

"You wiped your plate clean last night," said his grandmother. "What d'you suggest? We haven't got enough for ourselves: you'll have to get rid of her."

Sito tugged the crust end off a loaf and threw it out of the door. His grandmother aimed a slap at his head but he dodged her and sat down.

"Here have some bread before this fool gives it all to an animal," she said to Davina as she cut one of the long loaves in two and split the two halves into four with her hands. In complete silence she picked up each quarter and poured thick green olive oil onto the warm bread. Then she sprinkled salt over the oil and set the four rations out on the board. They ate in silence.

Eventually, after they had eaten and were drinking bitter, sugarless chicory coffee out of thick glass tumblers, the grandmother looked at her grandson and said, "What did you bring her here for?"

The boy responded with a shrug. "She was running away."

"Running away?"

Davina nodded.

"So you weren't good enough for her ladyship, either!"

"Gran!"

"No, I'm going to tell her and then we'll all be straight."

Isabel Heredia looked hard at Davina, it wasn't hate and it wasn't revenge: it was what she felt she had to say. "He married you, abroad, and brought you here because none of the nice girls in town would have him after he'd flaunted this silly madam around with him in the street." She indicated Maribel with a square hand but never took her eyes off Davina's face. "When they were younger than this streak of bacon sitting here," she indicating her much loved Sito, "they - I mean my daughter and her *señorito* - would go around together in the town, arm in arm in plain light of day! We told her, we threatened her; her uncles would have done for him if I'd let them. We said he just wanted his way with a pretty girl and he'd ditch her the minute she was expecting. Which he did. But then he came sniffing around again, didn't he?"

She looked at her daughter. Maribel stared into her coffee, tears rolling down her cheeks.

"Oh, he loved her," she continued, "said he couldn't live without her, wanted to marry her but his mammy wouldn't let him." She took a slurp of coffee. "Sito, your sister should be listening to this, go and wake her up."

"No Gran, let her sleep. She doesn't need your venom."

"It's not venom boy, it's the mortal truth. Your mother has lost her good name and all her chances, and we haven't got anything to live on but what you can bring in because . . ."

"Mammy, that's enough," begged Maribel.

"Well," continued her mother, still staring straight at Davina, determined to finish one way or an other, "after he'd been seen with his arms around a girl from this side of town, and half gypsy into the bargain, that was that as far as the nice girls were concerned. None of them was going to be second choice to his bit of black stuff and everyone knowing it." The woman folded her arms, "And all this time his precious mother was on at him about the family name and the family business or I'm the Queen of Sheba. So there you are. He needed a wife for the family name, he found you in foreign parts and you was the only one in town that didn't know about our Maribel. But what you are doing here, when you've got his widow's pension, a big house to live in and his daughter to marry off into money and look after you in your old age, defeats me."

"She's not his daughter."

Three faces turned to her. The old lady's mouth opened and shut. "What?"

"Marina, my daughter, is not his child. I was pregnant when I married him."

The old lady started to chuckle. Her double chins started to wobble, then she placed her hands on her knees and she laughed so loud her face turned red and Sito had to get her a cup of water to stop her choking. She drank the water and wiped her face with her skirt, settled herself back into her chair and looked at Alfonso's widow with new eyes.

"You can stay," she said. "Whatever you need, count on Isabel Heredia."

"Thank you," replied Davina in a whisper. "Please, would you let me have a few moments on my own, I need to gather my thoughts and decide what to do next."

The laughter had woken Maribel's daughter. She put a tousled head around the door and said, "What's the matter?"

"Nothing's the matter, child," replied her grandmother, beckoning her into the room. "Come here and meet your new auntie."

Chapter 25

Davina was woken about ten o'clock by a commotion in the main room. It sounded like Sito and he was saying, "She'll have to stay here now."

"Don't be stupid, she's mad. She'll set fire to this house, as well." It was a man's voice with a heavy Andalusian accent.

"She's not mad." It was the grandmother. "But you're right, she can't stay. She's only here until she decides what to do."

"I'll take her down to get a boat in El Puerto," said the man.

"No, too many people know her, they'll tell the police – you can't hide a face like hers, she's as English as English." It was Sito's voice, he sounded very like his father.

"Well she can't go back to that house - she'll have to go back where she came from to start with. She certainly isn't staying here, not in this house, not in this town. Paco, take her to Gibraltar."

"What! Me? She's none of my business. Anyway it's miles away."

"People do the journey every week, twice a week – tobacco, whisky, dried fish. Take beans and flour with you. Take brandy and change it for some decent rum, I used to like a drop of rum."

"I'm not going anywhere – I've got work for the next month

with the harvest. I'm not giving that up for anybody."

"Anyway," intervened Sito, "how's she going to get to Gibraltar? We haven't got a car and it'd take a week to walk it – even if she could – which she can't."

 He was seriously regretting his charity; planning at the back of his mind how to slip out unnoticed and not return until the woman had gone - but his grandmother had the bit between her teeth.

"You can take her. Paco will lend you two mules. Load them with panniers for regular business." It was an instruction not a suggestion.

"I'll have to fill in papers when we go through the villages."

"Then don't go through any villages."

"And what about bandoleros? There's a bunch of cut-throat outlaws on that road."

"They won't touch a boy and his mother."

"They will if she's got yellow hair and speaks with a funny accent."

"Then don't give her a reason to speak. We'll cover her hair and she's got that cape thing to cover the rest of her. Don't go anywhere people can get curious."

"We'll have to sleep in the open."

"So? It's not winter yet. It won't kill her. Do her good: she can find out what real life is like."

"Gran, you've got an answer for everything!"

"I was a widow before your mother was born, how d'you think we've survived this long?"

Sito abandoned his idea of escape; he valued his grandmother's respect above all things.

From across the room Paco said, "Getting the mules will be difficult. Juanito is using them for the grape harvest."

"Then hire a couple of others, or some horses for God's sake! She can pay – just don't say where the money has come from."

There was a silence. Doña Isabel had lost her patience and the men were trapped into an enterprise neither of them relished.

Davina got up, straightened her clothes and went to the door, she opened it quietly and said, "I can't pay anyone anything, I'm afraid, I don't have more than a few pesetas with me."

Isabel Heredia looked at her. "They say you stole the old lady's money and set fire to the house, and you and the girl have run away."

"Set fire to the house!"

The man called Paco said, "It's not burnt down, just the rooms over the street. The sisters were in the street running about like headless chickens. Then the fire brigade got there and asked them where their Ma was. Firemen had to carry the old lady out." He was laughing in spite of himself. "No one hurt . . ." He paused and was suddenly very serious, "Where's your girl? She wasn't in the house was she?"

"No."

"But she's not with you?"

"No."

The tone silenced him. "Right then, I'll see about those mules."

Paco looked at his sister and raised his eyebrows. She just nodded and indicated the door. He left without another word.

It wasn't a pair of mules to ride it was a leggy youngster pulling a rough wooden cart that stopped outside the Heredia doorway at eight o'clock that evening. Sito was up on the driving seat next to his uncle. Paco jumped down and picked up Davina's bag.

"D'you want this under the seat or in the back?"

"Under the seat, please."

"Right then, up you go."

Davina was hoisted into the cart. There were no embarrassing farewells. As Sito picked up the reins ready to move off, his grandmother said, "Hey wait. What's in the back?"

The sides of the cart were lined with rough hewn wooden boards and the back folded down on strong metal hinges. The cart itself was fully loaded and covered in hessian sacks weighted down with flat stones. Doña Isabel opened the back and lifted a sack. "Well praise the Lord! We'll have some of these."

There were earthy smelling potatoes in wooden crates, a box of sickly looking turnips, yellow pumpkins in a woven basket, and the rest of the cart was jam packed with melons. There were a number of the knobbly, misshapen rugby-football melons called toadskins and at least fifty glossy green watermelons the size of footballs. Doña Isabel pulled out an empty sack and Paco stuffed in a few kilos of potatoes, two pumpkins and a few melons.

"Not those toadskins, they give me indigestion," said the matriarch.

Paco and Sito rearranged the cargo and closed the back board. Maribel came running out of the house and handed her son a cotton bag. "Cheese, bread and chorizo," she said.

"Ha," said Paco, looking up at Davina, "you may get drenched and you'll have to sleep outdoors but we Heredias won't let you go hungry!"

Sito winked at his Grandmother, "Don't forget to feed my dog, Gran, she'll be whelping in a few days or so."

They set off for the first stage into the night. The newly shod mule clipped down the streets but they attracted no attention and within less than an hour they were out on the road to Medina Sidonia.

"How long will it take to get to Gibraltar?" asked Davina.

"Four, five days."

"Five days!"

"There's a lot of hills between here and the coast and this is a mule cart," said Alfonso's son. "Not one of your fancy cars. And she's young, only just trained; I promised not to work her too hard."

"What's her name?"

"Name? I don't know. Mule?"

Davina smiled a wry smile. The creature had an owner who didn't want to overwork her because she was so young, but she didn't have a name. Or perhaps she did and Sito was too embarrassed to tell.

"I shall call her Liberty," she said.

"Call her what you like, just watch her back legs, she's got a temper like my Gran and a kick to match."

"It's true then, what they say about mules."

"Of course it is."

That first night they traveled under a clear sky and a harvest moon until they were well away from Jerez. In the early hours of the morning Sito moved the mule off the road onto a stony track that led to a small reservoir. They pulled into a clearing among almond trees to make camp for the night. The ground was too damp to sleep on and they were too weary to empty the cart to sleep in it, so they arranged Davina's waterproof cape like a groundsheet under it and stuffed the sacks around the iron spokes of the wheels for warmth and protection from draughts. Using a long rope, Sito tied the mule to a tree and made a bed for himself along the narrow front seat.

Once she was wrapped into her cocoon Davina poked a hole between the sacks and looked out at the sky and the black-shadowed countryside around her. What an adventure! Then she heard the first wolf. The mule became restless. Sito got up and tied her closer to the cart.

"Sito."

"It's only a wolf, sounds a long way away. They won't come near us."

"No. All right. I was just worried about the mule."

"*Ai*, the English and their animals. Go to sleep, you must be tired."

"I suppose so. Goodnight."

"Goodnight."

"Sito."

"Now what?"

"Thank you."

"Goodnight, Señora!"

The next day they ate cheese and bread and watermelon for breakfast. They took it in turn to go down to the water to wash and then Davina spent a happy half hour or so collecting fallen almonds, which she tucked away in one of the empty sacks. It was a glorious morning. Sito moved the mule out into the clearing to graze and tied her to a tree stump. Liberty pulled at tussocks of grass and set larks bounding up around them. The boy set the cart to rights and began the task of sorting out the mule's harness. Davina collected the remains of their breakfast, climbed onto the running-board and stowed the food bag next to her carpet bag under their hard wooden seat. Suddenly Sito leapt up beside her as a group wild boar grunted out of the trees around them. The mule snorted and shot to the length of her tether.

"That was lucky," said Sito. "You wouldn't want to be on the ground with them so close."

"Are they that dangerous?" laughed Davina, somewhat taken aback by their size and fearsome tusks. I didn't know they were so big."

"Big and nasty. Don't you have them in England?"

"I think there used to be - like bears and wolves , but not any more."

The group of tusked boar shuffled off and Sito jumped back down on the ground to reorganize the harness and unravel the long reins.

"Are you happy to be are going back?" he said.

Davina looked around at her surroundings; clumps of low scraggy bushes, peppery smelling herbs, in the distance tall pines marched across a grey-pink horizon. The sky over Spain always seemed so much bigger than over England. She tried to visualize a Cornish sunrise. "I think I am. I shall definitely be happy to be back in our old house at Tamstock. It's so lovely. All covered in ivy and surrounded by hundreds of roses - like something out of a fairy tale."

"What's a fairy tale?"

"Well, it's a story about a young girl or a young boy, who has to leave his or her family home and they go through a series of difficult or dangerous situations with nasty witches, ugly people or monsters before they can get back to safety. Sometimes they are captured and locked up in castles and they have to escape. Sometimes there is a peasant boy, or a clever animal that helps them. Then they become rich or they marry the boy or girl of their dreams and live happily ever after."

"Sounds like a lot of nonsense."

"No, not all of it, Sito. The difficult situations – I think they may once have come from true stories and got very exaggerated in the re-telling. Or they are what my teacher, Mr. Jones, called metaphors. They mean something else more serious, like fables."

Because they had been chatting and busy about their chores they hadn't heard the sound of low branches being pushed aside, but the mule's long ears were moving this way and that and she shifted about nervously as Sito tried to pull on her harness. "Sshhh," he said, "there's a good girl, back up, back up, good girl, there you go – nearly done."

Then Sito picked up the sound, too. If it was the boar coming back they were in a pickle, he tried to buckle the bridle faster. "Quiet you silly . . ."

Then he heard something that wasn't an animal.

"If anybody comes near us don't speak," he said quietly to Davina. "Put that scarf on Gran gave you. And the cape. Keep covered up."

Davina scrambled around, pulling on the soggy cape, tying the cotton headscarf under her chin. Then, feeling very nervous, she went to stand by Sito. He put out an arm and pushed the hood of the cape over her head.

"Get in the cart."

"Why? What's the matter?"

"I don't know. Shut up."

The cart rocked as she climbed up onto the seat and she felt very vulnerable sitting there with a half-harnessed mule in front of her and no one at her side.

"We shouldn't have come so far off the road." Sito grumbled.

"No, my good friend it was not a good idea."

A short, heavy man with string tied around an oversized jacket wandered into the clearing. He moved very close to Sito and waved a very sharp-looking blade under the boy's chin. "Look," he said, "I've got a knife, so no hasty moves, eh."

Sito buried his head in the mule's warm brown neck and closed his hand over a rein. She still wasn't strapped into the traces, she could easily run off. He was scared.

The bandolero was pleased with the easy effect of his words and turned to Davina with a swagger. "Good morning, Señorita. Curro Gonzalez at your service." He doffed a greasy cap, bowed elaborately and took a step toward the running-board. "Have you anything in your cart to feed a hungry hunter this fine morning?"

Davina looked at him, her eyes like saucers. She looked at Sito for guidance but the boy kept his face hidden. Slowly she shook her head.

"What was that you said: 'Of course my good friend, here please have some bread and cheese and some of our wine, too'?"

Davina shook her head again. The bandolero was delighted with her apprehension and came closer to press his advantage. "Why not invite me up into your cart to share your company, darling?"

"Leave her alone," shouted Sito.

"Your boyfriend ith jealuth," lisped Curro Gonzalez reaching up to swing himself into the cart with his free arm. "You just tell him to keep quiet while we have a little cuddle, eh. You got a pretty face and I've got a lot more in my pants to give a girl a good time than him down there." He leered at Davina. "And what is that, eh?" he asked, noticing her bag stuffed under the seat.

"Sito!" Davina's eyes were fixed on the knife. It was wide and sharp.

Sito waited until the man lifted a foot onto the running-board then charged. He grabbed the outlaw round his middle, the knife flew out onto the rough grass and both men fell backwards. Sito rolled over trying to grab the knife. Suddenly there was a second outlaw standing over him.

"The boy wants a fight, Curro, let him have it!"

He kicked the knife out of Sito's reach then bent as if to help the boy to his feet and kicked him in the ribs. "That's just a start boy. Here's another, and another."

Sito rolled onto his stomach and got a rope soled boot in his head, his nose began to bleed and he started to cry with pain and frustration.

"Just a start boy, remember. Now get up and do as you're told."

Sito tried to get to his feet but the smaller man called Curro pushed him back to the ground and shoved the blade of the knife under his nose.

"Don't play with us boy. Get that mule harnessed and we'll have your cart and leave you alone. Mess around and you're dead and your girl is our pleasure for as long as she can still breathe. Now move."

Sito scrambled across the clearing to where the mule had bolted. She was stomping around snorting with the reins tangled round her legs. He started to reorganize the leathers and back the mule up to the traces again; his brain was a fuzz, he couldn't think straight; he said, "Leave her alone. She's my mother."

"What, the mule's your mother?" Curro scoffed. "Ah, no, you mean the little lady! Take a look at his 'mother' Tomás. See if she's still tender enough to satisfy us."

Davina, shaking with fright, tried to climb over into the cart among the crates and melons. The long cape wrapped itself round her legs and she fell as she caught a foot on the backrest of the seat. The men laughed.

"Hey," said the small one, "fancy leather shoes for a countrywoman." He advanced toward her waving his knife like a little flag and leered up over the side. Sito made another run at him but the tall one tripped him up and he was sprawled on the ground once more.

Then all the strategies Sito had learned in his rough childhood games came into play. He rolled himself under the front of the cart, scrambled out of the rear and jumped onto the neck of the knife bearing Curro.

The tall man folded his arms, laughed and left them to it. Then he noticed the mule and ran to grab her reins before she could run off. Liberty skittered round and dragged him off balance. Tomás made a lunge for her bridle to manoeuvre her back into the traces, but the mule was young and very unsettled by everything going on around her; she shifted her haunches from one side to the other and refused to back up. Holding on to the end of the long reins Tomás reached for the whip standing in its place on the running-board and lashed the mule across her neck. She squealed and lashed out with her hind legs catching him in the chest with two metal shod hooves. She kicked again and again. Tomás doubled over and fell to the ground in slow motion. The mule shot into the safety of the nearby trees.

Sito was trying to get Curro's knife. He had the outlaw trapped against the side of the cart and was smashing the man's hand against the wood. Then he misjudged and cut himself on the blade.

He fell back grasping his right hand.

Davina lost her patience. She picked up one of the heavy, rugby ball shaped melons and bashed it down on the bandolero's head. In the tussle for the knife the knot in the string that held his jacket together had got caught between the planks in the side of the cart. As he struggled to extract it Davina smashed the melon down on his head again.

"That is enough," she cried. "I have had enough of you bloody Spaniards." Whack.

The man's chin jabbed down against the metal frame of the cart. The melon split open. Davina grabbed another.

"I have had enough of you men!" Whack, whack. "Enough!" Whack. "Enough!" Whack. "All of you!" Whack "Trying to run my life." Whack. "Making me do what I don't want." Her hands moved up and down like an enraged piston. "Who the hell do you think you are?" "Whack. "Leave me alone!"

"Señora, Señora," cried Sito reaching up with a bloodstained hand. "Stop! Stop! I think he's dead."

Davina halted with the toadskin melon in mid air. The bandolero was completely still, his head was hooked at an unnatural angle over the side of the cart and his body was limp.

Davina sat back among the fruit and vegetables and burst into tears.

It was growing dark before Sito and his father's widow were able to converse in normal tones again. They had spoken only essential words as the mule was finally harnessed and hitched to the cart. As they turned to go back up the stony track Davina scrabbled among the fruit and vegetables and jettisoned the sack of almonds she had collected so happily only an hour before.

They made no attempt to cover their tracks. The two men, whom both assumed to be fatally injured if not already dead, lay where they had fallen in the pretty clearing by the reservoir.

The day moved into evening and as the sun dropped behind the warm red hills.

Sito said, "We shall have to stop soon. I'm hungry and this animal is tired out."

"Yes."

"There is a small town up over there, you could find a room for the night."

"No. I was happy enough last night until . . ."

Sito said no more. They pulled off the road, made a hasty fire, ate in virtual silence and settled down to rest as they had the night before. The next morning Davina was horrified to find she had slept soundly and felt tremendously well. She prepared a breakfast of cheese and bread and Sito tried to coax a little fire to boil some chicory coffee.

"Today we should see the coast then it will get flatter and easier for your Liberty."

Davina patted the young mare and fed her some crusts. "Good," she said, "eat up and let's go."

"What about the coffee?"

"Sito, that is not coffee!"

"It is in our house."

"Yes, sorry."

The mare was also refreshed and set off at a cracking pace. Sito said, "You started to tell me about England. Would I like it there?"

"That depends what you like? Do you prefer the city of the country?"

"I don't know. Tell me about London."

Davina conjured London fogs and double-decker buses, theatres, shops and tea and cakes in copper kettle cafes. A chill ran through her and she said, "You know, I think I must be made of strong stuff – like my Granny Dymond. When I think about it I have been in some horrible situations and come out unscathed, well almost, and then I let other people make decisions for me. Isn't that stupid?"

"Have you killed anyone else!?" Sito didn't know whether to be shocked or simply amazed.

"No, not me, but I have seen someone killed. Although, perhaps he survived. Do you think those two men - do you think they . . .?"

"What concerns you? That they are dead, suffering, or that you – we might be accused of murder? If it's the last forget it. The police and civil guard are far too busy with petty criminals and General Franco's war to worry about those two. Now tell me about what happened in London, or wherever it was, and forget them."

Davina started to tell him about what had happened in the tea room in London with Leo. She had just reached the point where the mad soldier had fired the first shot when Sito put a hand out to silence her. There was a woman sitting beside the road in front of them. She had a bundle in her arms and a basket on a long strap over her shoulder.

"Let her ride with us," said Davina.

"No."

"She's got a baby."

"She'll bring us trouble."

"Don't be mean. Ask her where she's going and how we can help her."

Reluctantly, Sito stopped the mule and got down to speak to the woman, who was no more than a girl and so exhausted she could barely answer him.

"This is Cristina," he said as he helped her up into cart. Davina took the child from her arms and patted the hard seat next to her. The girl smiled gratefully. Her face was haggard and tear stained, her breathing laboured as if she had bronchitis. The child was very tiny, only days old. It opened large dark eyes and surveyed Davina but did not cry.

"Boy or girl?" asked Davina.

"Boy. Jesus," said the young mother. "They've taken his father."

"Who has taken his father?"

The girl shook her head and tears rolled down her grimy cheeks.

"Shh," said Davina, "you don't need to tell us anything, just rest. I'll look after baby Jesus."

"Where's your mother?" demanded Sito. In his view girl who had recently given birth should not be in these circumstances; her family should be caring for her. It was suspicious. "Why are you on your own?"

"They shot my mother, and my brother. Over there." The girl pointed west, into the middle distance.

Davina froze. Had the world gone mad? Who would shoot a mother and her son? "Why?" she asked.

"For the field and the well. Someone told the men in the uniforms about my father and my husband because they want our field and well. I didn't see what happened, I was in bed and he . . ." she sobbed, looking down at her tiny infant. "One of them came into our room. He saw us – but he didn't tell them. They didn't touch the baby and me. We're alive but they took my ma and my brother and they shot them, and they took my husband and my father. They've . . . ."

"But this is barbarous; who are these people?"

"Señora," said Sito, "leave her alone."

"But . . ."

"But nothing. There are too many sides and too many unsettled debts. It's happening all the time now. People that want to get revenge, or want something they can't get any other way are telling the Civil Guard all sorts of vicious nonsense and lies, and the Guard tells – I don't know . . . If they think you're a red, or someone says you're a republican you're lost, haven't got a chance. Don't get involved, this is nothing to do with you."

Davina stared ahead of her. Nothing to do with her! Her daughter had gone away, followed a young republican into the thick of the war, she was in real danger. And she herself was not at all sure whose side she should be on.

The cart rolled on and the girl fell asleep with the steady rhythm. At midday they stopped at a roadside water trough for the mule to drink. Sito filled their water containers from the fountain. Davina was as stiff as a board and very uncomfortable with the child in her arms but it was now apparent that the mother was running a fever and needed a doctor. She had refused to tell them where she was going or wanted to go, or anything more about her husband, so they decided to carry on and leave her at the first convent or hospital they passed. Sito cleared a space for her among the potatoes and melons and they continued with her lying asleep or sobbing to herself in the back of the cart. Davina gave the baby water and a crust of hard bread to suck on, and in this way they reached the coast.

It was dusk of the fourth day when they finally identified the

Rock of Gibraltar rising out of a bed of low cloud like a crouched lion.

There was a queue a mile long or more. People of all sorts, in all manners of attire were waiting patiently to get into the British protectorate. Hundreds of Spanish civilians, Britons and hangers on were camped out on a no-man's-land that had once been a racecourse. Members of the Spanish civil guard ambled by on tired horses. Davina found their apathy unnerving.

The girl, Cristina, roused herself to feed her silent child then handed him back to the foreign lady and settled down again in her uncomfortable litter. Sito unharnessed the mule, tied her to the shafts and then disappeared to talk with peasants and Moroccans waiting to sell their merchandise across the barrier in Gibraltar the following day.

At some time during the interminable night a Spanish policeman shone a torch into Davina's face and demanded her papers. Sito emerged from under the wagon and spoke to him. He waved his identity card and said something about his wife and mother in the cart. His wife was suffering from the *gripe*; he thought his mother and the child had it too. The baby was feverish he said with a sad countenance, they needed a doctor, but he would have to sell the melons first. The young policeman traced his torch over the cart. Davina coughed and spat over the running board.

"Take your *peste* to the English," he said, and left them in peace.

Davina was fast asleep, her arms soldered into right angles around the baby, when Sito nudged her awake some time after dawn.

"She's worse," he said, nodding at the girl in the cart.

Davina turned stiffly in her seat. The girl's breathing was irregular and she was murmuring as if in the grip of a high fever.

"We'll have to leave her here, they won't let us in if she's sick," insisted Sito. "Unless I leave you here and you get in by yourself."

"No. No I am not going to abandon her here and what about this little innocent? What'll happen to him if his mother can't feed him?"

Sito reached into the back of the cart and shook the girl's shoulder, "Cristina, tell us, have you got any papers?"

"In my bag - all my documents."

"Good. Don't speak now unless you have to."

"Well, Señora," he said, looking up at Davina, "now it is up to you. I can take the girl back with me, leave her here at the nearest convent, if they'll have her, or you can get her into Gibraltar with you? The mule and I will be happy with a rest, a good meal and road back home."

Davina smiled. "Let's get to the front of the queue and see what's what. First of all this girl needs a doctor; it's probably post-natal fever. After that we might as well sell your wares, I think you deserve a little profit."

"But what are you going to do about her? Leave her here or in Gibraltar?"

"Well she'll be safer in Gibraltar than where she came from. Look Sito," Davina sighed, "some things are just meant to be. I have lost a husband and gained a son, I have lost a daughter and gained another – what do you want me to say?"

Sito laughed. "I cannot believe I can love the woman that made my mother's life so miserable. But I do." And he climbed back into the cart and gave Davina a big hug and a kiss. The baby woke up and started to cry.

Chapter 26

Leo noticed the woman in blue sitting on the front seat of a vegetable cart because she reminded him of a Madonna ikon. The cart was one of many making its way up the steep incline. They were letting in a lot more Spaniards it seemed. Not that the woman looked very Spanish.

He didn't stop to stare; he was on his morning round: popping into diverse cafés and bars for a coffee or a glass of wine, a small cigar and the time of day; gathering little gems from people such as Vincenzo from Genoa, who served excellent espresso and had a brother in Abyssinia. Leo knew a man who was very interested in Abyssinia and Mussolini. Manolo had a limp and a family in nearby La Linea, he kept a smoky little cave in the city walls and sold sharp, ice-cold *fino* in small, scratched tumblers. His brother was with the republicans in Malaga, at least he had been until Nationalist troops had moved in.

Albert from Brighton kept the newspaper kiosk outside the infirmary, his wife's cousin Fred was with the Yorkshires garrisoned on the island. They, according to Albert, were in serious training for a 'spot of trouble'. Franco's Nationalist warships had bombarded coastal towns during the summer and the Gibraltar racecourse had been converted into a refugee camp. They were trying to get all the refugees onto the Rock before there were further attacks, but it was a tight squeeze and each day it seemed as if their numbers increased.

Albert was bubbling with indignation; "Have you seen them? Hundreds coming in since the early hours! All these foreigners! I mean you used to know who was who on the Rock – us from England and the Spanish families that have been here for generations. But nowadays you don't know, you just don't know who you're talking to - gotta watch every word in case you criticize the wrong side. And who's in the right I'd like to know? Killing your own countrymen! It isn't natural. Our Fred says even the officers in the garrison can't say for sure who they should be siding with. And in the meantime – look at 'em, they're letting in anyone and everyone. Could be a lot of subversives and villains for all we know. Could be letting in whole cartloads of criminals! I dunno – the missus says we might as well go home. Find a nice little place in Hove. She's right, it won't be long before them gunboats are back to fire on *us*. That's what our Fred says anyway, and he oughta know, him being with the Yorkies. Mind you, sir," Albert leaned precariously out of his cubicle to impart a state secret, "our Fred says the Yorkies are taking it seriously." He nodded conspiratorially, as one who knew what was what.

Leo handed over his coins and nodded back, accepting the newsagent's confidence with humility, "Good to know we're in safe hands, Albert."

"I should hope we are! Because when there's trouble, sir, one thing always leads to another. You mark my words. One thing always leads to another."

"Indeed, Albert, indeed. Well, see you tomorrow."

Albert touched his forelock without thinking and Leo strolled off looking at the front page of his paper. The bachelor King of

England caught in the lens with a married American woman called Wallis Simpson; 'Birmingham Nail Factory Closes Down – three hundred lose jobs'; 'Strawberry Harvest Beats Records in Kent': not a word about the Spanish civil war, Home Rule for India, Hitler's Germany or the Italian invasion of Abyssinia. The British press suffered from collective xenophobia. He folded the broadsheet and tucked it under his arm. On his way up Main Street he would call in on Vijay at the 'Red Fort Bazaar' to enquire after his mother, a perennially ailing, white-garbed widow. Vijay's uncle was back in gaol for being too 'active' in the Congress Party. He was particularly concerned about this: English officers in the Indian Police Force had an unpleasant way of getting information out of detainees; once they got even a whisper of the name Kazan there would be no mercy until the truth was out, but that had always been a risk. Perhaps he was going soft. After that visit there would be no alternative but to return to the Oriental Curiosity Shop. Hopefully by then Arnold should have finished his morning's Morse practice; the tap, tap, tapping irritated him beyond measure.

"There's more Spanish coming in, Arnold. Country-folk - whole families of them. There'll be no water left by the end of the week if they go on like this."

"Someone has got to take them," replied Leo's senior partner, Arnold Mackay. "There but for grace of God, Leo. You wouldn't be so flippant if you were trying to escape cut-throat natives."

"It's not quite like that Arnold. Do you ever read the local newspapers?"

"Not anymore, I'm not getting mixed up in anyone's affairs ever again."

"In that case," said Leo, running a finger around the rim of a black marble vase, "why are you learning the Morse code?"

"I didn't say I wasn't interested in saving my skin - or yours, if push comes to shove. One day you might be very grateful."

Leo looked at Arnold and raised an eyebrow; "Are you planning more adventures for me?"

"No," Arnold replied, ignoring the reference, "I am not. I told you, I'm not interested in anything any more except putting enough in the bank for my pension."

Leo wondered if Arnold was being entirely truthful, was he by any chance reporting to anyone in London. The idea unnerved him for a moment then he saw that Arnold was also ruffled.

The small man pointed a stubby forefinger at a tray of exquisitely painted glasses; "She's not coming again today either," he said. "We'll have to do the dusting ourselves. Now where are you going?"

Leo picked up his hat from the counter and opened the shop door. "Down to the quay, the 'Star' is due in and the Barodas are on it. The Maharajah is a very interesting chap, remember? So is his wife - devoted to improving the lot of the illiterate zenana girls, which seems a little odd, even in these egalitarian times. I intend to invite them to our humble emporium. Her Highness will very likely spend a fortune if I can get her up here; she has a passion for the valuable and unusual. I'll check the small ads at the tobacconist on the way down - see if I can't get another Mrs. Mop for you before royalty arrives?"

"For me!"

"It's your shop Arnold, I'm just the sales rep.."

The door bell pinged. Leo was gone - again. He gets jumpier by the day, thought Arnold Mackay. "What's he up to?"

He lifted a feather duster from its hook in the broom cupboard and began to shift sprays of dust from one object to another. It was not a task he disliked. On his way around the shop he stopped to stroke the stuffed mongoose they had brought with so many other curios from India. Leaving Bombay was the hardest thing he had ever done. He poked the chicken feathers over the rearing brass cobra and let his mind drift back to the security of Sir Lionel's office and the comfort of Clive Craven's quiet friendship.

His life had taken an unexpected turn. Despite the Morse he was bored and lonely. He missed the cut and thrust of political intrigue. He missed little Mumtaz - and her friends, who had never charged him. She'd been fond of him too, not like a real girlfriend, of course, but doing it with Mumtaz was always . . . Well, no point dwelling on that, she belong to another lifetime. Leo was up to his old tricks, though, couldn't coop him up in a shop all day. It would be interesting to find out who was running him this time. "At least," he chuckled, as a feather tickled the fanny of a tiny ivory nautch girl contorting herself in gymnastic erotica, "the randy devil hasn't fixed himself up with a bit of tail yet."

Arnold paused, the duster hovered over the centre table, perhaps Leo was grieving for Kitty. And so he should. She had been an angel. He remembered their wedding, how she had gone so pink for a half-caste when Lady Hermione had held her hand and chatted to her. Leo ought to be grieving, not running up and down Main Street like a delivery donkey every ten minutes.

He flicked his wrist over the down-hill window display and met the eyes of a fat child splaying greasy fingers over the glass. "Shoo," he said, shaking the duster so all the accumulated particles descended over the trays of loose amethysts and agates. "Shoo, be off with you. Nasty little girl, go home!"

And what about *his* daughter, he thought. What about that

little one? Leo hadn't even mentioned her name, not even while they were still in Bombay packing for the voyage. He tutted and shook his head with dismay: he'd told the woman where to contact him. She had to tell him he said, no more hanging around, pretending not to exist: write to him, tell him. He'd given her the name of the hotel on Marine Drive. She had promised. Millicent Cleaver was too old to be looking after a toddler, anything might happen, and that bumbling old fool the Russian was worse than useless. Arnold opened the shop door and shook the feather duster into the street, as he did so he repeated one of Lionel Pinecoffin's terse aphorisms; "Mind everybody's business but mind your own first and last." A passer-by looked at him and quickened her pace.

*

The nurse evidently held a post with responsibility, there was a navy blue stripe around each of her cuffs. Her uniform appeared to be made of cardboard and she wore a cap starched in concrete with an expression to match.

"Her pulse is too fast and she has a fever," she said accusingly. "We shall have to admit her."

A porter and wheel chair were summoned. The porter helped the emaciated girl into the seat and tucked a rug over her knees. Davina bent down to place the baby in her arms.

"And what do you think you are doing?" The accent was broad Scots, the tone outraged authority.

"Giving her her baby," replied Davina, not daring to make eye contact.

"Are you mad? She is undoubtedly contagious, I repeat, undoubtedly contagious."

"But . . ."

"No buts here, missy . . ."

'Missy'! 'Missy'! Davina heard her mother's voice say, 'And who, precisely, are you calling missy?' She stood up straight and thrust the baby into the nurse's arms. "Then you hold him."

The nurse accepted the little bundle as a reflex action, and also, as she later told her indignant colleagues, because the blonde madam – her hair all over the place, speaking with a plum in her mouth and looking like a gypsy no less, the *woman*, certainly no lady, was perfectly capable of dropping him right there on the floor.

"We cannot have this child in the ward!"

"Well then you had better put him in the nursery or find him a wet nurse, because he needs to be fed." Davina began to march to the door of the infirmary.

The nurse, breaking a cardinal rule, ran after her, saying, "We cannot take this baby."

The new Davina, whose voice and manner were brisk and crisp, turned and looked the nightingale in the eye. "I am sorry, but *we* have done all *we* can do. This baby needs to be with his mother. A child should never be separated from its mother – no matter how good or bad one might judge them. I am not 'family' and I cannot look after this baby until his mother is recovered because I have got nowhere to live."

"But there are rules!"

"Yes, I'm sure there are. There is also your Christian duty. I have done mine, now you do yours. Get that poor girl better and don't take her child away from her, she's already lost her mother, her husband and goodness knows who else in this madness."

"Ah, so she's a Spaniard, from Spain. She's not even Gibraltarian."

"Neither am I, and neither are you, Nurse. Thank you. Goodbye."

Davina's hands were shaking and her heart was racing as she stepped out of the smell of disinfectant and back into the noisy street. Sito was lounging against the cart smoking a cigarette, but he threw it down and stubbed it with his foot the moment he caught sight of her face. He stepped forward to greet her, then shouted, "Hey!" and ran round the side of his cart - a group of boys were helping themselves to his cargo.

By the time he had chased them off, Davina had pulled her precious carpet bag from under the seat and was folding the waterproof cape over her arm, "I had better take this, you never know I might need it again one day."

"Are you going now?"

"Yes, my dear. You have to sell your goods," she gestured to the cart, "before they all get stolen, and I have to find a room for the night, and passage to England tomorrow."

"But . . ."

"My goodness, what a lot of buts today!" She was barely holding back the tears. The tension of the scene in the infirmary, the tiredness and the horrors of the events of the past week had suddenly caught up with her. Above all else, she didn't want to lose this boy who was her late husband's son.

Sito pulled a little notebook and a stub of pencil from a trouser pocket. "Tell me where you are going, Señora."

Davina took the notebook and opened the pages. It was full of scrawling, forward-leaning handwriting. She looked at Sito questioningly. He shrugged, "I write things down."

"So I see. I hope you haven't written anything about me."

"No," he lied.

Davina put the little book on the running board and wrote; *Crimphele House, Tamstock, Cornwall, England.* Then underneath she wrote; *Plymouth, then train to Callington.* "There is a telephone, but I've forgotten the number. About Marina . . . "

"I shall find her for you. You will see her again soon. And I will kill that stupid Pedro!"

"If they don't shoot him first."

"Hmm, that's true. When I find her, what do you want me to say?"

Davina sighed. "Oh, I don't know. Whatever you think is right. We have a lot of truths to tell, sooner or later. Tell her what you want her to know. But only if you think she is strong enough to take it. If you want to, and your grandmother agrees, come to England with her."

She did not say she didn't believe a word they were saying: that she couldn't believe she was going to see her daughter again or that he would ever leave Spain, so she put her arms around the boy's shoulders and hugged him. She was crying.

"Go now, and make sure you sell all those dreadful melons before you start back."

Davina arranged the cape over her arm and picked up her bag. "You haven't written anything about what happened, have you Sito?"

"What happened?"

"Oh," Davina waved a hand in the air, "just about everything." She tried to smile and said in English, "Bye- bye."

Leo noticed the woman struggling with the carpet bag for three reasons; she had a an unfashionable mass of long golden hair blowing quite romantically in the late summer breeze; she was carrying what appeared to be a waterproof cape on a bright sunny day, and because she was wearing the Madonna-blue dress. It was the woman he had seen earlier that morning. As he neared her he realized she was older than he had first assumed and, as their paths crossed, he realized the romantic hair was hanging quite loose, which was quite unusual for a woman of her age. Under other circumstances he might have found an excuse to speak, to help her with her heavy bag, but he had to exploit any possibility of the maharani viewing his new collection. Apart from that, indeed, on top of that, the Barodas were linked by marriage to the lavish spending, bright young things of Cooch Behar, who were among the P&O's best passengers: business was business.

Davina lugged the bag up the hill, stopping now and again to look in a shop window or examine the outside of the more modest hotels. She was also keeping an eye open for somewhere to sell what she now thought of as her 'loot' and some sort of shipping office. A bookseller's sign caught her attention: books in English, how wonderful, she would come back and buy. There was a copy of *Jane Eyre* . . . but all the prices were in sterling and she only had pesetas. She would have to change Doña Mercedes' housekeeping money at a bank. But selling had to be a priority. Unless she found a modest room first and took a risk on the value of her mother-in-law's baubles. Her head was spinning. Oh, God, what a mess. She took refuge on the edge of a water trough and tried to gather her thoughts. Gazing down the street at nothing in particular, she realized she hadn't eaten since very early that morning and then it had only been some bread and water, no wonder she was dizzy. In the distance a man stopped and seemed to look directly at her. Embarrassed, she instinctively tried to gather her hair into a bun but she had lost all her hairpins.

She flushed hot and cold; she hadn't put up her hair after that first night in the clearing, they would be on the ground, where she had slept under the cart: a little nest of English, straw-coloured hairpins. Evidence. Then a sneaking, unwanted doubt crawled into her head: what had Sito written down in his little book? He owed her no favours, she had after all been responsible for their recent poverty. Was he going to report her to the British police - tell them she was a thief, an arsonist and a murderess? "Oh God, will this never end?" she said aloud and got to her feet again. Then she heard her father say, "Come on Davy girl, where's your Granny Dymond spirit?"

The room was stuffy and flowery but not unpleasant. Pink curtains festooned with posies, a green flounced counterpane of oversized roses, a lingering odour of lavender polish.

"Yes, thank you, this will be fine," she said.

The landlady handed Davina a key and stood waiting.

"Oh, um, yes, sorry. I've only got Spanish money at the moment."

"No, no. Good heavens love, this is a boarding house, not the Ritz. I'm not after a tip, I was wondering if you would like a cup of tea, you look a bit a peaky."

Davina slumped on the soft bed, "That would be wonderful."

The landlady hobbled off down the landing and Davina sat staring at the curtains, trying to summon enough energy to open a window. She was asleep by the time the landlady returned.

Emma Sangster, who had had three husbands and never married one of them, knew what it was to be in what she called 'troubled times'. Quietly she placed the teacup on the bedside table and pulled the far side of the counterpane over her Davina's legs. "I said you looked done in," she muttered and closed the door softly behind her.

Davina slept until late in the afternoon and woke with a start. The room was stifling. She got up and staggered to the window. It opened onto a spectacular sea view. Gulls swooped down over rooftops and below there was the banging and clattering of the naval base. It was all so alien and all so strangely familiar. "I shall stay for as long as I can," she said to the Atlantic Ocean. "I shall stay and get myself sorted out. Then I'll go home and start again."

Suddenly she felt lighter, fresher, eager to be doing something so she stripped off and washed her hair with Sunlight soap and gave herself a thorough stand up bath at the chipped washstand. "And I shall buy some cologne, or maybe some real perfume," she said afterwards to the woman in the mirror.

*

Leo recognized her as the ikon lady on the cart, the moment she walked through the door. He also recognized her situation: she had come to sell, she was embarrassed, she needed money. He went forward. "Good morning, may I help you?"

Arnold was polishing silver candlesticks at the back of the shop. His head shot up as he heard Leo's voice. He hadn't heard that tone for a very long time. It was the old Leo playing the tiger. He shifted for a better view of the chase.

Davina held her carpet bag in her two hands before her. It was empty of everything now except the content of her mother-in-law's safe. She stared around the shop. It was full of the most magical items.

"What an Aladdin's cave!"

Leo smiled. "It is, isn't it."

"Watch it sweetheart – 'open sesame' and here's your demon genie," said Arnold to himself, confusing his stories.

Trying to delay the moment, Davina moved towards a big round table to get a closer look at the mother-of-pearl pill boxes, a Japanese lady in a glass case, jewel-handled paper-knives and golden thimbles. The bag bumped the edge of the table and she jumped back.

"Oh sorry. Gosh, I had better be careful here."

He knew the voice: the 'gosh'. Where? When? "Would you like to show me what you have brought us?"

There was a movement at the back of the shop. Davina scanned the shadows and located the head and shoulders of a short man behind a high counter. He nodded a sort of greeting.

"Over here," said Leo, indicating a leather-topped desk. He held out a chair, waited for the lady to make herself more comfortable, then lowered his large frame into a bentwood chair. "I'm sure you have something for us," he said, reassuringly.

Davina opened her bag and hurriedly removed some items from a side pocket. "I have these." She laid out some earrings.

"I hope you have their partners."

"What? Oh, yes. That was silly, here they are."

Leo picked up an eye glass and examined two sets of drop earrings.

"They are from Columbia – well the stones are," Davina gushed.

"Yes, yes. In white gold. Quite unusual. What else?"

Feeling a little more confident, Davina laid out two necklaces, a diamond brooch, a sapphire pendant and all the other little treasures she had snatched in her raid.

Leo examined each item carefully without speaking. The Colombian emeralds were of value, the rest was very ordinary. He removed the eye glass and portioned the items into two groups. Davina watched his hands and flushed scarlet. She looked up: eyes as green as . . . She thought her heart was going to explode.

"Well . . ." Leo started to say something.

"It's all macaroon. Scaramouch!" blurted Davina.

"Scaramouch?"

"What's the word for worthless diamonds?"

"Mackbar?"

"That's it. Mackbar. Base diamonds."

"Yes. Do you know about diamonds?"

"No. No, nothing. I – someone told me once." She wanted to escape, to be outside the shop and never come in. She began to scoop the gewgaws on the table together. "I'm sorry. I didn't mean to waste your time."

"Stop, please."

He tried to stay her hand with his but she snatched it away as if he were a leper. Confused, he said, "We shall be pleased to buy everything."

"Ai, ai, ai," murmured Arnold under his breath, "what price a leg over?"

Leo went to the till and removed the entire day's takings. Then added three twenty-pound notes from his own wallet. Arnold cleared his throat meaningfully. His partner ignored him.

"Now if you can just tell me your name and address, for our records, we shall be all fair and square." He took a sheet of paper from the desk drawer and sat down again to write, saying, "One hundred and sixty pounds to Miss? Mrs. . . ."

Davina stared at him.

"No receipt needed?" Leo cocked his head on one sided, questioningly.

It erased the last vestige of doubt. "No, thank you." Davina grabbed the money and crumpled it into her fist without looking at it. She stood up ready to go.

"Is there anything here in the shop you would like, perhaps?"

"I don't want to buy anything, thank you."

"As a small gift, I meant."

Arnold slammed a silver candlestick down on the counter, denting its base for ever. But he had no need to worry: the woman was at the door, as eager to leave as he was to see her go.

The shop bell pinged. She was gone. The small man sighed a dramatic sigh and was about to speak when he saw Leo lunge from his chair, grab the carpet bag and rush for the door.

"Quick, you've nearly lost her!" shouted Arnold with all his old sarcasm.

"D'you want to talk about it lovey?" said Emma Sangster. "I'm the only discreet landlady in the whole world. You can trust me not to tell a livin' soul. What you say stops in this kitchen, right here in this teapot. Anyway, no one's listened to a word I say since my boy Jacky went to France and never came home again." She poured tea into a wide eau de nil cup and rattled on, "I bought a budgie after that, back in 'fifteen. He never talked to me neither. He was a good listener, though, 'til he died. Got a bit seed stuck. I never got another one. Just lookin' at 'em now makes me think of that war."

"That's how it started," mumbled Davina, "with the war."

She began at the Armistice party and went on through two more cups of thick tea uninterrupted until she killed a man in a clearing by a reservoir and then traveled four more heart-stopping days in a mule cart with a girl probably suffering from typhus and her baby, and arrived on the Rock of Gibraltar only to come face to face with the father of her lost daughter.

There was a silence. Eventually Emma Sangster said, "And I thought I'd lived." She got up, "We need a brandy my girl, this tea'll rot our guts the way we're goin'."

She pulled a bottle from a peppery smelling sideboard and put two tumblers on the table. "So now what you goin' to do?"

"You tell me, Mrs. Sangster."

"Alright then. Tea might rot your gut but the leaves come in handy." She pointed at the dregs in Davina's cup, "Swill that lot round and tip it in the sink. That's it. Now hand it over 'ere and let's see what's what."

There was a rat-tat-tat on the back door.

"Sit down. Don't answer it, we're busy. Now, give me that cup."

As Davina handed her the cup, the door opened.

It was Leo. Behind him stood a policeman.

"I said give me the cup, not rub the sodding pot!" laughed Emma Sangster, too loudly. "Here sit down before you fall down, I'll deal with this."

Chapter 27

Emma Sangster, landlady of Roseland Guest House, Rosia Road, bustled to the door. "I've got a front door you know, what you two doing coming round the back like the baker's boy?"

The policeman saluted, the gentleman in the navy serge suit removed his hat.

"Come in if you must. Just watch yerselves, this lady has gone and picked up a touch of something very nasty – I shouldn't be surprised if it isn't highly contagious, so don't come too near."

Neither of the men moved to enter. The policeman eyed Davina with alarm but good manners overcame his desire to say what had to be said and be gone. "You first, sir," he said addressing the stranger at his side.

"No, no officer. You are in uniform and on duty, you first." Leo's eyes had registered the kitchen, the table and the state of the woman staring white-faced at the policeman before he had finished his words.

"Yes, right, I won't take up anybody's time," said the policeman, "I just need to ask Mrs. Sangster a couple of questions on behalf of the sergeant."

"Oh, come in, come on in. Shall I put the kettle on or are you really not stopping?" Emma Sangster spoke to the policeman but kept a beady on the big gent in the dark suit carrying her lodger's traveling bag. He was classy and no mistake.

The bobby removed his helmet and smoothed back his gingery hair. "D'you remember me, Mrs. Sangster? I stayed here a couple of years ago, with my missus, when our flat got flooded. Gordon MacRamsay, from Cardiff."

"Oh yes, the Welsh Scots. Pretty as a picture, your wife."

"That's what I tell her, Mrs. Sangster. Mind you she's put on a bit since she was here. Got a sweet tooth, and after the last nipper, well . . ."

"Another one, oh dear, are you wanting to stay again? I'm awful sorry I'm fully booked"

Davina looked at Mrs. Sangster, it wasn't true: why on earth should her landlady do herself out of business for a woman she didn't know – because it was perfectly clear, Emma Sangster was trying to protect her.

"Oh no, no, no, this is official, not um – err . . ." The Welshman swiveled his eyes in the direction of the lady sitting at the table and half-closed both eyes, meaningfully.

"Shall we go into the sitting room then, where it's private?"

· "Good idea."

Davina couldn't breathe: Sito had gone straight to the police. She wondered if they could hear the beating of her heart against her ribs – then she wondered if Emma Sangster wasn't right, she had picked up something nasty.

The man, who was her daughter's father, was standing by the sideboard examining a variety of nick-knacks and souvenirs. One by one he picked up a wooden lighthouse with razor shell inlays set on a cockle shell rock, from Scarborough; various vaguely identifiable animals with shell ears and tails from Southsea. He put each one back exactly in its place and stooped to look more closely at Our Lady of Lourdes, all done out in a crinoline of tiny periwinkles and clear varnish. Smiling he turned to look at her.

"Fascinating. Such a lot of work, such patience! I have brought you your bag, by the way," he indicating her traveling bag at his feet.

"Thank you."

"We do know each other, don't we?"

"Yes."

"You are the Dymond girl but I have to make a confession, I have forgotten your name. It begins with a D, only it's not Daphne or Dorothy." He shrugged and grinned a lopsided, one dimple grin. "Something beginning with D, though?"

"Davina."

"Of course, Davina; London and the uncut stones. I have never forgotten, and I have never done that since, you know - shown a girl how to judge diamonds. I should have guessed - 'mackbar'. I am getting forgetful in my old age."

"Middle age. We are middle-aged now."

"Actually, not quite, I am as old as the century and this is 1936, so not the middle. Well, yes, of the human span, I suppose. You don't look middle-aged at all."

"I certainly feel it today and a lot more. Mrs. Sangster is right; you had better not come too close."

"Look, I'd be blind not to see the effect that uniform had on you. Can I suggest that your fever demands immediate quarantine? Up you go to your room and no one to be admitted except the good lady and myself. You have after all, spent the last few days in my constant company, so I must be immune."

He was bossy and bustling, and Davina had no energy to stop him organizing her.

"I don't think that bobby is here for anything related to what one might call a personal nature, though," he continued. "There are at least two thousand refugees on the island, not enough drinking water and typhus has come in from across the border."

"That's where I have come from - across the border."

"Oh, right. Well, yes, good. There's serious fighting in Ronda and Seville and I don't know where else, you are much safer here. But you arrived at least a week ago, I can vouch for that, if necessary."

Davina looked at the man, why was he trying to help her? What could he know? She put a hand to her brow and pressed down on her eyes. "I'm sorry, I do feel very unwell."

"Up you go then."

Leo had her by the elbow and into the hall before she could reply.

"Can you manage the stairs alright? My God, what a carpet! Enough to make anyone dizzy. There you go."

She let him assist her up to her room but she was fast enough to close the door sharply in his face. For a moment she leaned her head against the painted wood then she turned and slumped to the floor on her bottom, like a rag doll. What? What the hell was she doing? How dare he barge in after nigh on twenty years and start telling her what to do. Her left temple throbbed, her left eye-lid flickered - she scrambled to her feet and just got to the basin in time. Migraine: hardly surprising. She closed the curtains, vomited again and staggered to fall face down on the bed.

When she awoke there was a fresh sea-breeze in the room and a vase of roses with a card tucked into them on her dressing table. As if by telepathy Emma Sangster appeared with a tray of lemonade and ginger biscuits. "You're awake then."

"Yes, I think so. What day is it?"

"Monday."

"Monday!" It was still only a week since Alfonso had died. "What happened on Sunday?"

"I made roast beef and Yorkshire pud and Mrs. Crabbe, who's got 'Bella-vista' two doors down, came in for a chat, oh and your Mr. Kazan came round in the afternoon with these nice roses. Now, can you get up? There's a bath running with some of my lavender bath salts and then he wants to see you."

"And you think I ought to see him."

"I do. He's got lovely manners, nice eyes, and a few bob in the bank by the look of him. And it's about time you had a bit of fun."

Davina sat up and drank some lemonade. Mrs. Sangster stood back, plump arms folded over her ample bosom. "Mind you," she chortled, "I always was a terrible judge of men."

Davina didn't hear her – she had remembered the policeman. "What did the policeman want?"

"Nothing to do with you dearie," replied the landlady, moving to the window to open the curtains. "The sergeant wants to stay here while they're doing up his new flat."

"Oh for heaven's sake! Sorry, what did you say about men?"

"Men? Can't remember. Come on then, up you get and into that nice bath. You'll feel brand new after."

They dined in a small sea front restaurant on the Mediterranean side of the Rock. They chatted about how Gibraltar felt like an island, about Arnold Mackay and laughed about his obsession for dusting and polishing, about rare items in the Oriental Curiosity Shop, about Spanish wine and the serious problem of drinking water, about absolutely everything except themselves. Coffee was served, Spanish brandy poured and darkness fell. Eventually the golden drink worked its magic, Davina finally felt the tension in her neck and shoulders relax, she leant back in her chair and smiled.

After a few moments of silence, Leo said, "I have three secrets I want you to know."

"That sounds like three too many and far too serious."

"That is why I have kept them secret."

He swilled the brandy around its globe and avoided looking at her. "I have a daughter, a father I do not want to meet and a fortune's worth of uncut stones in a bank vault."

Davina laughed. "Well, if you want to play 'truth, forfeit or dare', I have a daughter, who does not know her father; I've stolen jewels that unfortunately weren't worth a fortune; and I think I killed a man. So there. Oh, and I lost my virginity to a passing stranger when I was eighteen."

Leo looked at her and burst out laughing. "My lady, you leave me speechless."

"Good because I really, really do not want to continue this conversation."

The waiter came to the table with a box of Havana cigars and halted the macabre game.

Davina gazed out to sea while Leo selected a medium sized cigar, cut and lit it. For a few moments he puffed at the Cuban tobacco and stared at the profile of the Englishwoman across the table. Her eyes were glistening.

"I'm sorry," he said. "I just wanted you to know."

"My husband died just over a week ago, and my daughter has run off with her young man to join this damned war and it is all so dangerous . . . I'm sorry. It's too soon for me. I should like to go back to Mrs. Sangster's now. Tomorrow I have to organize my passage back to England."

"Tomorrow! Can't you stay a little longer?"

Davina shook her head without looking at him.

"I shall accompany you on the voyage then."

"No! I want to go home by myself."

Leo leaned across the table and patted her hand. "Sshhh, I'll pay the bill and we'll go."

They walked in silence up the steep streets of the Rock. Gharries were available but Davina wanted to walk. As they traversed the unusually silent town she said, "I'm sorry, I was being selfish. You wanted to tell me about your daughter."

"It's not important."

"Yes it is, you wanted me to know."

They stopped in the Alameda gardens and sat on a bench. The scent of jasmine hung like a zenana screen in the still night air, separating them from the real world. Leo told her about his old-fashioned courtship of Kitty; how he had asked her father for permission to marry her and how he had left to go traveling as soon as she was pregnant. He told her about his lively little girl called Elena and stopped at the letter from Millie Cleaver, unable to continue.

"You haven't been to see her, have you," asked Davina quietly.

"No."

"Do you want to?"

"It's difficult." Leo squeezed her hand. "They are with my father. She's quite safe. You don't understand - it's too much."

"Why Leo, why is it too much?"

"Because I have done the same to him – more or less. I knew he existed before I got to London and met you. I actually half knew about him when I was a boy in Bombay, various people insinuated – but they never actually told me outright – so – well I pretended I didn't know anything about him, pretended I hadn't got a father – because I had chosen someone else for that role. I didn't want to be a Russian, I wanted to be English. I didn't want to be one of the old enemies. So I ignored him."

There was a pause. Davina looked at Leo's hand holding hers. The fist was large, the fingers round and strong – she tried to imagine him as a boy. "So who looked after you when you were little?"

"Oh, I grew up in a British orphanage – and sort of spent a lot of time with a high ranking IPS family. That's why I speak the way I do. English people think I'm frightfully old-fashioned la-di-da, but it's just the way I learnt to speak, you see."

"So who is Millicent Cleaver?"

"How do you know about Millicent Cleaver?" Leo was cross, shocked.

"You just told me. You said 'Elena is all right because she's with Millicent Cleaver'."

"Did I? That's the brandy talking – take no notice."

A blackbird hopped among branches above them, pinking a warning, telling them to go home.

"Blackbirds always make me think of England. Whenever I hear them I can see them hopping around the sun dial in Tamstock," said Davina.

"Mmm?" Leo was elsewhere in his thoughts then he took both her hands in his and said, "I have been very naïve and very stupid. And I probably would have gone on being naïve and stupid about myself if I hadn't met you again. Sitting down there at that table, I realized what life might be like if we . . ." He faltered, his charm, his skill with words, his talent for getting what he wanted all forsook him in a moment of truth.

Davina took her hands from his and rolled her wedding ring around the third finger of her right hand. She had changed the ring onto her right hand when Alfonso told her to, when they were nearing the Spanish coastline back in 1919.

There was a sudden guffaw of laughter followed by expletives. A group of drunken sailors swayed down the centre of the gardens. One stopped to throw lewd comments at them but catching sight of the woman's white face in the lamplight turned away.

"Actually, I thoroughly dislike Gibraltar," said Leo watching them stagger off.

"Then go back to India, find your daughter and make peace with your father, if he will let you. Honestly Leo, I think we both need to sort ourselves out."

He sought her lips and kissed her. "Before what? If you are talking about priorities, this is what I suggest; I have a beautiful suite of rooms with spectacular views of the harbour, some new gramophone records . . ."

"Oh no," Davina laughed separating herself and straightening her dress. "Not so fast. Not this time."

"Ah, well, we have time. Now I have found you I am *not* going to let you run away again," he replied, grinning his dimpled grin. "Forget booking a passage anywhere tomorrow: I simply shan't let you go."

Davina turned and looked him in the face, lost for words. What gave him the right to give her orders? She had said she wanted to go home, back to England and he was treating the matter as a mere whim. Did all men adapt fact to suit their fictions?

Oblivious to her annoyance, Leo kissed her on the forehead and said, "I suppose you want me to escort you home now, like a proper gentleman."

"Absolutely. Like a proper gentleman."

They kissed again at the gate to Roseland. Davina put her arms up around his neck and was tempted, so very tempted to give in to his plans, but over his shoulder she glimpsed a bobby walking his evening beat. The uniform made her shudder. One day the Spanish police would trace her to Gibraltar.

The following day Davina reserved a berth on the 'Ranpurna' for the following Friday. The ship was returning to Tilbury, calling at Plymouth. By Tuesday she would be safely back in old Tamstock.

For each of the remaining days Davina met Leo in the afternoon. They dined together at the new Rock Hotel, where Leo did indeed have a beautiful a suite of rooms on the top floor. Their lovemaking was tranquil and joyous: as if they had been lovers for years who never tired of each other's face, of kissing eyelids and gently biting lower lips, of running hands over bodies that were now fuller and softer and so very easy to understand.

Leo loved the opulence of her breasts, their roundness, the hard, darkness of the nipples. He liked the texture and smell of her hair when it fanned out across the pillows. He assumed he was in love because he couldn't bear to be apart from her for a moment. But Davina insisted on returning to Roseland before each night was over. He begged her to stay, said all he wanted in the world was to awaken to the sun with her in his arms. She refused. She knew if she stayed the whole of one night she might never leave Gibraltar and she had good reasons to go. She told herself she must let her head rule her heart – this time.

It was Friday and they stood side by side on the quayside waiting for the 'Ranpurna' lighter.

Davina watched a swoop of raucous gulls heckling a fishing boat and her heart beat faster. She was facing the Atlantic, she pulled the ozone into her lungs and wanted to laugh and cry all once.

"Naturally we don't have to stay here in Gibraltar. I mean I don't *have* to live here. We can go wherever you want," said Leo.

"What?" She hadn't been listening.

"Look," he continued, "I know you said it was too soon for you, but I think even if I have only been in your life these few short days . . ."

Davina didn't hear the rest; she was lying in a young man's arms in a stuffy room behind velvet curtains; she was arching her back in the sweat and agony of childbirth; she was watching two sturdy legs and a bob of black hair whoosh down a slide - *Look Mamá, look.*

"Leo," she said, "you have been in my life for all my life. What are you saying?" She flung her arms up around his neck and hugged him until her feet came off the ground. "Are you asking me to . . .?"

"To stay. Of course. You'll stay?"

"No."

"But why?"

"I told you. We have to sort out our lives first. Go and find your daughter. Make sure she is all right. Don't just abandon her, she must miss you terribly. Then come to England. I want to see you by the river, I know it's silly, but if I see you in a real place – where I know I belong I'll know if I am doing the right thing or not."

"In that case," said Leo, hurt beyond words, "you had better have this now." He reached into an inner pocket and extracted a flat, square package wrapped in white linen.

"Please don't open it until you've passed Trafalgar."

Davina accepted the gift and began to stow it in her traveling bag. Leo winced and said, "Better keep it on you, just while you get aboard, bags get lost sometimes."

She started to put it in her handbag.

"No, really, much safer if it's actually on your person. Can you get it down the front of your dress?"

Davina laughed, "No much room there for this."

"Try, it'll be safer."

Davina opened her front buttons and pushed the package down as far as her waistband. She laughed, "I look like Mrs. Sangster now!"

She climbed awkwardly into the lighter and Leo waved her off then waited to see her board the old Asia Line vessel out in the bay. A sense of loss settled under his left rib cage. Losing so much in one single morning nearly unmanned him. He turned and strode away from the quay without looking back.

Davina defied Leo's instructions and opened the package as soon as the ship was under way. It was a white buckskin box lined with gold satin. Nestling among the gold fabric lay a necklace studded with tiny emeralds and pearls, there was a big pearl in the centre and below that a huge pear-shaped emerald. It was beautiful and obviously worth a fortune. She had never heard of the 'Empress Emerald'.

Chapter 28

Arnold heard the door bell and looked up: Leo, not a customer. He registered the harrowed expression and said nothing.

Leo went to the desk in the centre of the shop and sat down, hands palm down on the leather pad. Some minutes passed in silence. Arnold went on polishing the till, eventually he said, "She's gone then?"

"Mmm."

"For long?"

"For ever, I'm afraid."

"And is she that special?"

"More than special."

"And you let her get away, just like that."

"She wanted to get back to her home in England - she had her reasons."

"Well you're a fool. And a damned great fool at that," retorted Arnold.

Leo shrugged, "What could I do?"

"Do! What you do with every other bint and bibi worth the rogering; charm her prostrate and keep her there. Leo, you get all the girls you set your hat at. I've watched begums and mems make eyes at you with their husbands in the same room. Now, suddenly you're mooning around like a love-sick calf over losing a middle-aged Englishwoman that doesn't know one end of a lipstick from another. Where's the sense? She's neither rich or sophisticated or particularly gorgeous, not in your league at all, is she?"

"That's the point."

"And what about Kitty?" Arnold said quietly.

He had made his way round the counter and was standing next to a brass dancing Shiva, duster raised in his right hand, as frozen in action as the immobile dancing deity. He had spent the best part of thirty years feeling jealous of Leo Kazan: now he was about to see him crumble: he wanted to see the expression on his face, would he, could he cry? Vengeance is sweet and it is mine, he thought.

"Poor Kitty," he whispered. "What about poor Kitty?"

"Kitty died two years ago."

"On a Friday afternoon, I remember it well." Arnold shivered despite his cold-blooded intention. Poor, poor Kitty. *He* would have looked after her properly, he thought for the hundredth time, he wouldn't have gone away and left a treasure like that.

"You were there?" Leo's tone was accusatory.

"No, but as soon as I heard what was going on I tried to get there. Lionel came with me. We couldn't move - the streets were jam-packed in all directions. They started firing into the crowd. I did try. I've told you all this before. I tried to get there, so did Lionel."

"Tell me your version again."

"What d' you mean, *my* version? It's what happened."

Arnold paced to the back of the shop with as much dignity as his small frame could muster and put the yellow cloth in the broom cupboard.

Leo said, "Just, tell me again. Tell me why you think Elena might be with Millicent Cleaver."

"She *is* with Millicent Cleaver, the woman told you in her letter."

"So you know about the letter."

"Of course I do, I gave her your hotel address you fool. I know everything, remember? It's what Lionel trained me to do: minute and file and keep my eyes peeled."

Arnold came back to stand by Leo. "That day, when the rioting started Millie Cleaver was on her way to your father-in-law's shop for some ribbon, wool, God-knows-what, she was always hanging around. She's always been around, watching you, even when she was employed up-country she managed to keep tabs on you. Kitty was coming back from somewhere with the baby just as they threw the fire bomb in. She turned to the nearest woman, who happened to be Millie, pushed Elena into her arms and ran into the shop. Then they threw another fire bomb in . . ."

Arnold was angry. The police hadn't done anything to break up the demonstration in its early stages and three good people had died because of an English name painted on a shop window. And to top the lot, this oh so suave, oh so international, clever-arse Kazan hadn't been there. Away as usual on some glamorous mission, swanning around Europe, wining and dining traitors. Mr. Soviet Espionage Kazan, whose reports sent shivers down IPS backs and London ministers into huddles – he hadn't been there to prevent a bunch of chanting coolies throwing home-made fire bombs into the shop and home of a completely innocent – and half-Indian family. It made you want to puke. And now the bloody man was whimpering over the past because he'd fallen flat with a wench who hadn't been to a hairdresser in twenty years, pah! He turned to face his adversary in triumph.

Leo was lying hunched over the desk. Suddenly all Arnold's accumulated resentment disappeared. It dawned on him what Leo was actually trying to do; he wanted to set the past straight. Perhaps the Englishwoman had done him some good after all. Sorting out the past: he understood that. It was what he had had to do himself before he left Bombay: analyze the past and then file it away. No point leaving bits lying around to get muddled up with the present.

"Leo, it might be that Millie Cleaver knew about the demonstration – or she was worried when she saw what was happening, or maybe it was just divine coincidence. The fact is she's got your little girl, but she's no chicken, she can't look after her for ever."

Leo sat up and folded his arms. Tell me about Millie Cleaver: we'll go from there. I want to know everything. Lionel's dead, so you won't be breaking any confidences.

Arnold went to the shop door and turned the sign to 'closed'. Then he slowly walked up to the big man in the centre of the room, gingerly stretched out a short arm and patted him on the shoulder.

"You're right, it's time, isn't it? Time to get things clear."

Leo kept his head down but nodded.

"Would you like me to start from the beginning?"

Leo mumbled into his arms. Arnold inched onto the chair on the other side of the desk and gripped its arms, taking a deep breath he said, "Your real mother is in her mother's house in Goa. Her father died some time ago, but her mother, your grandmother is still alive. Your mother's called Catalina - you know that, it's on your birth certificate. She lives in her old bedroom surrounded by her Portuguese dollies.

"After they found her she was very ill, but they looked after her and she got better, but not completely. Physically she is fine, but she'll never be right in the head. Under the circumstances it's probably a blessing."

Leo looked up, his green eyes were glistening. "So who the hell is Millicent Cleaver?"

"Her father was a botanist working for the Royal Society or something, bad-tempered old devil. He had a daughter by his Indian housekeeper, who died when the girl was very young. He sent the child to an up-state boarding school; she was clever, so they turned her into a governess – wasn't much else she could have done."

Arnold paused to light a cigarette. He was playing for time, because now he had to start what he thought of as Millie Cleaver's confession. He had a choice; he could say she had *found* Leo – or he could tell the truth. He decided on the truth. So he started to repeat from memory what he had written down for Lionel Pinecoffin, it wasn't so hard, he had been in the room taking notes while she spoke. He started from the moment this single woman in her mid-thirties offered to hold a baby on a Goa to Bombay train and ended the day Leo sailed for England in 1918. He told Leo exactly what Millie Cleaver had told Lionel, and what he had seen for himself. He did not however, mention his personal opinion on why Leonid Kazan had never made a serious attempt to reclaim his son, nor did he mention Lionel Pinecoffin's specific instructions regarding Leo's real identity – or his own envy.

*

Davina sat on the platform watching the early autumn rain flatten the plants in the station-master's window box across the track. She felt chilly and conspicuous in her foreign summer frock and old-fashioned cape. A gaggle of farmers' wives waddled down the platform carrying oversize wicker baskets covered in red gingham cloths. They each wore a bright headscarf and looked as if they had just stepped out of a Beatrix Potter colour-plate. As the country train chuntered into the station and came to a noisy halt, Jemima Puddleduck ushered her companions into a carriage, then held the door open until Davina had lugged in her much-traveled carpet bag.

"You on then m'dear? You look chilled to the bone. Had a nice holiday have you?"

"No. Yes. I suppose so."

The farmer's wife smiled at her. It was such a genuine, uncomplicated smile Davina wanted to hug her.

Five of the country wives settled themselves across the front bench seats of the carriage with their backs to the engine and the remaining four sat in the seats facing them. As one, they arranged their baskets on their laps and picked up their conversations where they had left off. Davina, in a middle seat, stared out of the window in a daze, not really registering anything until they slowed down for the next station, when she noticed the glorious profusion of fluffy hollyhocks and tall weeds lining the sidings. The station itself was immaculate; yellow marigolds in cut-down barrels, lobelia swinging bright and blue from hanging baskets. She was home and it was all so familiar and all so alien.

A young ticket inspector hopped into the carriage. One of the headscarves nudged another in the ribs, "Here he is Rose, your beau."

"Doris!"

"Morning officer," said one of the older ladies. "You polished your buttons this morning? We've got Rose with us, you know."

"Mabel!" simpered Rose, "Leave him alone."

"Morning ladies," said the young ticket inspector, trying to ignore their teasing, "tickets, please."

"Tickets?" said Jemima Puddleduck, "Oh my! Who bought the tickets? Any you girls got a ticket?"

The head scarves nodded left then right and then left again, in perfect unison. Davina had to put a hand over her mouth to stop herself laughing out loud. The ticket inspector, turned round to see who was watching his weekly humiliation, his face as red as pickled beetroot.

"We bought tickets last week, I got 'em 'ere somewhere, will they do?" Doris pushed her hand down into her basket and came up with the hairy, white root-end of a leek. The ladies chuckled with glee, "That's a leekit, mother!" said one. "He wants a teekit."

"Oh I got one of those," shouted a headscarf tucked into a corner seat. She pushed her hand under the cover of her basket and pulled out a round yellow disc. "Ah no, silly, this is a *tea biscuit*. What was it you wanted again, boy?"

"Come on now ladies, you're not the only travelers today. I got to punch other people's tickets before we get to Callington."

"Rose says you can punch her ticket as often as you like, boy," said Doris. Rose dropped her head over her basket, consumed with naughty giggles.

"Right then," the pink ticket inspector turned on his heel, walked two paces down the carriage and leant over to receive Davina's peace offering. He nodded his gratitude and went to stand by the door. There was a kafuffle in the rear seats and a headscarf called, "Here they are boy, I've found 'em."

The tickets were punched and the poor young inspector was rewarded with a bulbous currant bun and a pot of jam. The morning fun was over and everyone settled down to look at the scenery – big red-brown cows knee deep in mud, and hedgerows glistening with raindrops in the morning sun. The clouds parted as they only ever do over England, it was the start of a beautiful day.

Davina sighed with satisfaction and relief and wondered if she had had a nice holiday.

*

The voyage had become tedious two days out from Gibraltar. Leo was in no mood to socialize or occupy himself with any of his preferred on-board distractions. He had met no one interesting, no one who merited fleecing at cards. His dining companions were dull and worthy; a school principle, a senior cleric and an upper-ranking ICS officer. Their wives were dowdy and much taken with the related topics of hygiene and housing. They lamented the number of street children, but could identify no solution to the distressing sight of emaciated toddlers begging on the public highway. There was some mention of the European situation but as one of the wives pointed out, they were a long way from any possible front, and the Germans had surely learned their lesson after the last do.

Each evening, as soon as dessert was over, Leo was on his feet and making his excuses before he could be included in the gentlemen's smoking coterie; he really couldn't be bothered to be sociable. As a result of his self-imposed alienation the voyage seemed interminable and he became more and more edgy as his destination approached.

George Randall, the very pukka ICS wallah, waited until they had passed Port Said before he made his move. He and Leo coincided while taking a morning turn on deck. They stood together as the Gulf of Suez merged into the Red Sea.

"You've seen this a few times, I'd say," said Randall.

"Lost count," said Leo.

"Me too, but it's always a pleasure to get back into eastern waters. Home for you, eh?"

Leo cocked his head on one side, picking up the warning signal. "Yes and no."

"But you're more at home with Mother India than on our good King's chilly island."

"I live in Gibraltar, actually."

"Yes, I know. Mediterranean climate, very pleasant they tell me. Not so safe a fortress as it used to be, though. That chap Franco's got more about him than our government cares to admit. I'm told he could send in his Arab horsemen at midnight and have the whole bally garrison beheaded by sunrise."

"I think that's a bit of a picturesque overstatement. The British garrison is on alert and well prepared to protect itself, and us, or so I'm told."

George Randall heard a word that bode well - 'us'. Well, *carpe diem*, now was as good a moment as any so far, but then again there was an uncalled for animosity that might jeopardize his proposal. Maybe he should postpone it for a day or two, just to be on the safe side. It was hard to tell with these Eurasians, half the time they didn't know whose side they were on themselves. Hah, bit of a joke that, he thought and smiled to himself, pity he couldn't use it, but this was no time to upset tender sensibilities. The least little comment these days could spark off a scene that could, often did lead to some embarrassing moments. Testing times, one had to be very careful who one was talking to – if they weren't part of the Raj.

Even friendly natives, well-educated aristocrats in their own right, people with whom one had dined had been put under house arrest. Indeed, one really had to watch one's words more than ever before. Nehru was taking a much too strong a lead of the Congress party demanding total independence from Britain, and what with Jinnah giving the Moslems even more reasons to get fractious, one was literally walking on shards of glass. Not to mention the commies stirring up trouble for the sake of it. No doubt about it, Kazan was needed now more than ever before, none of his crew could say more than 'cheers' in Russian. Congress and the commies were most definitely in cahoots – as the chap himself had revealed years ago, of course. They needed anything he could find: prevention being better than cure, as the good ladies at dinner were so keen to point out. He opened a silver cigarette case and offered it to Leo, who declined.

"Curious coincidence," he said "I've got a letter for you from the India Office in my cabin."

"Me? I think not. I'm afraid you have mistaken me for someone else, I have an antique shop in Gibraltar, you know."

"Oh yes, I know that. And domiciled at the new Rock Hotel, I know that, too."

Leo was silent, watching a dhow plough its honest way through the coastal waters.

"Jolly fortunate coincidence being on the same ship. Of course you have an unusual name, but it was my wife who confirmed it. She used to take tea with Lady Hermione, when she first came out and I was very junior, before we went into the Punjab. In fact Joan was with Lady Hermione only a couple of weeks ago, we were staying with family in the West Country."

"Hermione Pinecoffin, I thought she was dead."

"Good heavens, no. Bright as a button, and still chattering

about you and that blessed leopard. Hermione has rather concertina-
ed time, if you know what I mean? She tends to forget she was a
grown woman, wife and mother and all that, when you were billeted
on them."

"That is incorrect. I was never billeted on them."

"No, but you were Lionel's golden boy, and unfortunately
Hermione prattles on about you all the time. That's one of the reasons
why you had to be rested, you know. No one was sure who she was
talking to. Went a bit loopy after poor Lionel passed away. Got stuck
in a time groove and just kept on repeating the same stories, some
of which were not for the public ear. I mean I know no one listens to
loopy old dames, but there again in Bombay she used to mix with all
sorts, and there were a constant stream of visitors after the funeral –
all colours and creeds, as they say. Not like Joan, she sticks with her
own. Anyway Hermione's safely back in the family home now, out
of the way. Pinecoffin must have told her everything that was going
on. Can't for the life of me think why. "

The triangular sails of the dhow shifted and the boat headed
back to shore. For one moment Leo was tempted to jump overboard
and swim to it: start a new life in a new land. Then he heard Davina's
soft voice say, *what about your little girl?* And a dark-haired, round
faced, adorable child called out *Daddy!* Davina was right, denying
the child was wrong.

He said, "What you say may be true, Mr. Randall, I cannot
verify it. However I was 'rested' as you put it, and as a consequence
my life has taken a different turn, for which I am very grateful. I
would like to leave the past in the past."

George Randall leant over the rail and flipped his cigarette
into the waves below. Avoiding eye contact he said, "As I mentioned
before, it was my wife who confirmed your identity. She also

remembers a young Sikh at about the same time – we were at a dreadful fundraiser -'17 or was it '18? Whatever, this young chap caused a quite a sensation among the ladies, positively gasping for him, they were. Wearing a pigeon egg ruby and eyes as green as emeralds, she said, which is another coincidence because that very night a priceless necklace, the 'Empress Emerald', disappeared. Do you remember?"

Leo smiled a one dimple smile. "I don't know how well you were acquainted with Sir Lionel, Mr. Randall, but it is quite clear to me that you are ICS and he was Political Service. Time for lunch, I think." He turned his back on the crass civil servant and walked slowly toward his cabin.

George Randall stood and stared at the retreating figure; well what was that supposed to mean, yea or a nay? Honestly, he was coming to positively dislike the man, which was a pity because he would have to work with him sooner or later. They needed his skills and that was that. A chameleon, they'd said in London, could get himself inside anywhere and not be noticed – he'd be able to find out what was really going on between the League and Congress, find out where Britain could exploit disagreements. Proper Indians didn't make good informers, they had all agreed on that in London - untrustworthy little beggars.

Chapter 29

Two ibis stretched their beaks symmetrically to the sky, two peacocks fanned their tails in ostentatious array, above them birds of paradise hopped among branches alive with all the leaves of Asia; the gates were a naturalist's dream in metalwork. Behind them, up a short graveled drive, was a rambling but surprisingly modest bungalow. The walls were painted white, the window frames green. Ivy and jasmine climbed to the roof and spilled out around corners, lilies opened their opulence for the touch of rain, bougainvillea and other garish blooms toppled over the garden walls. It was, thought Leo, exactly the sort of house he would like. Not too big, comfortable-looking and set in a jungle of plants, except he would have a special rose garden, too.

As he stood there, trying to find the energy to face the scene ahead, a Siamese cat insinuated itself under the gate and stopped to glare at Leo, annoyed that its moment of indignity had been observed then it arched its back, regained the poise of good breeding and sauntered self-importantly off down the hill. A dumpy little house-boy came rushing out of the front door in pursuit of the cat and stopped short when he saw Leo's huge profile behind the gate.

"Sir?" he said.

"I'm here to see Mr. Kazan. He's expecting me." And that, thought Leo, may or may not be true.

The boy pushed a hand between the curve of an iron branch and an ibis and held it flat for Leo's card. Then, without opening the gate he rushed inside and returned with the card on a silver salver. He opened the gate and led Leo round to the back of the house. There was a lawn on a terrace and in the centre of the lawn three people were playing French cricket. A large man dressed in an embroidered kurta was holding the bat to his feet; a little girl with a mop of thick black hair was laughing and pretending to throw the ball but not releasing it. A stick-like woman stood apart, her gaze fixed on the child.

The house-boy coughed. He opened his mouth to say, "Your visitor, sir," but Leo prevented him and took the silver salver. He signaled the boy to go and stood rooted to the spot.

The little girl jumped around her grandfather, trying to hit his legs with the tennis ball. He in turn, made exaggerated groans as he had to twist around with the bat and dared her to get him in Russian.

Millicent Cleaver saw him first. She gasped and put a hand to her mouth. Leonid Kazan looked up and while his attention was drawn to the tall figure standing across the lawn, Elena hit him sharply on the shin with her ball.

"Aiiiii!" It was a genuine yelp, he rubbed his leg then turned to Leo; "*Milosti prosim. Pricojedin'ajtec'.*"

"*Spasibo.*"

Staying in his own tongue, Leonid Kazan said, "She's too strong for her years." Then he stepped back and looked hard. It was his brother: his brother was dead . . . It was his son.

He turned to speak to Millie, whose face was as white as

the jasmine and Japanese wisteria behind her. "What's the matter woman?" he shouted jovially in English. "Here he is! Here he is at last! Come on, smile and be a warm welcome."

He turned back to Leo and held out the cricket bat, "Now you are here you can play. See if this little minx can get *you*."

Leo pocketed his card, placed the letter tray on the lawn and took the English cricket bat from his father. Millicent Cleaver watched them, her body rigid with tension.

The little girl watched their every move, looking for clues on how to behave; her beloved Millie was obviously worried by the man, was she frightened of him, too?

Leo took up his position, holding the bat at his knees to protect his feet. The child didn't move, he cocked his head on one side and winked at her.

"You've got eyes like my grandpa," she said in English.

"Mmm, and you've got eyes like me. What does that mean, do you think?"

She moved nearer to him and stared up into his face then she turned and ran flat out into the safety of Millie Cleaver's grey skirt. The woman bent down and whispered to her then gently prized the child's fingers open and turned her to face Leo.

"Go and say hello nicely, there's a good girl. He's your daddy."

Elena twisted back to hide in the safety of the long grey skirt. Slowly and gently Millie Cleaver turned her once more to face Leo and then gave her a nudge in the back. "Be a good girl for Daddy," she whispered.

Elena walked slowly across the immaculate lawn and stopped at the feet of the stranger; she took the bat from his hands and dropped it on the ground beside her, extended the plump fingers of her right hand and said, "How do you do. I'm very pleased to meet you."

"Give him a kiss!" shouted Leonid in Russian. "Give him a hug! Ask him what took him so long."

Elena lifted her arms shyly and Leo swung her into the air and settled her on the crook of his left arm. The child looked down at the adults around her and suddenly laughed out in delight, "He's like an elephant, Millie, a great big elephant."

Leo laughed too, but there were tears in his eyes.

*

Dearest Mamá,

By the time you get this I shall be in France, I hope. We have been in Barcelona for few weeks but Pedro has decided I cannot stay. I have been doing translating for some Welshmen and some Americans but now we are being bombarded all the time and Pedro is sending me across the border to Port Bou. He says his wife and baby need to be safe. Yes Mamá, you have got a married daughter and now you are going to be a Granny!!

Give my love to everyone and tell them I am quite safe, and as happy as it is possible to be under the circumstances.

All my love, and do not worry. I feel very well, not sick at all …

Davina rolled her hand over her swelling abdomen, '*not sick at all*', you lucky girl. Perhaps my darling, you are going to be a mother and sister in the very same month. She started to laugh with relief.

The outer envelope that had enclosed Marina's unopened

letter dropped to the floor. It was embossed with the García del Moral monogram and had been addressed in what looked exactly like Alfonso's forward slanting scrawl. So Sito was getting into the house and the bureau was intact – that meant the house had not burned to the ground at all. What was going on there? Why hadn't he popped in a few lines about himself and what was happening in Jerez? Marina said '*do not worry*'- dear lord there were so many things to worry about. Still it was the best Christmas present she had ever had.

Mary Peach put her head round the door, "I've left some mince pies in the kitchen. What's the matter?"

"Oh, Mary!"

The kind woman, who bore such a striking resemblance to Davina, crossed the room and gathered her cousin into her arms. "That's it my dear, have a good cry. It's what you need."

"Mary," sobbed Davina, "why are people so good to me these days? Nobody said anything nice to me for years and years and now, suddenly, when I don't deserve it, you are all being so good to me."

"Well I don't know anything about those Spaniards, good Christian folk they're s'posed to be, but you're back home now and you're lovely and we're going to look after you, don't you fret. Your baby is going to be as strong and healthy as a Cornishman should be."

Davina put her head back and laughed. She couldn't be sure what nationality his father was, Spanish or – whatever Leo was, but he would be born a Cornishman. She hugged Mary. "Thank you, you are an angel. Let's have a mince pie and a schooner of sherry – it is Christmas eve."

They moved into the kitchen. Davina removed the cloth

from the plate of sugary little pies and said, "How do you know it's a boy?"

"I don't know. Just seems like it'll be a boy."

It was a boy. He was born on a blustery night in May, when the wind rattled the Crimphele chimney pots like the devil himself was trying to get in. A perfectly healthy baby with every baby's deep blue eyes but his own special halo of spun gold hair.

The midwife said, "There you are m'dear, give him a cuddle and your milk'll flow easy."

"What you going to call him?" asked Mary Peach.

"I'd like to call him Tristan, but it seems – I don't know – can't decide."

"Nice name that. A good Cornishman – ruined by an Irishwoman, though, if I remember right."

"Mary! I sometimes forget Parry Jones was your father. Tristan was a good Celt, wasn't he?"

"He was. Han'some and brave. Roll on your side a minute." She plumped Davina's feather pillows and said, "That better for you?"

Davina smiled, "Much better. Poor Tristan and Iseult. Trapped by love."

"Hmm. Love potion, weren't it? Not natural love. Mind you, that's a worse trap if you asks me."

Mary Peach held out her arms, "Now, give little Tristan to me and he can sleep here in his crib while you rest. Mrs. Jenkins and I'll go down for a cup of tea, if that's all right. Been a long night. You close your eyes, you got a busy time coming now."

The two women tiptoed out of her room and Davina rolled over to gaze at her new son. He was so beautiful. God bless him.

And, please God, take care of Marina and her baby, and keep these children safe from the outside world.

"Mary!"

Mary Peach stepped back into the bedroom.

"Mary, are we born the way we are, or does life make us?"

"Bit of both, I'd say. Look at me: born to skivvy and I always goes for the poshest dress in the shop."

"Ah, you know then?"

"Oh, I know. Your witch Morrigan made sure of that years ago."

"Morgana La Fey: she wasn't completely bad. She had a baby, it died."

The two women were silent for a moment, examining their private memories.

"Was it awful, finding out?" asked Davina, quietly.

"Could have been worse; I knew my pa loved me, and then when I saw how your ma couldn't be bothered with you neither, well it didn't matter so much then. Sorry about that. You had a tough old time of it down here by yourself."

"Did I? I didn't realize it at the time."

"I think we are born who we are, but life makes us what we become in the end, if you see what I mean?"

"Like poor old Morrigan."

"She weren't so poor – your family looked after her pretty well. Your pa even rented a cottage down here when she retired."

"Did he? He didn't tell me that."

"No, well he had a soft heart, for all your mother . . . Anyway, I think we make our own destiny, one way or another. And if it's not what we want well we've only got ourselves to blame."

"Yes, I think you're right. It just took me thirty-five years to find out."

"Well that's normal. Most women seems to spend their young days trying to be someone they think they ought to be: that they'd like to be, so they go along with what other people want and expect from them. Then, when they're married and they got the kids to look after, all that goes out the window and they're just themselves. And one day they see the fancy ideas they used to have don't fit in real life: bit like finding you can't squeeze into your best frock anymore. But that don't matter , cuz with the little ones around there's no need for it anyway. And so that's that. You are what you are. Happens about mid-thirties, I'd say. Leastways it does round these parts."

"Mary Peach, how did you become so wise?"

Mary Peach sighed a long, heartfelt sigh. "I ain't wise, I just seen a bit too much of life, it's rubbed off the illusions. Being married to a boozer does that to you. And I've got my Gwenny to think of. I sometimes wonder if she isn't a bit simple."

"But Gwendolyn is gorgeous; she is as pretty as . . ."

"As is a constant worry to her ma that she don't fall in the same man trap as I did."

"*We* did."

"Yes well, enough of this philosophizing. That little one is safe here with a proper mother to love him and a fine roof over his head. Get some sleep, while he'll let you."

Chapter 30

The peace of the summer morning was cut to shreds as yet another bomber squadron took to the air. Davina kept her eyes focused on dead-heading the roses in the lower garden. She had on two occasions watched what were now called 'dog fights'; on the first occasion the English plane came tumbling back down to earth, on the second she saw the skirmish up over the estuary, then within seconds both planes appeared to plunge head first into the sea. Once a plane had flown so low over the house she had seen the pilot's helmet and goggles. Her one greatest fear was that the war would come crashing down on her own hard won peace: that her beautiful old house sitting comfortably by the river dressed in summer wisteria mauve would be violated by the world of men.

It had taken her a long time to settle and then a long time to learn how to enjoy independence. She had spent most of her life on her own in one way or another, so being in the old house with just Tristan for company did not worry her. Mary Peach and her daughter, Gwenny, gave her hand with the housekeeping so she did have some company. She plodded along, coping with her situation until one morning, for no apparent reason, she awoke, stretched her arms up to the ceiling and sighed, "Heaven." No one to answer to, no one to criticize or nag her and a whole day to do whatever she wanted. From that moment on the little rituals of daily life became a pleasure. Save for persistent worries about Marina's well being and less persistent but more intrusive, invasive replays of words spoken by Leo she was content.

One of the RAF squadron had turned and was charging back inland, trailing smoke like a black parachute. She instinctively ducked. "No, please no," she gasped. "Tristan! Tristan, where are you?"

Tristan, had lost interest in the real life battles raging above him, he was far more interested in his own games. He raised a caterpillar arm and called, "Here," from somewhere among the jungle of roses and rhododendrons that surrounded the old house.

"Come over here, sweetheart."

"In a minute."

Davina smiled and returned to her pruning, there was no point going in doors – if the plane did crash and they were inside it would be infinitely worse. Another plane was suddenly overhead: she kept her eyes focused on her hands, dropping each dead bloom into her garden trug, making room for regeneration.

She did look up, however, when the post boy wheeled his bicycle round the wooden door.

"Alright then?" It was a question requiring no answer, his normal salutation. "Got a bundle for you this mornin', Mrs. Moral," he continued, waving a handful of buff and white envelopes in his hand, "and a telegram from your daughter."

Davina tucked her flower trug up onto her left arm, pulled off her gardening gloves and stepped out from among the thorny bushes. There was a big cream envelope from Alfonso's lawyers, the document inside would require careful reading; a letter from the

Dymond accountants, Matthew was a self-obsessed, surly devil but he kept her informed about the business and she received a monthly income for her share in the Bristol sherry business. The third envelope was small and bore an Indian stamp. She placed these unopened among the cracked rose hips in her flower trug. The Indian stamp had made her tummy turn but the flimsy brown telegram made her hands shake. She tore it open; PEDRO SENT TO LABOUR CAMP COMING TO YOU NOW.

"Good news then is it?"

"Yes, Billy. Not excellent news, not for my daughter but good news for me."

"Alright then. I'll be off, bye."

Davina read the telegram again and popped it into the pocket of her flowery summer frock. She would read the other letters later. She wouldn't open the envelope with the Indian stamp until she was alone in her own room. She pulled her gloves back on and returned to the roses.

"Mummy!"

"Yes dear."

Round little Tristan, his golden curls tucked away under a yellow sou'wester, staggered down the path from the house wearing gumboots and carrying his favourite book of bird stories.

"Mummy look, I'm the duckly ugling."

"No you're not, silly," laughed Davina. Stepping back onto the path and bending down she gathered him to her. "You are a very beautiful and very hot little boy. You are not ugly in the very least. Take that hat off sweetheart; you'll boil in this sun."

"Alright then," Tristan mimicked Billy the post boy exactly. He struggled out of her arms and scuttled back in the direction of the kitchen and Mary Peach's preparations for lunch.

Davina moved on up the row of dry, brown petals and seed heads, pushing her hair away from her face with the back of her hand, she continued with her gardening, speculating on the contents of her letters.

She felt, did not see, the garden door open once more. And she knew who was standing there. He had arrived before she had even opened his letter. His first letter. Well, the second, counting the note she had received in London. He was absurdly well dressed for a Cornish summer morning.

Suddenly Tristan was beside her again, tugging at her skirt. He was wearing a black woollen hat and had a white tea towel tied around his neck. Ignoring the man at the garden door he pulled at her skirt with one hand and indicated behind him with the other.

"Look, Mummy, look," he insisted until she followed him to a vast lavender bush, in the midst of which lay a nest of sticks and unraveled wool.

Having achieved his objective, Tristan acknowledged the presence of the stranger. "Who's that?" he said.

"You had better ask him."

Tristan looked up at her for reassurance and when she nodded he ran off down the path and gazed up at the tall stranger.

The stranger felt his stomach lurch. It was exactly, exactly as he remembered. A woman and child in a terraced garden full of roses. It was exactly, exactly what he wanted.

"Come and look," said the boy. "I've made a nest."

Leo came to stand beside Davina. She smiled at him. She had eyes as blue as the summer sky and freckles; Leo reached for her hand. Davina bit her lip, not knowing whether to laugh or cry.

"Look!" demanded Tristan.

They stared down at the mess of twigs and wool. It was very like a real nest. A nest containing three silver apostle spoons, some gold toffee papers, two fancy hair pins and a beautiful necklace, its emeralds and pearls glinting in the sunlight.

"Are you my daddy?" asked the boy.

The big man hunkered down beside the child and poked a finger into the nest. "Well it certainly looks like it."

"Alright then." Tristan gave the dark man a kiss on the cheek and skipped off up the path singing, "I'm a little magpie, black and white, here's my nest, shiny bright."

Davina and Leo looked at each other and burst out laughing.

"Introductions over," said Davina.

Leo picked the necklace out of the nest and stood up.

"It's stolen property," said Davina.

"A magpie?"

"One or two, along the way. It's famous – infamous."

"Oh."

"I read about it in an article on famous jewel thefts the day I went to see the doctor, because I was expecting Tristan. There was even a picture."

"And?"

"Oh, someone stole it from a maharani and then when it reappeared it was stolen again."

"You haven't done anything about it then?"

"No. At the time my life was quite complicated enough without getting involved with police. I assume the person that 'acquired' it sold it to you for the same reasons I came to your shop: that made me think. Anyway I'm never going to have a reason to wear the dratted thing, so unless a little magpie, black and white, chooses to put it in his shiny nest and shows it to anybody else, I think it is quite safe here.

"Good."

"Let me show you the garden."

They wandered around the rhododendrons, along the paths between the fruit bushes and the area set aside for vegetables. Davina named plants and chattered about how long it had taken her to get the garden back into shape after years of neglect. Then she said, "Now, what about you?"

"Oh, a lot of 'complications', mostly no longer complicated, thank goodness. Elena is staying with my father and Millie; they have moved up to the hills permanently. My father has taken out Indian citizenship and adopted the religion of our forbears. It suits him. He dispenses wisdom over a hookah and goes to the mosque every day. So he has plenty of new acquaintances and he's as happy as a dispossessed person can be. Millie has a child to care for and she's doing it remarkably well for her age, as far as I can see. We found a lovely *ayah*, too, and Elena has taken to her, which helps. They have plenty of other domestic help, of course. So Elena is safe, going to an English school and content for now."

"And you?"

"Well, I ran into a little difficulty with your countrymen. They confiscated my passport and tried to bully me into working for them."

"So how did you get here now?"

"It's all rather strange. I showed them my true colours, you see. I realized that I belonged to my mother's country and joined the Indian National Congress party – to do what I could for independence. I never was British, anyway. Doing that made me an enemy, but it meant they left me alone – except they had me watched day and night – but I'm rather used to that. I was afraid, to be honest, they would find an excuse to put me in jail. I couldn't have borne that, but they didn't, then out of the blue, after making at least a hundred attempts to get back to England to see you, I am informed that Mr. Churchill wants to 'consult' me and I've got to get to England as fast as possible. So I was put on a plane three days ago and via various military bases on the way, here I am."

"Mr. Churchill! Gosh."

"Gosh indeed, except he's going to say something rather stronger than that, when he hears the answer to what I think he's going to ask me. Mr. Churchill does not have a very high opinion of us Indians."

"You are going to London?"

"No, he's somewhere down here on the Helford River – a perfect coincidence."

"Mummy!" piped Tristan, trotting towards them. "Aunt Mary says is the man staying for lunch?"

"Are you?" asked Davina.

"If I may?"

"Good. I have a lot I want to tell you now, but it will have to wait until our little magpie is out of earshot."

Tristan had arrived at the site of his nest. "Don't take anything, please," he said, looking at Leo. "It's *my* nest."

"You need a biscuit tin."

The little boy cocked his head on one side, considering the suggestion.

"To put things in?"

Leo nodded and the child grinned.

"Are you going to stay with us now?" he asked.

"If mummy will let me."

"Alright then. Lunch is ready. Come on."

Tristan stepped between Davina and Leo, put one hand in his mother's hand and the other in his father's and tugged them toward the house. "Come on, I'm hungry."

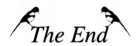

The End

Lightning Source UK Ltd.
Milton Keynes UK
14 March 2010
151371UK00001B/16/P